The Discovery
of the Austral Continent
by a Flying Man;
or, The French Daedalus

FROM THE SAME AUTHOR

Posthumous Correspondence (3 vols.) ISBNs 978-61227-513-0; 514-7 & 515-4.

The Discovery
of the Austral Continent
by a Flying Man;
or, The French Daedalus

by
Nicolas Restif de la Bretonne

Translated, annotated and introduced by
Brian Stableford

A Black Coat Press Book

Visit our website at www.blackcoatpress.com

ISBN 978-1-61227-512-3. First Printing. May 2016. Published by Black Coat Press, an imprint of Hollywood Comics.com, LLC, P.O. Box 17270, Encino, CA 91416. All rights reserved.

Introduction

La Découverte australe par un homme-volant, ou Le Dédale français, here translated as *The Discovery of the Austral Continent by a Flying Man; or, The French Daedalus*, was originally published in 1781, in a set of four volumes that also contained four shorter works, with a title-page falsely claiming to have been printed in Leipzig. A pre-title page announces it as the second in a series of the *Oeuvres posthumes de N *******, as La Découverte australe, ou Les Antipodes*, and the more elaborate title page does not indicate any author's name. The preface is signed "T. Joly," who poses as an editor of a work attributed to his "friend Dulis," and the notes in the original version of the text are variously signed by Joly and Dulis. The book was actually the work of Nicolas Restif de La Bretonne, who subsequently made no secret of having written the book, referring to it in more than one of his subsequent quasi-autobiographical writings and including his own name within the text twice, albeit written backwards.

The formula of presentation linked the work to Restif's 1780 novel *La Malédiction paternelle, lettres sincères et véritables de N******* à ses parents, ses amis et ses maîtresses, avec les réponses; recueilli et publié par Timothée Joly, son exécuteur testamentaire* [The Paternal Curse; Sincere and Veritable Letters by N******* to his parents, friends and mistresses, with the Responses, collected and published by Timothée Joly, the executor of his will], also allegedly published in Leipzig, but actually published by the widow Duchesne, the real publisher of *La Découverte australe*; its central character is Dulis, alias N******* [Nicolas].

The present translation of *La Découverte australe* is the first of four volumes, the next three of which will contain a translation of a loosely-connected work in the same genre of "*le merveilleux*" [the marvelous], *Les Posthumes: Lettres reçues après la mort du mari par sa femme, qui le croit à Florence, par feu Cazotte* [The Posthumous: Letters received after the death of a husband by his wife, who believes him to be in Florence, by the late Cazotte], originally published in Paris by Duchêne (the son of the widow Duchesne) in 1802, translated as *Posthumous Correspondence.*

When he published *La Découverte australe*, the author was forty-six years old, having been born on 23 October 1734 in Sacy, in the Yonne. He was the son of Edmé Rétif, a peasant farmer, but a very well-off peasant farmer, who also served the functions of a local magistrate; he was thus in much the same social situation as the one in which we initially find Victorin, the hero of *La Découverte australe*, except that his family was much larger; Nicolas was the eldest of the eight children of his father's second marriage, following a first that had been almost as prolific, two of the sons of which had taken holy orders.

In 1742 the family moved on to land that Edmé Rétif had recently bought, which included a field called La Bretonne; it was sold again later, but that did not prevent Nicolas from adding it to his signature, in a tongue-in-cheek fashion, in order to give it an aristocratic implication, further enhanced by changing Rétif to the more upmarket Restif, although he sometimes reverted to the earlier spelling. His first schoolmaster detected signs of intellectual promise in him, which led his father to place him, in 1746, under the tutelage of his stepbrother, Abbé Thomas, initially in Bicêtre, but subsequently, as a side-effect of upheavals caused by a crusade against the Jansenist heresy, in Auxerre.

It was while he was under Abbé Thomas' tutelage that Nicolas fell in love for the first time, with the daughter of a notary, Jeanette Rousseau—the first of many mostly-hopeless infatuations. Indeed, his supposedly-excessive interest in young women was one of the reasons Abbé Thomas gave for getting rid of his pupil in 1750, the other being insubordination. Although his father had hoped until then that Nicolas

6

would also go into the church, that expectation was dashed, and Restif was to go on to cultivate a deep and abiding loathing for the clergy. It was also in that period that he began writing, beginning a diary of sorts from which he was later to draw details of his autobiography, writing various poems and a comedy in Latin imitative of his favorite classical author, Terence.

Nicolas found great pleasure in writing, and his exercises in poetry soon became voluminous. His first venture into autobiography—or, as he put it, his first account of his "adventures"—was in that form, begun in 1753 and concluded in 1755, by which time it ran to four thousand lines. That was preceded, however, by another substantial poem, tentatively entitled *Les Douze mois ou Mes Douze travaux* [The Twelve Months, or My Twelve Labors], which was a long daydream fantasy in which the protagonist, having done a favor for the king, is rewarded with a plot of land enclosed by a high wall, containing a vast aviary and twelve beautiful young women, where he lives as if in an Earthly Paradise. That fantasy too was to recur resoundingly in his later work, vaguely echoed in the *Découverte australe*, but much more robustly recovered in a work to be described in the companion volume to this one.

After being sent home by Abbé Thomas, Nicolas tended sheep on his father's farm for a while, before being apprenticed to a printer in Auxerre in July 1751, where he naturally fell hopelessly in love with his employer's wife. Having served his apprenticeship and learned the trade, he went to Paris in 1754 and became a typesetter at the Imprimerie Royale du Louvre for a year before moving on to various other employers, constantly shifting in the context of a long battle fought by the government against the activities of illicit printers of subversive posters, pamphlets and books.

Nicolas returned to Auxerre for a while in 1760, and there he married Agnès Lebègue, with whom he eventually had four daughters, Agnès, Marie, Elisabeth and Marion (or Marie-Anne). The couple returned to Paris in 1761, where Nicolas again worked for various printers as a typesetter until

1767, with a brief interruption following his father's death in 1763. In 1765 he assisted Pierre Nougaret with the publication of *Lucette ou le Progrès du libertinage* [Lucette; or, The Progress of Libertinage] in the hope that the latter might reciprocate by assisting him with the publication of his own first novel, *La Famille vertueuse* [The Virtuous Family], but the friendship rapidly turned sour, and then to intense mutual hatred. Having become "Restif de La Bretonne," he contrived to get that novel published in 1767, and effectively became a full-time writer thereafter—initially assisted by the fact that his wife worked selling fabrics—pouring out a long series of prose works, eventually amassing a total that many of his contemporaries and subsequent historians thought excessive.

For a long time it was very difficult to count the number of works that Restif produced under various signatures, many of them in multi-volume series that were often subsequently augmented by additional volumes, but the final count, according to the most conscientiously detailed modern study, Pierre Testud's *Rétif de La Bretonne et la création littéraire* (1977), was a hundred and eighty-seven volumes, comprising forty-four titles, and totaling some fifty-seven thousand pages. That is the equivalent of some ten or twelve million words, in thirty-five years, although the last decade and a half were severely disrupted by the Revolution, which affected his production as well as temporarily devastating the possibilities of publication. That total would not seem so very vast to the numerous 19th and 20th century writers who routinely produced more than a million words a year for long periods, and sometimes twice as many, but it has to be borne in mind not only that Restif was presumably writing with goose-quills, but also that he insisted on typesetting all his own works.

The latter factor is an important thing to bear in mind, because it made Restif unique in literary history, and allowed him to develop various idiosyncrasies in orthography that some of his readers have found annoying. His detractors—who were and always have been numerous—sometimes joked that he kept his typesetting equipment in his bedroom and that he often composed directly to type without bothering with an intermediary manuscript, and they were probably not entirely sure themselves whether there might not be some truth in the allegation. Even if there was none, Restif was certainly in a very unusual situation of being able to continue his creative process to the very brink of production, to an even greater extent than authors who habitually made extensive amendments to their proofs.

Restif's early works include a riposte to Nougaret, *Lucile, ou le Progrès de la vertu* [Lucile; or, The Progress of Virtue] (1768) and *Le Pied de Fanchette, ou le Soulier couleur de rose* [Fanchette's Foot, or the Pink Shoe] (1769), which earned him the distinction, when psychologists began searching for technical terms to describe various sexual deviations, of encouraging some of them to name shoe-fetishism "retifism," as they had named sadism after the Marquis de Sade—whom Restif loathed sufficiently to write an *Anti-Justine* (1798), in an attempt to demonstrate that pornography could and ought to be virtuous and life-enhancing rather than vicious and depraved.

Whole books have been written on the subject of whether Restif was or was not a shoe-fetishist, pointlessly, as he clearly was not: a fetishist, in the psychiatric sense, is someone who substitutes the fetish object for the "real" desired object; while Restif certainly appreciated a dainty foot and found high-heeled shoes sexy, there was never the slightest doubt that what he lusted after, incessantly and obsessively, was the real thing, and not any kind of substitute. The other three books he published in 1769 did, however, include *Le Pornographe* [a neologism signifying "Writing About Sex"— *not* "pornography" in the pejorative sense that the term subsequently acquired], a utopian tract offering practical proposals for the legalization and organization of prostitution in the interests of public order and morality—the first of several such tracts addressing various specific issues of concern, including *Le Mimographe* [Writing about the Theater] (1770), *Les Gynographes* [Writings about Women] (1777), addressing the social role and status of women, and the more generally political *L'Andrographe* [Writing about Men] (1782; also known, more accurately, as *L'Anthropographe* [Writing About Humans])

Restif's first considerable success was the quasi-autobiographical *Le Paysan perverti* [The Corrupted Peasant] (1775), which detailed the educative and corrupting effects of life in Paris on an emigrant from a humble principal background, and to which he eventually added an inevitable feminine counterpart, *La Paysanne pervertie*, in 1784. By then, the success of the earlier volume had been outstripped by *Les Contemporaines, ou Aventures des plus jolies femmes de l'Age présent* [Contemporaries; or, The Adventures of the Prettiest Women of the Present Era] (1780), a collection of short stories detailing the problematic lives of young women of various estates, to which he continued to add further series under various other titles for the rest of his career. In the meantime, however, he was already working on his intended masterpiece: his multi-volume autobiography, to which he refers in the frame narrative of *La Découverte australe* as *Compère Nicolas* [Friend Nicolas], but which eventually appeared as *Monsieur Nicolas ou Le Coeur humain dévoilé* [Monsieur Nicolas; or, The Human Heart Laid Bare] (sixteen volumes, 1794-97).

The frame narrative of *La Découverte australe*, which provides a kind of self-portrait of the author circa 1780, also lays bare one of the existential cancers that was eating away at the author's soul during the period of his initial success: the distress caused by his wife's adultery, and his suspicion that at least one of his daughters was not actually his. From 1768 onwards, the couple were estranged, although still living together, and in 1778, when Marion was found a place, Agnès went back to live with her father. It was then that Restif, temporarily left alone (two of his daughters eventually came back to live with him), took to prowling the streets of Paris—particularly the Île Saint-Louis—by night, terming himself "le hibou" [the owl] and accumulating the observations that were later to provide the raw material for another of his most famous works of quasi-autobiographical fiction, *Les Nuits de Paris ou le spectateur nocturne* [Parisian Nights; or, The Nocturnal Spectator] (four volumes 1788; augmented by others at intervals until 1794). He claimed in the text that he began writing on walls and bridges in that period—thus making an important contribution to the history of modern graffiti—but given the implausibility of many of the other "adventures" described in the text, the claim has to be taken with a pinch of salt.

La Découverte australe itself was, according to *Monsieur Nicolas*, begun when Restif was confined to bed suffering one of his recurrent bouts of ill-heath, in 1778, before he began work on *Les Contemporaines*. It was a deliberately self-indulgent exercise, redeveloping one of his childhood daydreams, of what he might do if he were able to fly. That initial draft was probably restricted to the story of Victorin's adventures in preparing for and carrying out the abduction and seduction of his beloved Christine. He set the manuscript aside while he wrote the short stories making up *Les Contemporaines*, and although he does not say so, it was probably when he took it up again thereafter that he added the frame narrative and the second half of the story, describing Victorin's removal of his utopian community from the Inaccessible Mountain to the South Seas, his subsequent exploration of the archipelagoes of the southern seas, and the remarkable discoveries he makes there. That second part transformed the nature of the narrative very considerably, and made the book unique, not only within the pattern of the author's productivity, but within the context of French imaginative fiction to that date.

As a printer, Restif was very familiar with the peculiar pattern of French publishing in the 18th century, whereby publications printed legally had to be licensed by the royal censors: a law honored far more in the breach than the observance, as 18th century Paris was awash with illicit publications of all kinds, especially the scurrilous, the scandalous, the anti-clerical and the politically subversive. Some such books were printed in Belgium, Holland and elsewhere, and then imported to Paris, but most were simply printed clandestinely on the spot, with fake title-pages claiming to have been printed elsewhere; they were often anonymous or pseudonymous.

Some works challenging political and religious orthodoxy were licensed; Jean-Jacques Rousseau's publication, for instance, were above board, but those of most of the *philosophes* were not; Voltaire's *contes philosophiques* were all beyond the official pale to begin with. Restif's early works were licensed, although one or two of them must have hung in the balance of uncertainty, but he presumably devised the series of "posthumous works of N*******" specifically to accommodate works that he knew to be incapable of winning the approval of the censors, which the *Découverte australe* had no chance of doing.

Almost all works of imaginative fiction were banished to the strange twilight existence of unlicensed texts, especially anything with a philosophical bent that might smack of heresy—an old tradition in France, going back to Cyrano de Bergerac, whose trilogy of fantastic satires *L'Autre monde*, written circa 1650, lost its third volume and part of its second to pious thieves, while the parts that escaped were only published posthumously, in severally bowdlerized form (the texts were not fully restored until 1920).

Voltaire was pursued more relentlessly by the clergy than anyone else, but even writers who made far more conscientious attempts to be diplomatic had to tread very carefully. Voltaire's most prolific contemporary as a writer of philosophical tales Charles-François Tiphaigne de La Roche—a much more conservative individual who disapproved of his rival—advertised on the title pages of some of his major works that they were published, all anonymously, in "Luneville" (*Amilec*, 1753), "Babylon" (*Giphantie*, 1760) and

"Pekin" (*L'Empire des Zaziris*, 1761).[1] Restif never made any mention of Tiphaigne's work, but that does not necessarily mean that he did not read it; Pierre Testud points out that the account given of *Monsieur Nicolas'* reading does not correspond very closely with the notes that Restif made in his diaries, and omits a great deal of downmarket work that the author clearly enjoyed but apparently did not think good for his image.

Because of the partiality of his accounts of his reading it is difficult to determine what other works of imaginative fiction belonging to this shadowy tradition of marginal texts Restif might have read before writing *La Découverte australe*, although we can be reasonably sure that they included Voltaire's *Micromégas* (1752; the title page's claim that it was published in Berlin in 1750 is false), and some of the earlier dream-fantasies by his friend Louis-Sébastien Mercier, including the anonymous utopian vision of future Paris *L'An deux mille quatre cent quarante* (1774). He might well, however, have come across Gabriel Foigny's *La Terre australe connue* [The Austral Land Discovered] (1676, reprinted several times, including an edition in 1732), in which he would certainly have been interested, in that it deals with the discovery in an austral land of a population of hermaphrodites who, by virtue of the absence of sexual inequality, have been able to establish a perfectly egalitarian communistic society based on reason and mathematics. He might also have read Simon Tyssot de Patot's anonymous *Voyages et aventures de Jacques Massé* (allegedly 1710 but probably later),[2] which also features a previously-undiscovered austral land that is host to an orderly and relatively happy human society possessed of a strange mythology of its origins and a complex religious history.

---

[1] Available from Black Coat press in *Amilec*, ISBN 978-1-61227-033-3
[2] Available from Black Coat Press in *The Strange Voyages of Jacques Massé and Pierre de Mésange*, ISBN 9768-1-61227-370-9.

Both of the last-named texts make use, as *La Découverte australe* does, of the unknown Terra Australis, initially hypothesized in antiquity, and repopularized in the 16th century by geographers who thought the world map unbalanced, and in need to a southern continent to "equilibrate" it, much as the Americas had provided a continent to fill a western hemisphere previously suspected to be oceanic. Those who believed in Terra Australis and placed it speculatively in their maps included Gerardus Mercator in 1538. Navigators in the 17th century who glimpsed new lands in the southern hemisphere, including Abel Tasman, often assumed that they were parts of the land-mass in question.

Alexander Dalrymple of the British East India Company found documents in the mid-18th century that led him to produce an elaborate second-hand description of the hypothetical "continent," which prompted the British admiralty to instruct James Cook to go and find it when he went to Tahiti to observe a transit of Venus. He looked hard, first in the *Endeavor* in 1769-70 and then in the *Resolution* in 1773-74, but he failed to find it—although he did find Botany Bay, on what turned out to be the eastern coast of "New Holland," and numerous small islands, and his quest attracted a good deal of publicity. Restif read the published accounts of his voyages, which he was careful to integrate into the story of *La Découverte australe*, in order to explain why Cook had not found the mini-empire that Victorin had by then allegedly established in various southern archipelagoes as yet unknown in Europe.

Another fringe text of which Restif might have been aware is Marie-Anne Roumier-Robert's interplanetary tour fantasy *Voyages de Milord Céton dans les sept planettes, ou Le Nouveau Mentor,*[3] first published in four volumes, allegedly in The Hague in 1765-66, with the by-line *"traduits par Madame de R.R."* One book that he certainly read, however, and which made a very deep impression on him, was Benoît

---

[3] Available from Black Coat Press as *The Voyages of Lord Seaton to the Seven Planets*, ISBN 978-1-61227-446-1.

de Maillet's *Telliamed*, first published in 1748—ten years after the author's death—ostensibly in Amsterdam, although Restif probably read the third edition, allegedly published in The Hague in 1755, which restored some of the text removed from the first edition, although the full text was not recovered from the manuscripts until the 1960s. The 1755 edition was sold in Paris by Nicolas Duchesne, or Duchêne, who was probably its actual printer, and whose widow became Restif's principal publisher after his death in 1765, followed in her turn by their son.

Telliamed's full title was *Telliamed ou Entretiens d'un philosophe indien avec un missionnaire François sur la diminution de la mer, la formation de la terre, l'origine de l'homme, etc.*, first translated into English as *Telliamed; or, Conversations Between and Indian Philosopher and a French Missionary on the Diminution of the Sea, The Formation of the Earth, the Origin of Men and Animals, and Other Subjects Relating to Natural History and Philosophy* (the definitive English edition, published in 1968, abridges the subtitle). The author, who uses the hypothetical Indian philosopher—the name is his own spelled backwards—as a mouthpiece for his theses, was a diplomat and amateur geologist who used his foreign postings to study local rocks; he came to the conclusion that all of them had been formed by processes of sedimentation extending over billions of years, and that waters that had originally covered the Earth's surface entirely had gradually diminished, freeing the land, whereupon life forms that had first emerged in the sea began a slow invasion of the land, adapting by degrees to the new environments thus made available.

That account of the evolution of the Earth was not only controversial because it contradicted Biblical chronology but because it suggested that all the animals currently existing on land, including humans, were the product of a gradual process of progressive evolution rather than having been created individually, and that any "deluges" that had occurred in the interim were merely natural punctuation marks rather the crucial episodes of godly wrath.

Maillet's account of the Earth's development is placed within the context of a broader cosmogony, which explains the origin of the earth within the "vortex" of a rotating sun, in a manner by then conventional, following on from the speculations of René Descartes and various others, but Maillet complicated his account of the subsequent evolution of solar systems considerably. He suggested that when a sun has burned off most of its mass and energy, much of which is deposited on its planets, it migrates to the other part of the vortex and is replaced at the center by one of the plants, all of which migrate gradually toward that center, which then ignites, thus creating a continuous cycle in which all the worldly elements go through similar processes of evolution, including similar evolutions of life.

It was not until the 1960s that publication of de Maillet's full manuscript allowed scholars to glimpse exactly how close he had come to a theory of evolution by natural selection, but the 1755 edition did leave in place the stress on adaptation to changing environments as a key motor of evolution, which was subsequently taken up by the Chevalier de Lamarck. Restif was, however, writing long before Lamarck published his *Philosophie zoologique* (1809), so he was obliged as well as perfectly free to make up his own theory of evolution for the purposes of his literary flights of fancy, and although his theory now seems bizarre, especially in the inspiration it takes from various mythological sources, within its historical context is was a genuine triumph of extrapolative imagination, and he cannot be blamed for taking it as seriously as he eventually came to do—especially as his taking it seriously led him to increasingly bold and far-reaching extrapolations. In *La Découverte australe* they remain relatively modest, even in the account of supposed advanced scientific knowledge given to Victorin's grandson by a Megapatagon sage, but they subsequently took on mind-boggling dimensions in *Les Posthumes*.

Another book that Restif definitely read, because reference is made to it in *Les Posthumes*, although he might conceivably not have done so before writing *La Découverte australe,* is *Les Hommes volans* [The Flying Men] (1763; allegedly published in London but advertised on the title page as being available from "la veuve Brunet," who was the Académie Française's printer), the French translation of Robert Paltock's *The Life and Adventures of Peter Wilkins* (1751). It would have been unnecessary for him to get the idea of artificial wings therefrom, as he was well aware of the famous mythological precedent cited in his subtitle, but if he saw the book during the 1760s or 1770s it might have helped prompt him to revisit his childhood daydreams. It is, however, worth noting that *La Découverte australe* was published three years before the Montgolfier brothers reignited the dream of human flight in no uncertain terms and ushered in a new era of fantasies embracing the notion. Restif's description of the mechanism of Victorin's wings is, moreover, a masterly combination of the detailed and the vague, fully adapted to an era of technical innovation. In that context, the ingenious Victorin seems a worthy successor of the machine-maker and automaton-builder Jacques de Vaucanson, who was still alive and living in Paris in 1781.

By virtue of the deft combination of that technological element with the theoretical element derived principally from Maillet, *La Découverte australe* is undoubtedly the most significant work of science-based speculative fiction produced before the 1789 Revolution, and it remained so for some time thereafter. Although its cosmogony and evolutionary theory eventually turned out to be mistaken, and no one has yet found a means of devising artificial wings akin to those that allow Victorin to fly, that should not detract from the novel's imaginative achievement, seen as a work of art in its own right. The fact that it served as a springboard for further imaginative endeavors was, in effect, a bonus, albeit a significant one.

The manner in which the attempt to rationalize the day-dream fantasy that gave birth to *La Découverte australe* became a launching-pad for further thought was initially illustrated by the first edition of the book, which not only contains the novel but four other works, which take up part of the third volume and all of the fourth.

The first of those supplements is a long essay on "Cosmogénies ou systèmes de la formation de l'univers suivant les anciens et les modernes" [Cosmogonies; or Systems of the Formation of the Universe According to Ancient and Modern Writers], which places Maillet's cosmogony in its broader historical context. The account progresses from a comprehensive survey of classical systems to those of Descartes and Isaac Newton before claiming that "Monsieur de Buffon has effaced all the other philosophers by the beauty, the clarity and the seductive light in which he presents his system" in *Les Epoques de Nature* (1778; tr. as *The Epochs of Nature*). Restif links the Comte de Buffon's work to *Telliamed* because of its latent evolutionism, although Buffon was nervously diplomatic in his refusal to embrace the idea too forcefully with regard to human beings. Restif then goes on to elaborate his own suggested elaboration and modification of his synthesis of Maillet and Buffon, as sketched out in *La Découverte australe* by the Metapatagon sage.

The second supplement is the satirical "Lettre d'un singe aux animaux de son espèce, avec des notes philosophiques," [A Monkey's Letter to the Animals of his Species, with Philosophical Notes] in which the letter-writer offers advice to his fellows on the tactics and necessity of self-improvement toward humanity and membership in a great confraternity of intelligent beings—which, according to the preface, "would have completed the revelation of the author's objective, if I had not made it perfectly graspable." The letter is supplemented by a very elaborate set of notes signed by the fictitious T. Joly.

The third and longest of the supplements is a "Dissertation sur les Hommes-brutes" [Dissertation on Brutal Humans], which is a massive survey of legendary and folkloristic accounts of exotic species of humans and beings hybridizing human and animal features, greatly expanding the brief survey contained in *Telliamed*. In essence, it tries hard to offers justifications for taking seriously the plausibility of *La Découverte australe*'s representation of various kinds of mythical humans, including some not featured in the main narrative—tailed humans, monopods, albinos and marine humans—as well as the nocturnal people, savages and giants akin to the patagons, plus such hybrids as bear-people, swine-people, bull-people, beaver-people etc., etc., placing them within the evolutionary theory sketched out in the main narrative. The sum of all that is, according to Joly: "a system supported with every appearance of conviction, but whose real goal will not escape [the reader]: my friend wants to guide all living beings to a universal and general confraternity."

The fourth and most eccentric addition to the collection is a set of six "diatribes" represented as speeches made by guests at a salon, entitled "La Séance chez une amatrice" [A Session in the Home of an Amatrice, the final word being a improvised feminine of "amateur," referring to a salon-hostess]. The sequence opens with "L'Homme de nuit" [The Night People], which insists once again on the plausibility of some of the different human species discussed in the previous items, but in a more poetic style than the earnest dissertation. "L'Iatromachie" [Iatromachy, referring to medicine], argues, trenchantly and sardonically, with the aid of a great deal of Latin, that much supposed medical knowledge is mere superstition, expanding a contention briefly made by the Megapatagonian sage. "La Raptomachie; dialogue serio-comico-amphigourique" [Raptomachy; a serio-comic-amphigoric dialogue; the prefix relates to seizure, as in raptor] is a farcical conversational exchange whose participants get progressively drunk and incoherent as they discuss various matters. "La Loterie" [The Lottery] is a tongue-in-cheek recommendation of the use of lotteries in arranging marriages, which is partly echoed in the marriage customs of the

Megapatagonians. The final two pieces are both exotic exercises in music criticism; "*L'Olympiade, Armide*, etc." deals with the operatic performances in question, the second of which providing a natural link to the brief apologue "Gluck et les Loups" [Gluck and the Wolves"], in which Restif's favorite composer attempts to charm a pack of wolves after the fashion of Orpheus. The combination appears to have been stitched together arbitrarily, and attached to *La Découverte australe* more because the author had nothing else to do with them than because of their peripheral linkages with its text.

Interestingly, the joint preface to the second, third and fourth addenda, signed, like the general preface, by T. Joly, lists several other titles in the projected set of "posthumous works" to which the pre-title page of volume one attributed *La Découverte Australe*: *Le Conte de Prince O-Ribo*; *Le Hibou*; *Les Métamorphoses*; and *Les Préjugés*. The first title refers to a novel that Restif subsequently published as *Les Veillées du Marais, or Histoire du grand prince Oribeau, roi de Momminie, au pays d'Evinland, et de la vertueuse princesse Oribelle, de Lagenie; tirée des anciennes annales irlandaises et récemment translatée en français par Nichols Donneraill, du comté de Korke, descendant de l'auteur* [Evenings in the Marsh; or, The Story of the great Prince Oribeau of Evinland and the virtuous Princess Oribelle of Lagenie; taken from old Irish sources and recently translated into French by Nichols Donneraill of the county of Cork, a descendant of the author] (1785), which is a didactic fantasy with some elements of the marvelous, describing the exemplary education of Prince Oribeau. The second presumably refers to the project that ultimately emerged as *Les Nuits de Paris*. The third might be the work advertised as *Les Mille-et-une métamorphoses*, which appears as number one in a long list of books Restif allegedly still intended to write, featured in the supplementary material to *Les Posthumes* in 1802, none of which he actually wrote; the twenty-fourth item on the latter list is *Les Préjugés justifiés*, which might be the fourth item initially envisaged as a work by N*******.

The research invested in "Cosmogénies" and "Dissertation sur les hommes-brutes" is both varied and intensive, and illustrates an aspect of Restif's tendency to obsession rather different from the one displayed in his relentless production of fiction, more akin to the earnest insistence of his plans for utopian reform; both essays demonstrate that once he got a bee in his bonnet, he tended to pursue it assiduously, as far as it would go. That was certainly what he did with his own cosmogonic thesis; he eventually developed it even more extensively in non-fictional form in volumes supplementary to *Monsieur Nicolas*, which bore the separate title of *La Philosophie de Monsieur Nicolas* (1796), the first part of which detail his "physics," but before then he had extrapolated it very elaborately in graphic fictional form, in his account of the cosmic voyages and futuristic explorations of Multipliandre in *Les Posthumes*, first penned in 1787-89, although not actually published until 1802: the strangest work of fiction ever penned by anyone, and the most far reaching imaginative endeavor ever attempted.

Restif produced a third adventure in the marvelous in 1896, but that was never published, and the story of the further developments of the speculative elements of *La Découverte australe*—an episode of biography as tortured as any of those that Restif labored to dramatize, but which he did not live to write—will be taken up in the introduction to the companion volume.

This translation was made from the version of the text of *La Découverte australe* reprinted in the Robert Laffont anthology *Voyages aux pays de nulle part* (1990), which is abridged, slightly amended and shorn of all of the supplementary material except for a few of the footnotes. I am not sure when the abridgement and amendment were first carried out, or by whom, although it would be very odd if the alterations to the literary satire contained in the final section were made in the modern era; the Bibliothèque Nationale catalogue includes two printings of the text in 1781, only one of which bears the fake Leipzig place of publication, and it might be the case that the other, acknowledged as the work of the widow Duchesne, was diplomatically altered by the author/typesetter, but the versions available on line all reproduce the "Leipzig text," so I cannot check. At any rate, I have replaced most of the additional text and footnotes contained in the first edition, and I have detailed the significant amendments in my own footnotes, taking the extra material from the copies of the first edition reproduced on Google Books.

Although it could certainly be argued that it would have been more scrupulous to reprint the entire contents of the first edition, including the elaborate prefatory material as well as the supplements, it did not seem to me that the additional material especially the long essays—which would have made the text much longer—really belongs in the same volume as the novel; the supplements do not add anything substantial to the enjoyment of the work as an example of classic speculative fiction, whereas the novel itself is a coherent and organized text that can be read and savored independently of what now, inevitably, seem to be hopeless and not entirely serious attempts to justify its inventions rationally. Although the arguments employed by the author in support of his text now seem impotent, however, it does seem to me that it might not be irrelevant to offer some comment on the peculiar evolutionary theory that he devised, intermediate between those of Maillet and Lamarck, so I have added a brief apologetic afterword of my own.

Brian Stableford

BOOK ONE

I

In the month of December 1776 I took the Lyon diligence in order to return to Paris. There were eight of us in the vehicle: a Benedictine, an actor, two actresses, an advocate, a merchant, a person of unknown profession and myself—not to mention a monkey, six dogs, three parrots, two parakeets, an Angola goat and the various human individuals garnishing the imperial.

The Benedictine was the greatest consumer of Spanish tobacco in Europe, the best of gourmets and the finest connoisseur of choice morsels. One of the two actresses, who played queens, was as libertine as R***, whom she resembled facially, to the extent that I initially mistook her for her, and as malevolent as La S***.[4] The soubrette was serious, melancholy, regular in her speech and almost as amiable as the delicate Fannier. The actor was a tragedian, as handsome a man as P***il, who played as badly, with a conceit and insolence that might but ought not to be compared with ******. The advocate, whom I recognized in spite of his disguise, was a famous man whom I hold in scant esteem and like even less, loathed and persecuted, a persecutor and even a calumniator. The merchant was a good man, very rich, very simple, drinking well, eating well and sleeping even better, snoring for four, and tak-

---

[4] The satirical passages in *Les Posthumes* reveal that Restif, who did not approve of actresses in general, had a particular distaste for "Mademoiselle Raucourt (Francoise Saucerette) and "Madame Sainval" (Claire de Sainval).

ing almost as much tobacco as the Benedictine, with whom he conversed about worldly matters.

The unknown quantity was a man neither young nor old, neither handsome not ugly, neither fat nor thin, neither tall not short, who did not appear to be either rich or poor, who neither talked too much nor too little, and all of whose actions announced that he neither loved nor hated anyone in the world.

There remains "me." That "me" is an eccentric, too singular to describe in a few words. Imagine a small man, who holds himself so awkwardly that he seems counterfeit, of sad and dreamy expression, his head sunk between his shoulders, his vague and indeterminate gait representing a living specimen of a Guianan Acephale;[5] who alone, as in society, conversed with his own thoughts, to the point of bursting into laughter, crying out and weeping without the company being able to suspect the reason; timid and brutal to excess; loving pleasure and disdaining out of pride the objects that procure it; preaching tolerance and not being able to suffer the slightest contradiction, etc. That is my portrait, unflattering, at the bottom of which one could put: L-g-t, but I declare that it is not me...

I had soon had enough of the monk, the actor and even the merchant; the two actresses had soon had enough of me; so that after two days, there was only the unknown quantity with whom I found that I could converse. Thanks to his character, he tolerated me as much as I desired. Gradually, we formed a

---

[5] Author's note: "Men of America of whom Cortal speaks on page 58 of his *Voyages*, whose head is in the chest." The reference presumably intends to indicate Francisco Coreal's *Voyages aux indes occidentales* (1722), although it is false, no such reference occurring on p.58 of any volume of the rather humdrum text. The fact that Restif did his own typesetting did not make him any less likely to make typographical errors, especially in rendering proper names; the mysterious P***il might similarly be misrendered, the actor N****** has in mind perhaps being Beaumesnil.

bond, and as I have a few good qualities that I have not mentioned, he treated me as a friend.

It was toward the evening of the fourth day when he finally asked me: "Who are you?"

I replied to his question with the portrait I have just traced.

"That's exactly what I wanted," he said, "and not your condition or estate."

I replied to that.

"I call myself Friend Nicolas. I've been a shepherd, a vine-grower, a gardener, a laborer, a student, an apprentice monk, an artisan in a city, married, cuckolded, libertine, sage, stupid, intelligent, ignorant and philosophical; finally, I'm an author. I've written numerous works; most of which were bad, but I sensed it; I had the good sense to be ashamed of them and to tell myself that I had only published them out of the necessity of living and feeding my own children and my wife's—for after all, I really am what I said I am, children don't make themselves, and someone has to nourish them.

"The most important of my works is *Compère Nicolas*; which is to say, my own life. I anatomize there the human heart, and I hope that that book, made at my own expense, will be the most useful of books, in that I dissect myself unsparingly, thus sacrificing myself, a new Curtius, to the utility of my peers. I'm composing another, entitled *Le Hibou*, and another..."[6]

The unknown quantity interrupted me, with a half-smile, and said: "You're what I need; you can be my historiographer. I have the most singular things to tell you. It's not a matter of rendering them plausible, because they aren't. I speak French as you do, I have no more accent than you, I'm neither whiter not blacker, and yet there is between my homeland and yours the entire diameter of the terrestrial globe. I was born in the

---

[6] The final sentence is omitted from the Laffont edition.

austral hemisphere, at 00 degrees from the equator and 00 degrees of longitude,[7] on an island called Île Christine."

He fell silent. I looked at him in astonishment, but as he continued to remain silent, I spoke again, full of various thoughts.

"What!" I said. "Is it possible that Nature duplicates herself in the two hemispheres, and that at the same latitude, one finds not only the same plants and the same animals, but also the same humans, the same empires, and people speaking the same languages! Oh, if that were so it would be a fine discovery, and your story would be marvelous enough, and interesting enough, to make me a fortune and get me out of the poverty in which I've been languishing since my father's curse—for you should know that I've been cursed, and it's for that reason that I'm poor and a cuckold.

The Austral man shook his head and asked me why I had been cursed. I told him my story, such as it is found in certain letters that only ought to be published after my death.[8] He shook his head again, but he made no reply to my story.

We were approaching the capital, and as our conversation had been very particular we wanted, out of politeness, before separating, not to allow our traveling companions to take away a bad impression of us. We paid them compliments and made eulogies of them; they returned them, with the exception of the malevolent actress, who savored incense but never incensed anyone herself; she thought she merited everything and owed nothing.

Finally, we arrived. The Benedictine got up first in order to get down; he shook his robe and caused us each to sneeze six times, with the exception of the merchant. We separated with as much indifference as if we had never met. The actor

---

[7] The author does not mean zero degrees; he uses the formula 00 to replace omitted numbers as he uses asterisks (and, occasionally, dots and hyphens) to replace omitted letters in words; I have retained his formula rather than substituting asterisks.

[8] i.e., those contained in novel *La Malédiction paternelle.*

and the actresses went to lodge at the Carrousel, the Benedictine at Saint-Germain-des-Prés, the advocate in the Rue de la Calandre, the merchant in the Rue des Bourdonnais, and the dogs, the parrots and the goats probably followed their mistresses. As for me, I took the unknown quantity home, not forgetting his monkey, which appeared to me to be very singular.

When we were sorted and rested, we resumed out conversation with more liberty than in the Lyon diligence.

"I don't want to leave you in error," the Austral man said to me. "The inhabitants of the Antarctic hemisphere are absolutely different from the humans of this one; everything is clear-cut in those isolated climes, because everything there has remained as it emerged from the hands of Nature. Instead of the people having, as in Europe, Asia and even in Africa, amalgamated themselves, so to speak, and improved themselves—or, at least, the most perfect have annihilated those of the same species who appeared to them to be a hindrance, or deformed, etc.—in the southern hemisphere, it's entirely the opposite. Nothing there is mixed, the half-perfected beings have remained so to this today; with the consequence that the sight of them is alarming, and Europeans would not fail to destroy them.

"It's for that reason that we have decided to keep our homeland hidden. There is a law that applies to all foreigners who have landed there, either in a vessel in good condition or by way of shipwreck; they are retained, without ever being able to return home. However, they are accorded a treatment that ought not to leave them any regrets; they enjoy all the advantages of citizens without being forced to work; it's only their children who are returned to the common order. By the same token, we only have one good ship, which is always equipped by the State; it's always confided to princes of the blood, whom it's impossible to deceive, for reasons you'll soon know—for I'm going to tell you a story that will astonish you."

He left it there for the first day, and as he had excited my curiosity to an inexpressible point, I waited for the next day with a great deal of impatience. It finally arrived, that morrow so much desired; we had chocolate, and after the breakfast, my man said to me:

"I am French by origin, as are almost all my compatriots. We live in a beautiful island beyond the Tropic of Capricorn, which we have named after our first queen, who is still alive. It is under the same meridian as France; we have days and nights of the same hours as here. I've told you that there's a law that renders distant journeys by the inhabitants impossible. Thus, you can believe that I'm traveling with the consent of the leaders of my nation.

"Of all the men I've encountered thus far, in the six months that I've been traveling in the southern provinces of France, you are the only one in whom I thought I could confide, because I hope that you will help me in my research. It's neither treasures nor wealth that are the goal of my voyage; it has a much more important objective. I want to make contact with a scholar of the first order, a philosopher above the common run, like J.-J. Rousseau, Monsieur de Voltaire or Monsieur de Buffon, and convince him to allow himself to be taken with me by those of our princes of the blood who have the faculty of making use of artificial wings, and traveling all over the world.

"Today, I shall tell you the story of the sage mortal to whom we owe the origin of the best government there is in the world, but before then, I'd like you to tell me certain things I don't know. Which of your great men, for example, would consent to allow himself to be taken to the Austral lands?

"That question," I said, "isn't very difficult. The greatest men are Monsieur de Voltaire, Monsieur Rousseau and Monsieur de Buffon; there is also Monsieur Franklin here, an envoy of the United States of America, who might suit your purpose, but there isn't any likelihood that he would abandon the interests of his own country in order to satisfy another. As for Monsieur de Voltaire, he's too old; younger, you could have had him easily, but...he's too witty. That fine fault is scarcely tolerable in this land, where one can have all possible wit with impunity; I imagine that in your land, he wouldn't catch on. Monsieur de Buffon might be more suitable, but he's sufficient well-off here not to want to leave us. There remains Monsieur Rousseau. I believe you could have him easily. He complains about us, and would willingly abandon us. But in order that his disappearance shouldn't make too much noise, it's necessary to come to some arrangement with him. He could appear to die. Monsieur le Marquis de Girardin, to whose estate he has retired, can erect his tomb, and on the very day that his sudden death is afflicting all Europe with his loss—very real for us—your princes of the blood will have taken him away.

The Australian embraced me joyfully. In order not to keep the reader in suspense I shall say very briefly that the abduction in question was carried out with perfect ease; only J.-J. Rousseau's friends were informed of it, and me. I shall keep silent as long as I live, and this story will only appear after my death. Thus, Posterity will know that the cenotaph in Ermenonville is empty.[9]

The Australian then began speaking, in these terms, to tell me the extraordinary facts you are about to read.

---

[9] Rousseau died—or, according to N******, pretended to die—in 1778.

It was about seventy years ago that a young man from the Dauphiné found the secret of flying—like the birds, because it's necessary to explain that in French.[11] And the motive that gave him such a keen desire to fly was amour.

Victorin—that was the Dauphinois' name—the son of a simple procurator fiscal, had fallen madly in love with the beautiful Christine, the daughter of his Seigneur. Christine was beauty personified, or at least, the most beautiful thing that Victorin had seen. He thought of nothing but her; he was desiccated by love, and as that sentiment was unsustained by any hope, it was a frightful torture. The young man only sought solitude, and when he found himself in some beautiful landscape, between hills crowned with woods, it seemed to him that he was breathing the air of liberty, the ancient and sweet equality of human beings—for there is nothing in the world that more efficaciously restores a man to his natural state than open country, fertile and surrounded by woods or fallow land. He experienced then a delightful sentiment, unknown in inhabited locales—especially here, where everything in parkland and there are "no trespassing" signs everywhere.

There was a domestic in the procurator fiscal's household who was a rather bad lot—which is to say idle—but who was a great reader, named Jean Vezinier. The fellow had read the beautiful and veridical histories of Fortunatus, who, by the virtue of his little hat, transported himself and his beauty anywhere he wished; that of Michel Morin, of the *Mariage de la*

---

[10] The chapter breaks in the main text are not in the first edition, but the manner in which they break up the text make it more reader-friendly than the various devices used in the original version.

[11] It is necessary to explain it because in French, *le secret de voler* could also mean "the secret of stealing."

Mort avec Creusefosse, and the birth of little Morats, their children, who ate earth instead of bread, etc.[12] It was to that fellow, whose intelligence was ornamented by so much fine knowledge, that Victorin confessed that his great desire was to have wings and to fly.

Jean Vezinier listened gravely, and after having reflected for three-quarters of an hour, he replied: "It's not impossible."

Victorin, transported, leapt for joy, and begged Vezinier, who had a great deal of talent for all petty works of invention, to lend a hand to the project, and see what they might accomplish.

In consequence, they hid themselves away, in order to steal as much time as possible from useful occupations. They made wheels that locked together; they complicated the movements, and succeeded in making a wooden wheel that operated two canvas wings. The heavy machine could lift a man off the ground but it required a very tiring effort to make the wheel spin. The inventive Jean Vezinier resolved to try it out anyway, not wanting to imperil his master's son.

They went up a mountain, climbed on to a crag, and Vezinier abandoned himself to the wind. He had given his wings a curvature, like those of birds, but the ensemble of his made it resemble fairly closely a large bat. He encountered an inconvenience that he had not anticipated; having no progressive impulsion, they could only follow the wind. He nevertheless flew some distance, which transported young Victorin

---

[12] *Fortunatus* was a chapbook, whose story is cobbled together from various legends and folktales, first published in German in the early 16th century, which enjoyed enormous popularity in various versions and several other languages. The character of Michel Morin was featured in an oft-reprinted early 18th century humorous text cast in the form of a funeral oration for a cowherd who fell out of a tree; he then began to crop up in other texts. The title [Le] *Mariage de la Mort avec Creusefosse* [The Marriage of Death and Gravedigger] appears to be fictitious.

with joy. He imagined, on seeing Jean Vezinier fly, that with a further adjustment and lighter wings, it would be possible to give himself a progressive movement, an ascending movement to lift himself, and a descending one in order to land.

Jean flew as far as his strength would permit, but was exhausted in less than a quarter of an hour, and let himself fall to the ground by slowing his speed. Victorin ran to him and prevented him from hurting himself when he landed, because he was falling horizontally, face forwards.

After that trial, Victorin and Jean Vezinier only talked about their wings, and what they would do when they could fly long distances. Victorin only breathed for Christine, and wanted to go find an island or an inaccessible mountain in order to take her there and live with her, but Jean Vezinier had many other ideas. He wanted to avenge himself on his enemies, and kill them from high in the air. He wanted to carry off the daughters of the town, who had disdained him as a husband because of his idleness, and enjoy them at his whim, in order to return them to their parents dishonored. He wanted, above all, a certain Edmée Boissard, the daughter of the schoolmaster and the prettiest of the marriageable girls, who had preferred the Maréchal's son to him. Victorin did not approve of those dispositions, and often reproached him for them, but as he needed Vezinier, he dared not criticize him too much.

Finally, they perfected their wings, and after a few additions, and having substituted taffeta for canvas, they succeeded in giving them a progressive horizontal, and even retrograde, movement; and in rising up and descending perpendicularly at will. They went to try them out in the country, in a deserted spot.

They both took off together, but misfortune caused Jean Vezinier's mechanism to break, and he fell from a height into a pond, where he drowned. Victorin was not strong enough to help him; he returned to the house, where he recounted the domestic's accident, without saying anything about the cause. People ran to the pond, and pulled Vezinier out, but they did not understand anything of the muddy machine to which he was harnessed. Victorin, who had his reasons, cut it into pieces in order to got rid of it, and broke the wheels dexterously, in order that they would be incomprehensible. Jean was taken back to the house, absolutely drowned. They might have been able to recall him to life had they known about discoveries recently made in France, but the help that was administered then only finished him off.

So, Victorin was alone, and abandoned to his own genius. He often returned to the same solitude in order to dream about his project, think about Christine, and slake his young soul's thirst with the ambrosia of liberty.

One day, when he was in a distant place, he saw two big birds—they were storks—separated from their flock by some accident. The two birds were flying side by side in search of food. Victorin admired them.

"Oh, if I could fly like them," he exclaimed, "that would be worth as much as nobility in Christine's eyes. I'd carry her away, I'd adore her, I'd give her anything she wanted; I'd build her a nice comfortable nest on a sheer crag, out of the reach of men. How happy we'd be! For I love her as much as she would love me, and when, after ten years, we'd have pretty children as beautiful as her, I'd go to find Monsieur de ***, her father, taking him one of my daughters, bearing a strong resemblance to her mother, and I'd say to him: 'Look, Monsieur, here's your daughter rejuvenated, whom I'm returning to you.'

"And he'd say to me: 'How's that, Victorin? Where have you been for ten year?' But I wouldn't tell him anything, and, immediately deploying my wings, which he wouldn't have seen because I'd have hidden them behind my back, I'd fly away, and he'd be very astonished.

"And he'd ask my daughter, whom we'd have educated very well: 'Who are you, beautiful child, and where have you come from?'

And she'd reply: 'From the home of my father and mother, Monseigneur, who love one another very tenderly, and are lodged in a beautiful nest of gold, silver and silk, constructed on a very high rock.'

"'And who is your father?'

"'You've just seen him, Monseigneur.'

"'And your mother?'

"'Her name is Christine de ***, Monseigneur.

"And immediately, Monsieur de *** would embrace her, with tears in his eyes, saying to her 'Ah! That's my daughter.' But he'd be angry with me, because I'd abducted her and I'm not a gentleman. And he'd say: 'Where is this nest?'

"And the little one would say: 'I don't know, Monseigneur, because my Papa, who is a Flying Man, brought me here through the air; but don't be angry, Monseigneur, and have pity on me.'

"And Monsieur de *** would look at my daughter, who would resemble Mademoiselle Christine, and he'd kiss her, calling her his dear daughter. And then he'd ask how his demoiselle is with me. And my daughter would tell him how I love her mother; how I hasten to do everything that might please her; how I serve her; how I never let her want for anything; how I nourish her on the best birds, and good white bread from the city, and how I hunt and work every day for her, so well that she also loves me with all her heart.

"And when he'd heard all that he'd say; 'Oh, if I could only see my poor daughter!'"

It was thus that young Victorin soothed his troubles for a few hours—but they only came back afterwards with more violence, for when he was in the midst of his pleasant chimera, his intelligence would wake up suddenly and he would say, tearfully: "Alas, all that isn't true!"

In his profound melancholy, he sought solitude even more, and no one would ever have seen him, if the desire he had to see Christine had not forced him to go to the château frequently.

One day, when he was in the garden, Christine arrived there with her chambermaid. Victorin was intoxicated by the pleasure of looking at her. Christine wanted a bouquet of white roses that grew high on the bush. The chambermaid tried to pick them, but she pricked her finger and made it bleed, and, having perceived Victorin, she called to him:

"You're more dexterous than me, Monsieur Victorin; pick some of these roses for my young mistress."

Victorin launched himself into the rose bush, tore his sleeves, his ruff and his hands; the blood flowed, but he picked the roses and presented them to Christine, trembling with pleasure.

"My God, Monsieur Victorin," the Beauty said to him, "you're wounded!"

And she took her handkerchief, which she soaked in his blood; she even pulled out a little thorn that had remained stuck in his flesh. Victorin fainted with pleasure. They thought it was the pain, and the beautiful Christine let two tears fall upon him, which reanimated him. He smiled as he came round, which reassured Christine, and caused her natural and sympathetic tone to be succeeded by the attitude of disdain that the daughter of a provincial nobleman cannot, in all conscience, prevent herself from having toward her inferiors. But that attitude only inflamed Victorin's heart further; he noticed above all that the beautiful Christine had just put a rose on her bosom, the heart of which was stained with his blood.

He watched her draw away, in the fashion of a lightly built nymph treading the grass of the boscage with delicate feet.

Scarcely had Christine quit Victorin than the young man found one of those butterflies with a proboscis that suck flowers without landing on them, and whose flight seems continuous. He tried to catch the insect alive, and when he held it, he tried to divine the mechanism of its flight by examining the movement of its wings. He spent a long time in that meditation, and when he thought that he had penetrated nature's secret, he began his trials.

Two entire years of arduous labor, which Jean Vezinier would doubtless have abridged, produced nothing but deformation and scant effect, by comparison with what he wanted to achieve and with the perfection of nature. Meanwhile, Christine increased in age and beauty. There was talk of her marrying. Victorian shivered, and redoubled his efforts. He examined all kinds of flight, of insects as well as birds. That of the butterfly appeared to him to be facile to imitate, but it required too powerful a spring and overly large wings. He returned to that of the grouse, which approached his hovering butterfly's genre of flight, and re-examined its articulation. That of geese and big birds appeared facile, but it is heavy and requires denser air—which is to say, condensed by cold, like that which reigns at a great height.

He made all those reflections, even though he was a simple peasant, alone and unaided. What can love not achieve! Oh, that alone was the inventor of all the arts!

Finally, Victorin perfected Jean Vezinier's invention; his machine gave him, by virtue of the rapid movement of its mechanism, the flight of the grouse to lift himself from the ground, and, by means of a slower movement, the flight of the great birds of passage, which only beat the air with a regular and distinct tempo. He composed his wings of the lightest silk fabric and sustained them with struts of whalebone, stronger at the point of origin, which, tapering gradually, closely resembled the ribs of bird's feathers.

He took those improved wings into the deserted countryside to make a new full-scale trial. He had tried previously in his father's courtyard, during mass on Sundays when everyone was at church, but he had not dared to fly high, either for fear of being seen by children or the fear of some accident that might have forced him to receive help and betray his secret.

He left for the solitary location in the morning, determined to run every risk, and to go up as high as possible, even if he lost his life in the trial. To lose Christine would have been a far worse misfortune!

Having arrived on an isolated hill, Victorin fitted his wings.

A broad and sturdy strap, which he had had prepared by the harness-maker, circled his waist. Two others, smaller, attached to his knee-boots, garnished each leg and thigh laterally and then passed through a leather buckle fixed to the belt. Two broad bands continued over his ribs and joined a hood that was fitted to his shoulders by four straps through which his arms passed. Two strong mobile strips of whalebone, the bases of which were supported by the boots, in order that the feet could activate them, continued over the ribs, contained by little rings of oiled boxwood and rising all the way to the head, in order that the taffeta of the wings could be prolonged that far.

The wings, attached to the two exterior lateral straps, were placed in such a fashion that they bore the man in his entire length, including the head and half the legs. A kind of sharply tapered parasol, retained in its extension by six silk threads, served to enable him to lean forward, aiding him to lift his head, or to adopt an entirely perpendicular stance.

As the Flying Man had to be able to make use of both hands, the mechanism that gave movement to the wings was activated by two straps that passed under the sole of each foot in such a way that, in order to fly, it was necessary to make the ordinary action of walking—a movement that could, in consequence, be accelerated and slowed down at will. The two feet each gave a complete movement to both wings; they dilated them and caused them to beat simultaneously, but by virtue of the effect of a little mechanism, the right foot operated the extension of the closed parasol, and the left foot brought it back while opening it.

The mechanism was executed by the two collateral struts of whalebone, moved by a wheel with two notches that passed under the feet, and which, turning in the same direction, pulled the left whalebone and, in continuing, hooked on to a button of the right whalebone in order to drive it. The same springs could also be moved with the hand.

Flight was rendered stationary and perpendicular by a certain compression of the wings, effected by the two strings, which came under the armpits and passed into a chin-strap, to which the head gave movement; the effect of the two strings was to lower the tip of the parasol and direct it in all possible directions.

The components of the flying machine were only made of boxwood, but they were not overly fatigued, with the exception of two teeth and their supports that were made of polished steel softened by an unctuous substance; the only part subject to wearing away by friction was the strap that moved the spring of the wings; it was made of silk, but of much greater strength, and the Flying Man always had several of them in his pocket; he checked it every time he took off, and never waited until it was too worn to replace it. The advantage that it had was that, once he was in the air, the silken strap suffered so little fatigue that it was sufficient for a long-haul voyage.

After a few weeks of experiments, Victorin found a means of fitting a second mechanism to his machine, similar to the first but weaker, capable in case of an accident of sustaining him in the air while he fitted another strap to the principal device.

So, Victorin arrived on a hill, climbed up on a small rock, and first gave his wings that rapid movement of the flight of a grouse. He rose above the ground thus with sufficient facility. His lack of habituation to finding himself in the air made him dizzy, however; he could only go higher by closing his eyes.

He soon felt a fairly considerable degree of cold, and most of all, he found that he was soaring with so much ease that the slightest movement of his legs gave the wings the strength to sustain him. He opened his eyes momentarily, and saw that he was at a prodigious height. He tugged then on the two strings designed to move the tapered parasol in all directions, and directed the tip downwards, which caused him to descend rather rapidly.

When he saw that he was near the ground, he held it horizontally in order to get back to the hill and the rock, from which he was more than two leagues distant, although he had only been flying for fifteen minutes, so rapid had his flight been. He landed there, folding up the taffetas of the legs and doubling the erectile movement.

Victorin was therefore able, by means of the direction of the parasol, to give his wings three kinds of flight: erectile, which lifted him from the ground, depressive,[13] which brought him back to it, and horizontal by which one moved forward. With practice, the Flying Man could combine those three directions by means of almost simultaneous movements.

After various trials that crowned his success, Victorin folded up his artificial wings and went home very content. He rectified certain defects he had noticed, and, full of confidence, dared one night to carry out a considerable journey.

There was the most beautiful moonlight. Victorin emerged from his bedroom without being seen by anyone, and from the courtyard of the paternal house, by means of his parasol, rose above the buildings.

The semi-darkness enabled him to be less frightened by the height at which he found himself, with the consequence that he resolved to pass over Christine's father's château. He directed his flight, following the terrestrial road, of which he never lost sight, and came above the fortunate abode of the object of his adoration. He could still see a light therein, and tried to get closer to the window—but the noise of his wings and the mechanism, in the silence of the night, was so loud that it woke up the château's dogs; they started barking, making a frightful racket. Everyone put their heads out of the widows, and Victorin had the pleasure of seeing Christine.

The old Seigneur had looked up, and was very surprised to see a bird so huge that he had never heard mention of one like it. Monsieur de ***, who feared losing sight of it, shouted for someone to bring him his double-barreled shotgun. It was brought and Victorin, to his regret, was obliged to draw away.

---

[13] I have retained literal transcriptions of *érecteur* and *dépresseur*; the erotic analogies are clearly intentional.

When he was at a great height, he began to sing, words that the more sonorous air of the elevated region rendered quite intelligible:

Beautiful Christine, whom I adore,
And whose attractions are so sweet,
Must I then draw away from thee?
I hoped to linger until dawn
In this place embellished
By your lovely presence.
I flee, having been dismissed
But I conserve the resonance.

The entire château heard that stanza, and it caused the greatest astonishment, but no one could tell where the singing voice was coming from. They searched everywhere, but in vain. Finally, the beautiful Christine went back to her room, and Victorin, no longer having any hope of seeing the sovereign of his thoughts, directed his flight toward the nearest city, which was seven leagues away. He arrived there in less than an hour, and lifted a young woman away from libertines who had attacked her.[14] He deposited her in her home through the window that she indicated to him, although half-fainted in fear, believed him to be the Devil, and then an Angel—which made a great deal of noise the next day.

Content with that trial, he returned to his father's house, went back to his bedroom, and went to bed.

In the morning he examined the silken strap that activated the mechanism; he found it almost worn away and was alarmed; he spent all day finding the mechanism the support

---

[14] The casual rescue of damsels in distress was later to become a standard part of the repertoire of "the nocturnal spectator"— the protagonist of Restif's quasi-autobiographical series of anecdotes *Les Nuits de Paris*, and, at a much later date, a standard element of the stereotyped role of the comic book superhero.

that I mentioned, in order to avoid falling to earth and breaking his neck, like poor Jean Vezinier, if that essential strap should fail.

Meanwhile, the nocturnal adventure caused a great deal of fuss at the château, the city and throughout the locale. A hundred people who had not seen or heard anything were nevertheless sure that they had seen the great bird. The stanza he had sung was repeated, copied in every possible fashion except the correct one. Victorin laughed a great deal secretly, and understood how popular rumors are made. He went to the château the same day and, having learned that Mademoiselle Christine was in the garden, went there, and did not take long to find himself within range of being seen by her.

As soon as she noticed him, she made him a sign to approach.

"Well, Monsieur Victorin, did you see the great bird too?"

"Yes, Mademoiselle, and better than anyone else, I can assure you."

"Not better than Papa and me, for we saw it as I can see you."

"I won't dispute what you say, Mademoiselle, but I saw it very well and heard its song, for I remembered it and made a copy."

"Let me see," said Christine. "That way, I'll know whether you really saw it, for of the thirty people who tried to repeat it to me this morning, there wasn't one who got it right."

Christine took the song from Victorin's hands, and read it with astonishment.

"That's it exactly," she said, blushing slightly. "But where were you, then?"

"I assure you, Mademoiselle, that I didn't set foot outside my father's house, but as the bird that sang it was very high, it was audible a long way away."

"Are you in your right mind?" Christine replied. "You're trying to tell me that it was the big bird that sang it? You won't make me believe that, or that you weren't in the vicinity of the château. I don't like to be told lies."

"I'm only telling the exact truth, Mademoiselle, when I assure you that I didn't take a single step outside my father's house; I respect you too much to lie to you."

"That's singular," said Christine to her chambermaid, "for I believe him; Victorin isn't a liar." To the son of the procurator fiscal she said: "Do you mind if I keep your copy?"

"It would give me a pleasure, Mademoiselle, greater than I could have hoped."

"There are more beautiful roses, but I warn you that if you sustain a single scratch, I won't take them."

Victorin ran to the bush of white roses; he picked the most beautiful ones, without pricking himself, or at least without being seen to do so, and brought them to Christine, who put them on her bosom. She had scarcely done so when the most beautiful came away from its pedicle and fell. Victorin hastened to pick it up, but could not return it; he raised it swiftly to his lips twice, and then ran to pick another.

Christine had noticed what he had done and blushed, but Victorin was such a handsome fellow that she was not annoyed by it. The young man brought back a beautiful rose, which Christine received with embarrassment. She continued her walk, asking Victorin to tell her the common names of the different plants that ornamented the garden.

What happy moments! Victorin thought he was in heaven.

Finally Christine went back in, and the amorous young man had to return to the procurator fiscal's house.

Ravishing chimeras occupied him on the way. He imagined that he had abducted Christine, that he had taken her to a charming and inaccessible place; that he was loved there, and that they lived happily, in complete liberty. That idea made him shiver, and he formed the resolution to try to effectuate it.

In order to succeed in that more easily, he asked his father, who was rich, to place him in the city with a procurator, in order to learn a little practical law, a science absolutely necessary in rural areas in order not to be devoured by seigneurial law,[15] much harsher than higher law. That was precisely the intention of the procurator fiscal; his son was only falling in with his views by making that request, which drew praise.

Victorin was fitted out with new and fashionable clothes. He was given a small sum of money, and when everything was ready, the day of his departure was fixed. It was the day before, but Victorin was not asleep As his province was the Dauphiné, the town of ***, its chief place, was only five or six leagues away from the Inaccessible Mountain, thus named because the mountain was shaped like an inverted sugar-loaf.

Giving the pretext of going hunting, Victorian had departed one morning before dawn with his wings and provisions for the day. As soon as he was in the country he had flown to the Inaccessible Mountain and had arrived there as dawn broke. He had found on the mountain a very agreeable esplanade with a little stream that filtered between the rocks and reentered the ground almost as soon as it had emerged. A soft lawn carpeted the charming location. On the northern side, a rather profound cavern was visible, and on the southern side, the steep sides of the mountain were garnished with bushes, most all covered with the nests of a thousand different birds. There were also some wild trees, among them a chestnut-tree. A swarm of bees was buzzing around a rock with a southern exposure, sufficiently deeply fissured to lodge those useful insects.

Victorin spent the day in that lovely place, where he had the satisfaction of perceiving a few wild goats. When the heat of the day reached its highest intensity, he explored his new domain, in order to make sure that it did not contain any venomous beasts. He did, in fact, find a few snakes, which he killed. Then he flew over the rocks covering the cavern, where

---

[15] *Basse-justice* [seigneurial law] was a hangover from feudal times, which enabled minor offences to be judged and penalized by the lord of the manor rather than being submitted to *haut-justice* [the high court].

he discovered another esplanade that appeared to him to be a very agreeable place for the summer, because of the coolness and shade that the rocks maintained there. He alighted there and explored it; he did not find any venomous reptile, but a great many turtle-doves and wood-pigeons.

There were five or six little springs, which appeared to be produced by the crater of an ancient volcano, filed with ice that only melted in period of the most intense heat, because the sun's rays could not penetrate into it; the crater formed a natural glacier. He drank the water and found it excellent.

This, he said to himself, *will be my summer palace; it's here that the beautiful Christine will preserve the lilies of her complexion. The other esplanade will be my abode in winter, spring and autumn.*

After having examined everything he had a meal, which he would have liked to share with Christine, and having re-covered his strength, he rose up to a fearful height, trying to fly more boldly than ever. He came down again rapidly, striving to vary the direction of the pointed parasol, and seizing large pieces of rock in both hands as he rose, while his feet operated the erector very swiftly. He returned to horizontal flight by means of his chin, without releasing his burden, and maintained his flight at a sufficiently great height not to be seen by people down below.

All his trials succeeded fairly well, albeit after he had re-commenced several times; and when night fell he returned to the parental home, which was an hour and a half away at the most. Transported by joy at his discovery, he resolved to em-ploy all of the night that remained to him before his departure for the city in carrying various items to the Inaccessible Mountain, such as all the agricultural implements, clothes and linen he could procure. He also took chickens, rabbits and even two lambs, a male and a female.

He did more; having perceived in the courtyard of the château one evening a great deal of linen belonging to Christine and her chambermaid—slips, stockings, etc.—that had been hung out to dry after being bleached (which was only done once a year) he stole it during the night, formed several packages, and, in three trips, ferried to the Inaccessible Mountain almost all of it that belonged to the Seigneur's daughter. They were a great fuss at the château the next day; searches were carried out, various people were accused, but as it was impossible to discover any proof, the linen not being found anywhere, either at the merchants in the city or at the fairs, no one could be seriously harassed.

After that significant coup, Victorin went to spend an entire day on the mountain, which he would have been able to regard as his petty empire if he had not had a sovereign himself who did not even allow him to dispose of her person. He carried out further flights carrying heavy burdens. He arranged comfortable retreats for his chickens and his lambs, which took him very little time because he found a great many shelters under the rocks. He then began to cultivate a little patch of land, preparing it to plant vine-stocks, which he proposed to uproot from his father's garden—which he did the following night; and as the holes were prepared he only had to carry them in wicker baskets, which he put into the ground with them, in order that they could be taken out again easily.

He then reflected that it would be necessary to put someone there to look after his lambs, chickens etc, which might otherwise be lost, or at least go wild. In the town there was a sister-in-law of Jean Vezinier's, widowed very young and without children. The woman had not been very sage after her husband's death, and it was believed that her brother-in-law, Jean, who had seduced her first, At any rate, the woman had had a bastard daughter, whom she had nourished and brought up herself, but the unfortunate child was exposed to the scorn and ridicule of other children, which mortified her mother greatly. Victorian thought that it would give those two creatures pleasure to be carried to the Inaccessible Mountain, where he would nourish them and not only make them responsible for the care of the animals but cultivating a garden and beginning to sow a plot with wheat.

Having made that resolution, he put the plan into execution. One evening, while walking in the town, he perceived La Vezinier alone with her daughter, taking the air at their door without daring to chat to the neighbors. He went to them and told them that he had to talk to them but that, not that, wanting to be seen, they had to go to a remote place that he would indicate to them. While they went there Victorin fitted his wings and rose into the air. As he had told the mother and daughter to climb on to a rock, in order that he could see them at a distance and not have to hail them, he fell upon them and carried them both away, by means of broad straps that he wound around them under their armpits.

They lost consciousness out of fright, and Victorin, redoubling his effort, went with his burden to the Inaccessible Mountain in less than an hour. He set them down there with provisions that he brought for them, threw water in their faces, and when he saw them coming round, he flew away without being seen. As the mother could read, however, he set out on a piece of paper what she had to do.

When she recovered, the woman read the note; she saw the promise that they would not be left without food and would soon be given company, which consoled her slightly. She had a strange idea about her abduction, however, when she found herself in a land without inhabitants; she thought she had been brought there by the Devil as a punishment for her past conduct. Nevertheless, she did as she was ordered and set to work with her daughter. Victorin brought them more provisions from time to time, by night, without showing himself.

For himself, having returned to his father's house, he went to bed and slept rather late. Everything causes a sensation in a little town; the next day, he heard everyone talking about the disappearance of La Vezinier and her daughter. It was said that he had gone away out of displeasure, but people were very surprised that they had not sold their property, or even their utensils. All the wells were searched, for fear that they had been thrown into one; enquiries were made in the neighboring villages and on the roads, but nothing was discovered. It was then that good souls said that the Devil had taken them away, which was soon regarded as certain by all the old wives in the region.

By means of these preparations, Victorin had a fixed and determined plan. He did not fail to present himself every day in the gardens of the château and to try to render himself agreeable to Christine by his attentions. He succeeded in that. On the eve of his departure from the city he had seen the Seigneur's daughter during the day, and on encountering him, she had smiled at him in a very obliging manner. He followed her without affectation. The beautiful Christine, either deliberately or accidentally, dropped her fan and carried on walking. Victorin picked it up and ran to give it back to her, but on the way he lifted it to his lips five or six times, and Christine perceived it. Even so, she received it in a gracious fashion.

She was alone at that moment. She asked him questions. She asked him whether he had a mistress.

"Yes. Mademoiselle."

"Is she beautiful?"

"Like the fresh dew of the morning."

"Does she love you?" And she added, precipitately: "Oh, undoubtedly!"

"Alas, no," said Victorin, with a sigh.

"She's either not much of a connoisseur, then, or very proud."

"Yes, Madame, she's proud, but she has reason to be. I'm nothing compared with her."

"She's a great Lady, then?"

"She's more than that, Mademoiselle; she's Beauty personified; a King wouldn't be too great for her."

"You're piquing my curiosity. So where is this Beauty hiding?"

"Among the lilies and the roses; she lives in charming places, which she embellishes further."

"You've read romances then, Monsieur Victorin?"

"Yes, Mademoiselle; I've read *Cyrus, Polexandre, Clélie, Astrée* and *La Princesse de Clèves*, which pleased me even more."[16]

"I suspected as much, to hear you talk."

"Oh, Mademoiselle, it's a great honor that you do me."

"It's necessary to read the English authors: *Pamela, Clarissa, Grandison*."

"I don't have them."

"I'll tell Julienne to lend them to you. But don't become a Lovelace, at least!"

"As soon as you forbid me, Mademoiselle, I can assure you that I will not."[17]

Christine smiled at the naïve fashion in which Victorin replied to her. Having reached the end of the path, however, she perceived her father, her mother and a few friends nearby. Christine blushed at her familiarity with the son of the procurator fiscal. She adopted her disdainful attitude, still charming regardless, in order to say: "Adieu, Victorin."

The young man bowed to his companion and withdrew, as stylishly as he could, although he sensed that his peasant-like awkwardness had spoiled his reverence. He left the château, firmly resolved to neglect nothing in the city to acquire

---

[16] The first four titles are among the longest novels in existence: the ten volumes of *Artaméne ou le Grand Cyrus* (1649-1653), by Madeleine de Scudery but signed by her brother, total nearly two million words; she also wrote the kindred romance *Clélie* (1654-1660). *Polexandre* (1619-1637), by Marin Le Roy de Gomberville, is more in the vein of an adventure story. The classic pastoral novel *L'Astrée* (1607-1627) is by Honoré d'Urfé. The much shorter *La Princesse de Clèves* (1678), published anonymously but generally attributed to Madame de La Fayette, is a more intense and tightly-plotted novel of passion set in the court of Henri II.

[17] Lovelace is Clarissa Harlowe's abductor in the longest of the three novels by Samuel Richardson cited by Christine.

fine manners before executing his designs upon Mademoiselle Christine.

He left the next day on horseback, accompanied by one of his father's domestics, and arrived in the evening in ***, at the home of Maître Troismotsparligne, a *procureur* in the seneschal's court.

Victorin was a handsome fellow; lively colors animated his cheeks, and a masculine and robust attitude, devoid of harshness, combined with his natural beauty. His principal goal being to learn fine manners, in order to render himself agreeable to Christine when he had abducted her, he made that his first subject of study. In wanting to please, one pleases.

Madame Troismotsparligne was a well-made woman of about twenty-five, although her husband was well past fifty. At twenty paces, or even ten, she could pass for a pretty woman; the form of her face was agreeable, and her color was almost equal to Victorin's. Seen at close range, however, one found that she was much scarred by smallpox. Her walk was voluptuous, and even lascivious, her figure admirable; she had a pretty leg and a charming foot, so she took extremely good care of her adornment.

It was that woman who caused Victorin's first aggravations; Victorin, whose senses were new and vigorous, only needed a spark to catch fire. But what can true love not accomplish! Victorin resisted the attractions, the advances, the charms and the lures of the Procurator's wife, or he responded with some politeness, which was only to form his fine manners, because he knew that there is nothing like lessons from a woman to form a young man.

However,[18] he cast his eyes over the young men of condition who inhabited the city and searched for models among Christine's equals, convinced that the Latin proverb (for he

---

[18] The following episode is omitted in its entirety from the Laffont edition, in spite of its relevance to the following section; the Laffont text resumes with the line "On Saturdays he returned to the Inaccessible Mountain."

had learned the rudiment) *Similis simili gaudet*—one only pleases with those similar to oneself—is the truest of all proverbs.

There was then in that city of the Dauphiné, whose name is irrelevant here, a young gentleman who passed for the Corypheus of the locale. He was a handsome fellow, the son of a mother more than good, rich, conceited and putting all his merit into his clothes, his embroideries, his ruffles, his jewels and a very elegant carriage, in which he took pleasure in riding after dinner every day for two or three hours. It was that dandy whose acquaintance, and even amity, Victorin was ambitious to make. He had one sure mean of achieving that in an instant, which was to make him party to his invention, but the young clerk had no intention of doing that! As he had found the rare secret of flying through the air, though, he could surely find the more facile one of flying on the ground.

One day, Victorin encountered the fop on the rampart alone, beside his carriage, into which he was about to climb back and return to the beautiful streets of the city. "Monsieur," he said, going up to him casually, "I possess a secret which might perhaps give you pleasure; I can make your carriage move without horses."[19]

"Thos words excited the attention of the fop; he stopped, and seeing a well-dressed young man he asked who he was.

"I'm only a procurator's clerk," Victorin replied, "but I have brilliant hopes."

---

[19] Author's note: "Announcements have been seen in 1779 on the part of a man who possesses Victorin's second secret; my friend should not be accused of having credited it to his hero in imitation of that mechanician, since the manuscript is initialed by the late Monsieur de Mairobert, dead before the announcement. [Joly.]" The writer and royal censor Mathieu-Francois Pidansat de Mairobert committed suicide in March 1779. Restif knew him well and claimed in his autobiographical writings to mourn his death on its anniversary every year.

Meanwhile, the fop reflected for the first time, darting a glance at his horses. "A fine secret," he said, "that would make my carriage go without its most beautiful ornament!"

"That's not what I'm claiming, Monsieur," said Victorian. "Your horses would be accompanying the carriage, but they would only be hitched by the reins, and that would excite the admiration of the whole city."

At those words, the delighted fop, foolish, vain and arrogant as he was, threw his arms around the procurator's clerk and kissed him to both cheeks, calling him his dear friend. "When can you operate this marvel?" he asked him.

"You appreciate," Victorin replied, "that I'm not employing any magic..."

"When can it be done?" the fop interrupted, urgently.

"Not now; it's necessary for me to dispose my mechanisms in your carriage. I'll set to work tomorrow, and in a week, at the latest, you'll enjoy the pleasure of astonishing the city, being celebrated throughout the province, throughout the kingdom, Europe, and perhaps the world—for I want to give you the honor of the invention."

"Oh, it will be necessary not to communicate it to anyone!" cried the fop, pirouetting with joy.

From that moment on, Victorin became the intimate of the rich young man; he took him everywhere and introduced him into the best society of the city as a young man who had "brilliant hopes" and who could be received.

That was all that Victorin wanted. He adopted the tone of society, and became nothing less than an accomplished cavalier.

In the meantime, he worked on his new friend's carriage. A locksmith made him the mechanism, without knowing its purpose, and after the week for which he had asked, the machine was ready. The fop was effervescent with pleasure. He climbed into his carriage one Sunday at four o'clock in the afternoon, in the most beautiful weather; his coachman harnessed the horses; the traces were taken away, which amazed the man and made him think that his master was mad—but

Victorin has tested the machine, and by means of two seesaws set in motion by the carriage-driver's feet the wheels assumed the movement of a rapid trot. A lever placed within the reach of the hand permitted steering; but increasing the movement one could go uphill, and by slowing it down could descend without danger. The coachman looked at it stupidly at first; then he made the sign of the cross and cried that it was the Devil. His master threatened him, but the rogue would not climb back up. A few blows of the cane made him see reason.

At first no one paid attention to the marvel of the carriage, but Victorin was waiting for the vehicle with a few of his friends in the busiest square in the city; he pointed the phenomenon out to them. They drew closer, and ran after it in order to follow it and see the carriage. The populace imitated them; everything was in turmoil, and the fop, swearing, could not part the crowd; he retraced his steps, between two lines of admirers, and enjoyed all his glory. What a moment for a dandy! He could not contain himself; he overflowed with ease, glory, foolishness and pleasure.

After having shown off sufficiently he went home, too weary to do any more because of the movement he had been obliged to make with his feet in order to make the carriage go. I forgot to say that he had the horses removed before entering the courtyard, and that the movement of the carriage was not slowed down in the least by their absence, which completed confounding the incredulous.

One fraction of the sectors went away profoundly astonished, while the other—the ignorant populace—went home convinced that the fop had made a pact with the Devil.

You can imagine how many questions bombarded the possessor of such a fine secret in the circles in which he showed himself for the rest of the evening. His merit appeared a hundred times more brilliant, and many women virtuous enough until that moment to scorn his fatuity were finally disposed to lay down their arms to him. Did he take advantage of it? That is not part of my story.

"Who would have believed," said foolish old women, "that a man apparently so light-headed, so frivolous, was occupied with inventions capable of immortalizing him? See how often one is mistaken in the judgments one makes!"

Even sensible people were surprised, for no one thought about Victorin, who only had the appearance of a naively clever and very young man...

But it is time to get back to our hero.

On Saturdays he returned to the Inaccessible Mountain in order to take food to La Vezinier and her daughter—these voyages were made by night, but Victorin returned to spend Sunday afternoon in the city; he landed in a little wood and came back on foot—and occupy himself with putting the grotto into a fit state to receive Christine. He brought different things there, which he was able to procure by means of the presents that his friend the fop gave him in the first flush of his gratitude: a beautiful bed, chairs, tables, a chest of drawers, and even a sofa. He also brought silverware, fabrics, gauzes, etc.

When all of that was in the grotto he thought about consolidation; the southern esplanade could be entirely cultivated and furnish nourishment to thirty or forty people. That cultivation was proceeding very slowly in the hands of La Vezinier and her daughter; they needed an aide, and above all horses or oxen. Victorin knew a poor young man in his village who was in love with the daughter of a rich farmer, in whose employ he was a plowman and vine-grower. He abducted him one evening and brought him to the Inaccessible Mountain, after which he placed three horses and a plow there, wheat to sow, etc. He promised the poor fellow, who did not recognize him and mistook him for the Devil, like the woman and the bastard girl, to bring him his mistress, on condition that he treated her well. He showed him the provisions, ordered him to work to till the ground with the two women, and promised to visit him every week.

Victorin had taken care not to abduct the farmer's daughter, in order to ensure that no one suspected what had happened to the plowboy. He was also waiting for a favorable opportunity to seize her during the night, in order not to be seen by anyone, and that opportunity was hard to find, given that it took him at least an hour by night to come from the city to his village, and he could not make the journey very often.

Finally, however, chance favored him and his hopes; one evening, the young woman left all her own underwear and her mother's extended in the garden. Victorin arrived, saw it, and stole it, along with corsets, skirts, etc. The next day, he returned again and, having perceived the farmer hiding in one corner of the garden with his shotgun, his wife in the other and his servants dispersed, tried to find the daughter.

She was at the door of the house, a lantern in her hand. He swooped down on her, flying in an inverted arc; she uttered a feeble scream, and fainted. Victorin carried her away to the Inaccessible Mountain, on which he left her, after having alerted La Vezinier and the boy, enjoining the latter, under pain of his life, to respect her until he had found a means of marrying them.

That gave a great deal of pleasure to the poor boy, who saw in consequence that it was not the Devil who had carried him off, since the Devil only encourages us to evil. That was his reflection, and that of La Vezinier. Poor Cathos was very astonished, on coming round, to find herself in the arms of Joachim! He did all he could to convince her that it was not him who had abducted her; she could not believe any of it, and wanted to return to her father's house, until he made her see that that was impossible, and that they could not get out of the place where they were now living.

It was then autumn. Cathos was very surprised to find the two women there who had been believed to have drowned in a well. All three of them aided Joachim in his work and they sowed sufficient ground to nourish ten or twelve people. Victorin came to see them often, as much to bring them provisions as to encourage them to work. As for him, he had resolved to wait until the return of summer before abducting Christine, unless some suitor appeared who asked for her hand in marriage. But none presented himself who was agreeable, with the result that Victorin had time to embellish the dwelling that he destined for the sovereign of his thoughts, and even to prepare little Estates of which she would be the queen.

He transported a shoemaker and a hairdresser to the Inaccessible Mountain, the latter to serve as chambermaid, and a dressmaker, a tailor and a cook. Afterwards, reflecting that all those people might well have a desire for one another, one evening, he brought a priest, whom he informed of his intentions on the way. The Ecclesiastic told the new inhabitants of the Inaccessible Mountain to make their mutual choices, and that he would marry them. The plowboy married his Cathos, the shoemaker the cook and the tailor the dressmaker. There remained the hairdresser, to whom Victorin made the promise that he would soon find her an agreeable husband.

Victorin was so occupied with his own affairs that he did those of his procurator rather poorly. He often received reprimands, but the procurator's wife always took his side warmly. That did not please Maître Troismotsparligne at all, who resolved to get rid of a young man so well liked by his wife. In consequence he wrote a letter of very sharp complaints to Victorin's father, in which he asked him to come and fetch his son. The procurator's wife, who saw the address on the letter, suspected its contents; she made arrangements to take possession of it when the procurator gave it to the maidservant to take it to the post office, and wrote another in an entirely contrary tone. The procurator fiscal replied in consequence, and sent presents of game to the procurator, who did not understand it at all, but as his clerk had mended his ways somewhat, he decided to be patient.

For his part, Victorin saw the term approaching that he had fixed for the abduction of Christine; he perceived that the amity of the fop was cooling, and the presents were already drying up. He hastened to make all his arrangements for the execution of his important design. It is said—although I am not sure of it—that, penetrated by the last procedure of the procurator's wife, he testified his gratitude to her, but still with the view of completing his formation for Christine, and that he received various little gifts from her, which contributed more than a little to the ornamentation of the grotto of the Inaccessible Mountain.

Finally, he had a desire to pay a visit to his parents. The procurator wanted nothing better, and Victorin set off on horseback—but he had taken care, on the preceding nights, to take all his baggage to the grotto, with the exception of his wings. There is no need to depict here the reception that is parents gave him, thanks to the letter from the obliging wife of the procurator. Victorin responded to it, but yearned to go up to the château.

The opportunity presented itself that same evening, for a small matter that the procurator fiscal wanted to communicate to his Seigneur. He sent his son, because he was better spoken and better educated.

Victorin dressed up before presenting himself, with the exquisite taste in which fools excel—although he was not one—and which alone had made the reputation of the fop. He arrived brilliantly; he was announced. The Seigneur was at table with a numerous company.

"It's Victorin, the son of my procurator fiscal, Mesdames!"

"Send him in."

A handsome cavalier appeared. Christine's heart quivered. Kindly smiles brightened the faces of six ladies, who had already assumed disdainful expressions. Even the Seigneur, on seeing the well-dressed young peasant, who bowed with an infinite grace, could not forbid himself a sentiment of respect, or something closely resembling one, since the recognized Victorin and addressed him as "Monsieur."

The young man acquitted his commission in fine speech, and with intelligence.

"I'm very content with you," replied Christine's father. "You haven't wasted your time in the city, and I can see that I've been told the truth about the fine acquaintances you've made there…damn it! Do you know, Mesdames, that he was the intimate of the most elegant of the young gentlemen of ***?"

"Of whom?" asked a Lady from the city. "Of Monsieur de Bourbonne? Indeed, I recognize Monsieur! Everyone attributes a marvelous invention to him, by means of which Monsieur de B*** has had traveled all round the city several times, in a carriage that moves of its own accord."

"Moves of its own accord!" cried the other Ladies. "Oh, Monsieur, will you explain that to us?"

"Sit down here," the Seigneur said to him. "With your permission, Mesdames?"

"Oh, my God yes! Monsieur de B*** is well-known to us, and he's eaten with him very habitually," said the Lady from the city.

"Set a place!" cried the Master.

And Victorin, addressed as *Monsieur*, was seated beside Christine, of whom he seemed to be begging pardon for a very respectful gaze.

"Well," said the Seigneur, "tell us a little about this invention?"

"It's really Monsieur de B***'s" the young man replied, modestly.

"Oh, you're keeping the secret!" cried the Lady from the city. "Everyone knows that it's yours, and Monsieur de B*** admitted it to his mother."

"I might have helped him with it."

"My God, my dear Victorin," said the Seigneur, transported by joy, "you must make me one like it."

"I'll do more, Monsieur. Often, six horses can't pull a carriage with all the compost from the cesspit that's piled up in it; I'll make you a machine that will pull it with a single horse!"

"Oh, I'll let you off the other one," said the good Seigneur, again transported by joy. "That's the useful one! But my dear boy, do you know that your fortune's made, if you want it?"

"I have no ambition," Victorin replied, "and if the human heart were not susceptible to a gentler passion, I'd be perfectly happy in my estate..."

And his eyes turned involuntarily toward Christine, with an expression of respect and tenderness, which the young demoiselle probably sensed, for she blushed like a rose opening at the dawn of a beautiful day.

"You'll only have to make a trivial adjustment to Christine's carriage."

"Tomorrow," said the young man, ardently.

All the Ladies retained Victorin, and the men presented humble requests to him. He promised to do what he could."

The next day, he set to work for his Seigneur, and by means of the work that he got the locksmith and the cartwright to do, he had finished the machine in three days. He was going to try it out in the absence of the father and the daughter, but the beautiful individual found out, and witnessed that with the help of only two valets, the machine hauled a cart full of fertilizer out of a hollow that six strong horses could hardly draw on a flat surface. Young Victorin had a particular talent for mechanics, aided by that of Jean Vezinier, whom he had undoubtedly surpassed; their first attempt at their wings had been another masterpiece!

Victorin had returned to his father's house before the Seigneur arrived, wanting to leave the beautiful Christine the pleasure of telling him the story of what had happened; he had instructed her as to how to have the trial repeated, in order that she might amuse her father. The young demoiselle was not insensible to that delicacy. The good Seigneur, in his turn, was infinitely satisfied.

Meanwhile, Victorin was occupied with his favorite project. He continued to transport, every night, useful objects or mere items of commodity to the Inaccessible Mountain. He had the pleasure of seeing his farmer ready to harvest a fine crop. The previous spring, he had planted vines on a hillock, but until they bore fruit, he had had the strength, so powerful was his mechanism, to transport a few casks of Bordeaux and

Arbois wine. To make those journeys he found pretexts for visiting the neighborhood; he flew by night, arriving before daybreak, made his purchases and carried them away the following night, after taking care to place them conveniently during the evening.

Finally, everything was ready to receive Christine. The harvest was gathered in on the Inaccessible Mountain; Victorin had just finished a windmill to grind the wheat; all the necessary things had been constructed. He finally determined to abduct his mistress. A fortunate hazard even enabled him to take possession of a trunk that contained her most beautiful clothes.

Christine was due to go to the city. Victorin was so well informed that he knew that the Seigneur thought that sojourn necessary for his daughter. It was the eve of the departure and the carriage was loaded. Victorin had examined everything that same evening. He removed during darkness almost everything that belonged to his mistress, and made two trips to the Inaccessible Mountain that night. In the first he took the trunk, in the second he watched out for the moment when Christine would come out for the departure. It was bound to be early in the morning, because they wanted to arrive in the city in time for dinner.

He was not deceived in his expectation. At daybreak everyone was up and about in the Château de B***m**t. There was no moon and the obscurity was perfect. Victorin, who had done so many trial runs in abducting all the people of whom he had need to serve the sovereign of his will adequately, was hovering motionlessly above the château, much as an eagle with hooked talons lies in wait for a lamb that is commencing to bound into the flowery meadow in order to graze.

Christine finally appeared, preceded by her chambermaid, who was lighting her path, and accompanied by her father, who as swearing at the idle valets. She remained on the perron while her father and the chambermaid went down to the courtyard.

The moment was too precious not to be seized. Victorin, directing his erector parasol downwards, fell from the heights of the sky upon the beautiful Christine and lifted her up, saying to her: "Have no fear, divinity of my soul; I adore you; have no fear!"

But fear was the stronger. Christine, feeling herself lifted up by some kind of monster, uttered a piercing scream and fainted.

That scream was heard by her father, as well as the sound of Victorin's flight, which he mistook for the fall of a part of his château.

"Oh! My daughter has been crushed!" he cried. And he flew in the direction from which the scream had come. As he ran, his lantern went out—but everything was standing, nothing had fallen. He called to Christine, but Christine did not reply to his redoubled cries.

The domestics came running; they searched, they groped. Christine could no longer be found.

During that tumult, dawn broke; they thought that they would finally discover what they trembled to see: Christine crushed—but there was not the slightest trace of her! What dolor that was for a father idolatrous of a daughter so meritorious and so beautiful!

III

Meanwhile, Victorin was soaring on the waves of the sky, carrying his precious prey. Christine was still unconscious, and her lover hastened to arrive, for fear that if she recovered consciousness and saw herself so high up, she might experience too great a fright. He arrived on the Inaccessible Mountain at the instant when his beautiful mistress opened her eyes; he only just had time to take off his wings, also taking off his sailor's jacket, in order to come to her and reassure her.

"Where am I?" she said. "Victorin? Oh, how delighted I am to see you! It's you, then, who has saved me from the claws of the great bird that carried me off? Where is my father? Where is he, Victorin! How have you saved me?"

"Alas, adorable Christine, you are in the retreat of the great bird—but have no fear, so long as I am with you. I have been watching over your safety since the monster's first appearance, and I knew where it deposited the various persons it abducted.

"I read one day in the city that a certain Daedalus, wanting to escape from the island of Crete, made himself wings, and as I am rather inventive, I immediately began racking my brains to fabricate some for myself, since the thing was possible, and to watch over your safety by flying through the air like the birds. I had the good fortune to succeed in that, after various attempts of another kind.

"I came out of my father's house this morning to present my respects to you on your departure. I perceived the big bird; I suspected that it was meditating some evil deed. I deployed my wings, which were all ready, and hid. As soon as you appeared, my fears were only too well confirmed. The big bird swooped down upon you; it lifted you up, but I followed it here in order to snatch away its prey.

"We are on an inaccessible mountain; it deposited you here and flew away, doubtless not for long. But I have a secret to vanquish it, and as soon as it reappears, I shall go to attack it. The worst thing is that I can, in truth, get out of here myself, but I will never be able to take you with me. Thus, I shall be obliged to live here for as long as you remain here, and only go away at your orders, for the time that you specify. You shall lack nothing here, beautiful Christine; I shall make it a law to fulfill all your desires."

Christine was half-dead during this speech, which she did not have the strength to interrupt. Victorin begged her to enter the grotto, where she would be safer if the big bird came back. She consented, out of fear, and was nevertheless agreeably surprised to find therein an apartment as comfortable and well decorated as her own. Victorin left her there, on the pretext of going to see whether the big bird was returning and to fight it. In truth, it was to give instructions to his people and command them to keep the secret on pain of death.

He had not expected the good fortune that had just accompanied the abduction, but the ideas that Christine had adopted changed his plan of action, and instead of confessing his amour and making its excess the excuse for his crime, he wanted to appear to be her defender, win her heart gradually, and become her husband by her own choice as much as by necessity. Above all, he indoctrinated the hairdresser who was to serve as chambermaid; she had intelligence, and he promised her a husband if she were faithful to him, at the same time as he proved to her, as clear as daylight, that she could not avoid his vengeance if she betrayed him.

Having taking all these precautions, Victorin smeared himself with the blood of a few wood-pigeons, which he killed in order to prepare a nice dinner, and went back to Christine, seemingly fearful, to assure her that he had just wounded the big bird and driven it away, but that he could not be certain that it would not come back, not knowing whether or not its wounds were mortal.

Slightly reassured, Christine testified her gratitude to Victorin, who convinced her to take some refreshments while awaiting dinner. The chambermaid and the cook were introduced then, and came to offer their services to Christine, as they were in a condition inferior to her, and doubtless destined to serve her by the big bird, whose had abducted them expressly before her. Cathos appeared, as well as La Vezinier and her daughter, and all three were easily recognized by Christine, who made each of them recount every detail of their abduction. It was the same for all the rest.

Victorin listened to what was said from hiding, ready to show himself at the commencement of the slightest indiscretion, but he had reason to be content. He made that clear to the three women when he came back in. Afterwards, Christine having had something to eat, Victorin invited her to come and take a tour of her new domain—in order to take possession of it, he said, there being no appearance that the big bird, freshly wounded, would dare to come back so soon.

The beautiful Christine consented to that, and, supported by the happy Victorin, into whose arms she threw herself without the slightest complaint, as into a safe refuge, she visited the cultivated southern esplanade.

It was autumn; in addition to the planted vines, there were two or three large stocks at the foot of a rock aboriginal to the Inaccessible Mountain, from which beautiful grapes were hanging, because Victorin had pruned the stocks the previous year and cultivated them. He lifted Christine up in his amorous arms in order that she could pick the clusters that pleased her most for herself. Then he showed her the stream.

He showed her a few wild goats that had been domesticated, and which furnished very good milk because of the aromatic plants on which they were nourished. Then he took her to the four ewes, including the progeny of two that the big bird—so he said—had doubtless brought there pregnant. There were also two cows and a young male calf, as well as a horse and a mare for the labor. He showed her the natural hives that the bees had made in a rock covered in moss and sheltered from the north wind. But he put on a pretence of discovering all of that and, like her seeing it for the first time—which rendered the amusement keener.

Finally, appetite making itself felt, they returned to the grotto in order to dine there. That meal was charming for Victorin, but it ought not to be believed that Christine was tranquil; her tears flowed continually, in spite of the young man's attentions and the insistent cares of the chambermaid, who was tenderly attached to her from the start. She could not be consoled, and the approach of dusk frightened her a great deal. It was, however, demonstrated to her so clearly that she would be safe if she shut herself in, that she decided to go to bed.

Victorin promised that he would stand sentinel at her door, armed from head to toe, and her chambermaid slept with her. The other people of the Inaccessible Mountain occupied the access passages of the grotto, long since appropriated by them and very comfortable. All these arrangements tranquilized the timid Christine. She even told Victorin that she did not want him to risk his life or his health during the night, and that she begged him to conserve it for her sake, etc.

The next day, Victorian thought about procuring amusements. The work of the people was very light; everywhere that everyone lends a hand to the work, there is always time for pleasure. Fortunately, Christine had not seen the city and only knew country pleasures as yet, even though she was a demoiselle. There were, therefore, hours regulated for games and dances. Victorin had learned to play the violin, with the consequence that he was the soul of the party.

Gradually, Christine's tears became less bitter; her dolor was no longer anything but tender, caused more by anxiety for the health of the father she loved and the certainty that he was in despair at her loss than by her own fate. Adored by everyone surrounding her, served by a handsome young man to whom she was not indifferent, and to whom she believed that she owed her life, where could she have been happier?

She often begged Victorin to try to fly to her father's house, but he always put it off, under the pretext of fear of the big bird, which might only be waiting for his absence to swoop down on the Inaccessible Mountain and transport her to some unknown location. These reasons appeared sound. After six months, however, the tender Christine could no longer bear the anxieties that her father was causing her, and was visibly changing. Victorin, who left the Inaccessible Mountain almost every night in order to procure things he needed, had news of the worthy Seigneur, but could not give it to her.

Finally, one evening, it was agreed between Christine and him that he would leave in darkness without anyone knowing—even the chambermaid—and fly to the Château de B***m**t, and that she would not leave the grotto until he returned.

There was a proof that Victorin wanted to undertake. He hid himself in the depths of the grotto instead of leaving, in order to see whether he could count on the discretion of his mistress and that of his people, in case she talked to them. He had every reason to be content. No one doubted that he had gone, because they always heard the loud noise that his wings made when he took off—unless he went to take off from the top of a fairly distant rock: a circumstance of which everyone was unaware.

The following day, he presented himself before Christine as having arrived from the Château de B***m**t, which greatly surprised his people, and he gave her an account of what had happened since the abduction.

"Scarcely had you been abducted, Mademoiselle, than Monsieur your father, who could not have any suspicion of what had happened, searched for you and had others search for you everywhere. Imagine his astonishment and dolor when, in broad daylight, you were not found, dead or alive. The surprise was increased when it was found that your trunk, which had been in the carriage, and your most precious effects, had disappeared. The most bizarre suspicions arose in your father's mind, and changed his despair into fury—but so much the better! That is what saved him.

"Nor did it take long for people to think of me. As I was unable to be here and in my father's house, my disappearance caused me to be regarded as your abductor. Monsieur de

B***m**t had me tried, and I am presently hanged in effigy in the main square in Grenoble. That is what prevented me from showing myself to Monsieur your father and informing him of your fate. I have equipped myself with writing materials; you can write a letter one of these days; I will carry it on the first favorable opportunity and leave it on the balcony of the château, in order that your father, who never fails to go there to smoke his pipe when he gets up, will find it in the morning.

"It is necessary that I do not go right away, however, for I have certain proof that the big bird is still prowling around; I perceived, on landing on our mountain, a new inhabitant that can only have been brought by the bird. He is a very handsome fellow"—Victorin looked at the chambermaid—"who will suit Cocote very well, I believe, if Monsieur Bird judges it appropriate also to transport a priest here in order to marry her to the newcomer...but I am going astray from what Mademoiselle is burning to know. Monsieur your father is well; it will be sufficient to write him a letter to destroy all your suspicions and inform him of the exact truth, in order that I can be unhanged. The persons already abducted by the big bird will convince him..."

"Oh, my dear Victorin," said Christine, "my father has never wanted to believe any of that; he said that they were fables."

"You see, beautiful Christine!"

"Yes," she replied, weeping, "I see."

"Calm that dolor, which is killing me, adorable sovereign of all of us here, or I cannot answer for my life."

"I shall calm myself," she said, "but it is necessary to justify you with regard to a cherished father."

"That will not be as difficult as you believe; it is not as if the big bird has not been seen. So many people have seen it that it is no longer possible to doubt it, and your letter will therefore have its effect on your Papa."

"You console me, Victorin! Oh, how much gratitude I owe you! Dispose of my life."

"Yes, I would dispose of it, if it were possible—but it would be…to render it happy."

With that unexpected word, Victorin threw himself at her feet, and, having taken possession of one of her hands, which she abandoned to him, he covered it with burning kisses.

"Get up," she said to him, finally. "I have only you here. Alas, what would have become of me without my dear Victorin?"

"Oh, Madame, how you penetrate me with so much generosity...and if I could...but it is impossible to leave this mountain; all the power of the King of France and forty years of toil could not remove us from it. To try to lift you with a machine as frail as my wings would be to risk breaking us both on a rock...oh Madame, how our finest days will pass…!"

"I only regret yours."

"And I, Madame, mourn for you alone..."

While saying these words, Victorin devoured Christine's hands, which she did not make any move to withdraw. She was the daughter of a Seigneur, it is true, and Victorin was only the son of the procurator fiscal, but he was the king of the Inaccessible Mountain, and Christine was well aware of the fact that, although everyone only obeyed her, everything was done by virtue of him. Finally, the pride and prejudices of birth, no longer having any witnesses to sustain them, had gradually vanished before the affection that Victorin had always inspired.

The young man sensed his victory, but he veiled his joy beneath the flattering testimony of an entire devotion. He did not allow a glimpse of any pretention, and only his burning lips expressed his amour on Christine's white hands.

Eventually, she thought about withdrawing them, but it was without anger, and for the rest of the day, she appeared quite tranquil. She went for a walk with Victorin and her chambermaid.

The young lover had discovered a passage leading to the summer meadow some days before. It was very narrow, between two precipices. He had taken care to interlace as many branches of bushes as he had been able to bring together in order to reassure the sight. He took Christine over it, guiding her at every step, and pretended to discover that charming place, which appeared to have another climate, for the first time. The flowers and the lawn were as fresh as in spring, althhough it was then the month of July.

Christine was charmed by the discovery of that new domain, where the little flock of sheep and the milk-cows were taken the very next day.

"It will be our summer abode," Victorin said to her, "for as long as it pleases heaven to leave us here."

Meanwhile, Christine did not forget to write to her father. She composed the following letter:

Monsieur and very dear Father,

My greatest distress, in the misfortune that has overtaken me, is the pain that it has caused you. That is what has afflicted me more than all the rest, since I was abducted by the big bird that you had already glimpsed one evening. It is the same one that had previously carried off the two women who were thought to be drowned, as well as Cathos Denêvres and her father's plowboy, with a few other people of whom you have heard talk. I have found them all here, dear Father; the big bird has not done them any harm. But I do not know what it would have reserved for your daughter, for whom it appears that it had taken all those people, if, by a good fortune for which I cannot thank heaven enough, I had not had the help of your Victorin against it.

That excellent fellow, to whom we doubtless owe the conservation of my life, having watched out for the big bird after the stories, treated too scornfully, that were running around, has found the secret, thanks to the great skill that heaven has given him in mechanics, of making wings, following the big bird and discovering its retreat. He arrived here almost immediately after me, on the day of my abduction, and fought the big bird with so much courage that he succeeded in

68

chasing it away from the Inaccessible Mountain to which it had carried us all, and where we are well enough provided with the necessities of life.

In my particular case, I am respected by everyone as a sovereign; Victorin is my chief subject, and I know that it is to him that I owe all my authority. Furthermore, dear and respectable Father, you ought not to have any anxiety; Victorin keeps to his place and your daughter knows all that she owes him. That amiable young man alone has the faculty of leaving the Inaccessible Mountain, and uses it solely to serve me. He is the one who will bring you this letter. I beg you, my dear Father, to put your reply in the same place, in order that Victorin can take it, for he does not dare to speak to you, or even to show himself, because he knows that he has been unjustly hanged in effigy and that he has been convicted at trial.

You ought, therefore, dear Father, to keep your windows closed and not show yourself on the tower from which you love to discover what is happening in the countryside by means of your telescope, for otherwise, Victorin will never dare to take the risk of collecting your dear reply.

I am, with the most profound respect, very dear Father, your tender and submissive daughter,

Christine de B***m**t.

When the beautiful Christine had written her letter to her Father, she read it to Victorin, who was very flattered by that mark of confidence. She sealed it and handed it to him, to carry it as soon as it was convenient. The young man, who knew that the desires of beautiful women are urgent, departed the following night for the Chateau de B***m**t. Needless to say, the fear of being retained or discovered prevented him from showing himself at his father's house, but while Christine was writing her letter he had written one to his parents saying much the same things, with as much ingenuity as possible. He put the letter to his mistress' father on the worthy Seigneur's balcony, and the one to his own father on the sill of the window at which the procurator fiscal took the air every morning in order to dispose his stomach for the morning meal. After carrying out those two commissions he passed over the city of ***, where the priest lived who had already married his people, and carried him to the Inaccessible Mountain again.

When she awoke, Christine saw Victorin come in.

"Your orders have been carried out, Madame, and Monsieur your father is doubtless reading your letter at this moment."

"Oh, my dear Victorin, how obliged I am to you for your promptitude."

"That isn't all, Madame. As soon as I left the mountain, the big bird came back; there is another newcomer in your domicile."

"Who is he?"

"A priest, Madame; thus, your chambermaid, who has had time to get to know her lover, and who appears to love him, can marry him today, if her beautiful mistress will permit it. Everyone will be happy here, Madame..."

"Oh, Victorin! But we shall keep the priest; it has been a long time since we have heard mass..."

"That is a pleasant idea, but what if the big bird takes him from us, even in broad daylight, as it has done once before?"

"You're right, Victorin."

"Oh, Madame, if only I were worthy of you!"

"Listen to me, Victorin: seriously, are we here for life? You would not deceive me?"

"My God, yes, Madame, unfortunately for you...because...for myself, I am happy wherever you are."

"In that case, Victorin..."

"Speak, Madame! Oh, if I were your equal, you would not be reduced to explaining yourself first—but respect will close my mouth eternally. In any case, Madame, count on the fact that you will always have in me a lover as submissive as tender. Make my happiness; I will almost dare to answer for yours."

"But Victorin, what would my father say?"

70

"We shall persuade him, Madame. I shall only ever present myself before him after having done striking deeds, and served the State, by means of my faculty of flight. And who knows whether I might not perhaps find, with the aid of a powerful king, some means of getting you away from here? Decide my fate, adorable Christine!"

"Monsieur," said the beautiful individual, seeing him on his knees, "I cannot doubt your sincerity, for I know very well that, in addition to owing you everything, I depend absolutely on your will here, and that it is by an effect of your generosity that I command. You are the king of this little society; thus, you are the master. Dispose of my fate yourself."

"Me! Madame, Oh, Madame, I would a thousand times rather be eternally unhappy! Me, dispose of my sovereign! Me, who would put my entire life, my glory and my happiness entirely in your dependency! Let us wait, Madame, and if misfortune determines that the big bird takes the priest away again, I shall be able to suffer, without complaint, even for my entire life."

"What!" said Christine, softened. "You do not know what the language of a young woman who abandons her destiny to you signifies? Well, it is me who is giving myself to my benefactor, to my friend. You can tell the priest..."

Victorin was on his knees; delicious tears were inundating his cheeks; he kissed Christine's hand, transported. After having received, to his great delight, that first pledge of his happiness, he ran to see the priest and all the arrangements were made for the sovereign's wedding. A rock garnished with flowers was the altar. The priest imitated sacerdotal garments as best he could with what was given to him; he offered the sacrifice, whose substance he had prepared personally, and Victorin was finally united with the beautiful Christine, the daughter of his Seigneur, whom he had loved so tenderly and so respectfully for such a long time.

Things were concluded so promptly that Christine only made a very natural reflection afterwards, which was that she ought to have informed her father and waited for his consent—but her husband attempted to dispel that regret by the ardor of his kisses. And to give evidence that the marriage would not slow down his attentions to his wife, he went as soon as the second night to look for Christine's father's reply.

He only advanced with the greatest precaution, and did well, for any less and he might have been doomed, and the beautiful Christine too, for without him, no one would ever have been able to release her from the Inaccessible Mountain—and doubtless its inhabitants, having no more to fear from Victorin, whom they believed to be a sorcerer, would not have taken long to shake off the yoke of subordination, and God knows how things would have gone in the little colony!

Victorin, therefore, maintained a great height for a part of the night, examining everything carefully, and approached silently by means of a slow and gentle movement of his wings. He discovered the worthy Seigneur, seconded by his men, hiding in the darkness within rifle-range of the balcony. It appeared that they would all have fired at the same time, in order that they would not miss Victorin.

They did not disband until daybreak; then everyone withdrew. Victorin took advantage of the opportunity to take possession of the letter attached to the balcony; the noise he made alerted the Seigneur, who appeared almost immediately at his window, but the flying man was moving away. The Seigneur fired both barrels of his rifle at hazard, and so nearly hit the target that Victorin heard the pellets whistling past. He resolved not to risk his life again for a letter, and flattered himself that he would make his reasoning persuasive to Christine, to whom the quality of husband rendered him dearer than ever.

He arrived at the Inaccessible Mountain in daylight, with the consequence that he was seen in the air by a number of people who were about in the country or traveling. There was no longer any talk of anything throughout the Dauphiné but the big bird that abducted young women, and it became as famous as the Beast of Gévaudan did subsequently.[20] There were even people who claimed to have seen it at such close range that they could specify its dimensions—to wit, that it had a wingspan of a hundred meters. It was attributed a hooked beak as thick and long as an elephant's trunk, etc.

All the inhabitants of the Inaccessible Mountain were penetrated with respect on seeing their master in the air. However, he did not think it appropriate to descend into their midst, for one small reason. That was that, having resolved to keep the priest, at Christine's request, he was bringing him a housekeeper.

As he was coming back by day he had perceived a young woman alone on the high road to Lyon, who was going from one village to another in the course of her work, for she was a dressmaker. Not seeing any obvious danger, and presuming that two groups of peasants and travelers who were ahead of her and behind her would be witnesses to the marvel, he swooped down upon her in a reversed arc, as rapid as lightning, and carried her off. He had the pleasure of hearing the

---

[20] The Bête du Gévaudan [Beast of Gévaudan] was deemed responsible for a number of fatal attacks carried out in what is nowadays the region of Lozère and the Haute-Loire between 1764 and 1767, attributed to a giant wolf or dog allegedly possessed of huge teeth and a long tail. More than a hundred deaths were blamed on the beast, and Louis XV eventually rent two professional wolf-hunters to hunt it with bloodhounds; when they failed to unearth it he sent his own chief huntsman, who did kill an unusually large wolf, but without putting a stop to the attacks attributed to the beast. A local hunter was eventually credited, at least by local legend, with having killed the beast with a silver bullet. Theories as to what really happened abounded for many years; Élie Berthet's feuilleton novel *La Bête du Gévaudan* (1858) featured both a wolf and a man suffering the delusion of being a werewolf, and numerous modern werewolf stories reference the incident.

cries that the peasants uttered to make him let go, as if he had been an animal.

He deposited the unconscious girl in the summer meadow, and when he had taken off his wings he went to help her and bring her round. He reassured her, telling her that he had chased the big bird away; then he took her to the other side of the rock, where he introduced her to his wife.

Obviously, it was extremely important that Christine did not suspect that her husband could carry such a burden; she would surely have become suspicious of him; at the very least she would have wanted to see her father, and all Victorin's happiness would have been destroyed. The priest, who was fully informed, and a few other inhabitants of the Inaccessible Mountain, refrained from talking; they believed Victorin to be a powerful magician from whom nothing was hidden.

When everyone was tranquil and the young housekeeper had been handed over to the priest, who took her to his grotto, Victorin, alone with his wife, told her about the danger he had run. Then he gave her the letter from her father, conceived in these terms:

If I did not believe that you had been forced to write me this letter, my dear daughter, I would think that you were trying to deceive me with dreams and fables devoid of plausibility. Everyone knows that the Inaccessible Mountain is uninhabitable and uninhabited. In truth, a few hunters claim to have seen wild goats there, but they have been contradicted by others.

I believe, therefore, that your abductor, the traitor Victorin, is keeping you in some deserted place, or in some thieves' cavern, where you must have a great deal to mourn, with a wretch of that species. That is what breaks my heart, and what I desire the most is that you will not receive this letter, my plan being to lie in wait for the scoundrel and to capture him, dead or alive.

If any life remains in him, after my men or I have shot him, we shall make him confess where you are, and I shall save you. Oh, my dear child, have I raised you for that vile peasant, who perhaps...that idea makes me despair. The local people here think he is a sorcerer; personally, I think he is only a blackguard, but very wily.

Adieu, my poor Christine. If you receive this letter—for which I scarcely hope—think of conserving the dignity of our blood, even at the expense of your life. I kiss you, my dear daughter, while suffocating with grief.

Your unfortunate father,

Annibal de B***m**t.

P.S. As for you, little scoundrel Victorin, if you escape me tonight, sooner or later the justice of heaven will cause you to fall into my hands. I promise you then a good and prompt punishment, unless, coming very rapidly to your senses, you immediately return my daughter to me.

Christine was very distressed by that letter, but she was slightly reassured by thinking that her father was mistaken about Victorin, as about all the rest. Thus, after having shed a few tears, she sought consolation in her husband's arms.

There is no need to go to great lengths regarding the life that she led for several years in that charming abode. She was adored there by everyone, as much for her generosity—nothing renders one good like misfortune—as by virtue of the authority that her husband gave her. She had three children, two boys and a girl. She nourished them, raised them and found a new happiness in their caresses. It is true that they were charming. Then again, there is no mother so tender toward her children, and happier because of them, than a woman who is adored by her husband. Victorin did not belie that; on the contrary, he appeared to become even more affectionate day by day, and he sometimes said to his wife:

"I am more demonstrative now, my charming love, because I know that you must attribute my caresses more to a veritable and respectful tenderness now than in the beginning; I was waiting until time had revealed to you the full extent of the immortal sentiments that attach me to you, and unlike the happiness of other husbands, which diminishes, mine, on the contrary, is incessantly increased."

Christine kissed her husband tenderly, and did her best to show him how happy he rendered her.

"Alas, my dear husband," she said, "how foolish is the pretended difference of conditions: it was with you that happiness awaited me. But neither I nor my father, who has always desired my happiness, would ever have taken that route to reach it. It needed very extraordinary events to bring us to where we are. Today, you are so dear to me that, whatever desire I have to obtain news of my excellent father, I would not want you, for anything in the world, to take the risk. What would become of me without you? Yes, my dear husband, I bless my fate—but I repeat, how many things it required to procure it, such as it is!"

"It only required amour, charming wife," Victorin said to her. "My companion, my love, why should I have secrets from you? Oh, for a long time now I would no longer have had any, if I had not feared diminishing your happiness. I have waited for these charming pledges of our tenderness, in order to be in a fit state to plead our cause with your father before confessing all my secrets to you."

"What are you going to tell me, then, my love?"

"That my amour has done everything: that it was what caused me to invent the wings with which I fly; that it was the desire to possess you that has been the sole motive; that there is no big bird; that I was me who abducted you...

"Now you know everything, adorable Christine, hate in me, if you can, the father of these charming children"

He set himself on his knees.

"No, no, dear husband, I will not hate you. On the contrary, I will love you more. Oh, how many things I discover now! It was you who put here everyone that I see, in order to compose me a little empire and make me a sovereign! What love has ever equaled yours? However, my very dear spouse, you have done well to wait until time had proven its constancy and purity to me, in order to make the confession you have made. It is very sweet to be unable to doubt that one is loved for oneself, and that it is not a frivolous and temporary infatuation that one has inspired! Come, my dear children, your father was very dear to me, but he is dearer to me than ever today; he makes me love you more, and I love him more because of you."

After this tender effusion, Christine, more tranquil, had her husband recount all the details of his conduct. He was sincere, except that he did not say a word about the wife of procurator Troismotsparligne. He did not forget his frequent excursions by night to procure the things that the Inaccessible Mountain lacked.

Christine was touched by so much effort of which she had been unaware. But when he told her the story of the peril he had run in order to obtain her father's reply, Christine, frightened, renewed her promise never to demand that he return there.

"At present, my dear wife," he added, "I have another project that I shall communicate to you, and which I shall carry out as soon as you consent to it. It is the only means of getting us out of here with honor, and with your father's consent. Our sovereign is at war with the English; I propose to go and offer him my services, which might be of the greatest importance, and when I have had the good fortune to render him an essential one, you shall be the recompense that I demand. With the recommendation of the sovereign himself, your father will make it an honor to accept me as a son-in-law; my nobility will be of the highest species, since it will be for services rendered to the State, and you shall see how happy we will be! I shall obtain the concession of this mountain from the king, and it will be your country house. We shall embellish it..."

Christine interrupted him with her caresses, throwing herself into his arms and saying a thousand tender things. However, starting to think about their separation and the dangers that her husband might run, she made him confirm his word that he would only depart when she appeared to desire it. Things being thus agreed, the two spouses emerged from their grotto with their children and went to take a little walk, the most agreeable that they had yet had together. They resolved to keep the secret of everything from their people, and since they were happy, to leave them in their situation.

In fact, those good folk—to wit, the laborer and his Cathos; the shoemaker and the cook; the tailor and the dress-maker; the barber-secretary and the chambermaid; La Vezinier, her daughter, and the husband that Victorin had pro-vided for the latter, a burly Limousin, an excellent mason; the Ecclesiastic and his young housekeeper—were all in an agree-able situation. They lived in abundance and in pleasure: little work, incessantly repeated amusements, a lovely abode, excel-lent air and good nourishment. They practiced gardening for their amusement, and even the cultivation of vines, which pro-tected them from the reproaches that the laborer might have been able to make them. The latter, for his part, although he had the hardest work, was pampered by all the others; he was furnished with dairy products, fruits, salad, which he liked a great deal, eggs, and above all wine, as soon as the vines could produce it.

Each couple had very pretty children, in great enough number. All that youth amused the parents, who delighted in seeing the children frolic together. The good Ecclesiastic was also very content with his housekeeper; they lived together in the greatest intimacy, and as there were no envious individuals on the Inaccessible Mountain, no one thought any the worse of them for it. Thus far, there was only La Vezinier who was not happy; Victorin had made her the curé's deputy housekeeper, which gave her a certain status.

What a charming Republic! It must, then, be necessary for people to be so restricted in number to be happy![21] There was no vice on the Inaccessible Mountain, and all the virtues

---

[21] Author's note: "A great and beautiful truth! Never can a society too numerous or a State too vast be happy."

were seen to reign there: fraternal amity, mutual support, zeal, love and kindness; all the individuals existed as much in the others as in themselves. The slightest indisposition of one member alarmed the entire society; the children were equally cherished; they were everyone's, and yet each was loved as a unique child.

One sensed that there could not be any self-interest there, nor any other vice. Vices would have been folly there, and humans are never, ever vicious unless the social regime in which they live is bad enough for vice to be advantageous. O legislators, fools who want to render others wise, how often you merit our scorn! In any case, virtue, on the Inaccessible Mountain was quite natural.

I repeat, any society sufficiently limited for the individuals therein to be equal, all acquainted with one another, all needing one another, is necessarily happy and virtuous. That is the nub of the matter; I do not know whether any other moralist has found it.

Victorin's departure depended absolutely on Christine. She yearned to see her dear husband illustrious, but she shivered at the mere idea of their separation. A thousand frightful dangers were offered to her timid imagination, so she always held back. For his part, the tender Victorin was in no hurry to leave a spouse who adored him; he only dissipated her fears weakly, and contented himself with showing that he was always ready to do what she desired most. In the meantime, he devoted himself to rendering his little State happy.

He took a long time about it, for ten years after the confidence—which is to say, after sixteen years of marriage and at least seventeen of residence on the Inaccessible Mountain—he had not left to become illustrious. By then, the most charming youth of both sexes was seen on the fortunate mountain. Victorin organized a new esplanade there, like that of the south, equally large but higher up, which had a kind of small lake in the middle. He had the ground tilled, even lending a hand to it himself, and everyone did likewise. The following year, he established ten young couples there, who found that they had a sufficient share of land to live there in abundance.

He opened an easy path between the two populations, by means of blowing up a rock with gunpowder.[22] All of his family and the inhabitants were present at that operation, but they were sheltered by the entrance to a cavern. Only Victorin, fuse in hand, hovered with his wings deployed, and was easily able to remove himself from danger. He stocked the little lake with fish, which was a great help to the little colony in nourishing them for a part of the year.

His fashion of going to make his purchases was to fly from the Inaccessible Mountain by night, before daybreak, and to land in a wood near a large city. He had discovered a safe place between two rocks where he left his wings. Then he went to the city wearing peasant costume in order to buy the things he needed. He spent the day there; when he left at dusk he returned to his wood, from which he flew away with his burden. Observe that if anyone had found his wings, they would not have been able to make use of them, because he always took the mainspring away with him in his pocket. Thus, whatever happened, he would easily have been able to make others, in less than a single night.

But one embarrassment remained: how did he acquire money? What I have not said is that everyone on the Inaccessible Mountain worked. The shoemaker, the tailor, the young people—everyone was busy, and the surplus of their labor was confided to Victorin, who gave them in exchange all the petty commodities that they might lack. Even the good Ecclesiastic devoted himself to composing canticles, and his pious songs, like those of Père Marin, were taken by Victorin to sell to the

---

[22] Note in the first edition, omitted from the Laffont edition: "The noise made by the explosion of the powder on that occasions greatly intrigued physicists, who wrote in all the journals of the era that there had been a terrible thunderclap in the Dauphiné when the sky was serene. [Joly]"

publishers of Lyon, where they were hailed as those of a new Adam de Nevers.[23]

The hairdresser devised the prettiest bonnets and the most seductive hair-designs, almost as fashionable as those *en-herisson, en-griffe, à-lapandoure, en-chignon-double* or *bouillonnée*, etc. etc. The two dressmakers made Polish, Circassian and Levite skirts, bustles and thigh-pads, and other fashionable accoutrements no less elegant. Victorin took them all over the realm, and good taste was in such ferment there that it has since been entirely renewed in Paris, where he made a fortune. For the air is so pure on the Inaccessible Mountain that minds are extraordinarily inventive there.

For his own count, Victorin made various curious and very useful machines, and once having procured the tools became, without a Master, one of the most skillful clockmakers in Europe. He made the most beautiful and most accurate marine watch that has ever been seen; he flew all the way to London to sell it, but often repented of it thereafter, the buyer having profited from that fine invention to establish his glory,[24] at

---

[23] "Père Marin" is Marin Mersenne (1588-1648), a French theologian and musicologist who did pioneering scientific work in the field of acoustics in *L'Harmonie universelle* (1637) and also made a substantial contribution to the development of reflecting telescopes. Adam Billaut, better known as Maître Adam (1602-1662), of Nevers, was a carpenter by profession, but built a great reputation as a poet and songwriter; his work was much admired by Corneille and Voltaire.

[24] This sly reference is to the English clockmaker John Harrison (1693-1776), who labored throughout the 1730s and 1740s trying to perfect a marine chronometer that would keep time well enough to permit the accurate calculation of longitude, then a key problem in navigation, and hence world trade. Harrison actually based the escapement of his famous "sea watches" of the 1760s on a model pioneered by John Jeffreys. He never received the mammoth prize that he spent all his life trying to win, and was very shabbily treated by Parliament.

the expense of that of your artists—but I restore it here to the French nation.

You can see why he had no lack of money. I could easily believe, after that example, that the first monarchs were merchants and machine-makers, skillful men who were respected for their wealth and their utility.

IV

Meanwhile, the children of the sovereigns of Mount Inaccessible grew up. They were within two years of marriageable age—which is to say, between thirteen and fifteen. The elder son was a handsome young man, the living portrait of his grandfather, which his mother had often told him. The younger resembled Victorin, and his mother a little, which rendered him very pleasing. As for the daughter, she was Christine herself, as she had been when her husband had abducted her. Those three lovable creatures were endowed with a thousand perfections, which completed the happiness of their parents.

One day, De B***m**t —the elder son, to whom Victorin had given the name of the worthy Seigneur, his father-in-law—said to Christine: "It seems to me, my dear Maman, that if I saw my grandfather, I would be well able to persuade him that he should pardon my father for a sin that was not one, since it has made your happiness, and that is all my grandfather wanted!"

"You're right, my son, but how can that happen?"

"I'll speak about it to Papa, who will be able to teach me to fly like him."

Christine trembled. "My God, don't attempt that, my son! There's no one but your father in the whole world who has strength and skill enough for that."

Young Sophie joined in with her mother: "Oh, my brother, you'll fall!"

But little Alexandre, the younger son, started smiling. "I wouldn't fall, and if Papa wanted to teach me...you'd see, my sister. And in fact...but I can't say anything."

"Speak, my son," Christine said to him. "What have you done?"

"Dear little Maman, I can't hide anything from you, I love you so much. I saw Papa's wings one day, and I made myself similar ones, with his old ones. Would you like to see me fly? I amuse myself with that when I'm alone."

"Oh, my son, I forbid you to do that!"

"Peace, peace, little Maman. I'll fly low, very low, and you'll see."

Christine let him do it, fully determined to prevent him from flying if there were the slightest danger. The little fellow—he was thirteen—put on his wings, activated his lifting parasol, and rose up with two flaps to the height of the treetops. His mother uttered a piercing scream, but the little rogue, directing his flight in a straight line, captured a woodpigeon, which he brought to her.

Christine, half-terrified and half-delighted, hugged the foolhardy child to her maternal bosom, saying to him: "I don't want you to use your wings again until your father has shown you how."

As for little Sophie, she was delighted, and but for the presence of her mother, she would gladly have asked her brother to do it again.

As soon as Victorin returned, he was told about the escapade. He went pale, for he adored his wife once again in her children.

"Let me see your wings, my son."

Alexandre presented them to him triumphantly—but the father did not find the safety-device that he had only added himself after a mishap, and, showing him his own, he said to him: "You see, imprudent youth, on what your life depends? If your strap had failed, what would have supported you?" On seeing Christine frightened, he added: "It's true that it's sound, but in the end, you're nevertheless culpable of having risked the life of our son, who is dearer to us than ourselves..."

The child begged his father's pardon, and especially that of his tender mother, and promised never to do anything stupid again. Victorin immediately made him start work on a safety-device, giving him several thongs and straps, and the next day, when the device was fitted, he permitted him to go up in the air. The child did so with as much boldness as if he were really a bird.

Victorin had not yet thought of teaching his children to make use of wings like his own—far from it; he had always taken the greatest care to hide them. Seeing that the secret was out, however, he understood that there was no other means of elevating his family above the other inhabitants of the mountain than giving them the exclusive faculty of flight. He explained his ideas on that subject to them, and made them sense how important it was that such a secret should not be divulged. The next day, he gave lessons in flight to his wife and daughter, for he found Alexandre so naturally adept that he abandoned his brother's instruction to him, nevertheless reserving it for himself to preside over the first lessons for fear of an accident.

Within a month, the entire family of the sovereign of the Inaccessible Mountain was able to make use of artificial wings. Sophie was almost as bold as her younger brother, and often caused her mother to tremble. She, in spite of her science, only ever dared to take off in company with her husband.

It was then that the elder son again brought up the proposition of going to see his grandfather. Alexandre and Sophie wanted to accompany him, but Victorin and Christine told them that it was necessary first to ascertain the dispositions of their grandfather, and that, in any case, it would be easier to liberate one if he were detained as an impostor than to liberate three. Young De B***m**t therefore departed before dawn on a beautiful moonlit night, guided by his father and accompanied by his brother and sister.

All four came down in a place familiar to Victorin, to which he had taken a richly-harnessed horse earlier that night. It was in a copse close to the château Victorin took off his elder son's wings, and dressed him as a young cavalier, and after giving him some final advice he returned with the other two children to the Inaccessible Mountain. They found Christine in tears there, and had to make a great deal of effort to console her.

Alas, there is no perfect happiness. It seemed that no pain ought to afflict that happy wife, in remaining tranquil on her mountain, but she had a father; she wanted to add a further degree to the happiness she already enjoyed, and made sacrifices to that pleasant hope.

Meanwhile, young De B***m**t, left in the copse, emerged in daylight mounted on his lovely horse, and went straight to his grandfather's château. As he arrived at the gate, Christine's father opened the window of his balcony in order to smoke his pipe there. He perceived the handsome cavalier, and hastened to go to meet him personally. His beauty, his youth, his features, the richness of his clothing and the harness of his horse astonished the old man and moved him prodigiously.

"Be welcome, Monsieur," he said, "for you can only be the bearer of good news."

"At least, Monsieur," the young man replied, "be sure that I wish you all good things at once."

The old man offered him his hand, without making any reply, and took him to the best room in the château, where he sat him down and asked him what he would like for breakfast. The young man had been warned by his mother that in his grandfather's reception room there were family portraits, including one of her, between those of her father and her mother. De B***m**t, replying to the old Seigneur that he had a good appetite and that the choice of food was indifferent to him, searched those paintings with his eyes. He had time to examine them while his grandfather was giving his instructions—with the consequence that when the old man returned to him, he found him with a tear in his eye as he studied Christine's portrait.

"What's the matter, young Cavalier?"

"Alas, Monsieur, I'm looking at this portrait; it's that of a person who is very dear to me."

"Very dear!" And the old man, studying his young guest in his turn, shuddered as he spoke. "That's my daughter."

"It's Maman."

"Yours, Monsieur!"

"Recognize your blood, Monsieur. I am the eldest son of Christine de B***m**t, and I am assured that I resemble my grandfather."

"Oh, my dear son! But where is my daughter? Who is her husband?"

"You should not blush, Monsieur, for she is the wife of a sovereign, and although his Estates are not very vast, he is the absolute master there, at the same time as he is the beloved Father of his subjects."

"Sovereign?"

"Yes, my dear Father—allow me to give you such a sweet name."

"Oh, my Son! Yes, I recognize you; you are my blood, my portrait. I would recognize you even if you were Victorin's son."

"Dear Seigneur and Father, so I am, but what you have said is nonetheless true, and when it pleases you to come to my father's Estates, I shall take you there. You will see there a daughter who only breathes for you and who, perfectly happy with her husband and her children, nevertheless finds that she misses her father."

"You have brothers and sisters?"

"I have one brother and one sister: Sophie de B***m**t —for we bear your name; my father wanted that. Sophie is charming, and you would believe that you were looking at my mother, when she was with you—to the point that my father and mother have often said that, if they respected you less, they would have been able to abduct you, after having procured you a deep sleep, and when you awoke, persuaded you that everything that has happened was only a dream, introducing Sophie to you as your Christine, dressed as she was on the day she disappeared."

"Oh, my Son, how you make me desire to see them all! For in the end, since Victorin is a sovereign, even if only of a shanty, I ought no longer to bear a grudge against him, and his alliance honors me. Come on then, let's eat, and we'll leave this very day."

"It cannot be until tonight, Seigneur my dear grandfather; my father, who brought me as far as a nearby copse, will come to seek information of me, and I will tell him about your generous dispositions in our regard.

The day was therefore spent in pleasures. The old Seigneur could not weary of admiring his grandson, and being subjugated by his nature—and prejudice, ancient hatreds and projects of vengeance all yielded to the delightful sentiment of paternity. Thus, he showed young De B***m**t, under that name, to all his vassals; he would have been capable of showing him to the whole world.

However, a reflection occurred to him in the evening. "How were your father and mother married?"

"By the ministry of a priest, who is still with us, my dear Papa."

"Ah! I'm glad. I shall give my ratification as soon as I see them, and all will be said."

Finally, night fell. The anxiety of Victorin and Christine for their son did not fail to make them all depart under the veil of darkness, for the Château de B***m**t. Christine made the journey beside her husband.

They arrived at midnight. Their elder son was waiting for them in the copse, alone. As soon as he heard the sound of their wings, he shivered with joy, rose up in the air, and shouted to them: "Success!"—that was the word they had agreed—"Let's go to the château."

They went there immediately, and all five of them landed on the large balcony. They promptly took off their wings, and their elder son went to announce them to his grandfather.

It is impossible to describe the joy of the old Seigneur at the sight of his daughter, still almost as youthful as when he had lost her. He did not say a word, but he pressed her against his paternal heart. Sophie and Alexandre had their turn. The old man wept over Sophie; she resembled feature for feature Christine de la T*** d'A*** his wife, when he had married her.

Thus prepared, his heart opened without difficulty when he saw Victorin kneeling before him, eyes lowered, with the countenance of a culpable individual. He put his arms around him and called him his son-in-law. Afterwards, he heard with pleasure everything that Christine told him about the happiness that her dear spouse had enabled her to enjoy.

After that interesting story, the first thing the Seigneur said was: "Someone fetch me the notary." He ratified the marriage, and declared by the same document that young De B***m**t, his grandson, was his sole heir—his son-in-law and his daughter having told him that they had no need of fortune.

When everything was thus arranged, Victorin proposed to his father-in-law that they take advantage of the darkness to go to his Estates.

"Gladly, my son-in-law!" exclaimed the old man. "But by what carriage?"

"By the one that brought us, Papa," said Christine.

"Let's go, my children."

The five flyers refitted their wings; they went on to the balcony, and the old man, after having given the necessary orders in his house, put himself in the arms of his son-in-law, who lifted him up like a feather. Christine and the three children flew through the air beside them, and in less than an hour they arrived at the Inaccessible Mountain.

It was no longer in a grotto that the sovereign was lodged; the mason he had abducted, and to whom he had given La Vezinier's daughter as a wife, had taught his art to all the young people. They had built beside the steam, backed up against the rick, a palace in the Corinthian style, very well distributed. To the summit of the rock, which had been flattened, earth had been carried, and a charming garden formed there. It was there that Victorin landed with his father-in-law and his family. They went to bed on arriving, deferring the visit to the mountain and all the details until the old Seigneur woke up.

He did not sleep long; curiosity, pleasure and joy scarcely permitted him a few hours of repose.

First he admired the garden, into which a suction pulp caused water to rise. Then he went down into the palace, richly ornamented; from there, he went to visit the habitations. He was surprised to find a very well kept chapel garnished with all the necessary things. He especially admired the beauty of the young inhabitants, which was doubtless due to the purity of the air, and especially the exemption from disagreeable passions, for beauty is natural to humans, as well as bounty. Then he was shown the summer esplanade, where there was only one house, but vast, capable of containing all the inhabitants. It was a place of pleasure, where people went to pass the time destined for games during every summer, shielded from the heat.

After his dinner, the old man watched the games that took place every day when everyone had finished their work, unless the Republic had common and urgent projects, as when the palace and the chapel had been built, or when a dwelling had to be prepared for a new household, for then everyone worked zealously and unrelentingly—work being a pleasure, in any case, for people as reasonable and obliging toward one another.

The worthy Seigneur spent all day traveling through his son-in-law's Estates, and was delighted. By means of an excellent telescope, he easily recognized the location of the Inaccessible Mountain by the surrounding places that were familiar to him. He even discovered his château from the sheer point of a rock to which his son-in-law carried him, and where he was surrounded by his entire family, for fear that he might suffer from dizziness.

"It is here, dear Papa," Victorin said to him, "that for some time I have been showing your dwelling to my beloved spouse and my dear children, and they would pay you a tribute in tenderness and rears—especially your affectionate daughter."

"All that you tell me enchants me, my son-in-law, and even if you were not a sovereign I would still give you my daughter. Have you not returned her to me in the young and charming person of your Sophie, who is also mine?"

They came down from the rock and went to supper.

The next day, Victorin made his father-in-law party to the laws that he had established in his little sovereignty. They were so beautiful and so just that it was impossible to admire too much the fact that the son of a simple procurator fiscal had acquired so much wisdom. But nobility does not give merit and intelligence, although merit and intelligence can give nobility—that is a truth that ought to be more widely acknowledged. If the Great cared to reflect that they do not really have any rights, and that it is reasons of general utility that have conserved those that they enjoy, they would be less vain, less harsh and less egotistical. If magistrates thought that they only exist for the people, and not the people for them, they would doubtless have more integrity, be less cruel toward the culpable, etc.

Victorin's laws were very simple; each case only being indicated by a single word or phrase:

Murder: thrown from the top of the mountain to the bottom.

Theft: impossible.

Calumny, or *slander*: deprivation of public pleasures.

Property: common.

Adultery: slave of the husband for two years.

Rape: slave of the victim, for as long as she might wish.

Blows given: the chief shall render the talion.

Disobedient child: condemned to live apart from his comrades.

Bad son or daughter: sequestered and condemned to celibacy until their reform is certain.

Incorrigibles: precipitated.

Good deeds, services rendered: honored, recompensed by marks of distinction.

The most capable for work: shall have the choice of the most beautiful young women for spouses.

If a husband and wife do not agree: the entire Republic shall assemble with its Chief, and the marriage will be dissolved if reconciliation is impossible, provided that it is not too inconvenient, but the spouses shall be separated for a year, without being able to think of others.

"I am very content with those laws," said Christine's father to his son-in-law, "but they would not be sufficient in our country, where personal interest and the prizes that the rich have overturn everything. Well, my son, you only need, to be a great sovereign, to have large Estates. However, there is one thing here that gives me pleasure, and that is that you are safer than all the princes of Germany or Italy, whose Estates are a thousand times vaster than yours. They only have a precarious authority, and yours is absolute."

"I do not limit myself to this point of the globe, Father," Victorin replied. "Now that I am reconciled with you, and the happiness of my wife and myself is complete, great ideas are coming to me. In a short while from now, I want to undertake a voyage with my younger son, to the Austral lands, far from any country discovered by ambitious Europeans; and when I have found an island like Tinian, or those of Juan Fernandez, I shall transport my colony there. As I shall take the shortest route, after my discovery, and shall have no detours to make, I shall not take long in that voyage. It will be necessary, however, that the first two inhabitants my son and I transport there will find an easy subsistence, because we cannot take enough provisions. Once the point is assured, I can answer to you for the fact that Christine de B***m**t will be the first sovereign of a great realm; for such is my respect and my tenderness for her that I want her to be proclaimed a Queen. Those, Seigneur, are your son-in-law's plans.

Weeping with joy the old man embraced Victorin.

"Fulfill your high destiny, my Son," he said to him. "Oh, I can see that the man who was able to make wings, and form a little State on the Inaccessible Mountain, is also capable of forming a great Realm. It is only a matter of less to more... Go, go—make me happy for ever..."

"I can also do very fine things. Seigneur and Father," Victorin continued. "For example, I can go to offer my services to the King, in the present war. I can carry orders, gives information to the fleets we have at sea; what good might I not do by warning our squadrons about all the movements of the enemy? Finally, I could also render myself the arbiter of differences between kings and nations, and forbid war, either by threatening the first to be turbulent with great misfortunes, or by abducting the motor of those vast quarrels that plunge entire nations into mourning. I would only have to sequester five or six of those Messieurs, as many English, Germans, Portuguese, Muscovites, etc., for the others, frightened, not to dare to do anything after a prohibition by the Flying Man."

"You're right, my son-in-law. That project is worth more than that of Abbé Saint-Pierre[25] or those of J.-J. Rousseau, and that is the true means of establishing a universal peace!"

"I was amusing myself the other day composing a speech, such as I would like to pronounce to two armies ready to do battle. It seems to me that, supported by a few striking blows, such as those I have just mentioned, it might make a very great impression:

---

[25] Charles Castel, Abbé de Saint-Pierre (1658-1743) was the first person to propose the establishment of an international organization to maintain peace, in *Project pour rendre la paix perpétuelle en Europe* (1713). He was kicked out of the Académie because of his reformist ideas—including a graduated income tax, free public education for males and females and the state funding of transportation systems to facilitate commerce—and his subsequent political activities were suppressed by Louis XV. He had a considerable influence on Rousseau.

"*Are these men that I see ready to destroy one another? No, no, they cannot be men! Humans, those beings endowed with reason, are guided, held back and achieve explanations thereby. Only the lion and the tiger, whose blood is always inflamed by a fever of bitter bile, can only defend their rights by tearing one another apart. But Humans, made in the image of the divinity, employ other means...*

"*No, these are not men that I see, or they are madmen. O Madmen, listen to me! Listen to the Flying Man, who can crush you with a hail of stones, who can annihilate your insensate leaders! Listen to me Madmen. Twenty thousand or thirty thousand of you are about to perish in battle; when they are dead, which of the two parties will be right? The stronger, no doubt! So, wretches, is to blind force that you are going to surrender the decision of your interests? Abjuring reason, which brings humans close to the divine, it is as atheists, or rather as brutes that you want to conduct yourselves!*

"*Madmen! And you have laws that condemn murderers and thieves to death! The foremost and most ferocious of murderers, who merit a thousand wheels and a thousand pyres, are your generals, who are blaspheming Nature in ordering murder, blaspheming the Divinity in consecrating injustice and degrading human beings in reducing them to behave like beasts, when they are endowed with reason, and can argue with dignity.*

"*O infamous wretches, you must fear reason, because if you did not fear it you would employ it, you would rely upon it; or, if you are too prejudiced, too obfuscated, you would refer to disinterested arbiters. But you do not want reason, or justice. And yet, God is justice itself; you are therefore apostate against the Divinity! Wretches! And you have laws against atheists, against murderers, and you have a religion, priests and altars! Is that derision? Are you mocking the Divinity?*

"*You are not men, and I do not know you. No, you are not men. Fight—and instantly, I shall direct my blows against the principals of the two armies; their criminal lives will pay for the insults they are delivering to Nature. Dare to begin! I, the Flying Man, order you to explain yourselves, to state your grievances, to demand reparations, as reasonable beings do. Let the one of the two nations that does not accede to what is just be immediately withered by the scorn of the entire world. If it takes up arms first, then let all the other nations reject it like a ferocious beast, until it becomes reasonable again.*"

"Good, my son-in-law! Stand firm!" cried the old Seigneur, transported with pleasure at seeing his daughter's husband as the arbiter of nations, and armies, which is worse.

"*I, the Flying Man,*" Victorin continued, "*accept your arbitrage, this time: draw up respective statements, short and clear, in which nothing is contrary to the truth, and put them under that rock there; I shall take them, and will bring you my response.*

"That, my dear Seigneur and Father, is the speech I have prepared, and which I shall perhaps make some day."

"It is very fine, my son-in-law, and I shall be particularly pleased if you serve the fatherland against those pirates the English. But the most important and most urgent thing is the establishment of your realm in the Austral lands. Captain Halley, when he came back in 1700,[26] had found nothing worthwhile, but perhaps he was mistaken and you will see a hundred times better than him. Then my daughter will be truly a Queen." And the old man stood up joyfully, in order to embrace his son-in-law.

---

[26] The reference is to the astronomer Edmond Halley, who was given command of the *Paramour* in 1698 in order to carry out investigations in the South Atlantic of the variations of the compass: the first purely scientific expedition by an English naval vessel. The crew proved insubordinate, questioning his ability to command, so Halley was commissioned as a captain in the Royal Navy, and managed to carry out the mission at the second attempt in 1699-1700. He never visited the South Pacific, so it is not surprising that he found nothing of relevance to Victorin's scheme.

Such were the matters about which Victorin conversed with his father-in-law during the latter's sojourn on the Inaccessible Mountain. Finally, after a week, he took the worthy Seigneur back to his home, at about ten o'clock in the evening. He was accompanied by his entire family, but no one in the château saw anything. His daughter and grandchildren helped put him to bed; then they embraced him and returned to their mountain.

Imagine the surprise of Monsieur de B***m**t's domestics when they saw their master smoking his pipe on his balcony the following morning! They could not believe their eyes, and took him for a phantom. But soon his loud voice had summoned them all to give them his orders, and they could not doubt the realty of his return. No one dared speak to him about it, however, for the worthy Seigneur was a little fierce, except for an old housekeeper who had been in the house for a few years longer than her master.

"Oh, Monsieur, when did you come back, then?"

"Yesterday evening, my good woman."

"No one saw you then?"

"Of course—you were all so fast asleep that my entire château could have been carried away without waking you up."

"Did you have a good voyage, Monsieur?"

"Very good, my god woman; I've seen my daughter, my grandchildren, my son-in-law—but a son-in-law…suffice it to say that I am well content with him, and I could not have found such a match in the entire kingdom."

"Oh, Monsieur, so much the better, my dear Master! It's necessary not to listen to rumors, though, for everyone thinks that it's Victorin!"

"Good! It's a prince that my daughter has married, and she'll be even more of a princess before long."

"God be praised, Monsieur!"

"So be it, my good woman. But go about your business, and let me occupy myself with important matters."

I believe that the worthy Seigneur wanted to work on the legislation of the future realm of his daughter the Queen, but what he imagined, which was doubtless very fine, has not been divulged.

Let us return to the Inaccessible Mountain.

Christine had been a witness several times to the conversations of her father and her husband, about her future royalty. After the worthy Seigneur's departure, at the first moment of tranquility, she said, laughing: "Was all that you said about the Austral lands and an island like Tinian or Fernandez serious, my love?"

"What do you mean, serious, my dear spouse? Very serious! I would not lie to your father."

"So you think, then, that we would be happier there than here?"

"It's not for the sake of happiness, my dear wife—that, for me, is in any place that you inhabit—but for glory and utility. We shall found a new people, which will perhaps be famous one day. We shall first give it the arts and the sciences, in such a fashion that it will not lose them."

"I fear, my love, that this great project cannot be realized in every point. For one thing, to make a great society, common sense tells me that it would be necessary to put into it all the vices that are widespread in the world. Otherwise, if the citizens are like those here, limited in their views and virtuous, they will fall prey to the first European society that discovers them. It would be necessary for you to make them warriors— which is to say, wicked—in order that they should not be slaves. It would be necessary for them to have ships, and to engage in commerce. If they were content with their own productions, and did not leave their homeland, I believe that they would gradually degenerate. Even here, I remark that there is a great deal of innocence, or exemption from vice, but there is little energy; if it were not for your laws, and the exercises you have established—in brief, if you were not the soul of the inhabitants of our mountain—they would become torpid."

"That is very well observed, my dear companion, and I know that you have a great deal of intelligence, but if glorious things were accomplished without risk, without danger and without difficulty, where would the merit be? The glory is in overcoming them, and that's what I hope to do. In any case, we have children, for whom this establishment is becoming too narrow.

"First, I shall work to discover my island, or my continent—it doesn't matter which, provided that it is uninhabited, or, at least, that there are no powerful nations there to which our proximity would be inconvenient. If I find the latter, I shall refrain from making them known to Europeans. I shall try to discover a fertile land, between the fortieth or the forty-fifth degrees, which, according to the voyagers I have read, are almost equivalent to the fiftieth in our northern hemisphere, for it is at that latitude that humans are most human.

"When we are well-established I shall convey the arts and sciences to the peoples, but I shall take great care to recommend that they avoid long distance navigations. I shall try to ensure that they do not leave their coasts, and that they advance very little in the direction of the equator.

"All my difficulty during this voyage, dear wife, is in separating myself from you. But I will leave you our elder son and our daughter. De B***m**t will take my place here; he will often bring your worthy father here, as well as mine, whom I have had my reasons for not seeing yet. You sense them; I wanted to spare the delicacy of your father and leave him the liberty to talk to his son-in-law in the terms that suited him."

"Are you going to leave soon, then?"

"I have already made my preparations. We need more powerful wings—long-haul wings, so to speak—in order to carry our provisions. We shall take another pair, lighter, for when we reach the country, and for going hunting."

Christine was very sorry about the prompt departure, but it gave so much pleasure to her father that Victorin was going to complete his determination that he left in mid-September with his younger so, moistened by the tears of Christine, his elder son and the lovely Sophie. As for the father-in-law, he was so transported by joy that he gave them his blessing.

V

The two Flying Men, equipped with their powerful wings, rose into the air from the highest point of the Inaccessible Mountain at ten o'clock in the evening, each carrying a basket of provisions attached to the leather strap surrounding the waist. That gave them the appearance, seen from below, of two birds of an incomparable stoutness. They flew directly southwards, taking for a reference-point the meridian marked by the stars of Capricorn's tail.

It only took them eight nights to reach the equator, and as they flew ever higher as the heat increased, they were not inconvenienced by it. On the contrary; they sometimes had difficulty protecting themselves from the cold by night, for they rested by day on sheer mountains, sleeping with their heads pillowed by their basket of provisions.

Few people were able to pay attention to them during their journey; the darkness at their departure and the high altitude that they maintained thereafter caused them to pass in the eyes of peasants for a tiny cloud; as for the people of cities, they saw nothing—except for those of Cairo in Egypt, because the Flying Men had come down lower in order to examine a huge crocodile asleep beside the Nile. Their appearance caused a general alarm throughout the city among Muslims, Copts and Jews; the first thought that Mohammed had come in person to punish them for their frequent revolts and the second that it was the end of the world; as for the Jews, they opened all their windows and started crying "Messiah! Messiah! Adonai!" All of them were very astonished, however, when they saw the two Flying Men pass over without stopping, and going to the highest of the pyramids, on which they perched.

As dawn approached on the twelfth night, Victorin and his son reached the tropic of Capricorn, having that constellation at their zenith. They traveled a further twenty or twenty-five degrees on subsequent nights, searching on the same parallel as France for a country that would suit them. They first perceived an island so large that they took it, on the first voyage, for a continent, but as it was inhabited they left it. Twenty leagues from there, at 00 degrees of latitude and longitude, they found another, as large as England, Scotland and Ireland combined, situated on the same meridian as France, with the consequence that the hours of the day were the same there, and there were seasons that were diametrically opposed.

Victorin and his son flew over that island for several days. It was covered with woods, although there were grasslands of a sort, and an infinity of placid animals, such as bison, buffalo and oxen, various species of deer, and wild goats. One animal resembled a zebra or a donkey, another was similar to a horse; the only carnivorous species was a kind of tiger or jackal[27] of the smallest species, but very numerous, which only attacked the large animals when they were languishing of old age. They did not see any humans.

It was only on the third day, toward dusk, that young Alexandre discovered a near-human creature on the island. It was a kind of naked man who was observing them from the entrance to a cavern. He pointed him out to his father, who, having taken up his night-telescope[28] and made use of the focusing mechanism, perceived several other naked men and women lying face down.

"There are only savages on this island," Victorin said to his son, "and they seem to me to be very small in number. We

---

[27] The word I have translated as "jackal" is "*Jagal*," which does not exist in French, but is probably a corruption of *chacal* [jackal]; N****** often uses the word *tigre* [tiger] rather vaguely, seemingly meaning any big cat rather than a tiger narrowly defined, and probably intends to imply non-feline carnivores in general by the second term.

[28] Author's note: "A kind of telescope invented in England for discovering ships at night." Night-vision binoculars were not actually invented until the 20th century.

can settle here. Let's choose a fortifiable open space, in order to locate our first inhabitants there."

They set about visiting the heights of the island, flying very low with their light wings, but not without precaution. They found a mountain that seemed to them to be absolutely deserted, on top of which there was a plain and a lake. They landed there and stowed their baskets safely in an inaccessible grotto, from which they cleared out a few small carnivores and where they spent the night.

The next day, armed with good sabers and pistols, they went hunting. They killed a few birds, which they cooked in a pot they had brought, and made a broth that fortified them considerably. They sought by that means to stretch their supplies of biscuit. They also found a species of breadfruit, which resembled chestnut for taste.. They collected a supply, after having made sure of its salubrity by the simple means of feeding it to the animals.

Every day they became bolder, always going a little further, taking care to mark the trees in order to find their way back to their grotto. They did not spare the jackals, which they killed with saber-thrusts; with regard to the other animals, they only took what was necessary.

Finally, on the eighth or tenth day on the island, they found a beaten track. They followed it, listening carefully as they went. It took them to a spring, around which they saw a large quantity of unknown animals, which started in surprise on seeing them but did not run away.

They continued to follow the path, convinced that habitations could not be far away. They did not take long to arrive at its terminus: it was a grotto closed by tree-branches crudely cut with stones. They looked into it, but the obscurity as so profound that they could not see anything. Having heard some movement, however, they were afraid, put their light wings in readiness, and drew away rapidly on foot. They got back to their mountain without having discovered anything.

"But father," said Alexandre, "I think the people of this land resemble bats! We don't see anything, and everything is profoundly silent during the day, but I assure you that every night I hear something like human voices and cries. Let's keep watch for them; in order to do that, let's go to sleep now so that we can wake up at midnight."

Victorin had already thought of that, but could not divine what species the people of Île Christine—that was the name he had given it—were. He approved of his son's reflection, and in the middle of the night they both took up positions in a safe place, from which they could observe everything. Scarcely were they there than they saw five or six of the island's inhabitants, with their women and children, advancing in their direction.

The savages looked at the grotto, and pronounced a few words, in squeaky voices similar to those of mice, but much louder. Victorin understood by their speech, and what he could grasp of their gestures, that his abode was not a mystery for the inhabitants of the island, but what surprised him infinitely was that they ran with the same vivacity and collected fruits, exactly as if they could see clearly. They had wooden hooks to pull branches toward them.

He then saw others arrive in large number; they all talked to one another amiably. Then they made a meal of breadfruits, and when first light announced the imminent return of daylight, they went away. The two Europeans followed them at a distance, and saw them go back into their cavern.

As they were considering that singular conduct, two savages—a man and a woman—who were walking tentatively, although daylight was beginning to brighten, bumped into them. They were very frightened, but soon reassured on seeing that they were alone; they took possession of the man, in spite of his mouse-like cries, and took him to their rock.

On the way, they encountered another savage, whom their prisoner did not see, although he was not far away, but they let him pass, and observed that he too was groping his way, with his eyes closed.

As soon as they had arrived at the rock they examined the savage. He was a young man about twenty years old, russet-white, with very long eyelashes. He could see a little once he was in the grotto in the rock, and showed signs of great fear. Victorin and his son tried to reassure him, making gestures of amity, and offering him food, but he seemed insensible to everything, and wanted to go to sleep. They put him on a bed of moss, where he did not take long to become somnolent, and where he stayed without moving until dusk, at which time he woke up briskly. Victorin and his son presented themselves, and the savage was again very frightened; he only sought an issue in order to escape. They offered him cooked meat and breadfruit to eat, but he did not want to touch them, and seemed tremulous.

"I see what the savages of this island are, my son," said Victorin then. "They're night-people, of which it's claimed that there are only a few accidental individuals—but it appears that they really are a race, which other men have annihilated everywhere they have encountered them, and which only subsist in countries where only they are found. Well, we shall make a law by which it is expressly forbidden to do them any harm. They do not appear to be malevolent. Let's set this one free, and let's be on our guard henceforth, and see what happens."

Victorin immediately opened the entrance to the grotto, and the night-man escaped as swiftly as an arrow. The two Europeans, equipped with their wings and having placed their baskets on an inaccessible rock, followed their prisoner, who did not take long to encounter a troop of his compatriots. He stopped; they surrounded him, and they all commenced squeaking with a singular force. To each squeak from the prisoner all the other relied with shrill cries.

Finally, the prisoner squeaked alone for nearly ten minutes, after which all the others squeaked at the same time, and they all headed for the grotto, keeping in tight formation. But none of them thought of employing violence; they did not touch anything, and did not seem to be tempted to force an entry to the cavern. They only peered through a few gaps and signaled that they could not see the two strangers.

Victorin and his son deduced that the people were very gentle, and that they could live with them, but they also understood that it would be very difficult to domesticate them. They both coughed then, and showed themselves, in order to be seen. There was a strange movement in the troop; they gazed with astonishment, ready to flee. But the young man who had been a prisoner appeared to reassure them; he even took a few steps forward, and invited the whole troop to follow him—but no one dared.

Then Victorin offered them, from a distance, the cooked meat and fruits. They appeared to desire them, and exhorted one another to go and take them, but no one was able to decide to take the first step. Even the prisoner, after taking twenty paces, was recalled by the others, and turned back. Finally, Victorin and his son, in order to astonish them more, flapped their wings and rose up into the air. Then the night-people uttered squeaks of terror, and they all fled. From all around, as they drew away, exceedingly shrill cries could be heard. After that experiment, the two Europeans retired to their grotto until daybreak.

Quite sure of having nothing to fear from the island's inhabitants while the sun was over the horizon, they visited it with greater confidence, sometimes flying and sometimes on foot. They found it to be very fertile.

While they were in the air they perceived a ship battered by a tempest. They proposed to render some assistance to the unfortunates ready to perish in the region, and flew over the liquid surface of the sea. They had scarcely reached it when the vessel hit a rock and was holed. The two Flying Men immediately landed on the rock and shouted in French to the crew not to be afraid, to go up on deck and cling to the rigging. They then attached a rope to the top of the mast and, making use of all the power of their large wings, they towed the vessel near to a place where the rock was dry. They moored it by the masts, and invited the crew to climb on to it by means of the ropes. That was easily done.

Fortunately, the ship was French. At first, the sight of certain death had caused them to carry out the orders of the Flying Men without any great attention; when fleeing death, one sees nothing else. When they were a little more tranquil on the rock, however, the surprise of the passengers and sailors was strange, on seeing themselves rescued, four thousand leagues from their homeland, by men who could speak French and fly in the air. Questions were put off, however; the danger was not entirely past.

The two Flying Men carried all the passengers to land on Île Christine, two by two—which is to say, four per trip. When everyone was safe, the sea calmed down, and, the crew having rested, four were taken back to the vessel in order to put the launch to sea and save whatever they could of the provisions. They found several crates of biscuit in good condition, wine, wheat, eau-de-vie and tools; it was only the gunpowder that had been completely lost. They also saved a good deal of merchandise, which, although damp, could still be useful. It was only after they had taken everything they could from the vessel, and the sea finished breaking it up, that the shipwreck victims looked closely at the Flying Men.

They revealed who they were, careful only to mention Seigneur de B***m**t, as whose son and grandson they identified themselves, in order to be more respected. There had only been two women aboard the ship; the youngest and most amiable of the officers, chosen by the Flying Men, drew lots for them, and all the others swore to conserve them in possession of their spouses.

Afterwards, the Flying Men enlightened them with regard to the inhabitants of the island, and proposed to the crew that they make accommodation with the daughters of the nocturnal savages, convinced that they would give birth to a mixed race that could be domesticated. All of that was executed subsequently, for during the first nights, they thought of nothing but taking repose and, during the day, of establishing themselves with a degree of comfort. Then they began to till the ground, employing the principles of the new cultivation, and sowed a part of the grain recovered from the vessel.

While awaiting the harvest, they decided to ration the biscuit, and that they would live on breadfruits, game and dairy products—for they soon discovered that they could domesticate the wild goats and cattle. They also found birds resembling guinea-fowl, which furnished eggs. They made a garden; the few seeds they had were sown, and the Flying Men offered to bring them other kinds.

When the new colony was in progress, the men of the crew went to the great cavern of the night-people, and chose the prettiest young women there, whom they brought back in daylight in order that they would be more docile in the dark. Pleasure domesticated those spouses in a relatively short time, although the men still appeared impossible to discipline, trembling at the mere sight of day-people; it was only the two European women at whom they seemed to gaze with pleasure.

When all the shipwreck victims were in a tolerable situation, Victorin and his son told them that they were returning to Europe to accomplish what had been the motive for their voyage. Everyone asked them for what they desired most, and they departed charged with commissions.

On the way back, they passed over the diamond mines of the realm of Golconda, where they chose some of the largest stones, after having frightened the guards and the merchants. Then they flew into the air and went to England, where they sold them. They bought a superb ship with the money, which they took to the port of Brest, where they left it at anchor.

They finally returned to the Inaccessible Mountain six months after having left it—which is to say, around the twenty-fifth of March. They found the worthy Seigneur de B***m**t there, who no longer left, in order to calm the anxieties of his daughter.

The success of their voyage caused the old Seigneur an inexpressible joy. When he learned about the advantage that his son-in-law had taken of the shipwrecked French vessel, and the marriages already effected between the crew and the night-women, he could not moderate himself, and he was the first to set his knee on the ground before his daughter, saluting her as a Queen and calling her Majesty. To put the cap on his delight, they told him about the diamonds of Golconda and the ship purchased in order to take all the inhabitants of the Inaccessible Mountain away at once, along with many other people—as many artisans as artists—whom they would carefully refrain from informing of their destination.

The worthy Seigneur did not want to stay for two minutes more on the Inaccessible Mountain; he begged his grandson to take him home in order to sell his château and all his property, and to buy trade goods with the price.

All of that was easily done, and in order not to pause over the details, which you can figure out as well as me, I shall tell you briefly that everyone left the Inaccessible Mountain one fine night, as soon as they could; that carriages were ready to receive the emigrants; that Victorin brought his father the procurator fiscal, with his brothers, his sisters, his cousins and as many of his relatives as he could; and that they all went to the port of Brest, where their beautiful ship was waiting for them. They embarked artists and artisans of all kinds, with their wives and children, under the pretext of going to Cayenne; they set off in good weather with a fair wind, and once they were at sea, Victorin and his son rose up into the air, where they held on to a rope attached to the masts of the ship in order to steer it, as Castor and Pollux had done among the ancients.

They found by that means the shortest passages, as yet unknown; not having use of a compass, the crew had no idea where they were. One of the three Victorins, and sometimes Sophie, flew close to the water, sounding it by hand, in order to avoid sandbanks and rocks; and finally, after three months of navigation, they landed happily—which is to say, without any loss, although not without difficulty—on Île Christine.

There they were received with inexpressible delight by the other colonists, who had just brought in their first harvest and had their first child. When she set foot on land, Christine was proclaimed Queen. A palace and comfortable houses were built; everyone set their hands to work, cultivating, tilling, hunting, collecting breadfruits, etc.

The laws of the Inaccessible Mountain were established on the island, and they worked very well there, because Victorin maintained a kind of equality there, in spite of his father-in-law, who wanted a peerage of Barons, Comtes, Marquises and even Ducs and chivalric orders, although he did not take long to see reason. The worthy procurator fiscal also wanted officers of the law, and they had something similar, but which nevertheless differed in several respects.

Finally, I shall tell you that the night-women gave birth to rather particular hybrids, more-or-less resembling day-people; but they hoped to improve the new species by alliances, while abandoning the nocturnal race entirely to itself, the day-men only taking wives therefrom in cases of the most urgent necessity.

That is the state in which things were for the first six months after the arrival of Victorin and his family—which is to say, until the first harvest; after which everyone, having been an agriculturalist, reverted to their particular occupations, either in the arts or the sciences.

The first city, or the first town, of Île Christine had three hundred inhabitants, including the people from the first wrecked ship, the people of the Inaccessible Mountain, who formed a veritable nobility by virtue of their mores and the affection that the sovereigns and their children had for them, and finally, the artists and artisans embarked. The ship that had brought Christine's veritable subjects was confided to the guard of the youth of the Inaccessible Mountain, with a strict prohibition on allowing any of the other inhabitants access to it; and for greater security, Victorin and his son removed its sails. The vessel was destined for commerce with a large neighboring island, which Victorin and Alexandre had reconnoitered before deciding on that of the night-people.

A cargo of trade goods from the large island was compiled after a few years, when the artisans and workers of Île

Christine had worked hard enough to have more utensils that the inhabitants required. Victorin and his son had made several voyages in order to reconnoiter the nearest nation; it was in accordance with their observations that the vessel was laden with various products, and works of art of the greatest perfection—in brief, it was furnished anything that might be an object of commerce. That was the idea they had in mind.

The peoples of la-Victorique—that is the name they gave to the large island, which would henceforth be the chief place of the Fifth Continent—are all Patagons of a sort, some twelve or fifteen feet tall.[29] They are so mild-mannered that one does not see the slightest quarrel among them. Victorin and his son observed them for a long time before daring to descend anywhere, but when they were close to the ground, they perceived that scant attention was paid to them. They soon discovered the reason when they saw large birds, some kind of condor, flying close by. Finally, the father and son came down on an eminence, and made arrangements to be able to make excursions into the country from there.

While they were admiring that new country and its inhabitants, they perceived a young girl about ten feet tall—she was twelve years old—who came around two trees and put out a hand to seize them. They drew away a little and, as they were equipped with their light wings, they rose a few feet into the air. The girl picked up a stone to throw at them, but a

---

[29] "Patagons" were a mythical race first reported by members of the crew of Ferdinand Magellan, supposedly observed on the coast of South America during the circumnavigation of the world that he undertook in the 1520s; they were said to be giants between twelve and fifteen feet tall. Antonio Pigafetta, who provided the elaborate written account of their alleged discovery, did not explain why Magellan called the giants "Patagons," but the name Patagonia was subsequently attached to their supposed homeland. Numerous later voyagers also reported seeing giants in the region, although the reported sizes of the people in question gradually diminished over time. Opinions vary as to whether Pigafetta was deluded or simply lying, but his account certainly influenced later observers as well as providing a rich resource for future litterateurs.

twelve-foot woman, apparently her mother, stopped her from doing so, and began calling to the two Flying Men, as the people of that country call to birds—a fashion which only different from that of France in being louder.

Victorin and Alexandre thought they could go to her, and approached, giving marks of submission and joy—which gave great pleasure to the tall woman and to her daughter. Victorin went to perch on the woman's shoulder, and Alexandre on the daughter's, who seemed to quiver with joy, without daring to touch him. Then they flew away and came back several times, and when the two woman went back home, they followed them.

The women arrived at a huge house, entirely constructed of wood, where they lived with men even taller than the women, to whom the latter talked a great deal, while displaying them. The men appeared to pay little attention to them, however. They sat down at table, as they do in that country—which is to say that everyone took a place on wooden beams that served as benches, and the mother and daughter distributed breadfruits and roots, as well as a kind of pâté, with which each of them filled a big wooden bowl. When all that was eaten, everyone lay down on leaves and moss, underneath the place they had occupied for supper. Only the young girl thought of giving some nourishment to the two Flying Men; they took it from her hand, which caused the benevolent child a keen joy.

They left the next day; the abode seemed tedious to them. Humans, accustomed to being rulers of nature, are not at ease with beings who appear to regard them the disdain of a physical superiority for which there is no consolation, compared with which the civil superiority that your princes and even your kings have only gives rise to a slight sensation. Considering things in their true perspective, one can console oneself for that: I have as much strength, I can savor the same pleasures, I live as much without the assistance that is foreign to them, they are all my equals, etc.—but a being who can take two or three men in his hand and hold hem there like birds, debases us in some way. It is therefore not surprising that the giants of old, who were widespread in the ancient continent, were gradually destroyed by the little people; if la-Victorique were populated by Europeans, the Patagons who live there today would not survive for three centuries.

On returning home, Victorin and his son published their discovery, but they could not found any speculation of commerce thereon. It was only after three or four voyages, which familiarized them with the Patagons, and the Patagons with them, that they decided to take their various products there, of which they had shown specimens, and which had proved agreeable. They made sure, above all, that the products were in proportion to the size of the people with whom they wanted to trade.

The vessel laden with merchandise thus arrived in the abode of the Austral Patagons, who marveled to see them, and which gave them a high opinion of the little people. They seemed particularly charmed to see that the crew of the vessel was entirely composed of dwarfs, made exactly like them, and devoid of wings. They negotiated by means of sign language, and succeeded, within a month, in learning one another's languages passably.

It was then that the reason, the industry and the science of the little people put them in high esteem among the Patagons. They admired all our arts and all our inventions, and although some of them regarded them as an effect of our weakness, others—the greater number, although not the wisest—were truly enchanted by them. The secret of making use of artificial wings, above all, seemed admirable to them, but Victorin carefully refrained from enlightening them in that regard. As for the ship, they did not seem tempted to construct one; they said that their land was sufficient, and that it was crazy to employ means that Nature has not given us to go in search of other dwellings—that humans, like plants, ought to remain attached to their native soil, and could only be denatured by quitting it.

Those reasons did not appear excellent to Victorin, who thought it much better to be a sovereign in Île Christine than a procurator fiscal in the Dauphiné, or even the king of the Inaccessible Mountain, from which it was impossible to expand and which would soon have been unable to nourish all its inhabitants, with the consequence that the expelled would have revealed everything. Thus, he had not left anyone behind, and since his departure the mountain has been absolutely uninhabited, as it had been before.

They brought back from the land of the Patagons, or la-Victorique, metals that were not found on Île Christine, especially platinum, which was abundant there almost at ground level. That from la-Victorique is much more fusible and more malleable than that from America, so it has the same value today in Île Christine as gold has in Europe. Beautiful works of art are made with it, and all the money in the land. They also brought back elephants' tusks of prodigious size, of which beautiful things were made, even including bed-posts. They also discovered a metal resembling copper, but which is not subject to verdigris, as ours is; there was no silver or tin, but they found a little iron and a kind of lead.

They tried to make trenchant implements out of that iron, and succeeded quite well, although it is not as good as that from our lands. That is why Victorin proposed to make a voyage to the boreal lands from time to time, in order to exchange the products of Île Christine and la-Victorique for steel. But he changed his opinion thereafter, not wishing to divulge the mines of his hemisphere, and he procures iron and steel by the means of the Patagons, who exploit their mines themselves. Thus, one does not see in Europe either Austral platinum or the new copper. Victorin reflected that those metals might excite the cupidity of Europeans, and he is reserving that branch of commerce for the time when Île Christine, sufficiently populated, can serve as a barrier to the New World.

I thought I ought to give you these ideas about the new People before entering into detail about its progress and its internal government.

Some time after the first voyage of the ship to la-Victorique, Queen Christine and her husband thought about a marriage for their elder son. They suggested it to him, telling him tenderly that, being the most eligible party in the realm, he could choose among all the young women the one that appeared to him to be the most beautiful and the most deserving. In response to that proposition, however, the young man remained silent, and even seemed a little sad. A month went by without him making any reply. That reserve in a hot-blooded young man gave rise to some anxiety; Christine spoke about it to the worthy Seigneur, her father, who, departing from his prejudices, replied to her:

"Why, that's quite astonishing! Whom do you want your son to marry? The daughter of your chambermaid or your shoemaker, apparently? They're the two most accomplished in the entire realm! But do you think that my blood, a boy who resembles me and doubtless has my inclinations, can swallow that?"

"But my dear Seigneur and Father," Christine replied, "what do you want us to do? There's no other means of marrying him, and it will also be necessary to give Sophie to one of our subjects, and for Alexandre to marry..."

"Why? Parbleu! Your Majesty has very short sight, for a sovereign. Let the father and the two sons leave for Europe; it will only take ten or twelve days for them to arrive. Let them choose two of the most illustrious princesses, and bring them here, where your sons will marry them. As for Sophie, I don't think that it will be any more difficult to go and find her some king's son for a husband—not an elder son, whom it's necessary to leave to his people, but a younger one."

"Wouldn't that antagonize the colony, Father?"

"On the contrary, Madam! Your Majesty ought to be convinced that it would increase respect, whereas familiarity could only destroy it..."

"It's necessary to discuss it with my husband."

"Yes, Madame, and I'll take charge of explaining Your Majesty's intentions to your august spouse the king," said Christine's father, emphatically, although perfectly seriously.

Victorin had also remarked his son's reverie, and it caused him more serious anxieties than anyone else. That reverie had commenced after the first voyage of the ship to la-Victorique. He had even made a discovery: three hours being sufficient to fly from Île Christine to la-Victorique, his son returned there quite frequently in secret—but he could not imagine what attracted him to the land of the giants.

Without giving any evidence of his anxieties to his wife the Queen, when she talked to him about abducting a princess, he contented himself with replying that he wanted to set an example for the inhabitants of Île Christine by showing them that they would follow, like them, the system of equality. That reason seemed good to the Queen—who, in any case, never had an opinion opposed to her husband's, and she promised to settle things with her father the worthy Seigneur.

For his part, Victorin charged Alexandre with attempting to penetrate his elder brother's dispositions. The young man strove to do so, but without success. However, as he sought every opportunity to converse with his brother in private, he perceived that he was going to la-Victorique. He followed him there, taking great care not to be perceived.

The elder brother flew directly to the habitation of the Patagone girl who had been the first to see the father and the younger son on their first visit to the island. Alexandre observed that the girl was waiting for her brother, that she received him in her arms, and that she took him away with her, caressing him a great deal. He saw that his brother returned those caresses; in the end, he had no doubt that they were lovers. That discovery appeared very extraordinary to him. He set off back to Île Christine immediately, and went to tell his father what he had seen.

Victorin immediately assembled the entire royal family: the Queen, Princess Sophie, his father-in-law, his father, his mother, his brothers and his sisters, to whom he added the Ecclesiastic, and he explained to them what had happened.

The good Seigneur was of the opinion that the inclination had something grand about it, and that it was preferable to an alliance with a subject; and that, in any case, by virtue of that marriage the royal family would achieve a stature above that of the people.

The Ecclesiastic, who was at least an archbishop, if not more, added gravely that:

"There is no doubt of the fact, on reading the writings of Homer attentively, and even those of the Latin poets, that the ancient kings of the Greeks, their Heroes and their Gods were only giants. The amours of Jupiter were only the passing fancies of that giant for women of common stature, and the heroes who emerged from that commerce were intermediate men who participated in giantism via their father and the small race via their mother—which is also confirmed by our sacred writings, for such were the turbulent men of which they speak who were the issue of the sons of God and the daughters of men. Such was, among the Greeks, Hercules, infinitely superior to his brother Eurystheus, although born of the same mother but not the same father, that of Hercules being a giant; also, the mother of the hero had a great deal of difficulty bringing him into the world, as Ovid says; the father of Eurystheus being, on the contrary, a common man named Amphitryon. Such was Bacchus, but Semele, his mother, was less fortunate than Alcmene, her overly large infant obliging her to deliver him after seven months, and she died of it—whence came the fable that she had seen Jupiter in all his glory, a fable that presents another meaning, which my character prevents me from explaining to you, etc."

The good Seigneur found that savant discourse admirable. It made no impression on Christine, but Victorin thought about it, and he resolved to see whether such a marriage was possible. He waited for the return of his elder son, who did not take long to reappear, and in whom everything announced that his amours had not had an unfortunate outcome.

Victorin went to him with a kindly expression; he made him understand that he was aware of the dispositions of his heart, and went so far as to ask him, in the name of the affection that he had for him, to take him entirely into his confidence, in order that he could work for his happiness, in whatever outcome it might consist.

Such an affectionate speech had its effect. Although blushing, the young man replied to his father:

"I would be unworthy of so much generosity, Seigneur, if I did not open my heart to you completely. You know that I was very well received among the Patagons, during our voyage there for commerce. The young person who was the first to see you and my brother, in particular, showed me a great deal of affection, and as soon as we could understand a few words of one another's languages, she assured me that, if I wanted to be hers, no Patagon would ever mean anything to her. That is what she made me understand clearly.

"You know how charming she is, and how well made she is; my heart could not resist. I told her that I was the elder son of the chief of the little people. She replied to me that among them, all people are equal, that her father is highly esteemed in his nation; and that if I were more than other little people, that brought us closer together. We agreed to see one another frequently. When we left, she seemed very afflicted; I told her that by means of my wings, a unique prerogative of my family, I could come to see her nearly every day. I have not failed to do that, Father.

"I cannot express to you how much I love, and am beloved, but I am not dissimulating the difficulties from myself: would you consent, and would my mother consent, to my taking such a wife? Would it not injure her in the eyes of the Nation? Even if your generosity overcame all obstacles for me, would the Patagons, who regard us as scarcely human, see with a kindly eye one of their daughters given to a pygmy, by comparison with them? Those, my dear Seigneur and Father, are the questions I asked myself, without being able to overcome the penchant inspired in me by the beautiful Ishmichtris.

"I find in the grandeur of loving such a young woman that all the princesses and all the beauties in the world seem to be nothing by comparison. However, Father, I hope so much of your generosity that I dare to count on your particular consent, and even on your taking steps with regard to the Patagons."

Although he had expected it, Victorin remained very surprised by his son's speech. After some tumultuous reflection, he summoned De B***m**t again.

"Don't talk to anyone else about what you've just confided to me," he said to him, "for fear that we might become the laughing-stock of our compatriots if we don't succeed. I admit to you, my son, that the grandeur of your views pleases me, and I presume that you will also have, for particular reasons, the consent of your maternal grandfather. But in looking further ahead, it seems to me that if we succeed in uniting the two nations by marriages, we shall aggrandize our species. I'll think about all of that. At the moment, it's only a matter of you. We'll soon go together to the Patagon isle, and I'll sound out the principals of the nation."

Young De B***m**t was transported by joy on finding his father's sentiments in such conformity with his own, but instead of waiting, he went immediately to la-Victorique to inform his mistress of what his father was going to do. Ishmichtris was delighted. She took her lover to her mother, to whom she had already confessed her inclination, and begged her to intercede on their behalf with her father and other fathers of the nation.

Ouflichflo listened to her daughter indulgently; she caressed little De B***m**t, whom she carried on her wrist like a hunting hawk, and all three of them went to the great Horkhoumhannloch, Ishmichtris' father. Without any circumlocution, Ouflichflo put the proposal of the marriage to him.

As soon as he had heard it, it was evident that he wanted to laugh, but spirits do not circulate as rapidly in those large bodies as in ours, and they saw his features gradually become reconfigured and his eyes become animated, and it only burst forth five minutes after his wife had spoken.

This is an approximate translation of his response:

"My dear itimikhili (wife), no one shall accuse our daughter of being rhamca (lubricious); on the contrary, all of the noble and powerful nation of Ppotkhogans (Patagons) will praise her, as being very mitimhipipi (sober in amour). But for myself, what appears to me at present to be of major consideration is that I shall have ouoûnbjîh (honey-bees) for grandchildren, and that will be rather funny. All we lack is to give the sister of this mijhi-titi-mhan (pretty little man) to our son, the big Skhapopantighô, but that can't be, because what would happen to the mijhi-titi-mofti (pretty little woman) is what happened to the nhiti-mofti (night-woman) from Sunhichdhômbah (Nocturnal Isle—the Patagon name for Île Christine) who died pregnant by the Ppotkhogan who had abducted her."

"My dear khratakhahboul (husband)," replied the worthy Ouflichflo, "I like this lilimhi (jewel); let's give our bikhijhi (daughter) to him; he'll make her happy, no matter how."

"Ha-Limiféqui (my wife), I can't decide such a thing without consulting our Oh-Mahn-oh (heads of families); it will only take me ten orhomhodho (circles, or years) to see them all; I'll give you their response immediately."

Women are passionate everywhere, even among the Patagons; the worthy Ouflichflo became impatient.

"I want a response immediately," she said, "or you're going to annoy me, make my cry and lose my appetite completely."

"Come, come, my dear limiféqui, I'll only go to talk to my neighbors, and in ten vhicilli (moons, or months) I'll be able to give you an answer."

"Ten vhicilli! Then I won't drink, or eat, or sleep from now until your ten vhillici!"

"Ha-Oh (my God) you're prompt, my limiféqui. Oh well, I'll only take ten ikirikoh (suns, or days), to see our neighbors—I can't go any faster than that!"

"I won't give you ten tabalah (hours), nor ten thathatha (minutes, or pulse-beats). You have to call two or three ohmhan-oh right now, and that will be settled."

"Oh, all right! I'll do it!" said the great Horkhoumhannlock, simply.

Two of three heads-of-families were summoned immediately, and the case was put to them for a decision, in the presence of their wives. Those grave individuals listened attentively; then they looked at one another; then, taking four minutes, one of them made a sign indicating that he wanted to speak; the others turned toward him, taking three minutes. Their wives were seething with impatience.

Finally, the great Ombomboboukikah, the oldest, said: "The case is grave; it's a matter of an alliance with an inferior species, which, although endowed with reason, appears to us, by virtue of its vivacity, its levity and its beauty, more like women. So, it's necessary to assemble the nation and take twenty orhomhodho to deliberate."

The others were of the same opinion, with the exception of one, who opined for thirty circles.

Fortunately, the women lost patience, and they terrified those grave individuals so much that it was decided by them that the marriage would take place within ten suns, at the latest. They all took young De B***m**t in their arms and caressed him in stifling fashion.

One particular reason caused the women to favor the passion of the beautiful Ishmichtris, which was that there were far fewer men than women in Patagonia, which meant that each man had at least three wives. Apparently, that was also the reason that had determined the young Patagone; she had calculated that the amiable little man was equal to about a third of a Patagon, and thus, having him all to herself, it would amount to the same thing.

Young De B***m**t, heaped with caresses, departed at top speed to return to Sunhichdhômbah, or Île Christine. He found his father, who was waiting for him in order to leave. The young man gave him an account of the journey he had just made to inform his mistress; that gave Victorin a great deal of pleasure and changed his resolution. He put off the departure until the following day, and that same evening, he assembled the chiefs of his colony, to whom he made the following clever speech:

"Dear compatriots, I have the honor of being your chief, and although we are all equal in his happy colony, since we are all human, you regard me as its founder. But I do not want the advantages of my position without the difficulties, the responsibilities and the sacrifices. You are all happy, by virtue of honest, affectionate conduct; it is necessary that my family and I go further, in order to merit the consideration with which you honor us; we must seek to ensure your repose, your tranquility and your commerce with neighboring nations.

"Fellow citizens, I am meditating, since my son is of an age to marry, a great scheme, a scheme that will astonish you, the success of which appears to me to be uncertain, but the advantages of which would be immense. This is it: you have charming daughters; my son is amiable; it is not that amour could not determine him for one of them, but I have the certainty that he has not yet opened his heart for any. My plan is that he sacrifice himself, and, for the good of the State, that he should take a wife among the giant species that is our neighbor. That alliance will bring us the greatest of goods, peace, and friendship with powerful men.

"That, my dear fellow citizens, is what my son and I have decided to do for the public good. Speak, and let the chiefs of the colony say freely what they think."

A murmur of applause immediately went up; the chiefs surrounded the god Seigneur, the father of the Queen, and asked him to give the thanks of the nation to the father and the son.

"It is with delight," exclaimed the old man, "that I am charged by truly French hearts to testify to the king, my son-in-law, and the hereditary prince, the dauphin, my grandson, the great veneration that their noble and generous resolution has inspired in the chiefs of the colony. Go, immortal heroes, go consummate your task; it is the wish of all the inhabitants of Île Christine, and above all, it is mine!"

The Queen was present. She embraced her son, with tears in her eyes, saying to him: "Obey your father and your grandfather."

Victorin spoke again. "As for my other two children, I propose my daughter as a prize for the most meritorious young man of the colony, the one who will distinguish himself by the qualities of heart and mind, combined with a pleasant face. All the young men of the colony, sage and well-made, at least two years older than my Sophie, may contend for her hand; and the one who, as well as gaining her heart, obtains the esteem of her mother, mine, and the suffrage of the nation, whoever he may be, will become her husband. As for my younger son, he is as devoted to the public good as his brother, and we shall think about him after the marriage of his elder."

The next morning, Victorin and his two sons flew to Patagonia and descended at the home of the beautiful Ishmichtris' parents. They were received by the worthy Ouflichflo with testimonies of the most tender affection. And as, in that land, only women are asked for their daughters' hands in marriage, and dispose of them at will, Victorin's request was made and agreed right away.

The issue that caused the longest discussion was the residence of the newlyweds on Sunhichdhômbah; they did not want to consent to that, saying that it was the land of the tlîtilhiti-mahn (human bats). The king of Île Christine, however, having spelled out his grand plans, explained that he hoped that the Patagone alliance might aggrandize his species, and furthermore, having been keenly supported by the future, Patagone ladies might go there and be convinced to marry by men—for in that land, the men appear to decide everything, but actually decide nothing; whereas, on the contrary, women appear to do nothing, but actually do everything, *as is the case here*.

The day being fixed for the celebration, it was agreed that it would take place in the fashion of both nations, that the entire family of the groom with be there, and that the Patagon nation would be aggregated, of which it would henceforth be considered a member, in consideration of the alliance.

Victorin and his son, very satisfied, returned home in order to work on the preparations. Beautiful rose-green-and-gold fabrics were made in order to make several polonaises for the bride, for it had been decided that she would wear French costume. When the new fabrics were finished, specimens were brought to her, and skillful dressmakers from Île Christine, with the most fashionable merchants and the shoemaker, went to Patagonia to take the measurements of the beautiful Ishmichtris, and inquire as to her taste, or inspire it. The seamstresses were very well received, and by means of small stepladders like those in libraries, they took the dimensions of the vast body of the beauty, who, having reached her fifteenth year, as already three-quarters of her full height—for the Patagons continue growing until twenty-five.

A bonnet was constructed for her in the form of a frigate, with rigging, cannons, masts, sails, etc., which was a delight because, the bonnet being vast, objects could be detailed there with grace. Ishmichtris was very content with it. But that adornment was only for the day of the marriage; another was made, more becoming and less vast, in the most exquisite taste, for the day after. They tried her in a sheath-dress, which closely resembled present-day polonaises, and had none of the poor form that maladroit seamstresses are beginning to give them, and by means of the stitching and the bustle that was fitted to it, the beautiful Patagonian would have been able to hide and entire regiment of soldiers clad in the Prussian fashion under her skirts.

The only embarrassment was finding sufficiently large plumes; the fashion merchants explained that to the mother of the bride.

"It's only that you lack?" she replied to them. "Why didn't you say?" Ishmichtris' brother, the burly Skhapopanthighoh, was sent out hunting, and killed a kind of ostrich, whose wing-feathers were as long as marine rushes.

They fashioned them as best they could and dyed them different colors, and succeeded in making a head-dress that was fitted to Ishmichtris' head with platinum wires and pins like little crowbars.

The greatest problem was curling the hair; the beautiful Patagonian's tresses were so long and coarse that the two most experienced hairdressers of Île Christine, previously famous in Paris, could only succeed in crimping them with difficulty. Nevertheless, they succeeded, so expert were they. One of them put her entire arm into a curl, around which her comrade rolled it, with the result that every curl bore a strong resemblance to the cylinders that roll the grass in your sterile gardens.

As for footwear, the Parisian shoemaker had the art of giving grace to the beauty's vast shoes; he observed all the proportions so well, made the toe so sharp, the heel so thin and the arch so high that when Ishmichtris was in silk stockings and white droguet socks, even the Frenchwomen agreed that her foot was the daintiest that a woman of her stature could have.

The day when the two costumes were finished—it was the day before the wedding—the neighborhood was assembled to see the beautiful Ishmichtris. She came out of a lovely cabin formed by the branches of neighboring trees and constructed expressly. All of Patagon society was assembled in front of the door, women on one side and men on the other. Only Ishmichtris' father had been curious enough to stay where his daughter was being adorned. The seamstresses, ten in number, coiffed as highly as possible with ostrich plumes and wearing shoes with six-inch heels, hip-pads, bustles, etc., preceded her. The Patagons, on seeing them, declared that the dwarfs of Sunhichdhômbah Island were not so dwarfish!

At the sight of her, the entire assembly was mute with astonishment; even the Patagons stood there open-mouthed. She advanced majestically between two lines of her relatives and fellow citizens, bowing graciously to each of them, as she had been taught to do by the great Marcel—brought among the artists when the Inaccessible Mountain had been abandoned, and doubtless assumed in Paris to be dead.[30] The entirety of Patagon society was enchanted by her grace, but slightly humiliated by her hauteur—in the physical sense of the word; she infinitely surpassed all that there was of tallness among the tallest Patagonians.

Young De B***m**t did not make the diplomatic mistake of following his mistress; he put himself between her and the male and female artists who had contributed to her adornment, and as, with his wings and his stilts, he surpassed them in height, he seemed less disproportionate.

"What!" said the women. "Isn't your intended tall enough already, that you have to make her bigger still!"

"She can't be too tall, Mesdames," the young man replied. "My sentiments for her are so respectful and so tender that I am glad to see her shine, astonish and eclipse everyone."

"Oh, how tender Frishmishmhan (French) husbands are!" cried all the Patagons. "Our relative was not wrong to take one, nor her parents to consent to it!"

"Oh, how stupid they are!" muttered a Patagon, between his teeth.

"Less than you," replied one of his wives, who had overheard him. "They bear the yoke with a good grace, and not with the air of enchained slaves. What would you do if you only had one wife? We'd see you crawling at our feet."

After that show parade, the beautiful Ishmichtris went home, and remained dressed as she as for the rest of the day, as much to satisfy the curiosity of her friends as to become accustomed to it.

Finally, the great day arrived. Victorin, his wife, his father-in-law, his father, his family, and the chiefs of all the tribes of Île Christine went to la-Victorique to witness the illustrious marriage. In order that his troop should seem less ridiculous in the eyes of the Patagons, Victorin had charged a

---

[30] François Marcel, the famous doyen of the Académie Royale de Danse, died—or was assumed to have died—in 1759.

Cocosate—an inhabitant of the hills of Gascony—to make stilts that would increase the height of each man by about four feet. They were soon ready, and people had practiced every day, in order to be able to walk as easily with that machine as the peasants of the sandy heaths that one sees in Bordeaux resting on the awnings of shops, or on the sills of first-floor windows. That idea was very good, and made a favorable impression on the Patagons; at any rate, it rendered conversation more comfortable; people could talk to one another without the giants being obliged to bend double to hear what the Christinians were saying.

They had arrived on the beautiful ship, which Victorin had kept in good condition. They had brought the Ecclesiastic. As for the Patagons, they have no priests, properly speaking; it is the most ancient of the elders who bring to the Sun and the Earth the simple and natural homage of the nation, which only happens once a year for the sun, at the summer solstice, and once a year for the earth, at the winter solstice.

BOOK TWO

I

It is not that those huge men believe that the Sun and the Earth are the divine principle, but they regard them as the two foremost visible entities, relative to us: the Sun is the father, the Earth the mother; the Moon is like an aunt, etc. They say that we ought to address our homage directly to the Sun and the Earth, the only ones worthy to bear it to the universal God, whom they know, while we do not, etc.

But I shall return to the marriage of the elder son of Victorin and Christine de B***m**t, who is marrying a giantess.

The marriage ceremony was august and simple. The most excellent Elder, a hundred and sixty years old—for those giants live much longer than our species—united the two spouses and asked them the following questions, the responses to which they had rehearsed:

The Patagon Elder: Why have you come before me?

Response: To join us in the bond of marriage.

T.P.E.: Why are you marrying?

R.: Because love has spoken to our hearts.

T.P.E.: What did it say?

R.: Unite yourselves, and you will know delights.

T.P.E.: Do you desire delights, then?

R.: Yes, venerable Elder, for pleasure is the perfect development of the existence of every living being.

T.P.E.: Is it a sterile pleasure or a fecund pleasure that you desire?

R.: It is a fecund pleasure, for sterile pleasure is not true pleasure.

T.P.E.: What will your pleasure produce?

R. The masterpiece of Nature, a human being.

T.P.E.: O my children, think hard! Nothing is holier than the pleasure of marriage that produces a human being! Do not profane it with quarrels and dissents. Which of the two is the chief?

R.: The man, as the divine Sun is the husband and chief of the Earth, the Moon and the other planets, his wives.

T.P.E. to the Wife: Think, my daughter, to be submissive to your husband, for the man is the producer, and the woman is merely the developer; she only gives the body, and the man gives the soul and life. Thus, the omnipotent Sun warms you, illuminates you and rejoices you. Let the beneficent Earth offer you agreeable meadows and cool shade, let her furnish you with succulent fruits, limpid springs and beds of flowers on which to taste delights. Thus you bless and love the Sun and the Earth, as I love you and bless you. Let the Sun warm the husband with his divine fire, let the Earth form a bed of moss for the wife, that she receive there softly the first fruit of your marriage. O Sun, O Earth, unite your children! Are you united by heart?

R.: Yes, holy Elder.

T.P.E.: Be so in body, by the holy authority of the entire nation, which I exercise at this moment.

Such is the Patagon formula, to which was added, for the circumstance, two halves of a sphere, which the Patagon Elder brought together, saying: "Thus be united forever the nations of the two spouses!"

The European marriage ceremony followed—which appeared very sensible to the Patagons, who thought it appropriate that the marriage ought to be made in accordance with both rites. Afterwards, the spouses and the numerous assembly came down from the high rock on which the celebration had taken place, in order to go and eat and amuse themselves in a large meadow, where tables had been set up.

First they were served a Patagon soup in platinum caul-drons, like the saltpeter cauldrons that can be seen here in the Arsenal. They were carved and sculpted; the marriage that had just been made was sculpted there, in accordance with the designs of a Megapatagon artist (I shall tell you about that admirable people in due course), who had taken great care to represent the young prince of the Île Christine with the height given to him by his stilts, while hiding them with his wings. After that there were various diversions, such as those I shall describe to you before long. Then they were served the broth, crowned with a kind of parsley and cress, in which the various birds were found that had give the soup an excellent taste.

The Christinians were served in ordinary flat dishes.

A roasted hippopotamus veal was then set before each Patagon, one alone of which sufficed for all the Christinians. Then each of them was served a condor, each thigh of which weighed twenty-five pounds. After that came a giant serpent a hundred feet long, cooked in wine, which was found to be delicious. Finally, to complete their satiation, they were given the livers of young elephants, well-spiced. Every Patagon drank a quantity of wine equivalent to two hogsheads of Bur-gundy.

For the Christinians, each had his two bottles, which was about a quarter of a draught for the Patagons. They ate little feet from the Île Christine, and other trifles that the Patagons gazed at pityingly, comparing them to flies.

At dessert they had the fruits of the two countries. The Patagons' were exquisite; one of them was shared between all the Christinians, while the largest from the Île Christine, brought from Europe with our apricots, peaches, plums, ap-ples, etc. were swallowed a dozen at a time at the Patagon table, where the peach stones were regarded as little pips.

When the meal was over, the diversions were prepared. A Patagonian instrument played a prelude. It was a sort of marine trumpet made from a followed-out fir-trunk, twenty-five feet long and six in circumference.[31] It was the most beautiful marine trumpet that had ever been seen.

As soon as the instrument went into action, the Patagons were seen, with their two hogsheads of wine inside them—not to mention the hippopotamus, the serpent, the elephant liver, etc.—starting to move with the rhythm, and when they had heard it played for an hour, they were ready to dance. What a dance! One might have thought they were bell-towers going up and down. The young, much more prompt, danced to other instruments a trifle softer, for the beautiful marine trumpet was reserved for men—like the instrument, the most powerfully and most nobly made.

As for the Christinians, deafened by the marine trumpet and the other Patagonian instruments, they drew away as far as possible in order to dance to the violin and other European instruments. A few Patagons of both sexes followed them out of curiosity, and lay down in order to try to hear our tunes; they agreed that they were very harmonious, but they only heard them as we hear the drone of evening mosquitoes.

The groom and the bride danced by turns in both assemblies, and it must be admitted that the poor prince suffered a great deal from the marine trumpet, but he pretended to find it admirable, and by means of a good loudhailer, which his younger brother—the most skillful mechanician in the world—had fabricated for him, he never ceased to compliment the Patagons on it.

"You're too kind," Ishmichtris whispered to him, "but you're wise to flatter them; these big men generally have depths of pride that make them scornful of anything smaller

---

[31] A marine trumpet, or tromba marina, is a stringed instrument shaped like an elongated truncated cone, about six feet long (although the Patagon version is presumably much longer), resting on a triangular base. It was often played by nuns in the Renaissance period, and was allegedly misnamed a trumpet because women were not allowed to play the trumpet, and were obliged to employ the stringed instrument instead.

than themselves. If you praise their nasty instrument, they will think you have some reason; continue to laud their prejudices."

"Dear wife," the young prince replied, "I admire every day the extent of your philosophy. What you have just said is recognized among Europeans, where evidence of it is seen every day. Men taller in stature than their peers by a foot— which is almost nothing—scorn other men, naturally, and almost without intending to; they scarcely deign to treat them fairly. Those that are greater in intelligence are even more scornful of others—if you saw how they treat them! It would move you to pity."

I shall refrain from taking those philosophical conversations between the newlyweds any further. They said many other excellent things, which might seem to you to be out of place.

After everyone had amused themselves, dusk fell. The Christinians went to supper, while the Patagons, who only eat once every twenty-four hours, went to bed, in order to complete their digestion tranquilly.

The new wife sat down at table for form's sake; then she was taken to the nuptial bed by her mother and the oldest of the women of the mahn-mouhh (household). I think it might be interesting to report the ceremony of putting the bride to bed, as it is practiced in Patagonia. The mother and the doyenne of the nation each take one of her arms, and present her to the husband, saying:

"Beneficent Sun, here is an Earth that we present to you, in order that you might warm her with your rays and fecundate her by means of the principle of life that is within you. Cherish her and love her, for she cherishes you, loves you and respects you. Take care of her delicacy, for a woman is not a man." (Here Ishmichtris' mother smiled, on looking at the stature of her son-in-law, even though he was still on his stilts.) "We have given her to you because you are the most agreeable of masters; treat her as the most beloved and most faithful of servants, who would give her blood and her life for you. My daughter, swear faith, fidelity and obedience to your Master."

"Dear Khrahakhaboul (husband), I swear an eternal attachment to you, and since, in conformity with the laws of your nation, you will only have me for a wife, I shall love you three times as much as I would love a Ppotkhogan (Patagon) husband."

Upon that response—not dictated—the two Patagone ladies embraced the young bride, and her husband launched himself upon her nascent bosom, on which he sat, and from which he could kiss her entirely at his ease. The two ladies then recited the customary prayer:

"May the Sun, father of the day, and the Earth, mother of the night, during which repose and the sweetness of guiguimhitlhi (amour) are savored, love you and favor you both, without your ever having the long disputes that the Sun sometimes has with the Earth, or the Earth with the Moon, her younger sister, when the one or the other two femimisisibim (eclipse one another)."

After having kissed the two spouses, the good Ouflichflo and old Manimhilititi withdrew, walking backwards, and closed the door on them, saying to them: "Tomorrow, at avikikikoh (dawn) we shall come to congratulate you."

As soon as they had gone, the young prince had the Christinian seamstresses come in to undress his wife and put everything in order; that only took an hour, which seemed like a century.

Finally, he found himself alone with the beautiful Ishmichtris, whose youth and innocence promised him the sweetest pleasures. He savored them, those inexpressible delights, and made his companion share them, in spite of the sarcasms of young Patagons; and the beauty, very content, considering the delicacy of her dear little husband, moderated his renascent ardor, and obliged him to go to sleep on her bosom.

The two ladies did not fail to return the following morning, followed by Queen Christine. Trophies of the young prince's victory were found, and, as is the custom in Patagonia, just as in Turkey, they were carried in triumph. They were put at the end of a fifty-meter pole and Ishmicgtris' nearest relative, six years of age, mounted on a giraffe and followed by a chorus of young women, carried them throughout the habitation. That caused many Patagon tongues to fall silent!

The celebrations continued for three days, after which Victorin asked for permission to withdraw. It was granted to him, with regret, for the little people had succeeded in making themselves liked by the big ones, because of their intelligence and politeness. If it had not been for the disproportion, Ishmichtris' brother, the huge Skhapopantighô, could very well have come to an arrangement with Sophie, but there was absolutely no means.

On the other hand, several young Patagons wanted to imitate Ishmichtris, but their mothers, more experienced, dissuaded them. In any case, Victorin wanted to conserve the advantages of the Patagone alliance for his family alone. Thus, of all the young giantesses who testified amity to the Christinians, the only one who was accommodated was the pretty Mikitikîpi, Ishmichtris' cousin, who was destined for Victorian's second son, the inventive Alexandre.

They left during the night of the fourth day in the ship, taking the new bride with them, who shed a few tears on quitting her dear parents. They arrived that same evening on Île Christine, where the young princess was lodged in a palace appropriate to her grandeur.

I shall say right away that nine months after the marriage, Ishmichtris gave birth to a beautiful son two and a half feet tall—which was about half the height of Patagon infants. Alexandre immediately carried the news to Patagonia, with the exact dimensions of the child; it gave a great deal of pleasure to the Patagonian ladies, who saw that of the two races, an intermediate was about to be born, which was closer to them. There was great rejoicing on la-Victorique as well as on Île Christine.

Subsequently, the princess had five more children, which was two more than Patagone wives were accustomed to have. Finally, to say everything right away, Alexandre, like his brother, married the beautiful Mitikitipi, and she bore him eight children. Sophie married the most meritorious of the Christinians, her paternal cousin.

The two giantesses were good wives, and care was taken, in future, to marry the children of the two brothers to one another, without giving them either Patagons or Christinians, in order to maintain the intermediate race in just proportion, which was to ensure its beauty in the eyes of both nations—for the Patagons found them dainty without being pygmies, and the Christinians majestic, without being colossal.

Now that you are tranquil about all of that, I shall pass on to other things.

Having married his children, Victorin lived happily on Île Christine; death had not yet taken anyone away from him, and he enjoyed the inexpressible pleasure of having for witnesses to his glory his father, his mother and the worthy Seigneur, his wife's father. He enjoyed, I assure you, the happiness of Christine herself, and he savored it with even more pleasure than his own.

He had been on the island for twenty years, and had seen all his endeavors prosper. What mortal was ever more fortunate? Ah, the supreme felicity, unknown in corrupt cities, but which I sense, is to have made one's lot, and to have for witnesses of that success the authors of one's days! To see their joy, the delightful sentiment that we inspire in them: to see them savoring the rejuvenating nectar of pious pride that they experience in saying to us: "my son!"—for glory of the son belongs to the father much more than the glory of the father belongs to the son.

The night-people lived tranquilly in their retreats, where no one troubled them. On the contrary, provisions were taken to them, which were abandoned at the entrance to their cavern; it was a kind of tribute that Victorin wanted to pay to the true proprietors of the island. If you want to give your people good mores, and enable them to be just, O Legislator, do not do as the Europeans; be just yourself with regard to weak and defenseless nations—for nothing would have been easier than to murder all the night-people one day, but Victorin made it a fundamental law to respect them.

He soon had reason to applaud his conduct, and he was to experience a warm satisfaction when he witnessed what I am about to recount.

After presents had been given to the night-people without interruption for several years, the latter, who had initially appeared to receive them without attention, or perhaps to regard them as a trap, were finally touched by gratitude. They understood that the day-people were only giving them the fruits of lands that they had cultivated, and which were theirs. They went far and wide in search of indigenous fruits; they caught goats and wild cattle, tethered them, and led them to the gate of the capital, Christineville.

The first time that all those things were found, the next morning, the inhabitants were extremely surprised. Victorin, who roamed during the night, flying, and who shared with his two sons the onerous function of watching over the security of his people, knew perfectly well that they were presents from the night-people. He was filled with joy, in spite of their small value, but he did not want to say anything. He make them collect the presents and carry them in triumph.

That evening, he had those destined for the night people augmented, and ordered that the principals of the nation should stay up, in order to discover the authors of the act of friendship. About two hours after midnight, the night-people were seen bringing further presents, and uttering cries of delight.

All the night-women formerly espoused by the men from the wrecked vessel accompanied the Elders, among whose number were the worthy Seigneur and Victorin's father, in spite of their extreme old age. The women were asked what the cries signified.

They ran to meet their compatriots, mingled with them, and when they had spoken to them, they came back dancing, carrying in their hands the most beautiful breadfruits on the island. They recounted that their nation had finally understood that the day-people wished them well, that they were rendering presents for presents, in order to maintain amity, and that they had composed a song that went, in the nocturnal language:

Mhi-rhi lhi, lhi, lhi, lhi, lhi (Day-people good, good, good, good, good)
Mhi-rhi ppih bhlhi khui appi (Day-people set us good example)
Mhi-rhi nhi-klhi vhappih (Day-people not nasty, you)
Mhih-rhi nhi-khrrih ppih (Day-people not killing us)
Mhih-rhi khuî-fhîh Mhihogherih (Day people liking greatly night-people)
Mhi-rhi ppih khuî-fhîh-brhi (Day-people we like greatly too).

"You can see, dear fellow citizens," said Queen Christine then, "whether my husband was not right in his conduct full of humanity? We have friends who might be useful to us; let us conserve them, by living with them in the most cordial fraternity."

Afterwards, Victorin, who had learned the squeaky language of the night-people, replied to them with a verse, which he had the night-women learn by heart and charged them to sing to their compatriots, which translated as:

The day-people are your brothers,
And want to be your friends;
Their sentiments are sincere,
Accept the compromise.
Night-people, have no fear;
By day we shall watch for you;
By night protect out enclosure

Humans should help one another.

He was careful to explain that verse to the night-women, and penetrate them with its true meaning, in order that they should pass the enlightenment on to their compatriots; and he had the satisfaction, after an hour, of seeing them come back with six elders and as many young people of each sex. The night-women married to day-men served as interpreters for the two nations, and although the night-people were infinitely limited in regard to intelligence, they nevertheless had the following conservation:

Night-Elder: "I see you, you see me, me every easy, are you also?"

Victorin: "We are very glad to see you, to talk to you, and we bless the happy moment that brings us together. We bless these good women of your nation, whom we have taken by necessity, but will be the link that connects us."

(It took the night-women a very long time to make the night-elder comprehend the last few words.)

Night-Elder: "You good, good, good."

Victorin extended his hand. The women explained what he wanted, and the old man, trembling, advanced a crooked and hairy paw. Victorian and he held one another thus for some time, and then the day-man exclaimed, with tears in his eyes: "O Sun, Father of the world, you have never illuminated an alliance as astonishing! O Earth, common mother, leap with joy on seeing the union of your children, whom insurmountable barriers seemed to have separated!"

The women also explained all that, although Victorin had pronounced it in both languages, French and the squeaky tongue—but I repeat, the intelligence of the night-people is so limited that the women emerged from their nation, a little more enlightened by their sojourn with their husbands, had a great deal of difficulty making it perfectly understood. Those people had never been able to see the sun; first light sufficed to chase them into their caverns.

After that solemn treaty, the night-people went home, accompanied by some of the female interpreters, to explain to their nation what had just happened, for some error on the part of the delegates was feared. The husbands of the women accompanied them in order to bring them back, but did not go into the cavern. After they had fulfilled their commission, they returned in daylight, guided by their husbands, because they could no longer see.

There was something rather singular about those households. In the morning, the husband got up and the wife went to bed; in the evening the wife got up, and did everything that was within her competence and range, while her husband slept. In any case, the tasks the women carried out were very minor; they were incapable of industry, but they cleaned the house and went to water the vegetable garden. That was the principal reason why it had been resolved not to take any more subsequently, but Victorin was glad that necessity had obliged it to be done initially.

As for the children produced by those marriages, they were very susceptible to education, and were given the best possible, with particular care. They had no other defect than blinking their eyes during the day, with an incessant and rapid movement of the eyelids, but which did not prevent them from seeing. They could also see by night, and it was resolved to obtain some consequent utility from that mixed race, by means of the faculty that they had in common with the women who had given birth to them. The children were, however, accustomed—in spite of a certain contrary enchant, very marked in some but less sensible in others—to sleep at night and to do as other people did during the day; and that habit became second nature to them.

That is what I have been glad to tell you about the mixture of the people of the day and the night. I will add that a good relationship has been maintained between the two nations. If a day-man loses his way by night, the nocturnal men guide him affectionately back to his door. In the same way, if anyone encounters a night-man surprised by the daylight, he is brought back amicably to his cavern.

Furthermore, the night-people having perceived that laborers took their oxen to pasture during the night, and that their children brought them back in the morning, they offered to take charge of that employment. In consequence, they pasture all the flocks and herds during the night, and faithfully bring them back to the entrance to Christineville and the country villages at dawn; today they even take them to the stables.

Such services have a considerable advantage; the livestock are not tormented by the heat or by flies, and they work or rest during the day without inconveniencing their masters by virtue of the care they would require.[32]

---

[32] The chapter does not end here in the first edition. The additional text reads:

"(Here Salocin-emde-fitér interrupted the Australian with an exclamation:'"Unfortunate Pervuians, who did not have Victorin for a conqueror instead of a Pizarro or a Cortez! We would see your happy and flourishing nation populating abandoned America today and furnishing us with the aid of a sincere amity in unknown climes. May all the evil fall upon your tyrants that they have done to you! Alas, without the event of the commencement of the century, my execration would be accomplished and that vile and superstitious nation would have almost as much to complain about as you!')

"The Australian smiled at that sharp remark, and continued."

The "event of the commencement of the century" to which Salocin-emde-fitér (each of whose names is spelled backwards) refers is the War of the Spanish Succession, which began in 1701.

II

In the bosom of prosperity Victorin, seeing his people increase prodigiously, his family happy, and his daughters-in-law fecund, as well as the amiable Sophie, who had married Antonin, the son of one of his paternal aunts, did not take long to seek to make new discoveries, seconded by his two sons—especially by Alexandre, the younger, who was full of activity and invention, and had greatly improved his father's wings.

One morning, after having left the administration of affairs to his elder son, under the authority of his mother, the two of them departed and followed a longitudinal route along the parallel of Île Christine, in an easterly direction. They traversed a great sea and saw the limits of la-Victorique, but they had not surpassed it by two degrees, or fifty leagues, when they found a vast island slightly smaller than Île Christine. As was their habit, they flew over the island for a few days in order to discover the inhabitants, but they only perceived animals, all walking on four feet. In truth, they saw some absolutely unknown species there.

Finally, they descended on a mountain and conjectured that the island was only populated, as yet, by night-people.

After having taken a few precautions for their safety, they took their light wings and took the risk of traveling some distance from their retreat. They found frayed tracks, which supported their initial idea, but the paths were covered by trees and so low that one could only move there on all fours. They dared not go into them, because it would have been impossible to take flight there.

While they were thus in suspense, Alexandre, more alert than Victorin, perceived a hairy four-footed animal closely resembling a monkey, which was reaching out a hooked hand toward his father. He uttered a cry, and as their light wings were in readiness, they rose up in the air to a height of twenty feet with a single thrust of the parasol. They hovered then, and saw emerging from the trees a hundred animals like the first, which watched them fly off, several of which raised themselves up on their hind feet.

Then they perceived that the animals, although covered with hair, nevertheless had a face intermediate between that of a monkey and a human. They even heard them talking to one another, while looking at one another in a manner perfectly resembling that of screeching monkeys. Those screeches, however, had a continuity that marked ideas in combination—in brief, a language.

"These are the people of this island," Victorian said to his son. "Humans can differ in the face, in the skin, in the habitude of the body, be diurnal or nocturnal, but that divine radiance, reason, is everywhere characteristic of them. These beings talk to one another; they understand one another; look, my son, they are deliberating, they are consulting one another; they are looking at us. And there is one standing upright, who seems to be mimicking us while pointing at us. Our artificial wings must overturn all their ideas; they would overturn those of many Europeans, if they were not in a position to examine them closely. Let us make signs of amity to them, and see whether they understand them."

At the same time, the two Flying Men landed in an open space, and from there they made various signs of amity to the monkey-men, who looked at them with astonishment at first. Victorin and his son took a few steps forward, pronouncing soft words in a caressant tone: "Come, come, my friends."

The monkey-men appeared to consult one another, and, after a mute counsel, accompanied by the single word: "Rrrhî," an old one advanced alone.

Victorin and his son thought that they ought to meet him half way, and they all examined one another with the greatest attention. When they were a few paces away, they tried to read the monkey-man's eyes. They found them hostile, which caused them to redouble their precautions.

They continued to approach, however, and when they were almost within touching range, they perceived that the other savages were moving, in order to come toward them. They made a sign with their hand bidding them to stay where they were, and the sign was understood, but Alexandre warned his father that they were surrounded, and that those behind them were tightening the circle. A sign contained them in the same fashion.

Finally, the two flying men and the old savage found themselves face to face. Victorin began making signs of amity and offering presents of fruits from Île Christine, which the old monkey-man seized avidly, considered, and ate. He found them good, to all appearances. Meanwhile, the troop of savages, at the slightest sign of inattention on their part, advanced gradually, believing that the flying men did not perceive it—but the later always contained them with a hand gesture; finally, they obliged them to draw back, by showing them that they were about to take off.

They continued to converse by means of signs with the old one, more occupied in eating than responding to them. They tried to interrogate him about his nation, to discover whether it had weapons, habitations and what its nourishment was, but the old one did not appear to understand them.

Eventually, the other uttered a kind of cry. Immediately, the old one returned to the troop, to whom he did not appear to say anything. But another monkey-man advanced alone; he was younger and seemed more vigorous. He approached slowly, stopped, and gazed, as if he were keeping watch on the movements of the two humans. Finally, in a moment when he thought they were less wary, he launched himself forward in order to grab one on them, but they eluded him. At the same time, the troop of monkey-men, who had been watching the movements of their envoy, had rushed forward to assist him with the rapidity of an arrow.

Victorin and his son understood by that that the monkey-men were naturally hostile. They could not see any other way to have some liaison with them and get to know them than to take away a few individuals that were still young and take them back to Île Christine, where they would be treated well and where attempts would be made to domesticate them, to learn their language and try to teach them a little French.

They carried out that project easily. They flew above Monkey Island, as they named it—just as they had initially named Île Christine Nocturnal Island—and, having perceived young monkey-people playing in an open space, they descended in their midst, frightening them. They chose a young male about fifteen or sixteen years old, and a female of the same age, whom they lifted up—not without difficulty, for it was necessary that they should not be injured. Finally, however, they flew all the way to Île Christine, where they deposited them in the care of young De B***m**t and his wife Ishmichtris, asking them to try everything to tame and domesticate them.

Afterwards, having embraced their family and renewed their provisions, they departed that same evening for another island, which was only separated from a larger one by a narrow strait a quarter of a league in breadth.

They sought, in accordance with their custom, to perch on a rock in order to spend the night there and obtain their repose. When daylight came, they flew over the island in order to discover its inhabitants. They did not see any, which did not astonish them. They went to land in an open space, and advanced, looking everywhere. They found paths, as on Monkey Island, and just as low. While they were examining them, to see whether they could find the imprint of a foot, they heard a plaintive bellowing. They raised their eyes and saw, under the trees, hidden in the foliage, bears of some kind, which were studying them. A short distance away, a male and female of the species were beginning to climb.

Alexandre immediately rose up to the height of the treetops, approaching that new species of being, which was absolutely unknown to him, as closely as possible. Those bears did not have elongated muzzles, like others, but rounded faces like that of a pug. Victorin remained on the ground, observing as best he could, while his son came so close to a young bear-cub that the latter, frightened, let itself fall. Alexandre launched himself forward to catch it in mid-air, and lifted it up. His father immediately took off, and they carried the cub away, while the bears uttered terrible cries and descended precipitately from the trees in order to go and hide.

When the two flyers had reached their rock, they put the bear-cub down, and made signs of amity while offering it different things to eat, but it was so frightened that it played dead and closed its eyes. The examined it easily, and quickly saw that its external conformation resembled that of a human, and that it was only its fur that was that of a bear. However, its fingers were armed with claws of a sort, and its nose, flattened between its two cheeks, strongly resembled that of a bear.

They kept it for as long as it was mortally anxious, but when it hazarded a few movements they took it down from the rock, put various things into it land, and set it free. It fled with a singular rapidity, running on two feet, and making plaintive cries similar to those of bears. Those cries attracted several of its fellows, which ran to it and, seeing that it was alone, appeared to ask it what was wrong. It showed them the rock and exhorted them to follow it.

At the sight of that reflective action, Victorian and Alexandre no longer had any doubt that they were human. They took off with the resolution to capture two of them, a male and a female, if possible, in order to take them to Île Christine.

They had a great deal of difficulty in so doing; the bear-cub they had taken was so frightened that it spread alarm throughout that part of the island that was uncovered. Having hidden for a few days, however, the two flyers had the leisure to study and select two young people, whom they abducted and carried to Île Christine.

They found that the monkey-boy and the monkey-girl had already made satisfactory progress. They were recognized by them, and even received a few marks of amity, which appeared to them to augur well. An incident had occurred, however that had nearly caused a misunderstanding between the day-people and the night-people.

The young male monkey-man, walking with his conductor one evening, had perceived a night-man who was going forth without suspicion; he had immediately launched himself upon him, and would have strangled him, uttering frightful cries, if several Christinians had not snatched him from his hands. The man, frightened and wounded, went to carry the alarm to his compatriots, who did not emerge from their caverns that night.

That was perceived, and the nocturnal women married to day-men were immediately sent to explain the cause of the incident and to assure them that it would not happen again. As for the young monkey-man, it appeared that he had a great horror of the night-people, and was very astonished, when he had been somewhat domesticated, that such monsters were tolerated. He made it understood that whenever the monkey-people found them they killed them. Attempts were made to bring him back to more humane sentiments, but the monkey-people are so brutal that there did not seem to be any possibility of inspiring a certain delicacy in him. The most primitive of negroes are geniuses by comparison with the monkey-people.

Victorin wanted the instruction of the two young people to continue, but he instructed that they should only be allowed to see the young bear-people with the greatest precaution, for fear that they might be enemies and seek to do one another harm.

After a few days rest, Victorin and his son took off once again to continue their discoveries. They took the same route, passing over Monkey Island and Bear Island, and crossed a wide expanse of sea, advancing in the direction of the pole. About the fiftieth degree of austral latitude, they perceived a ship; they waited for nightfall to approach it closely. They recognized then that it was Capitaine Bouvet's.[33] As Alexan-

---

[33] Jean-Baptiste Bouvet de Lozier (1705-1786), an officer attached to the French East India Company, who carried out extensive explorations in the South Atlantic. N****** seems

dre had heard that the English had recently invented an optical device for seeing vessels in darkness, he had no doubt that the Capitaine's ship would have a provision of those glasses and proposed to his father that he try to take possession of one.

To that effect, they watched for the moment that the pilot would make use of one. They did not have to wait very long. The Capitaine himself came on to the deck and aimed his binoculars. At the same instant, Alexandre, whose newly-invented wings made very little sound, skimmed the deck and took the instrument.

"Damn!" said the Capitaine. "The glasses have fallen in the water! I don't know where that gust of wind came from—the air's calm! It's necessary to beware of these sudden gusts in these parts." And he went back inside to fetch another pair of binoculars. While he was adjusting them, Victorin and Alexandre drew away, not wanting to be seen. That instrument is very useful to them for seeing by night, and even during the day, in the depths of forests.

The time for making discoveries in the vanity of the austral pole had not yet arrived; the two flying men saw nothing but a sea charged with ice. They came closer the equator, and came to land on an island neighboring that of the bear-people.

Although that island was almost contiguous with the other, its inhabitants were nevertheless somewhat different, with regard to the human species, although the animals were the same. It is to be presumed that the cause of the difference was that the animals crossed the strait by swimming and mingled, whereas the humans had apparently forbidden themselves any commerce with one another, and had not contracted any mixture.

Victorin and his son had no sooner landed on an eminence than they heard some two or three thousand dogs barking around them. They were frightened by that and remained on their guard. Then the beings that had uttered the barking

---

to have forgotten that he had already equipped Victorin and Alexandre with a night-telescope in chapter V.

sounds that had surprised them emerged from a bushy wood; some were walking on their hind feet and barking very loudly; others were running beside them on four feet.

The two men immediately rose twenty feet into the air, and from there they threw down some of their provisions to the humans who bore such a close resemblance to dogs—who devoured them instantly and immediately looked up at the flying men, barking at them, as if to ask for more. They threw more down. Then they made their various signs of amity, which were understood very well. All those beings had tails, and the males were covered with a fur similar to that of poodles, but shorter and less dense. The females, on the other hand, by virtue of their slim figure, bore a strong resemblance to the greyhounds beloved by your ladies.

Victorin and his son did not think it feasible to descend into the midst of that troop, but they proposed to abduct two, a male and a female, as they were accustomed to do, and take them to Île Christine in order for them to be educated. Before then, however, they took one of the dog-men with them for a few hours, whom they treated as well as they could, and then released.

The man did not run away, like the other beast-people; he followed them, wagging his tail and caressing them, but they left him, after giving him all imaginable marks of amity, in order that he could commence disposing his compatriots in their favor. That same day they took away a young male and a young female dog-person, giving them provisions, and took them to Île Christine. Afterwards the two flying men set forth again, directing their flight beyond the island of the dog-people, which they called Cynic Island.[34]

As soon as they were above the next island, Alexandre discovered its inhabitants.

---

[34] The word "cynic" derives from the Greek, meaning "dog-like"; it is unclear how and why it came to be applied to the followers of Diogenes, eventually acquiring other meanings in connection with their oft-misunderstood philosophy.

"Damn!" he said to his father. "Look at those vile people! Let's be wary. Let's land on that plain covered with rotting felled trees; we'll be able to see those Messieurs!"

They immediately landed, and the first thing they saw among the felled trees was a woman sitting on one of the trunks, who had six teats and was nursing as many children, which bore a considerable resemblance to suckling pigs. Further away was a pig-man, whose expression was extremely rebarbative. Alexandre started laughing.

Victorin, surprised, observed; he heard the woman caressing her children, who were suckling, almost exactly like a grunting sow.

"Apparently the humans here are pig-people," he said to his son, "they must be ugly, but not malevolent." At the same time, he drew nearer to the sow-woman, who, having heard their footsteps, raised her head, which had something of the face of a woman as well as the snout of a pig, looked at them, uttered a cry, and ran away on two feet, rather slowly because she was carrying her six children. As for the male, his flight was much more rapid.

Alexandre cut off her retreat and stood before her, offering her provisions with a kindly expression. The woman made an imploring gesture, and appeared to be offering herself to death in order to save her little ones. But Alexandre reassured her, giving her breadfruits, which she sniffed and ate. Then he gave her free passage and moved away from her. She seemed quite relaxed, and drew away very slowly, but often looking back. As soon as she had reached a wood whose trees, of a species similar to the oak, were standing, she grunted very loudly.

The male who had abandoned her came back, and frightful grunting sounds were immediately audible.

Nearly six hundred pig-people came out of the wood and moved toward the two flying men, walking on four feet but often raising themselves up on two in order to gaze and sniff. Victorin and his son flew up into a tree, where they perched. The pig-men came as far as the foot of the tree, and immediately started digging in the ground with their snouts, which were like a boar's, in order to fell the refuge of the unknown beings.

In order to save them the trouble, the flying men took off and hovered over the troop, which stopped work and stood upright in order to consider them. Then they started grunting at one another. Their sows, who were elongated, white and short-haired, bristled, which indicated that they were not tranquil. Finally, one of them leapt up, twisting her tail, grunted in a frightful manner, and fled. All the others followed, running and bounding—which made Alexandre laugh until he wept.

The flying men captured one of the laggards, in accordance with their custom, to whom they gave breadfruits to eat, and whom they domesticated in half a day, to the point that he came to sniff them and offer them his snout. They set him free in the evening, and he returned very slowly to his compatriots.

The following day, the Christinians abducted two young pig-people, one of each sex, and took them to Île Christine in order to educate them and render them capable of one day being the civilizers of their nation.

After that voyage, Alexandre had the satisfaction of seeing the beautiful Mikitikipi, his tall and dear wife, give him a son, who was named Skhapopantighô-Hermantin—but he only used the latter name in society, the other being too difficult, having only been given to the child out of consideration for the Patagon nation.

After the rejoicing that the birth in question occasioned throughout Île Christine and Patagonia, the father and son set forth again, accompanied by Alexandre's elder brother, although his wife did not want to be separated from him even for a few days, for she only took pleasure in spending time with him and raising their children.

I should inform you that the abducted children of the monkey-people, the bear-people and the dog-people made very great progress, and that everyone was very content with them, for beings of those species. Although incapable of the finesse of our reasoning, they nevertheless learned to read and write, and were all the better able to understand and express common ideas.

The young dog-people, in particular, made such rapid progress that marvels were expected of them, and that they might even approach the intelligence of perfect humans. They were affectionate, attached, and, in brief, infinitely amiable, but they could never master different pronunciations of barking, and remained far below the monkey-people, who had initially seemed more difficult to form.

Let us return to Victorin, flying through the air with his two sons.

They passed over Monkey Island, Bear Island, Cynic Island and Grunting Island, and that evening, after sixteen hours of rapid flight, they reached an unknown island between the forty-eighth and forty-ninth degree of latitude, which was in consequence much cooler than the preceding ones, but they did not notice that; it was then the month of January, which is the July of those climes.

They rested, had a meal and went to sleep, but they were woken up before dawn by a frightful bellowing sound. They looked around, and saw humans of a sort collecting and browsing the grass, which were calling to one another. They were covered with tawny hair, had long tails, and their foreheads were ornamented with beautiful and powerful horns, very long, straight, smooth and shiny.[35]

"Well, this is something else," said Alexandre to his father and brother. "There are horned people on this island. My brother isn't unfortunate, damn it—for his first voyage, it's very singular."

---

[35] Note from first edition, omitted from the Laffont text: "There have been men of this kind in our continent; they were called Cerastes and were destroyed some time before the Trojan War, in the same century in which Adonis lived on the isle of Cyprus and the famous battle took place that brought about the destruction of the centaurs, etc. Ovid's *Metamorphoses* talks about those horned people."

De B***m**t started laughing. "Fortunately, it's not a bad omen," he replied.

"Come, come, my sons," said Victorin. "The horned people are looking at us; let's study the effect that the first sight of us has on them."

In fact, the bull-people had just perceived the three voyagers, and they were contemplating them with astonishment, but without fear. They appeared to consult one another thereafter, without speaking or bellowing, merely by means of their gazes.

After a moment of that mute deliberation, they put the most vigorous males with the largest horns in a front line, behind which they formed a second line, and then another; finally the fourth line and the two subsequent ones were composed of women and heifer-girls, who were easily recognizable by the delicacy of their horns, of a very agreeable flesh color, whereas those of the men were maroon in color with black tips.

The entire troop then formed a dense circle around the three flying men in order to surround them, and advanced, tightening the circle by drawing the bull-men closer together.

When they were twenty paces away, nothing could be seen but a forest of horns, extremely close together. Then, one of the best-horned bull-men, whose expression was very grave, detached himself from the circle and advanced toward the three strangers, who braced themselves, ready to take off. He stopped ten paces away and began to bellow words loudly:

"*Meuûmh! Moûmh! Hoûmh-houah! Moûmh! Houĺh! Houaïh, hoûhoumh!*"

Neither Victorin, nor his elder son, nor Alexandre understood any of that, but the last thought that it was necessary to make some response, and he started to say: "*Moûh! Mouhoûh! Meûh…!*"

Either because those words really were in the horned language, or because the bull-man took them for some dialect of a language akin to his own, he lifted his tail, bounded three times, and returned toward his nation, to whom he bellowed the same words that Alexandre had just bellowed.

The entire troop responded with a general bellowing, after which the bull-man returned to his people. One of the most agreeable heifer-women of the species approached, holding in her hands three little bunches of fresh herbs that she had collected. She gave them to the bull-man, who brought them to the three voyagers, to whom he presented them as a sign of amity. They received them with marks of the keenest gratitude, and gave the bull-man in exchange a loaf of wheat-bread, which he taste, and then took it to the principals of his nation, who all ate some and appeared to find it excellent.

For their part, Alexandre, his father and his brother pretended to eat the grass that had been presented to them; that confirmed the amity of the savages, who judged in consequence that they were not carnivores. The flying men dared not allow themselves to be closely surrounded, however; Ishmichtris' husband in particular was very fearful. Alexandre offered to approach the bull-men, telling his father that in case of any accident they had the means to frighten the savages and rescue him. Victorin was reluctant to consent, but, vanquished by his son's insistence, he gave in.

Alexandre went forward, holding in his hands wheat-bread and a few fine fruits. The horned men waited for him; on seeing him approach, the women, in particular, moved to the front rank and looked at him closely. He was very well received. He was introduced to the principals, and reserved a piece of bread and a beautiful pana—that is the name of the breadfruit—for the prettiest and most apparent of the heifer-girls who had advanced very close to him. He offered those presents very gracefully.

The young woman blushed to the tips of her horns and appeared intimidated, but, seeing the affectionate expression of the hornless man, she received her present, which she tasted immediately and went to share with the rest of her companions.

153

As soon as Alexandre had given his present, all the bull-men bellowed, but that was a kind of applause, for one old man, whose horns were five feet long, who appeared to be the father of the young heifer-woman, emerged from the crowd and came to offer his hand to the young flying man. After a few testimonies of amity, Alexandre, who knew how anxious his father and brother were, saluted the bull-men and their wives, by putting his hand over his heart and his mouth, and drew away, while all the poor savages repeated the same sign. When he had rejoined his companions, they uttered a loud bellow, to which the three humans replied: "Moûh-Moûhh!" three times.

They were deliberating as to how they could abduct two of the savages without indisposing the nation when they perceived a movement in the troop of horned people. A moment later, they saw two men, the old man who had first approached them and the one who had given them marks of confidence, advancing toward them, leading the young heifer-woman by the hand. The old men handed her over to Alexandre, making signs very intelligibly that they were leaving her for him to enjoy.

He thanked them, and pretended to be delighted with their present, but he asked by means of signs, and bellowing a little, whether they would also confide a young man. He was understood, and the two old men brought one of the most handsome. The flying men lavished him with caresses. Then they made ready to fly away. The young man and the young woman were then very frightened, but they dared not run away; although trembling, they allowed themselves each to be encircled by a strap and lifted up into the air. At their departure, all their compatriots uttered horrible bellowing sounds, apparently to bid them adieu.

Victorin, his sons and the two savages arrived at Île Christine the following day at around noon; everyone there was even more astonished to see the two new creatures than the previous ones. They were put into the hands of a very skillful man who was educating the others, and had been formed himself by Monsieur l'Abbé de Lépée, the same one who had consecrated his talents to making reasonable people of deaf-mutes.[36]

The good Seigneur, Victorin's father-in-law, could not weary of admiring the two new pupils.

"Well, Procurator Fiscal," he said to his son-in-law's father, "would you ever have suspected that we would see what we have seen in our old age? It is, however, my daughter's beauty that was the cause of your son making wings in order to steal her from me, and enabled him to heap marvel upon marvel."

"Oh, yes indeed," replied the Procurator Fiscal—who had been given that responsibility on behalf of the crown, without changing its title, although it was entirely in favor of the people and equality—"but if my son had not had depths of merit and intelligence, amour would never have enabled him to find such beautiful things."

"You're right, but agree that Christine de..."

"I'll agree to anything, my dear Monsieur, and it isn't me who'll dispute with you against the wealth and honor brought to us by a daughter-in-law that I love more than myself, so we're in accord. But agree yourself that my son..."

"Of course! If your son had not had merit, would he have loved my daughter? It was by virtue of his merit that he sensed the full value of my Christine, and forced nature in order to obtain her; it's by virtue of his merit that he has even honored my nobility. I have no more desire to dispute with you against the merit of that worthy son-in-law, but it required Christine

---

[36] Abbé Charles-Michel de Lépée (1712-1789) developed an improved sign-language for use by the deaf, having observed that the one those in Paris had improvised for themselves was very primitive, but it never caught on outside the classroom. It was soon superseded in its turn in matters of detail, but his pupils spread the educational method far and wide, and it was an important stepping stone.

de B***m**t to elevate his soul to the degree that her own is elevated."

The Procurator Fiscal let the good Seigneur have the last word, and left the matter there.

Victorin and his sons stayed on Île Christine for an entire month, for affairs of State, and were witness to the progress of the various savages they had removed. All of them, with the exception of the last, were beginning to talk. The young dog-people, especially, had so much attention and docility for those who cared for them that they were extremely beloved. Their example did no harm to the other savages, who, when they were a little formed, wanted to imitate them.

The various different species of humans, however, had an invincible hatred against the night-people; they had to be locked up at night and watched very closely during the day, because they tried to introduce themselves into the caverns of the unfortunates—although it is necessary to except the young bull-people, in whom no evidence of hatred against the nocturnals was ever observed.

Finally, the three voyagers set forth again, taking the two young dog-people with them, whom they intended to restore to their own land on the return journey.

III

They advanced along the same parallel, always extending beyond their previous discovery. On the third day they reached a new island, which was a day and a half's flight to the west of the Nocturnal Island, on which they landed. They saw on that island birds that were absolutely unknown, and so tame that they came to settle on them and take food from their hands.

"It appears," said Alexandre, "that either there are no humans on this island, or that they are very inoffensive."

As he finished speaking he turned round, and saw species of hares, roe deer, red deer, etc., capering. He made signs to them, at which they gazed stupidly, and then went away, without appearing to communicate anything.

"They're only beasts," said Alexandre. "Is Nature more imperfect here than elsewhere, and has she not gone as far as producing brute-men, as in the other islands?"

He did not retain that idea for long, because, his elder brother having turned his head, he perceived a flock grazing near the seashore. De B***m**t showed them to his father. The three flying men went in that direction on foot, and, having got closer, saw three or four hundred animals covered in wool, like sheep, led by beings of the same species that had beautiful spirally curved horns like rams. Those animals were not browsing but collecting tender grass with their forepaws; they ate some of it and made girdles of the rest; then they put little bundles between the girdle and their skin.

To one side they distinctly perceived a young ram that was caressing a pretty young ewe in the most tender manner. They drew away from that happy couple in order to approach the flock. Alexandre decided to bleat. Immediately, they all assembled and huddled together. Alexandre could not see anything that might be frightening in the sheep-people. He collected a few handfuls of grass, put one to his mouth, and went to present the rest to them—but he nearly paid dearly for that temerity!

One of the strongest of the ram-men, seeing him approach, launched himself at him in the Breton fashion. Alexandre only just had time to impart a thrust to his parasol, which raised him up six feet. The ram-man, missing his target, went on to collide with a tree ten paces away, with so much force that he fractured his skull and fell stone dead.

Undiscouraged, Alexandre hovered over the flock, letting his grass fall, and a few mouthfuls of wheat-bread, which the young folk ate. As for the ram-men, they advanced proudly at the head of the flock, stamping their feet and ready to launch themselves forward like their comrade.

Victorin, who had observed everything, and who was retaining the two young dog-people beside him on a leash, decided to tell them to go and reckon with the ram-men. They immediately ran in that direction. The ram-men had no sooner seen them than they crowded together with the others in the flock.

Alexandre landed on the ground, approached, touched the ewe-women, who had no horns, caressing them and presenting them with tender grass and bread, with the result that he familiarized himself with them a little. He also gave bread to the men. He addressed himself in particular to the most apparent in the flock, and did so much by means of his caresses and the bread he gave him to eat that he persuaded him to approach his father and his brother.

One interesting remark that Alexandre made on that island is that Nature there was in a veritably touching state of innocence. There were no carnivorous species there, not even petty tigers or birds of prey. The sheep-people lived fraternally with the different species of animals. One often saw them in the midst of them, playing and rolling over without the slightest suspicion on either side, especially with respect to the goats of both sexes. Everywhere the flying men set foot, in spite of their singular apparel, they saw the animals—not only the domestic species but red deer, roe deer, etc.—come toward them rather than running away.

Then Victorin said to his sons, tenderly; "I thank God for having lived until this day, and for having come all the way to these climes distant from that of my birth, in order to see Nature in her original bounty! Oh, my children, you have not seen, as I have, a world of the wicked, of which the ferocious beasts of jungles are only the image. You have not seen them tearing one another apart, devouring one another, and justifying themselves thereafter on the necessity of good and evil, comparing the moral with the physical and arguing the one to excuse the other. Whatever need we have of fresh provisions, let us not soil this land by the murder of any of its inhabitants, and let us not be the first to commit an act of violence here!"

That speech by Victorin made a vivid impression on his two sons; they regarded the new island as the last and sacred refuge of primitive innocence. Alexandre, who had a very great intelligence, made another observation; he said that it seemed that we were on the Earth merely parasitic beings, like mistletoe on trees, or animalcules on animals, and in consequence an inconvenience for it, which ought to regard our destruction as a benefit...

Victorin shook his head, and his son fell silent.

The flying men did not stay for long on Sheep Island, which appeared to them to be very fertile; they took away two young people of the species, of whom Victorin and his elder son took charge, while Alexandre, on his own, went to return the young dog-people to Cynic Island. He stayed there for a while in order to see the commencement of the civilizing effects of those two individuals on their compatriots.

They appeared to him to be vey favorable, but the young flyer made the reflection that those two individuals would soon become brutes again if a family of humans were not established on the island with whom they could converse in the language spoken in their manner and in civilization. For it is necessary to observe that the different species of brute-men spoke the Christinian language very well in order to express

159

newly acquired ideas, but that for everything that there was a word in their own language they could not help employing it, which was already forming a different dialect for each nation; in addition, each had the pronunciation of their species, whether squeaky, simian, yapping, bellowing, bleating, etc.

In accordance with that idea, Alexandre went back to Île Christine, where he explained his reflections to his father. They were deemed very wise and, in consequence, the proposition was published to the sound of the trumpet throughout Île Christine that some people should go and inhabit Cynic Island by way of enfeoffment—which is to, assuming lordship over the land and all the beings of species inferior to Europeans, with the sole condition of recognizing the sovereignty of Île Christine and contributing at times and occasions to the needs of the State.

Several ambitious families presented themselves; they were the most turbulent on the island. They were made to draw lots, and those who were not favored were consoled with the promise of other islands, as soon as the two young people of each species removed therefrom were returned to the indigenous populations. The ship was equipped; it was loaded with provisions and everything necessary to the emigrants, and they set forth. Victorin and Alexandre directed the route of the vessel by the shortest and easiest course, while Ishmichtris' husband and his brother-in-law, Sophie's husband, flew at water-level taking soundings by hand.

They arrived after a week at Cynic Island, where it was found that the young people they had left there had been very sad. They were transported with joy on seeing true humans again, and they established themselves alongside the habitation that was built in haste for the governor and his family, composed of more than sixty individuals The latter were recommended to look after the two young people very carefully, who were of the greatest necessity in order to live on good terms with the natives, to learn their language, understand the range and extent of their intelligence, their dispositions, and, in brief, everything that could be obtained from them. The governor promised everything, and, as his interest was attached to it, he kept his word.

Victorin and his sons did not attempt any discovery during that voyage. They returned with the ship, visiting Bear Island and Monkey Island, where they found the savages more timid than during their first visit. After their arrival at Île Christine, lots were drawn for the governorship of Monkey Island; the ship was laden with the necessary things, and the governor was taken there, with the young native couple who were to serve to link them to the people of the land.

All the savage pupils were taken back successively in that fashion, and we shall leave them for some time, as well as the governors, before seeing the effects of Victorin's sage conduct. I shall continue the story of that indefatigable man's discoveries.

A month after having returned to their homeland the young ram-man and the young ewe-woman—who had appeared very stupid, so unintelligent that it was necessary to keep them for six months longer than the others to teach them the simplest things—the three Victorins took off, and went beyond Sheep Island, where they discovered nothing but sea.

They veered slightly to the north, and found a fairly large island toward the fifty-second degree of Austral latitude. The land appeared absolutely arid; they only discovered a few trees there. The summits of the mountains were covered with ice, and it was even seen in the plains. The flying men descended to that dead earth and searched for inhabitants. They saw a few animals, which were the reindeer of the locale, but somewhat different from those of the north.

They advanced on foot in order to warm themselves, although it was still the summer of the Antarctic pole, and they reached a cavern hollowed out in a rock, on the edge of a broad river, the only one on the island. The flying men heard noises inside it, which rendered them circumspect, not knowing what species of animal might be there.

While they were hesitating, their wings well disposed, Alexandre perceived small animals at the entrance of the cavern, closely resembling large rats, which, after having looked at them, turned and trotted away, and then came back in larger number, turning back almost immediately and continually recommencing that maneuver. He approached during one of their absences, and, at closer range, thought he recognized that they were beavers, which had formed a fine republic there. In fact, they had the fur and the tails.

He went to tell his father and elder brother about his discovery. All three of them lay in ambush on the river bank, face down, and when the beavers came out of the cavern to go to the water, Alexandre caught one of them. How surprised he was, though, to find that the animal had a face closely approaching the human, and to remark in its movements appearances that indicated a rational being!

It was a female; not only did she initially play dead, but, seeing that that was serving no purpose, she put her hands together in supplication, and appeared to be trying to excite his compassion by means of a little cry, extended and diversified, which was doubtless the language of her nation. Alexandre did not want to make her suffer any longer; he gave her breadfruit and carried her to the entrance to the cavern, where he perceived water. The little beaver-woman carried away her breadfruit, and did not come back for some ten minutes, after which she reappeared at the entrance to the cavern with a hundred of her compatriots, to whom she showed the three flyers, while talking with the greatest vivacity—which caused Victorin and his two sons to laugh a great deal.

Alexandre advanced very close to them in order to distribute breadfruit to them in small mouthfuls; they carried it away into the water, and ate it with appetite. Children, conducted by their mothers, ran from the depths of the cavern; they were given roasted chestnuts as well as breadfruit, on to which they threw themselves with a kind of voracity. The three flyers were soon surrounded by the entire little nation, several of whose members touched them.

Alexandre dared to venture into the cavern; he found that it communicated with the river by means of a tunnel that passed under the rock, by which the exterior water was connected to a stream that emerged in the depths of the cavern. Along that stream were the habitations of the beaver-people, disposed in such a way that the pygmies could keep their tails in the water, either while resting or eating, and during their sleep. He went to render an account of that discovery to his father and his brother, and urged them to come into the grotto. The little beaver-people did not appear to be frightened and were not disturbed by their presence.

The flying men admired the construction of the cells in which each family was lodged. There was, in truth, on each side, a communication door in order to go from one to the next, but it appeared only to serve for conversation. They ate tree-bark outside, which they soaked in the water.

When they had examined the new species sufficiently, the Christinian king and his sons withdrew. Victorin resolved to leave Beaver Island immediately without taking away any of the inhabitants, because he did not believe, in view of the rigor of the climate, the poverty and paltriness of the little people, that any commerce could be maintained with them. He even thought that any they carried away might die on the way. But Alexandre observed to him that it was necessary to know whether the beaver-people who died naturally might leave furs good enough to become objects of commerce, and whether the pygmies fought wars, etc.

He pleaded his case so well that his father permitted him to take away four of the youngest and return at top speed to Île Christine, while he and his elder son visited a few islands that they had glimpsed in the distance. Alexandre only took two days to reach Île Christine and a day and a half to return; he deposited the beaver-people there, recommending them briefly to the usual instructor of the beast-people, kissed his wife and children, went to salute his mother and departed again for the rendezvous.

Meanwhile, Victorin and his elder son had been on a large island covered with snow and mountains of ice, where they only found white bears, without any human creature. Alexandre joined them there; he could not believe that there were no humans on the island, inasmuch as it was fairly close to the lands of America and New Holland. He searched everywhere, in spite of the excessive cold, and found a few bones that appeared to have belongs to humans; but the bones were those of Europeans, who had doubtless all died of poverty in that rigorous abode, or who had been devoured by the white bears—more accurately named sea-martens—that they had seen there.[37]

The three flyers were about to leave when they heard a rifle shot. They were alarmed by it, and took off, flying in the direction of the sound at a certain height. At the entrance of a cave they perceived a man dressed in animal-skins, who stared at them. They went to land some distance away. Alexandre took off his wings in order to show that he was an ordinary man, and began making signs to the man.

The latter, transported by joy on seeing beings of his species, even though he did not understand how they could fly, responded to their signals and came straight toward them. When he was within voice range he shouted to them in French: "Who are you?"

"Frenchmen, and friends of humans," Alexandre replied.

Immediately the old men fell to his knees and raised his arms toward the havens, with a delighted expression. Then, seeing Alexandre advance—having put his wings back on—followed by his companions, he waited for them, When they had joined him, the old man looked at Victorin, and threw his

---

[37] There are, of course, no polar bears in the southern hemisphere, but Restif would not have hesitated to locate some there if he had thought it appropriate. *Fouines-de-mer*, which I have translated literally as "sea-martens," is an improvisation, suggesting that what he has in mind is something more akin to a wolverine than a bear; he cannot mean some kind of predatory seal, because the sea-martens require continuous ice to cross the sea.

arms around him, crying: "Yes, I recognize that it is a Frenchman I'm embracing! Great God be praised!"

Victorin returned his caresses, and explained briefly to the old man how they could fly. "But by what misfortune are you on this savage island?" he added.

"Alas, the old man replied, "you can see by my clothing that we have been languishing here for a long time—for I am not alone. I was the captain of the ***; my crew mutinied and abandoned me on this island with my wife and my two children, a boy and a girl, then aged five and six. The mutineers had the cruelty to leave me almost without provisions, but fortunately, a young cabin-boy, touched by compassion, found the means to throw a barrel of powder into the sea, which fell on an ice-floe and which I drew toward me. He added this rifle and a good sword.

"After the crime, the crew, no longer hoping for pardon and finding that they were too great in number to keep the secret, had decided to turn pirate. I knew that from the young cabin-boy, who, after having displeased them, was left on the island the following summer, after which they believed it certain that were dead—for I recognized them, having had the good fortune to bring away a telescope, and I hid in order to observe them. I went to help the child, whom the sea-martens would have devoured, as soon as the barbarians had returned to the ship. You can imagine what a consolation I was to him!

"But I ought to tell you the story of the manner in which I have survived with my family, in the twenty years since I was abandoned, until today. I'll do that in my grotto, where we shall be more comfortable than here."

The three flying men followed their host, who immediately made a signal to which his wife responded. She still had a few shreds of European clothing about her. There was also a pregnant young woman and another woman of an unknown species, for she had the tail and horns of a goat, with a very long-haired pelt. She was very mild and had a rather agreeable face. Two young men, clad in skins, had an almost savage appearance, one of them being armed with a sword and the other with a hatchet; the second was beside the goat-woman, the other the young woman still clad in the French fashion.

The Captain's wife thought she would die of joy on hearing her maternal tongue spoken by men who had just landed on their island.

They went into the grotto, where the strangers were invited to sit down next to a fire of fish-bones, and they were offered refreshments, such as they had—which is to say, dried fish, which served as bread; fresh fish, fried in whale oil; or another fatty fish; and cured sea-marten meat. For their part, Victorin and his sons set out their provisions, and offered bread to their hosts, who ate it weeping with joy.

After the meal, the Captain told the story that he had promised.

"Abandoned, as I told you, with few provisions and three people who had no hope of help except for me, I mastered my anguish and armed myself with courage. As soon as I had found this grotto I placed my wife and children in safety here, and I immediately thought about seeing how I could stretch out my provisions. I explored the island, without finding any carnivorous animals; it was summer, but there were birds, including a species of duck, wild geese, penguins, etc. I did not want to frighten them by killing any, so I only took their eggs, being careful not to strip the nests completely. I remarked that there were fish in abundance on the coast; I made a line, and I caught enough in the following days as we needed.

"I did not take long, however, to perceive that the island had inhabitants other than the birds and a few small animals the size of hares or rabbits, which had very beautiful fur. I discovered billy-goats of a sort, by their odor. I tried to catch one, convinced that if I could have a nanny-goat, its milk would be a great resource for us. I started looking out for them, at first with little success, but one day, when the weather was very fine—it was the summer of this region—I went from this coast to the southern coast, and perceived with astonishment billy-goats or satyrs fishing, either with lines or with wicker baskets of a sort, suspended from a rod. They often walked on two feet, and appeared to be talking from time to time in order to inform one another of things to be done.

"I examined them for more than an hour through my telescope. In the end, as I was already wearing a costume of animal skins, I risked going toward them. On perceiving me, they all made a movement of fear; then they gathered together and watched me. I made gestures of amity, while always keeping my rifle and sword at the ready. By means of gestures, I asked them for fish. After I had repeated them several times, they understood me, and one of them brought me a basket. I took it and went away. They watched me go, and I took care not to appear to turn round.

"When I was some distance away, some of them detached themselves from the troop and came after me. They followed me at a distance of fifty paces, and saw me enter my cavern. For my part, I observed them with my telescope. They made marks on the trees, and went back, running. I feared that I might be attacked, and made preparations for a defense, very annoyed at having let the goat-men see me, but I did not want to frighten my wife.

"The next day, I saw some of them prowling around my dwelling. I went fishing, well-armed; they watched me, and my conduct appeared to give them pleasure, because they believed that I was imitating them. They approached in order to watch my procedure and my line, and they showed considerable admiration. That was because my line was one from the ship, quite different from theirs and much more convenient. They went away when I returned here, and, although I offered them some of my fish, they did not approach.

"It was at that time that my little cabin-boy arrived. I was sorry for his misfortune, but it was a great consolation to me to have him. I formed his mind as much as it was in my power to do so, and I succeeded in making him an excellent subject. He accompanied my fishing and hunting. Even my son, then aged seven, came with us in order to harden him to fatigue at an early age.

"We spent ten years in that fashion, but it is necessary to tell you that during that time, we domesticated a few of the goat-people who came to see us. One of them had a daughter less deformed than her companions; my cabin-boy fell in love with her and married her. I had destined my daughter for him, but the faithful young man said to me one day: 'Captain, it's better that it's me who tries to see what might result from a mixture with the women of this land, and that your family, which will have and ought to have the empire of it, retains all the perfection of human form. So, marry your two children to one another; that's a necessity.'

"I confess that that reasoning made a profound impression on me. I had an infinite repugnance to see my son marry a goat-woman. I therefore yielded to the necessity; you can see the fruits of it. I have six grandchildren, and Maurice, my cabin-boy, will soon have twelve, because his wife almost always has twins. I have the consolation of seeing that those children take more after their father than their mother, and if fortune enables them to ally themselves with more perfect beings, the original deformity will not take long to disappear.

"It remains for me to tell you about a terrible catastrophe that occurred on the island five years ago—for I count the years exactly, by means of one winter and one summer. The winter is cruel in this climate. We are making our provisions at present because, with the exception of Maurice's wife, no one can set foot outside the cavern for about eight months. We scarcely have four or five moons of liberty with the demi-warmth that we're experiencing at present.

"A more rigorous winter made itself felt a few years ago. It was during that horrible season that the sea-martens came to the island for the first time, apparently because there was a continuity of ice between their usual abode and here. Those cruel animals devastated everything; they devoured the goat-people. We often heard piercing screams at the door of our cavern, but none of us could go to open it; we only conserved enough heat not to die of cold by huddling together, lying under animal skins, while the goat-woman, the only one of us who could get up, unfroze water for us and prepared our food.

"Summer finally returned, but what was our astonishment no longer to see the goat-people, or even any small animals! All of them had disappeared, including the birds—but on the other hand, we saw many sea-martens, which ran toward us. As we had conserved and carefully protected our powder, I loaded my rifle. My son took my sword and Maurice a carpenter's hatchet; we set our backs to our rock, and waited for the enemy. As soon as they were within range, I fired both barrels, and I killed seven of them. The others were still advancing; they were received by the sword, the hatchet and the bayonet that I had fitted to the end of my rifle. We killed all the assailants, and finished off the martens that were only wounded. We took them away then, removed the skins and cured the meat, which is edible enough if one is hungry.

"In the following days we went hunting again; we only encountered solitary martens, and in the course of the summer we killed absolutely all of them. Finally, we found two young people, a male and a female, of the goat race, ready to expire of need in a refuge from which they dared not emerge, and we took them with us. They have been very useful to us. They have a little summer habitation nearby, and during the cold they live with us and serve us.

"The following winter brought more sea-martens to the island, which, finding nothing to eat, threw themselves on the fish. In the summer we have continually destroyed them, and were planning to do as much this year for those that remain, but we can now conceive better hopes, generous compatriots."

Thus spoke the captain. Victorin replied to him that they would take him and his children, as well as those of the cabin boy, to Île Christine, entirely populated by Frenchmen, situated under a gentle sky, whose soil was fertile; and that the remains of the caprine race would be transported to Sheep Island. He added that they would begin by transporting three, of his choice, that very day. The captain nominated his wife, his son and one of his grandchildren.

Suffice it to say that those unfortunates were transported in that fashion four by four, because Victorin's son-in-law made other voyages, and that they are living very happily today on Île Christine. As for the goat-couple, they were welcomed on Sheep Island, and it was observed that the two species were disposed to love one another. Victorin did not neglect any opportunity to study Nature—in which his son Alexandre surpassed him, for one can say that the prince in question would be the most active and ingenious of men, if we did not have his son Prince Hermantin today; that young hero of Australia eclipses all who have preceded him.

Only a few degrees remained to be covered to complete the tour of the globe on the parallel of Île Christine, but Victorin, already weighed down by age, and having just lost his father-in-law and his father, who had both died in extreme old age—Christine's father was a hundred and three, the procurator fiscal a hundred and six—was no longer thinking about anything but enjoying repose, and occupying himself with not only governing Île Christine well but supervising the viceroys of Monkey, Bear, Cynic, Horned and Sheep Islands. He visited them, and saw with satisfaction the prosperity on the European families who were governing them, as well as the good understanding they had with the natives of the lands.

Victorin encouraged them, caressed the chiefs of the savages, and succeeded in making them comprehend that he was their Father, their first civilizer, their friend, their benefactor and their supreme chief. He returned to Île Christine with Alexandre, whom he made Procurator Fiscal of the Empire—which is to say, the most important person in the State after the King. Victorin charged that deserving son with encouraging the arts, investigating which of them they lacked, and even going to Europe to search for the men necessary to instruct the Christinians.

Alexandre found that all the necessary arts were strongly established on the island, including printing. He then observed that ease and equality were procuring an immense population, every father of a family having ten or twelve children—which came, in truth, from a singular custom, about which I have not yet said anything, which is that on all the islands, the Christinians contracted two marriages during their lifetime. The first, at the age of sixteen for men, was with women of thirty-two, which they maintained for sixteen years. The woman of forty-four[38] nevertheless remained in the household and served as a guide to the young wife, until that one quit her husband.

It was the old one that was charged with the care of the children, which all belonged to her, and who commanded the entire household as mistress, except for the young wife, over whose person she had no power. When the latter reached the age of thirty-one, she entered a communal house designed for that usage, and stayed there for the entire year, only seeing women and living a laborious life. At thirty-two, she was given a young man, who was her last husband, and whose household she governed for the rest of her days, with all the rights of wives.

Meanwhile, the men of forty-two did not remain deprived; they could remarry a young woman, but they were not obliged to that third marriage, as to the first two. However, those who contracted a third engagement were held in high esteem. They could even take for a simple concubine a woman of an inferior species, such as a nocturnal, or one of the others I have mentioned. Those alliances were not criticized, and even contributed to maintaining confraternity, but the government kept an eye on the hybrids in order to improve their existence. They were only permitted to marry women widowed by the death of their husband, aged at least thirty-two and not over forty, in order that they should still be in their prime and that the children should derive advantage from them. Hybrid young women had to marry hybrids or ally with

---

[38] The arithmetic of this ingenious system is a trifle puzzling, logic suggesting that this figure and the subsequent one of forty-two should both be forty-eight.

old men as concubines only, but at the third admixture they became legitimate wives.

As for the royal family, they could not conform to that custom because of the Patagone spouses they had to take, in default of princesses of the blood, as much to maintain it in its excellence as to maintain confraternity with the powerful nations of la-Victorique or Patagonia. Extreme care is taken of young princes; their intelligence is greatly exercised, and acquires extraordinary force; Alexandre's sons, most of all, have become excellent mechanicians, and fabricate wings superior even to their father's, etc.

It was with his sons and nephews that the said Alexandre made a voyage to France in order to abduct painters and sculptors, and even men of letters, musicians and actors. They only appeared there by night, and carried out their coups without being seen. You will recall that some twenty years ago, two great painters, two sculptors, two famous authors, an excellent musician, two actors—one a tragedian, the other a comedian—and an excellent dancer disappeared, whom all the world thought dead. They are not; they were abducted by Alexandre, his two nephews and his two sons, who carried them to Île Christine, where they train pupils and contribute to the pleasures of a nation that is in abundance, and which enjoys the most precious wealth of all: innocence and liberty.

IV

Before telling you what is happening now on Île Christine, it is necessary to finish itemizing the discoveries of Alexandre and his new comrades, his sons and nephews—for there were no more long voyages for his father, his brother and Sophie's husband; they only visited the discovered islands, and maintained good understanding and wellbeing thereon. They have taken infinite pains to perfect the nations of monkey-people, bear-people, dog-people, horned people, etc., and have gradually succeeded.

Oh, if, like the Spaniards, they had found Mexicans and Peruvians, what might they have made of them? What good fortune for those unfortunate peoples! On the contrary, what a misfortune it would have been for the brute-peoples of the Austral pole if the ferocious conquerors of Mexico had discovered Monkey Island, Bear Island, etc., or the land of the Patagons! Humiliated by the tall stature of the latter, they would have wanted to massacre all of them, and might perhaps have found the just salary of their barbarity among their neighbors, of whom I shall soon speak to you. Scorning and disdaining the imperfections of the semi-brutes, they would have devoted themselves to their destruction, as being beasts; or, if they had recognized something human in them, even crueler by virtue of fanaticism, they would have condemned them to the fire, as the issue of incubi and succubi, or as the product of ancient bestiality.

In fact, those beings are only humans who have not yet risen to the final degree of perfection, and in whom nature has arrested sooner, after having caused them to pass from the sea, the origin of all living beings ad plants, to the free and dry air; doubtless because the lands of the austral pole are divided into islands, and the beings that inhabit them are distant from any other species, they have not been able to improve themselves by admixture.[39]

The mixture of races is the means that Victorin employs. He made marriages between monkey-women and bear-men, and reciprocally between dog-men and monkey-women, bear-women, etc.; between bull-men and ewe-women; between the latter two species and night-men and night-women. Finally, he permitted Frenchmen to have a concubine of any species they wished, of their choice, in each inferior nation, on condition that the children produced thereby only marry among themselves and are destined to populate a small island situated twenty leagues from Île Christine, in the direction opposite to the one in which the discoveries were made. I shall speak about that soon.

Things being thus arranged, the great Victorin, first King of Île Christine by the consent of his wife, whom he had made Sovereign on arrival, found himself in the happiest situation. He had a fine opportunity in that instance to follow the arrangement that the first peoples of the Orient doubtless made in similar circumstances, when the species were not yet united into one, as the Egyptian scientists were informed long ago. That was to divide his people into castes, superior or inferior, according to their degree of perfection—to put, for example, the caste of the French at the head; to have it respected, served and nourished by the others. But he refrained!

He knew by experience, and better still by history, that sooner or later the class of idlers falls into scorn, and ends up being the victim of the industrious or warrior class. Work, commerce, war—in case of necessity—and administration, all

_____

[39] Author's note: "One might object here that if the austral pole had been populated before the septentrional pole, those humans might have degenerated, returning to animality via the scale of brutism, which ought to precede the destructive revolution; wise Nature not wishing intelligent Creation to be witness to the frightful upheavals that must precede the extinction of life on planets."

of that was the lot of the French; the law of labor was general and indispensable; only useful occupation was honored, idleness being declared infamous, as becoming degradation: a law infinitely wiser than those of Lycurgus, since in Sparta, all the work of primary utility was done by the helots, which was bound to debase those labors, the arts, métiers, even the sciences and urbanity, etc.—and that was, in fact, what happened.

As for the humans of an inferior species, not yet perfected, they only had occupations proportional to their intelligence, and those limits were intransgressible; it was not permitted to employ them for overly rude labor capable of brutalizing them further, even under the pretext of utility; whereas hybrids could be employed for almost anything, as if they had been French, with the exception of government. The pleasurable arts, above all, like acting, music, painting, sculpture, etc., were reserved to the families of French fathers and mothers, and those of the wrecked ship married to two wives of our species. But as those details ought to be brief in a story such as the one I promised you, I shall conclude them, and pass on to the continuation of Alexandre's discoveries.

For a long time, his goal had been to complete a tour of the world along the parallel of Île Christine, and to make it under all the other parallels. He fulfilled the first objective that year, the thirtieth of the reign of his father and mother on Île Christine.

He departed in spring and followed the route he had maintained with his father and elder brother. To the southwest of Sheep Island he found a beautiful island cut by valleys and verdant hills, whose terrain as rich and fertile; the pasturage there appeared excellent. Alexandre was accompanied by Hermantin, his elder son, and young Dagobert, the oldest of his nephews, both issues of Patagone mothers, and consequently of a strength superior to Europeans. I will not anticipate here the praise merited by Hermantin; doubtless he will pass into posterity as the hero of Australia, and will merit among the descendants of present day populations the same glory and the same celebrity as the Hercules, the Bacchuses and the Odins of the ancient peoples of the septentrional pole.

The three princes visited the island, in accordance with their custom. They did not observe any carnivorous beasts, but they found large ants, similar to those seen in the Antilles and Cayenne, whose anthills had the form of the steeple of a bell-tower. If they found an animal asleep they threw themselves upon it, killed it before it could shake them off, and devoured it. They cleaned up the cadavers of all the dead animals they encountered admirably, and various different skeletons were seen in the vicinity of their anthills, of such neatness that one might have mistaken them for imitations in ivory.

What surprised Alexandre greatly, however, was a skeleton that appeared to be that of a centaur. He was examining it, with his two companions, very curiously, when they heard the sound of footfalls that resembled those of an army. They immediately put themselves on guard; Hermantin even rose some twenty-five feet into the air in order to discover where the sound was coming from. He perceived a fine troop of cavaliers, who were running and bounding, whose horses were whinnying in a most extraordinary but very agreeable fashion.

Struck by that spectacle, he alerted his father and his cousin to it. All three of them rose into the air and flew toward the cavaliers, who were about a quarter of a league away. On approaching, however, they perceived that what they had mistaken for riders mounted on horses were nothing but a kind of animal walking on two feet, or sometimes on four, which bore a kind of equine mane on the neck, with an elongated head, albeit more human than equine, and whose feet were hoofed like horses, although their hands were more akin to a bear's paws.

All those beings were amusing themselves in the grass, at the approach of sunset, and especially making love, in a manner that resembled that of horses more closely than that of humans, for they had neither decency nor modesty. But the horse-people appeared to be all the happier by virtue of being closer to brutitude and animality. There was no anxiety; the articulate whinnies, which appeared to be a language of sorts, were only those of pleasure. The mare-women fled; the stallion-men pursued them and assailed them; each couple uttered the inarticulate whinnying of sensuality, to which the entire troop immediately responded.

The public joy was troubled by the flying men, who suddenly showed themselves above the troop. As soon as they were perceived, an old stallion-man uttered a whinny of alarm. Immediately, all the women fled into the nearby wood; only the males remained, and looked at the flying men proudly. Alexandre, struck by their fine appearance, came down almost to the ground and made signs of amity. They looked at him without fear.

Young Hermantin, impatient to see them at close range, went to land directly beside a young horse-man, to whom he presented some wheat-bread. The young centaur sniffed it, tasted it, and whinnied; several other young people of the nation came toward him. Hermantin gave them similar presents, caressing them with his hand. Alexandre and his nephew did the same, with more difficulty—but in the end, familiarity did not take long to be established, to the point that a general whinnying recalled all the mare-women. They approached timidly; the flyers distinguished among them a perfect equine-human form, very agreeable.

To cut the story short, finally, after a few days, Hermantin, who had made friends with a young centaur and a young mare-woman, presided them to allow themselves to be taken to Île Christine; that was done. The education of those young horse-people was quite easy, but their intelligence did not equal that of the young dog-people, even less that of the young monkey-people. However, there was one advantage that the beautiful species had; they were appropriate to certain kinds of heavy labor by virtue of their great strength.

After having deposited the two new pupils, Alexandre, Hermantin and Dagobert departed again to continue their discoveries. They soon found a new island at the same latitude as that of Horse Island, but much less favored by nature; thistles grew there in arid soil; there was also a kind of vine, which bore very small grapes. It could scarcely be traversed because of the sarmentous plants that cluttered the meager locations.

While the three flyers were examining the new land, they heard a very original conversation a few paces away from them. I shall only report the beginning of it—the dashes mark the alternation of the interlocutors:

Hhîhhhouh; hhânh, hhânhh!—Hhinnh! Hhouih! Hhânh-hhih—Hhrrhh! Hhîh hhôuh hhîh hhouih hhouiouhîmh hhâimhh! Hhi! Hihinnhinh-hhîh! etc.

Hermantin was curious to see the individuals who spoke that rustic and unpolished language. A thrust of the parasol raised him up ten feet; he hovered over the bushes and saw two beings behind a thicket of vine-stocks and brambles, one of whom was speaking to the other in even more eloquent language. The young female whose face was reminiscent of a donkey and a woman, was collecting tender thistles, which she was mixing with the new shoots of the wild vines, while the young male donkey, her lover, was employing in order to persuade her to satisfy him the double language that I mentioned. The young female, without quitting her occupation, listened and looked at him, smiling.

I am in a position to translate the language of Sire Aliboron:[40] *Hhîhhhouh; hhânh, hhânhh!* (I desire you. Let me, let me.) *Hhinnh! Hhouih! Hhânh-hhih.* (No Stop it. Leave me alone.) *Hhîh hhôuh hhîh hhouih hhouiouhîmh hhâimhh! Hhi! Hihinnhinh-hhîh!* (Oh, I'm going to make you listen to me. Let's go. Let me.) Such is the fine gallantry of Donkey Island,

---

[40] Aliboron, originally a gallicization of the name of the Arabic scientist Al-Biruni, also attributed to the medicinal plant known in English as black hellebore, and consequent to those associations applied generally to doctors, is the name given in one of Jean de La Fontaine's fables to "Buridan's ass," which figured in a parable attributed to the latter scholar in which, unable to choose between two identical bundles of hay set at equal distance to either side of it, the animal starved to death.

and I can't see that it is worth any less than gallantry else-where.

From words, the lover was doubtless about to progress to actions—for he was very ardent—and his mistress was smiling, when the latter, like all females in such circumstances, darted a glance around to be sure that she was unobserved. She perceived young Hermantin, who was watching from above a bush. Frightened, she bounded, kicked and fled. The young donkey-man, more courageous, remained, his eyes fixed upon the big bird.

Hermantin made signs to him, and started braying as best he could.—which made the donkey-man smile, apparently because Hermantin was murdering the language instead of speaking it. At the same time, Alexandre and his nephew Dagobert drew closer. They seized the young donkey-man while he was occupied with Hermantin, but they only retained him in order to treat him well.

While they were holding him, his inamorata came back timidly, and peered between the branches of the bushes. Hermantin, who perceived her, went to take her by surprise, and in spite of her efforts to escape him, he brought her to her lover. They caressed them both, giving them wheat-bread and chestnuts, of which they seemed passionately fond, for the young woman, having at first refused to touch the bread, had no sooner sniffed a chestnut than she threw herself upon it and ate as many of them as they would give her, staying voluntarily.

Alexandre thought that this new species ought to be transported to Île Christine; he sent them via his son and nephew, wanting to stay on Donkey Island in order to examine its singular inhabitants. He had no difficulty in finding them; when the two young people that he had ordered to be taken away were lifted up, they brayed so loudly that the entire island resounded with it. Immediately, the donkey-people came running from all directions, in order to see what was happening.

They did not find their two compatriots, but they perceived Alexandre, with astonishment, who made them signs of amity. They approached him rather stupidly, but as he had few provisions, he contented himself with offering them, as a sign of good understanding, vine-shoots that were still tender and thistle-hearts, which they ate. It did not require any more to acquire their familiarity. Furthermore, they were slow and stubborn, and during the two days he spent with them, while awaiting his companions, he only had reason to be content with the young ones, who seemed lively enough.

The donkey-men and women were very sober; they did not amuse themselves with games like the horse-people; the two sexes had only one penchant, that of amour, but that one was so powerful in them that it was worth all the others. Men, women and young people only respired lust; they all sought to satisfy it urgently, and surrendered themselves to it almost without measure once they had found it. It appeared that the whole species lived in community, and that the females caressed all the infants indifferently.

Alexandre sometimes remained in contemplation for hours, unable to prevent himself repeating incessantly: "But they're happy in their brutish state, these good donkey-people! They sense keenly, they enjoy themselves ecstatically; they easily find the object of their desire—what more is needed to be happy? Alas, what will we give them when we succeed in raising them to our degree of intelligence and reason? Will it not be a real loss for them, if they acquire at the same time our anxieties, our interested and base passions, our fatal science of good and evil, and the knowledge of death? Oh, what are we doing?"

It was thus that the prudent and sensitive Alexandre reflected during the two days that he remained alone on Donkey Island. He found, however, after mature examination, that the donkey-people might be useful, not to make Academicians, but vigorous porters. That idea was not put into execution, because sooner or later, it would have plunged the unfortunates into slavery.

The two young flyers, his companions, returned on the evening of the second day, and he found that on their way, Hermantin had held with his cousin Dagobert discussions of the same genre as his father's reflections. You shall see before long that it was also the sentiment of a population of sages that the young princes were to visit.

From Donkey Island the three flyers passed on to the discovery of another land, whose inhabitants were the most singular of those of which there had been question thus far. Alexandre and is companions searched there, as was their custom, for the being in which they were interested by preference, but all the trouble they took was unrewarded by success for a long time.

It is true that as they approached the island they had heard a noise like the croaking of huge frogs, and when they landed it had seemed to them that large wooden beams were thrown into a great lake that took up most of the island, which had no land except for a strip twenty or thirty yards wide, covered with trees and aquatic plants. There was every appearance that the lake was the crater of an ancient and immense volcano, since filled with water.

The flyers had landed in a lava ravine, which formed a natural entrance leading to the lake. They deposited their provisions there, and as they were extremely vigorous, Alexandre permitted the others to penetrate into the interior while he remained with the baskets.

When Hermantin and Dagobert were on the edge of the lake, they perceived a few amphibians, which launched themselves into the water, and several others that were swimming. Hermantin ran to try to catch one of the animals, but the sound of his footfalls, although light, had frightened them; they dived immediately, and were only seen again at long distance, near the middle of the lake. Unable to go after them, the two young flyers flew to the other shore, but scarcely had they risen a few hundred feet than a thousand heads emerged from the water to consider them.

They found nothing beyond the lake, and made the decision to travel along the kind of zone that constituted the island's soil. Two days of journeying did not reveal any living
being except birds. They only heard amphibians throwing
themselves into the water from time to time, with a loud
splash. Surprised by that repeated phenomenon, they resolved
to hide during the night, in order to try, with the aid of their
English binoculars that made objects visible in darkness, to
discover the inhabitants of the island, if there were any, or, at
least to see what the amphibians they could hear were like.

Their doubts were clarified on the first night. They saw
very clearly amphibian-people emerging from the lake and
going in search of fruits, herbs and roots on the land. They
saw them exchanging signs of intelligence, although they did
not appear to have any language. The amphibians had small
scales on the head instead of hair, and their digits, on the
hands as well as the feet, were united by membranes. They ate
on land, but several of them kept watch, doubtless because of
the appearance of the flying men; at the slightest sound the
sentinels heard, a *brrrr-rrré-ké-ké-koax-koax* caused the entire
troop to return to the water.

Alexandre did not believe that they could capture beings
so suspicious, who would, in any case, be intractable, like all
other amphibians. He had resolved to abandon them, and to
regard that kind of deformed island as deserted, and in consequence destined for the hybrids issued from Christinians and
concubines taken from the inferior species, but his elder son,
seconded by his cousin Dagobert, were fortunate enough to
capture a young frog-man and a young frog-woman while they
were delivering themselves to the pleasures of amour. They
enveloped them in a kind of net and carried them away, without doing them any harm, to Île Christine, by completing their
circuit of the globe rather than retracing their course.

Alexandre, left alone on the island, eventually got to
know its inhabitants, who gradually became accustomed to
seeing him, but, that mute company not being very amusing,

he occupied himself in philosophizing while awaiting his young comrades.

"There is every appearance," he thought, "that the human genre began in fishiness; perhaps it will even return by degrees to end there, if Monsieur de Buffon's theory regarding the gradual cooling of the globe is true, in preference to that of Telliamed, for in the case that the latter prevails, it is by drying out that the world will end, having begun with humidity. In the former case, by contrast, the world commenced by drying, to finish by freezing.

"Without pronouncing judgment between those two great philosophers, I see that the austral pole is much more aqueous than the septentrional pole; if Telliamed is right—which I desire—life has only just begun here; it will gradually dry out, it will be populated, and we shall have the honor of being the founders and the chiefs of the first and the most powerful of the civilized nations of this hemisphere. We are the creators of others; if they subsist, as I hope, their descendants will regard us as demigods.

"Considering Nature as it is visible here, Telliamed appears to me to be correct. If, however, the French naturalist is right, life will decline in the Austral hemisphere, and we can only hope for a short duration. But do the Patagons, more perfect than us, mark a languishing Nature?"

I shall not take these reflections any further; Hermantin, his illustrious son, will soon give us a more certain physics.

Alexandre's son and nephew having soon rejoined him, they told him that they had put the new species in a fine fishpond, whose edges were garnished with provisions that would be presented to them several times a day, and which they had begun to receive. What gave him extreme pleasure, however, was learning, by virtue of Hermantin's observations, that Île Christine was no more than fifty leagues away, and that in completing the circumnavigation of the globe, there was no other island on that parallel.

The three flyers therefore set off, directing their flight toward an island that was situated further to the north, which they found to be beautiful and verdant. They set out in quest of the beings that inhabited the fertile land, but they only saw birds and, on the coasts, ordinary fish. Their searches by night and day, at all hours, did not reveal anything to them, even terrestrial animals. They were obliged to return without having found anything to Île Christine, and they declared the last island absolutely deserted, especially relative to the human genre. It was, in consequence, destined for the hybrids—but it is necessary to observe that it was then the month of June, which is our December.

However, when, after three months, a second voyage there was carried out, in order to begin its cultivation, and the tillage commenced, a strange discovery was made.

Alexandre, with his sons and nephews, was at the head of the laborers. One day, it was very hot and they went to rest in the shade. Hermantin, having advanced cautiously toward a forest, perceived serpents of monstrous girth, but only ten or twelve feet in length, asleep in the sunlight. He informed his father and his comrades, who examined them, shivering. The monsters all had a head approaching the human, and when they awoke crawled with a prodigious vivacity. Sometimes they reared up and hissed in a frightening manner, darting out their forked tongues.

Alexander and his flying companions rose up into the air, in order to frighten the serpent-people and oblige them to return to their caverns. At the same time, they sacrificed a dog that they had brought, in order to discover whether the animals were venomous. They threw it into the midst of thirty of them, which, bolder than the others, had not fled, and were hissing while gazing at them. But the dog was swallowed by one of the singular beings, which obliged Alexandre to tell Hermantin to fetch a donkey and drop it into the group of serpent-people.

The monsters threw themselves upon it and bit it; then they sought to choke it by winding themselves around its body. Alexandre and his companions having thrown earth at them however, they fled in a fury to their holes, with the exception of one alone, which was so animated that it strove to launch itself into the air. They continued to throw earth at it, but instead of hiding in its hole, it raced toward the laborers. Alexandre and his companions pursued it, and having thrown a kind of net over its body, they wrapped it up therein, containing it, and examined it at their ease.

While they were surrounding it, however, horrible hissing sounds were heard from the direction of the forest, and they saw a serpent-female arrive, followed by a dozen others, some full-grown and others very young, which tried to hurl themselves on the people surrounding the serpent-man entangled in the net. The people drew away, unable to resist them. They broke through the mesh with their teeth and freed the prisoner, whom they took away to his hole.

Afterwards, the Christinians examined the bitten donkey, and did not perceive any inflammation, although it had several wounds, which healed in a few days. When they were thus assured that the serpent-people were not venomous, they were much less fearful of them, and it was proposed to fight them if they became too troublesome, and even to expel them entirely from the island, obliging them to confine themselves to another, not as large, that as nearby, all property in which would be abandoned to them, with a prohibition to disturb them there.

Alexandre's eldest son, whose natural talents even surpassed those of his father, and who had already improved by experimentation all the knowledge that he had received from him, was burning with desire to capture one of the serpent-people, or even two, one of each sex. He put so much care into it that he succeeded. One day, he surprised two that had each swallowed a lamb that he had left them for bait; he enveloped them in a net and carried them to Île Christine, where he deposited them in a walled enclosure, in which there was a hole to lodge them, garnished in its depths with solid masonry.

Those two singular beings eventually became accustomed to humans; they even produced children, but it was impossible to enable them to approach our intelligence, as with the other beast-people. Although, at the end of a summer, they were a little more docile and more intelligent, the torpor of the winter caused them to lose almost all that they had acquired; in the following spring, they appeared much more timid and suspicious than in the previous autumn.

As for those that had remained on the serpentine island, they could not acquire any degree of domestication; on the contrary, they were distressed, and were often found dead. All those considerations excited the pity of Hermantin and the other princes of the blood; they proposed to search in the vicinity of the equator for an island without human inhabitants, where the serpent-people could live tranquilly, and where they would even be sheltered from the annual torpor. They found what they were looking for between the fourteenth and fifteenth degrees.

They returned their two comrades to the serpent-people in mid-autumn, before the torpor, in order to mollify them—which happened, because they had believed them dead, and were delighted to see them again. In a matter of days, a complete change was perceived; they no longer fled when they saw humans. Advantage was taken of that disposition to persuade them to allow themselves to be transported in the ship; that was what the two pupils partly determined.

In order to embark them, advantage was taken of the enfeeblement and the kind of imbecility that preceded the torpor. As they got closer to the equator, it was perceived that they were reanimating; they were disembarked very cheerful, and were made to understand that they would be better off. That expectation was not mistaken; in truth, they seemed very ill-tempered at first, but they gradually softened under the governance of the nocturnal-hybrids sent there from Île Christine.

"If it had been decided to let a species die out, it would doubtless have been that of the serpent-people," Victorin said to his sons one day, "but we thought differently. What shame for the Europeans who, all of the same species, almost all related, scorn one another, degrade one another and inhumanely refuse them the necessities of life, even going so far as to massacre them! The unfortunates, who, only sensing their egotism,

186

their harshness and all their vices, communicate them to others and then react against themselves!

"Forms once varied in the northern hemisphere, as in this one. I read in my youth that there have been humans with the heads of oxen, horses, monkeys and dogs, the feet of goats, etc., which seemed incredible to me. What I have seen here has given me the key to those old stories, regarded as ridiculous fables by the superficial deciders of Europe..."

As soon as the serpentine island was free, more than six hundred hybrids of all species were sent there, who were given as governor one of Victorin's Dauphinois relatives. That population succeeded marvelously, and it had gradually improved over the last forty years, by means of the continual mixing of the races.

There still remained many parallels to travel either to the north or the south of Île Christine. Hermantin, the elder son of Alexandre, a vast and powerful genius, who had all the finesse and perfectibility of a Frenchman combined with the strength and solidity of a Patagon, formed the most far-reaching plans after his voyage to New Sepentine, and proposed to visit all the Austral parallels between the equator and the tropic of Capricorn. A vast sea strewn with islands separates the countries discovered by the Christinian heroes from America and Africa, but la-Victorique is so long, although not very wide and frequently cut by narrow straits—it is often only two leagues from one sea to the other—that it extends to the tenth degree; it is a delightful country, the surrounding sea tempering the extreme heat, and an eternal spring reigns there.[41] It is

---

[41] Note from the first edition omitted from the Laffont text: "A reason already given for the greater coldness of the Austral hemisphere, which is doubtless the true one, is that the sea covers it almost entirely, and one only finds island there. In the two theories of the central fire, or the solar fire being the only active one, the effect of the cause is the same: the water retains the emanations of the central fire, or impedes the reflection of solar radiation. As for the case of the greater quan-

one of those contiguous islands, situated between the 00 and 00th degrees, that is inhabited by a people about whom I shall have to tell you in concluding the list of discoveries: the largest, strongest and most intelligent people in the world, the Metapatagons.

The princes departed to make their tour of the world along the tropic in the month of March. There were six of them, without Alexandre: Hermantin and his son Clovis; Dagobert and Thierry, his nephews; and the two sons of his sister Sophie, Roland and Renaud. They took good strong wings, improved by Hermantin, and in order to have provisions more easily available they had the ship equipped, which followed them, and with which they arranged various rendez-vous at particular latitudes and longitudes—for the flying men could find the longitude marvelously, knowing exactly how much distance they could travel in an hour, with the consequence that they left it written on a simple rock on the coast of every island.

---

tity of seas in the Austral hemisphere, it is uniquely due to the exterior conformity of the globe. There is a third theory, that of the Megapatagons, in which everything is explained even better. [Dulis]"

V

At twenty-two degrees of north latitude, a little beyond the tropic of Capricorn, the flying men fund a very beautiful island on which they stopped, still with the same precautions as previously seen, although they were less necessary, for Hermantin and his young comrades were very different from Victorin and his two sons. It was midday when they landed; they searched for shade because the heat was excessive, and found some easily in a region covered with mangroves and the most beautiful trees.

They sat down some distance from a lake formed by a river that traversed it, almost as the Rhône traverses Lake Geneva. They had scarcely been tranquil there for an hour when they heard a heavy tread, as if several individuals were coming toward the lake. They hid themselves in order to be able to observe without being seen. Then they saw, with astonishment, huge mobile masses, some walking on two feet and others on four, with monstrous human heads, an elephant's trunk for a nose, and hands and feet that were nearly human, but covered with a hard and cracked skin like that of an elephant.

Those huge beings descended to the lake and plunged in mouth-deep, giving evidence of a great deal of pleasure in being there, whereas before they had seemed very sad, as if exhausted. After having bathed, they advanced toward one of the shores of the lake covered in shade, and went to sleep there in couples, each of the huge beings having another one beside it, less vast and less ugly, without tusks beside the mouth, as the ones that appeared to be male had, as well as little animals of the same species, which were doubtless children.

When they were all asleep, Hermantin and his comrades approached very closely, and recognized that they were monstrous composites of human and elephant. They were less surprised by that than if they had been the first such mixed beings they had seen. They could not weary of contemplating them, and they were even employing the assistance of their binoculars when a little elephant-boy, wanting to suckle at the teat, woke up his mother. The latter, on opening her eyes, perceived Hermantin beside her.

Now, elephant-women are very modest; she blushed with shame and anger at being studied at such close range; she sucked up water with her trunk and launched it at the curious individual, uttering a cry that woke the entire troop. Poor Hermantin, although drenched, tried to deploy his wings, but the water had made them so heavy and sticky that he could not take off Meanwhile, one of the strongest elephant-men came forward to capture him, and was about to seize him when the machine agitated the wings sufficiently to lift him five feet into the air. The elephant man, along with all his comrades, sucked up water and launched it against him through the air, but could not reach him.

The other flyers rose up into the air in imitation of Hermantin, which greatly astonished the inhabitants of Elephantida—that was the name the young flyers gave the island. They let the colossi launch their jets of water, and flew over their land, which they found densely populated on the banks of rivers and lakes, but deserted in all the dry but fertile places, which only had animals similar to those of China and India.

There was scarcely any means of establishing there, as in the other islands inhabited by "semi-brothers" or beast-men, a governor and masters of education. The elephant-people appeared to be proud, but as intelligence is infinitely superior to strength, it was merely a matter of knowing its range accurately to know what course of action they could take. The difficulty was not minor. How could they lift up two of those enormous masses and carry them away, not even to Île Christine but only to the ship, which had just reached the island?

Hermantin and his companions thought about it. In the end, they invented a machine capable of being carried by three of them, which would serve both as a trap to catch a young elephant-man and a means to transport him. They constructed it, tried it out on themselves and a few large animals, and after having perfected it, thy fund it capable of lifting up a young male. They immediately fabricated another to catch a young elephant-girl in the same way, in order that the male should not be chagrined far from his homeland. With things thus arranged, they watched for a favorable moment, which did not take long to present itself.

One evening, as the elephant-people were returning from the lake with their women and children, the flyers, hidden in the bushes, perceived an amorous young couple who were searching for an isolated place. They attached themselves to the two young people, who plunged into a very bushy thicket, where they devoted themselves to their tenderness. They were not interrupted, but when they were in the sensual abandonment that follows enjoyment, Hermantin and his comrades threw their nets over each of them, which enveloped them and impeded the free movement of their limbs.

Thus caught in the same trap, the six flying men lifted up the machine together and departed. Doubtless the two lovers would soon have broken through the net, but for the fear they experienced on seeing themselves in the air, which prevented them from continuing their efforts to free themselves, for they had already begun to rip the mesh. They therefore remained quiet, uttering plaintive cries from time to time, as much because of the cold they felt at the height at which their abductors were flying as because of their continuing fear of falling. They were carried in that fashion, not without difficulty, to the ship.

They arrived just in time, for the two lovers were dying. They were set down on the deck, and the ship set sail for Île Christine, where they were no sooner disembarked than they were placed in a valley abundantly warmed by the sun's rays, where they recovered somewhat. Many signs of amity were given to them, but without their being rendered entire liberty. It was not until they had begun to understand the French language, and they had been given a promise to return them to their homeland, that they were abandoned to themselves. As they loved one another, they were quite cheerful after that assurance, and lived happily.

They were found to have a great deal of intelligence, almost as much as the Europeans, which rendered their education very facile and very rapid. They had almost round feet, formed like those of elephants, which made them closely resemble the feet of the people of Mount Imaus in Asia,[42] massive legs, a very large head, and hands like feet with very short fingers. Their nose was a veritable elephant's trunk; that was one limb more than we have, which rendered them appropriate to the most difficult things. The man had tusks but the woman did not; her hide was also less coarse, and her visage quite agreeable, save for her trunk, which could not help rendering her eyes deformed. Moreover, both were well-proportioned, and they preferred walking on two feet to four.

They made it known that there had once been real elephants and little humans who resembled monkeys on Elephant Island, for they indicated, in order to explain what they meant, some inhabitants of Monkey Island who were then traveling on Île Christine on business, but they added that there were none any longer.

They were only kept one summer; Hermantin and his companions took them back at the autumnal equinox. When they arrived on Elephantida with their pupils, they disembarked them and went to hide in order to see the effect that the discourse of the young people would produce on their compatriots. After three days they saw the young male arrive alone at their retreat, who assured them that the elephant nation was completely satisfied with their conduct, and invited them to come into their midst in order to have the pleasure of seeing and conversing with them. Three flying men detached themselves and followed the young elephant-man, but the other

---

[42] Mount Imaus was an old name for the Himalaya; the people to whom the text refers are presumably the mythical Abarimon, described by Pliny the Elder in his *Natural History* as having feet orientated backwards.

three stayed behind out of prudence, in order to be able to rescue their comrades, with the crew of the vessel, in case of danger.

The three flyers were very well received by the elephant assembly, and as they understood a little of the simple language of that people, they were able to converse with them about the most ordinary things, such as nourishment, and the customs of the elephant-people and the Christinians, which the flyers compared. That gave an infinite pleasure to those good people. They sought thereafter to discover whether there was any means to link themselves commercially with the nation, but, although capable of skill, the elephant-people were lazy, and only thought about their most essential needs.

That determined Hermantin, on returning to his comrades, to adopt the project of obtaining the consent of the elephant nation to settle inhabitants in the dry areas; he went with two others, who had stayed with him to observe, to make that proposal, whose advantages for the elephant nation he extolled. He did it so forcefully that those simple folk expressed an extreme impatience to see the new inhabitants arrive, especially when they were assured that they would have no wings, a kind of limb—as they believed them to be—that inspired much more dread in them than their trunks inspired in the Christinians. To prove it to them, they were taken aboard the ship, all of whose crew they saw.

They were given various presents, of which the two pupils showed them the usage. The assurances of amity were renewed, and they separated.

On their return, the ship was equipped to transport a colony to Elephantida, and Christinians were disembarked there in large enough numbers to be able to defend themselves in case of attack. They built a town there, and tried to make the natives love them, in accordance with the principles that Victorin had inculcated in them. But I shall leave them to establish themselves and prosper, in the warm climate that the waters and forests rendered temperate, in order to continue to tell you about the discoveries of Hermantin and his companions.

After the voyage to Elephantida they undertook another, slightly further away from the equator, for they perceived that the entire part of the austral hemisphere that is between the equator and a few degrees of south latitude is occupied by negroes and by great apes already known in France. They followed the parallel of the tropic of Capricorn, between the twenty-fourth and thirtieth degrees of austral latitude, intending to rejoin the extremity of the land of the Patagons and to travel the entirety of the island chain discovered by Victorin and given his name, la-Victorique.

After having traversed a rather broad sea, they finally reached a large island about a hundred leagues long by thirty broad, which they took at first to be a continent, but when they had reached the middle of it they could see the sea on both sides. They handed in a safe place, and made arrangements to procure themselves a refuge there against the heat of the day and the dew of the night, which was extremely abundant in that climate.

The next morning, they went down into the plain and commenced their research. They saw various animals, all extremely timid, which fled to a considerable distance, without allowing themselves to be approached. They also saw very large serpents, which, as soon as they perceived them, began to hiss and appeared disposed for combat. The chattering birds made a horrible noise in the trees under which they passed.

"It appears," said Hermantin, "that the principal inhabitant of this island is very malevolent, for all Nature is fearful of it, and under arms. Let us be circumspect, and let everyone be ready either to run away or defend himself."

As he finished speaking he saw a herd of deer, which fled, and which, having seen then, thought about running into the sea, which as nearby. The men having turned aside, however, the animals passed by and traversed a river by swimming, beyond which they seemed more tranquil.

The Christinians continued on their way, and found a frayed path, which they followed. It led them to an absolutely bare region situated at the foot of a mountain that seemed to be dotted with caves, some natural, others improved by an intelligent hand. They observed that the paths that led to each of those caverns were soiled with blood; they even saw, by virtue of the fur left on the stones and a few bushes, that animals of the species they had seen fleeing and had crossed the river had been dragged along them.

All of that gave Hermantin and his companions a great deal to think about. They continued nevertheless to draw nearer to the caverns, and they perceived about every hundred paces a considerable pile of horns, of deer, chamois, bison, buffalo and other such animals—but they did not see any bones, which caused them to conjecture that the inhabitants of the caverns had good teeth, which could even crush bones.

While they were considering the horns, they were almost taken by surprise. Two inhabitants of the island, emerging from a cavern situated at the foot of the mountain, which they had not noticed, came toward them, crouching low. Fortunately, Hermantin glanced in their direction; he made the alarm signal and rose fifteen feet in the air with a single thrust of the parasol; the others imitated him and found themselves at least twenty-five feet away when the two savages, who had just launched themselves forward, reached the place that the Christinians had quit.

Nothing was so capable of inducing fear as those two beings! Imagine the horrible face of a furious lion, adapted to a hairy human body; a mouth split from ear to ear, with sharp teeth; hands and feet armed with claws; a thick mane instead of hair; and sparkling eyes, whose gaze announces thirst for blood and carnage.

Hermantin made those Messieurs a few signs of amity, which put them in a fury. They uttered articulate roars, which caused all the lion-people to come running out of the lairs in the mountain. Some came spattered with blood, others were still clutching pieces of animal in their claws, which they devoured as they walked. All of them began roaring on seeing the flying men above their heads. The latter threw down a few provisions of bread, cake, and even meat. The last appeared very agreeable to them; they looked at one another, after having sniffed it and tasted it; they even became milder. They also ate the bread, and especially the cake.

Then Hermantin resumed signs of amity, which obtained similar responses. The six flying men went to land on a rocky outcrop, sufficiently isolated not to lend itself to any surprise, and from there they made signs to the lion-people to send one of their number. Either they were difficult to comprehend, or those invited were very difficult to persuade. It was not until after more than an hour that the most powerful of the lion-men was seen to detach himself from the troop and come toward the flying men with all the signs of tranquility. But perfidy and cruelty were legible in his eyes. Hermantin was therefore on his guard as he approached him to offer his hand, and all his companions, with the exception of the youngest, hovered above him, well-armed.

The lion-man offered his claw; Hermantin as about to take it when he saw a lioness-woman approaching, rather pretty for that species. She leaned on the shoulder of the lion-man, gazing at Hermantin with a tender-ferocious expression. She examined his wings curiously, and appeared to be admiring them. But at the moment they least expected it, she embraced Hermantin's young comrade with her gaze and launched herself forward to carry him away. The five flyers held her back, and as the lion-man deployed his claws in order to help her, they were obliged to strike him lightly with their daggers.

The wounds made by those unknown weapons astonished the lion-man and penetrated him with fear. He looked at them, and touched a point, which wounded him and made him cry out. All his companions advanced to help him. Then Hermantin made them a sign to stop, and on their refusal, he ordered one of those who were hovering to fire a shotgun blast, which broke the arms of three of the most advanced and wounded several others.

At that unexpected blow, the frightened lioness-woman showed the wounded to the lion-man, doubtless to persuade him to withdraw. The entire troop stopped, and the lioness-women went to help the wounded, whose wounds they licked. The lion-man and woman who were near to the flying men asked humbly to withdraw, which they were permitted to do. All the others fled, leaving three wounded behind, which the lioness-women also abandoned.

The flying men, however, descended beside them, and as Hermantin knew surgery perfectly—that fine art, like medicine, was singularly affected by the princes of the blood, who exercised it gratis, putting their glory into the exercise of both professions as it is put elsewhere into the destructive art of war, beautiful carriages, ostentation and follies of every sort— he put an apparatus on to the broken arms, laid the wounded down on moss, and prescribed them rest by signs.

Their comrades observed from a distance; they came back to them once the flying men had moved away, and took care to bring them nourishment until they were fully healed.

From that moment on, Hermantin and his companions were feared by the lion-people, who drew away when the young prince went to bandage the wounded, but eventually, they stated to observe, while nevertheless keeping a certain distance.

When the three wounded were cured, the lion-men entered into a great rejoicing, and came to bring presents to the flying men, consisting of game. It is necessary to say that during the treatment, Hermantin and his companions had succeeded in teaching a little French to the wounded, and learning to understand some of their expressions. They were very coarse, and their language consisted of scarcely more than twenty or thirty words, with neither participles nor conjunctions.

M'r'hô-on-hhom signified game; *r'hhhômb* running; *hhoûhhamp*, catching; *hhîh-hoûmhp*, loving, desiring or wanting; *fhlloûfhlloûp* blood. The nouns only exist in the vocative and the verbs in the infinitive; a forward gesture marks the future; a backward gesture expresses the past; a claw on the head is for the present; those are the only tenses. There are no adjectives except good and bad, long and short, and even those are not words but signs; the first consists of placing the hand flat on the heart, the second of drawing it away from oneself; the third is traced on the hand from the wrist to the fingertips; for the fourth one places a finger in the tip of a claw—that sign also signifies soon, momentarily, today, etc., just as "long" marks the contrary. The sentiment of hatred or abhorrence is only a gesture, with a cry, *mm'hoûmp*, which, without a gesture, indicates refusal, not wanting, fleeing, etc. The tongue is therefore as easy to learn as it is imperfect and inexpressive, but gesturing nevertheless renders it capable of expressing enough things for intelligent beings to be able to render all the ideas of common life thereby.

On the day for the celebration of the convalescence of the wounded, Hermantin and his companions spoke to the lion-people in their own language; it was Hermantin who made, more in gestures than in words, the following speech:

"*Rrr'hôms* (brave) non-timid, strong, intolerant lion-people (*hhoûmp-houômp*), me bearing words liking you. *Me, my others. Me* wishing you well, lion-people; want peace, *amity*. Me man-man, *you* courageous lion-men. *Me* knowing, *you* far from knowing. Me wanting give you knowing. *Me wanting you* eating better, lying down better, chasing prey less (the sign for long expresses better, that for short, less). *Two* you coming *my* land; *other mes* knowing long, long. Making *them you* knowing long; making *two you* knowing *all you* knowing like *me, like other mes*."

Half of that crude speech was still in signs. The words in italics do not exist in the lion-human language. This is a translation:

"Brave, strong but impatient lion-people, I bring you words of amity. I and my companions wish you well. Lion-people, we only want peace and understanding. I am entirely human, you, on the contrary are half human and half lion. I possess a great deal of knowledge of which you have no idea;

198

that is knowledge that I would like to procure for you, and with it and by virtue of it, all the comforts of life, for nourishment as well as other commodities. If you would care to confide two of your siblings to me, I shall take them to my country, where knowledgeable men, my fellow citizens, will instruct them; afterwards, when they are formed, we shall return them, in order that they can instruct you in their turn, and render you all akin to me and my companions in the extent of useful knowledge."

This discourse was received with much joy on the part of the lion-people, who shouted that the human-human had spoken their language better than any lion-human had ever done. And from that moment on, amity was cemented. They consented to provide two young people, of each sex, to be carried to Île Christine and to receive instruction there for as long as necessary. That was done the following day, and the lion-people, having seen the flying men in the air with their pupils, whom they were transporting to the ship, they saluted them with roars of joy.

They returned them to Île Christine, where the lion-people excited a great deal of surprise. Nothing was neglected in their instruction, but they were very closely watched because of their carnivorous inclinations.

Hermantin and his companions rested for almost a year in the bosom of their families without undertaking further excursions.

Victorin and Christine were very old, but full of good sense, and above all happy. They saw the colony prospering, more in terms of virtues than riches, which were absolutely useless there—which demonstrated to them the folly of Europeans, who, in order to be happy, left virtue behind and ran after riches! Among the Christinians, by contrast, there was continual proof, never belied, that the only secret of public and individual wellbeing is justice toward all beings, even the animals; for if you are cruel toward those brothers inferior in perfection, you will soon be so to humans themselves.[43] The foundation of wellbeing was, therefore, a perfect equality of wealth, means and prerogatives; an exact relationship between occupations and consideration; a reciprocity between the duties of the chief and those of members, etc. But I shall explain all that shortly. Let us return to our lion-people.

A year was spent forming them; at the end of that time it was perceived that they had acquired all that they were capable of acquiring. They knew how to distinguish good from moral evil, to count as far as the number of days in a year by means of notches on a piece of wood, which could serve as the almanac of their nation; how to make fire, to boil water, to sow grain and even to make bread—which, without wishing to

---

[43] Note in the first edition, omitted from the Laffont edition: "I would be sorry if I were suspected of approving of the abuse that exists in Paris and, I believe, almost throughout the world, of nourishing as many dogs as people and having a host of futile birds, etc. there. I think, on the contrary, that the liberty to nourish dogs and birds should be greatly restricted, especially in big cities, firstly because those animals have the same nourishment as humans and there are many humans who lack the necessary; secondly because frightful accidents results from a large number of dogs, known to everyone; thirdly because those animals cause insalubrity—I know many houses whose staircases, and even the apartments, are fouled by dogs; fourthly, because they are useless, inconvenient because of their noise, and dangerous by virtue of the quarrels they occasion for a blow give by imprudence, carelessness of impatience; and fifthly because not only do they remove a portion of the nourishment of the people but they close the heart to fraternal love—I have often seen tender feminine hearts wide open to animals but closed to their husbands, children, relatives and domestics; I would annihilate any species that produced such great evil. All I want to say is that is necessary never to make the animals that one has suffer, but it is desirable that one only has necessary dogs and birds. [Dulis]"

displease Monsieur Linguet,[44] was for the lion-people the chief means of civilization.

Everything that demanded a greater combination of idea surpassed their conception. That knowledge was sufficient, however; the civilized young lion-people, seconded by a few Christinian families that were established in their homeland, for whom a fort was built and who were furnished with good weapons, succeeded in time in civilizing the lion-people to the degree that they could attain—but they never became mild of temperate.

Very few of the Christinians made lioness-women their concubines; they brought their teeth and claws into play at the slightest discontentment, and it was necessary to contain them by fear; besides which, the hybrids that resulted therefrom had a very cruel and almost undisciplinable infancy, which could only be tamed by the most severe punishments.

But the ferocity of the lion-people is nothing compared to that of the last people discovered in the Austral islands. I shall relate how that discovery was made.

----

[44] A note in the first edition, omitted from the Laffont edition along with the clause occasioning it, observes that "Linguet," in a item his *Annals,* "employs all his art to persuade us no longer to eat bread," and then indulges in a long and rambling complaint about numerous other matters of no relevance to the present text. The reference is to Simon-Nicolas Linguet (1736-1794), a journalist and advocate who became famous in the latter profession before being forced into exile for the caustic political expressions he permitted himself in the former. When Restif wrote the present text Linguet had returned to France and was imprisoned in the Bastille, writing his memoirs. Restif could not know that he would go on to even greater achievements when released, but, in spite of his complaints, he paid homage to Linguet later in the text.

VI

The ship had been equipped, as usual, to return to Lion Island and return the two pupils taken from the nation inhabiting it, with the Christinian families who were to have the government of it. As flying men traveled much more rapidly, they visited all the seas ahead and then returned to the vessel. In one of their excursions they found an island, the last one of considerable size in the entire hemisphere. There were other small ones, of which I have said nothing, all of which had their inhabitants, so small or so primitive that nothing could be done with them.

Such were Doe, Hare, Rabbit, Rat, Hedgehog, Mole and Troglodyte Islands, where there were tiny humans with all those mixtures. I shall not tell you about them. Colonies will be sent there eventually, if it is judged expedient, but always with the attention not to oppress the natives, or to leave them free. What can I tell you about Oyster Island, which has been discovered very recently, where one sees oysters half-similar to those that we eat and half-animal? It appears that on that island, situated in a high austral latitude but warmed by a volcano that fills it entirely, animality emerging from the sea to pass on to dry land has been halted and fixed at its first point of amelioration. What confirms that is that one sees marine plants there that were commencing to animalize themselves, but which have remained at that first degree of animalization.

But let us return to the isle recognized by Hermantin and his companions while returning to Lion Island; it is the last discovery of that genre about which I have to tell you. More important and more consoling things await us in la-Victorique, that isle so considerable that it could be regarded as the fifth continent of the world, if it were not cut up by frequent straits, and smaller than Europe.

It was Thierry who perceived it first. He cried: "New land!" Immediately, the six flying men sped in that direction with wings deployed. They were then at the 180th degree of longitude, counting Île Christine as zero, with the result that they had made half a circuit of the world, and it was midnight on the new island when it was noon at Île Christine; that is a singularity that it is as well to point out.

The Christinian princes, therefore, advanced toward that island, far away from the parallel of Lion Island, and about six degrees further north, situated in the middle of a vast sea, more than five hundred leagues from any other land in the direction of the equator, and more than a thousand in longitude in either direction. In the direction of the Antarctic pole there was no other land beyond it, everything on the same meridian being sea, and by following a straight line and passing over the pole and continuing, one found nothing but the most austral extremity of la-Victorique.

That has been verified since, for the Christinian princes, after several attempts, found the means to pass over the pole without being too afflicted by the cold, by means of certain precautions and the extreme bounty of their wings. They passed over it on 21 December 1774, the longest day of the austral year, and saw the spectacle of the sun rotating around the globe without any sensible declination in twenty-four hours. They observed, during that passage, that the air was, extraordinarily, colder at sea level than at a height of twenty-five feet, but that on rising higher the cold soon became insupportable. They are shortly to make the same voyage over the Arctic pole, and they will see how it differs from the Antarctic pole.

When the flying princes were no more than about two leagues from the new island, they paused on a rock projecting about fifty feet from the sea, from which Hermantin aimed his binoculars in order to reconnoiter the coast. He observed that it was very steep, cut almost vertically, which made him think that it might only be a large sterile and deserted rock.

It was toward the end of the day; the six flyers had a light meal, readjusted their mechanisms, fitted new straps, as if they suspected that some peril awaited them, and departed.

When they were no more than half a league from the island, they saw clearly that it was very high along all the coast
that they had discovered; at a quarter of a league they perceived above it a host of large birds, whose flight had the appearance of that of bats. Finally, they came close enough to
distinguish with their binoculars that the birds in question
were flying men. Then they stopped short, in order to deliberate.

The result of their deliberation was that they should wait
for the dead of night before visiting the island, and that they
would turn back in order to wait on the rock, because they
might be surrounded by those barbaric flyers and over-
whelmed by numbers. So they went back there, and when the
obscurity was complete, the five princes approached Flyer
Island, observing everything with the nocturnal binoculars I
have previously mentioned.

They were advancing in great enough security, having no
doubt that the inhabitants of the isle were at rest, when they
heard a cry similar to those of the night-people of Île Christine. At the same time, they saw around them humans of a
sort, who had only the upper bodies thereof, and were surrounded by a pellicle that served them as wings, by means of
which they were flying with the greatest rapidity. They drive
them back easily with a kind of pike, with which they had
equipped themselves for the first time, those bat-people having
no limb of which they could make use, except for their
mouths, with which they caught the large scarabs or stag-
beetles, cockchafers etc. of which their nourishment consisted.

Reassured by the timidity of their adversaries, the three
princes advanced into the interior of the island, but without
setting foot on the ground. They reached a mountain, in the
lairs of which they heard unpleasant cries closely resembling
the cry of a screech-owl, but much more powerful. As they
flew over the mountain they saw large birds rise up that had
feathers, a human head with a nose like a cat and a kind of
short beak, which made as if to attack them—but the princes

frightened them with a few pistol-shots, which, in having felled several, caused all the owl-people to flee.

Freed of those enemies, Hermantin and his companions landed in the plain, and tried to find habitations. They saw several, but high above a wood entirely composed of large trees that appeared to be pruned and cleared by art; they found that in each of the trees there was a kind of nest composed of strong branches and covered by a canopy of earth kneaded with moss, in a form similar to that of the nest of crows or magpies.

They visited that new kind of city, all the houses of which were tightly sealed, having only one opening on top to allow the passage of air. Each one might have had some ten feet of free space in every dimension in the interior, and it appeared that they might contain two couples. They were situated at the top of the stem of the tree, and their supports were interlaced with a great deal of artistry in the stoutest branches. All the trees were fruit-trees, and bore a kind of chestnut that was then ripe, which marked intelligence in the inhabitants, whoever they were.

The Christinian princes could not weary of examining those large nests, and ardently desired to see some of the beings who lived in them. They were satisfied, but not without danger.

Those people went to bed early, as all avian populations do, and got up very early. Scarcely had first light indicated the renascence of the day than the winged savages opened the doors of their nests, from which they emerged in a host, with exceedingly shrill cries. The Christinian princes only had a second to react and assume a defensive posture. Fortunately, they were initially mistaken for bird-men.

They rose up to a considerable height. Eventually, however, they were noticed, and, as the daylight increased, recognized fully. The bird-people attempted to surround them. They had no means of fleeing; the enemy was assailing them from all sides; no other route remained than that to the cold higher regions. The six princes rose up as far as it was possible for them to support the privation of warmth, and from there they defended themselves with their long pikes against the bird-people, who rose up fluttering to their altitude and immediately descended again, after attempting to deliver a thrust with their hooked and bony beak or a long thorn that they held in their hand.

The Christinians wounded several of them, including a very determined male and female. There were, however, some that took no part in the combat, which frightened the owl-people and the bat-people to the extent of causing them to emerge from their retreats. Meanwhile, the princes drew away from the island, still fighting. They were so hotly pursued that several of their wounded adversaries fell into the sea, where they were immediately devoured by large flying fish.

The pursuit ended at the rocks that I mentioned initially, after which the Christinians made use of their pistols, which caused twenty of their enemies to fall into the sea. It was then that all the others returned, uttering piercing cries, so shrill that the princes thought that they might lose their sense of hearing.

That perilous attempt made them take the resolution to go and rejoin the ship and to enter the island in force. It was a deviation from their plan of justice and tranquility, but all humans have passions. They were irritated against the bird-people, not making the reflection that the sight of them might merely have astonished them at first, and that they might have been pursued at the first moment out of simple curiosity.

They rejoined the ship, therefore, and brought it to the coast of Flyer Island. The sight of the vessel attracted a swarm of bird-people all around it, who circled it uttering those insupportable cries. However, the princes, having calmed down somewhat, were careful not to fire at them; they were content to have a salvo of canons fired, which cleared the air of all avian species within a minute.

Afterwards, they disembarked tranquilly, and advanced into the island, which they found to be covered with various species of fruit-trees, especially acorn-bearing oaks, planted in dry places in order that they might be more fruitful. The soil, although untilled, nevertheless offered evidence of industrious hands everywhere.

They soon reached one of the towns situated in the trees, which I have mentioned. They perceived the bird-people, their heads protruding from their nests, watching them. They made them signs of amity, to which they did not respond. The winged princes then rose up to the height of the nests and repeated the signs, offering the bird-people bread and fruits, but no one took any. They all retreated into their nests and closed the entrance if one of the princes drew closer to it.

Finally, however, a bird-child, less timid than the others, took a piece of bread and allowed himself to be touched. He even emerged from the nest, and started flying with the princes, who have him a thousand caresses, in the view of all his compatriots.

They saw then the singular structure of those humans. They have almost human heads, but their nose is a kind of bony beak, in which nostrils are pierced, as in the beaks of bids. Instead of hair they have a tuft of feathers. Their wings are their arms, the wrist remaining disengaged, and the longest plumes emerge from the elbows. They have tails as long as that of a peacock; their legs, thin and stuff, are terminated by a foot in the form of a bird's. Their body is covered with little feathers similar to hair, and changing like that of the heads of ducks.

Their movement to take flight is that of a human running in order to jump, the arms being forcefully active. It follows that the bird-people can only pick up light objects in their hands, such as their nourishment; they even stumble slightly in bringing it to their mouths. They live, principally, on fruits and flying fish; they pick the former from the trees and catch the latter by skimming the surface of the sea. They recover themselves first; then, when both hands and feet are full, they fly to their nests to empty them. They sometimes carry weapons to use against the large flying fish, their enemies; they are long, hard and pointed thorns, with which they pierce them in mid-air. Their principal defense, however, is their bony beak, and then their feet, armed with curved talons like those of birds of prey.

All the animals on that island are winged. Sheep can be seen there, goats, donkeys, horses, deer, hares and even pigs; all of them can fly more or less easily, although the snakes and frogs there can only fly in leaps and bounds. But all of them yield to humans in the force and elevation of their flight.

After having established a link of amity with the inhabitants by means of the child they had caressed, and emboldened somewhat by the bird-people's lack of power, the Christinian princes visited the entire island. In a great river they even found flying crocodiles and hippopotamuses, but the latter only made use of their wings to accelerate their walk, by extending them when they saw themselves pursued. It appears that the sea, in that region of the globe, was originally populated entirely by flying fish of all species, which, in passing from the water to dry land, have all retained their wings.

They succeeded quite easily in domesticating the bird-child, as well as five of his comrades of both sexes, and they took all six to the ship. As two of them were adults, that gave rose to an event that caused a strange surprise: the most formed young bird-woman laid two eggs, and sat on them. They had not paid any attention to generation while they were on the island, although they had seen couplings that took place there is broad daylight, often in mid-air, within sight of everyone, but they had not observed what resulted therefrom.

The young bird-woman sat on the eggs for nine weeks, as many on the ship as on Lion Island, and a chick emerged from each egg,[45] one male and the other female; so it was observed that the bird-people all unite in couples, and that a

---

[45] Note from first edition, absent from the Laffont edition: "The birth of Pollux and Helen, Castor and Clytemnestra, issued from two eggs laid by Leda, appears to be the residue of an ancient tradition relative to these bird-people, of whom Ovid speaks in his *Metamorpohoses*. [Dulis]"

cock-man does not have two females at the same time; but they couple every year, like partridges and turtle-doves.

I have anticipated the order of events in order to conclude that which concerns the bird-people; now it is necessary to revert to the continuation of the voyage of the flying princes and the ship.

They reached Lion Island on the coast opposite the one where they had landed on coming from Île Christine. They found a natural harbor, very advantageously situated, went into it and dropped anchor. The six princes, in the meantime, rose up into the air in order to reconnoiter the locale and trace a route for the families that were to settle on the island. They were quite astonished, however, to find inhabitants quite different from those they had seen during their first voyage. They were no longer lion-people but tiger-people, leopard-people, cat-people, etc.

They visited the entire region, populated by extremely ferocious beings, and eventually perceived that Lion Island is divided into three by two arms of the sea, much as Ireland is separated from England, but by a wider channel. They found the lion-people again on the principal island. In consequence, they brought the ship around to reach the port situated in the west of the island, where they disembarked.

The lion pupils were greeted by their compatriots with inexpressible transports of joy, and their happy return, as well as the conversations they had with their nation, finished consolidating the good understanding between the human-people and the lion-people. The Christinians established themselves, and were aided in many things, for the transport of materials, by the lion-people, who, far from requesting a retribution, also brought game and fruits.

When the Christinian families were settled, and they had sowed crops, etc., Hermantin and his companions wanted to visit the land of the tiger-people. They discussed it with the lion pupils, who told them that in order to do so, it was necessary to be accompanied by the strongest and most vigorous of the lion-men. The princes thought that advice very reasonable, and accepted it with pleasure, charmed by the intelligence and good will of their pupils. The latter spoke to their nation, whose members were flattered by that mark of confidence. Twelve of the most valiant were chosen; the pupils instructed them, and a week later, they forth. The two pupils guided their comrades, and they passed over the arm of the sea in the ship's launch.

As soon as the tiger-people who lived on the coast saw strangers arriving, they came running, but having seen the lion-men, they dared not attack them, however much they wanted to do so. They contented themselves with gathering in large number and keeping a certain distance. Hermantin and the two pupils then made signs of amity, but the ferocious beings took no account of them. They had game sent to them via two lion-men. They waited for them, surrounded them, and tried to hurl themselves upon them, but the latter lashed out at them, and their comrades, seeing hem attacked, could not be held back; they raced to rescue them, and tore into pieces all the tiger-men they could catch, whose blood they drank.

The two pupils did not take part in that feast; on the contrary, they tried to calm their compatriots and bring them back. They succeeded in that, when there was no longer a single tiger-man on the battlefield. That event threw fear into all of Tigeria, and Leopardia, which was adjacent to it. As soon as the lion-man troop appeared, everyone fled.

Finally, the princes and the pupils succeeded in making the lion-men understand that it was necessary to act gently and try to trap a few young people that could be educated. As soon as the lion-men understood what was desired of them, they did not take long to accomplish it. They captured several young tiger-people, who were brought, half-dead with fear, to Hermantin and his companions. They wanted to try to domesticate them a little by means of good treatment, but as soon as they no longer saw the lion-men, they tried to tear everything apart, and as soon as they reappeared, they played dead. Hunger reckoned with them somewhat, however, and on the third day they took food gladly. They were subsequently given, along with two young leopard-people, to the instructor who had come to Lion Island with the Christinian families, because it was important to try to pacify those ferocious peoples.

It was thus that the last voyage of the Christinian princes of the blood in the unknown austral islands concluded. After everything was arranged on Lion Island, and the human families were solidly established and respected, the princes left and the ship returned, but Hermantin promised to visit every year with his companions, and never to fail.

On their return to Île Christine the princes spent time studying medicine, chemistry, physics, mathematics and all of philosophy, in order to unwind from their endeavors. In the intervals, they visited the islands, and often went to see the Patagons, whom they made party to their discoveries. Those colossi were not surprised by them; nothing astonishes them, and admiration is an impulse of the soul that they hardly know. But they said for their part that there were, to the south of their lands, other Patagons taller, stronger and yet more lively and more enlightened than them.

Those oft-repeated remarks gave Hermantin and his companions a keen desire to travel the whole extent of la-Victorique, but they were retained from day to day by the immense details with which they were charged with regard to the needs of the new colonies, for, as I have said, the Christian princes of the blood are simultaneously the most laborious, most useful and most universally obliging of citizens, and those who have the most important and most numerous occupations, which entitles them to solid and durable consideration. In the end, however, they found the time to visit la-Victorique.

After having out all their affairs in order and arranged for their substitution in their employments during their absence by enlightened lieutenants, they took their leave of their respectable grandfather Victorin and their grandmother Queen Christine, the hereditary prince their father and uncle, and his wife the tall Ishmichris, Prince Alexandre and his wife the tall Mikitikipi, and Princess Sophie and her husband. Then they set forth for Patagonia. The ship was to follow them and skirt the coast while the princes flew over the lands and the mountains.

They commenced by obtaining indications from the Patagons, whose language they understood perfectly. They were told that the further one went eastwards along the coast, drawing nearer to the equator all the way to the 00 degree, the more people were found to be strong, vigorous, intelligent, cultivating useful sciences, and virtuous.

The princes left Micropatagonia—as I shall call the coast neighboring Île Christine—and flew for about a day and a half in the direction of the rising sun, always slanting toward the equator—which was equivalent to some seven hundred and fifty leagues. They landed five or six times in order to rest, and did indeed perceive that at each station, enlightenment was augmented, but they did not find it sufficient different to warrant stopping.

Finally, they arrived at the oriental extremity of the almost-contiguous sequence of islands that composed what they called la-Victorique, or Patagonia. The coasts in question have been perceived by navigators without having been recognized; that beautiful island lies to the 00th degree of south latitude. Hermantin, who had been as far as Europe with his father, could not see that country without astonishment. It represented France in its coasts, its mountains, its rivers its forests and even its cities; the austral part resembles the boreal part of your country; beyond it there are two large islands that are absolutely similar to the British Isles,[46] as well as a few small intermediaries.

There were Alps that separated the country from another resembling Italy, and Pyrenees behind which was found a region like Spain. Those resemblances were so striking that Hermantin did not know what to think at first, but he knew the map too well to think that he had reached Europe. He merely

---

[46] Author's note: "They were the islands of lions, tigers and leopards previously mentioned."

observed that everything there was on a smaller scale, since that austral continent of sorts is scarcely equal to France. Everything corresponding to vast Asia and Africa is filled by the ocean, with the exception of a few islands recently discovered by Captain Cook, an account of which he has given.[47]

After having admired the resemblance between that beautiful country and the one where his grandfather had originated, and traveled over it in rapid flight, Hermantin and his companions returned to land in the capital of the country that resembled France, situated at 00 degrees thirty minutes of southern latitude and on the 180th degree of longitude, counting the observatory of Christineville as a baseline—which is to say, precisely below Île Christine and at the antipodes of Paris, which has the same meridian as Christineville, at nearly 00 degrees of latitude. But those 00 degrees make almost no difference, given that they are compensated by the lesser elevation of the lands in the direction of the austral pole. Thus, one can say that the city of Sirap, in the land of the Metapatagons, is situated almost diametrically opposite that of Paris. The temperature of the region is delightful, the seasons there are

---

[47] Cook's first voyage, made in 1768-71, took him to the Pacific in order to observe and record a transit of Venus from Tahiti. His orders from the Admiralty were then to search the south Pacific for the postulated Terra Australis. He mapped the coastline of what is now known as New Zealand and travelled westwards to the coast of what is now Australia, becoming the first European to reach its eastern coat, in 1770 and discovering Botany Bay. He published his journals of the voyage after his return, and became a national hero. He set out in search of Terra Australis again in 1772-75, charting the entire eastern seaboard of Australia before heading southwards in search of the hypothetical continent. He landed on various other islands before returning to New Zealand, and then made a final sweep across the south Atlantic. His third voyage, from 1776-79, took him in search of the north-west passage, and concluded in his death in what is now Hawaii.

perfectly equal, and the soil very fertile, which comes from various causes, of which the extinction of several volcanoes is the principal one.

Having landed in a square that closely resembled the Place Vendôme, Hermantin and his companions were immediately surrounded by the Megapatagons that lived in the nearby houses, but that was less by virtue of curiosity, in spite of the extreme difference in height, as to hasten to offer them lodgings and everything they might need; that was done without ostentation, with great sincerity. Meanwhile, the tall people admired the flyers' wings, and said to one another: "There is much intelligence in that invention, and it gives a high opinion of the strangers."[48]

Hermantin wanted to make a speech to that respectable nation, but did not know what language to use. At hazard, he employed that of the Patagons; he soon perceived that it was not that of the country, but that it was understood, for replies were made to him in that language although the inhabitants, between themselves, used the language of which I have quoted a few words.

The following is the Patagonian speech that Hermantin made when he saw himself surrounded by a numerous assembly of both sexes, women on one side and men on the other, dressed in a rather singular manner, for their coiffures resembled our shoes, and their footwear had, for the men, the form of a hat, or a bonnet for the women.

---

[48] Restif renders this sample of Megapatagonian speech in French written backwards, and then gives a "translation" in which the words are reversed so as to become comprehensible. There does not seem to be any point in reproducing the inverted French, and it would give the wrong impression to render the speeches in inverted English, so I have been content to reproduce the "translations" without the preliminary gobbledygook, as Restif goes on to do himself.

BOOK THREE

I

"You who are welcoming us, illustrious inhabitants of the most beautiful country in the world, the greatest and wisest of people, my brothers and I have come from a very distant country to enjoy your profitable conversation and your superior enlightenment. All of Patagonia resounds with your praise, and although we are not Patagons, as you can see by our stature, we are related to that respectable nation by way of our mothers. For you know, excellent people, that the Patagonia from which we come is neighbor to another island, once called Nocturnal Island and now Île Christine, after our grandmother, and that that island is situated at a hundred and eighty degrees of longitude from your country—which is to say, half the circumference of the globe, which is about 4,500 leagues, and on the 00th degree of latitude.

"The country where we originated, however, is infinitely more distant; it is at the other pole, and it is necessary to traverse the torrid zone in order to go there. That is what our grandfather, the engineer Victorin, did in order to come in the direction of the austral pole, where he established an empire of the French—which is to say, of the most civilized nation of Europe, Asia, Africa and America. His extreme sagacity determined his fate; he was the original inventor of the artificial wings with which we fly, and which his sons have improved. He comports himself in his empire as a wise and just prince. He has not oppressed the natives either of different islands or his own, although they are of species inferior to ours, and, in consequence, absolutely disproportionate with you, illustrious

Metapatagons. Far from oppressing them, he has, on the contrary, established laws that are advantageous to them, and which can only ameliorate their lot. He has enlightened them, to the extent that they are susceptible to be, and he takes truly paternal care of them, either personally or by way of people of his blood.

"As for us, illustrious Metapatagons, we have come here on his orders, in order to instruct ourselves, to profit from your examples and your sage institutions, and to try to take advantage of the sublime lessons that you are in a position to give us."

A venerable old man replied to him: "Flying travelers, we see you with pleasure; as we do not have to blush at our manners, our fashions, our works, our pleasures, our customs and, in consequence, our mores, we can only be charmed to welcome strangers. Everyone is welcome in this land, but we like people, above all, who show signs of an extraordinary merit. We shall give you an opportunity to show us yours. Afterwards, we shall teach you our arts, our sciences, our customs, and everything that it might please you to know. But before then, we would like to know you perfectly, and for that, you must tell us about your opinions and your laws; you must acquaint us with the customs of your nation, either orally or by means of those books you have brought with you. It will be necessary to tell us in detail your knowledge of every genre— in brief, to give us a complete account of the mores of your homeland."

The old man made this speech in very good Patagonian, infinitely more elegant and smoother that that spoken in the Patagonia near to Île Christine, and yet easy to understand, even for Hermantin and his companions, so natural was it. Afterwards, a middle-aged Megapatagon, who appeared to be the old man's son, said something to him in the particular language I have mentioned. I shall simply write the words, convinced that they will soon be understood, since I understood them myself without interpretation.

"These strangers appear to me to have a great deal of intelligence; their eyes announce it to me. It appears from their clothing, the invention of the wings that enable them to fly and the jewels they wear, that the arts are cultivated among them. I would like, Father, to be charged with educating them in our usages, accompanying them and penetrating their dispositions, in order to discover whether or not they cultivate the dangerous arts that have done so much harm to the peoples of the boreal pole, rumor of which has reached us, whether or not they have bad customs, and whether or not the vices of the heart are proportional in them to the enlightenment of their minds I observe that their features are in perfect opposition to ours; perhaps they are our moral and physical antipodes? Perhaps it would be dangerous to leave them entirely at liberty to see and converse with our young people? But I submit that observation to your elevated prudence."

"It is just, my son, but have no fear; virtue is too much loved here, and too pleasant, for anyone to abandon it. Our young people will not follow foreign usages and fashions; without being slavishly imitative, they have a noble pride in always wanting to be themselves, and only every changing for the better."

That language might appears a trifle unpolished on first reading,[49] but I'm sure that it will soon be as soft, as clear and as easy to understand as French. I do not fear going too far, because I'm sure of what I'm saying. Hermantin understood that speech perfectly, and said with a noble frankness to the old man, in the antipodean language that the speech of the two illustrious Megapatagons was full of reason and equity.

That gave an advantageous idea of his penetration, without, however, causing those intelligent people much astonishment.

---

[49] This comment implies that the speeches might originally have been rendered in the text in inverted French, and that the artifice might only have been abandoned on second thoughts.

The old man and the middle-aged man that I have just mentioned were appointed to instruct and accompany the flying voyagers. The old man was named Noffub[50] and the younger one Teugnil. The former was a sage, profoundly knowledgeable, of solid intelligence, serious without being misanthropic, the latter a man celebrated among the people for the mildness of his mores and the generosity of his character. Noffub was to initiate the voyagers in the physics and metaphysics of the Metapatagons, the other to acquaint them with usages customs and mores. It was the old man who began.

Hermantin and his comrades were taken to a simple but cheerful house, in which everything was useful and comfortable, and nothing was superfluous. Arrangements were made to supply all their needs, and all the citizens were told to favor them, which everyone did with a readiness worthy of a wise and hospitable nation. From the next day on, the aged Noffub and his son Teugnil, who had only quit them the previous evening when they went to bed, came to find them again, bringing with them various presents, including aliments and curiosities.

After breakfast, the old man asked a few questions of the flying voyagers about the usages of Europe, religion, sciences and the theory of the world, and sounded them out on their knowledge of physics. Hermantin replied, in accordance with the ingenious system of the French Pliny, for they had the works of that naturalist on Île Christine, where they were available to everyone. He talked about the *Époques de la na-*

---

[50] Author's note: "By an exclusive privilege, the man that these letters designate is equally sage in both hemispheres, even at the antipodes; it is as well to be aware of that." The significance of the note is easily understood by reversing the names, although the invocation of Linguet is a trifle surprising in view of the criticisms made of him in a previous note.

ture and the antiquity of the world,[51] a theory so simple that it was not necessary to plagiarize it from anyone, no matter what a certain Monsieur Tebog might say.[52] He explained the central heat in accordance with Monsieur de Buffon.

At that point in his discourse the old man started to smile, while looking at his son. Hermantin noticed that and stopped to asking the venerable Noffub whether he thought it implausible.

"To answer you," said the old man, "it would be necessary for me to read the books that treat your doctrine."

Hermantin had a Buffon, among other books, which he handed to the Megapatagon sage. The old man kept them for several days, after which he returned them.

"I shall now explain our doctrine to you," he told him, "which is a little less conjectural, and more probable than yours, more in conformity with the ordinary march of nature—in brief, more worthy of the animator-prince.

"It appears that your great French philosopher is of the opinion that stars, suns and planets are masses of dead matter, some inflamed and others extinct and that it is possible that these vast bodies, once cooled, remain inanimate masses, in-

---

[51] The Comte de Buffon published *Les Époques de la nature* in 1778, as part of a seven volume supplement to his natural history; it became the most celebrated of all his works.

[52] Nicolas Gobet, archivist and secretary of the Comte d'Artois, accused Buffon in the July 1779 issue of the *Journal de Littérature, des Science et des Arts*, of having plagiarized in the *Époques de la nature* an unpublished manuscript by Nicolas Boulanger (1722-1759) entitled *Anecdotes de la nature*. Buffon did have a copy, as Denis Diderot also had, and probably did take some inspiration from it, but the charge of plagiarism was excessive. Although several other works by Boulanger were published posthumously, the *Anecdotes* was not, so he has never received credit for his geological work, which was presumably ground-breaking, and would certainly make an interesting comparison with *Telliamed*.

capable of nourishing any living creature—which, according to him, is already the circumstance in which our Moon has been in for 2,318 years, the fifth satellite of Saturn for about 26,000 years, Mars for 18,506 years; that the fourth satellite of Saturn will lose the vivifying faculty in 1,693 years, which is nothing, etc.[53]

"Your philosopher has even calculated, in accordance with his principles and his hypothesis how long life will last on the planets now populated with living beings; for example, for the Earth we have another 48,093 years, approximately. That hypothesis might satisfy superficial minds such as the Europeans who seem to like the work done and who refer everything to their Doctors, but we, who have better instruments, and above all more powerful organs, and, in consequence, saner heads, regard all of that supposedly admirable system as an absurdity, capable of impressing children but not of satisfying mature adults.

"What! Nature has organized a gnat, and has made formless masses of the Earth and the Sun! The waters of the sea, rain, the eruptions of volcanoes, meteors—everything announces that the Earth is a living being, which transpires, and for which those things are necessary emanations. Everything on its surface is animate; Nature has set before our eyes, to serve as objects of comparison, visible animals living on other animals, and others almost invisible, which are insensible to the animal that nourishes them; she has placed us on the route;

---

[53] These figures are derived from a table in which Buffon estimates the duration of the existence of organic nature on the known bodies in the solar system based on his estimates of the date at which the planets emerged from the sun (as a result of a cometary impact, in his thesis) and the rate at which they would have lost the internal heat that they carried away. Earth is actually credited there with an estimated future duration of life of 93,291 years, out of a total duration of 132,140, rather than the figure that Noffub cites, although it makes no difference to his argument.

reason has sensed that goal of Nature, and we have drawn our own conclusions from it: living beings, we are the mites of the animate being that bears us, and which exists in its own right before existing for us. There is further possibility, that we might be no more than inconvenient animalcules of which it cleans itself completely from time to time, without ever destroying the seed, because it is within itself, and we are really an accessory to its existence.

"What an immense desert your philosopher makes of the universe, and how petty he renders in your eyes the Being of Beings, the sovereign principle of all! Friends, believe us, everything in Nature is alive; the Great Being only has for ministers beings that approach his infinite perfection. The Earth is alive; she is organized; she has her own central heat, but that heat is an effect of life and not a temporary approximation of the Sun, or what has been detached from him. She might once have been united with him, as well as the other planets and the comets, but she is nevertheless a separate individual, distinct from the Sun, as a son is from his father. It is, therefore, not a heat of incandescence that she has, but a vital heat.

"For it is certain that the Sun itself is not proportionately hotter than any other animate body; it is by a particular virtue, by a generative power, that the solar emanations, in falling on the planets, produce light there and a fecundating fermentation, which we call heat. In truth, the Sun is much hotter than the Earth; that is because the latter, which is female, has no fermentative and productive sperm, the exclusive prerogative of males, which always puts man so far above woman.

"Also, the rays that descend from the Sun have no sensible heat, it requires mixture with the planetary emanations to produce light and heat, an effect that only extends upwards for a short distance; darkness, relative to us, reigns not only between the suns but also between the planets, and forms what we call the azure of the skies, which is nothing other than a black background tinted blue by the mass of our atmosphere; "sky" is a word empty of meaning, and only expresses an optical error.

"It follows that the Earth only receives from the Sun, which is her father and her male, an animal heat, which penetrates her entirely; she receives the emanations continually, and sends them back, as do the other planets; that circulation is what maintains without diminution the movement, heat and life of the Sun himself."

Hermantin, sensing how plausible and satisfying that system was, redoubled his attention.

"Do not believe," the old man continued, "that those vast bodies are inert masses; they live and die, but the beings that exist on their epidermis will perhaps have been destroyed several times during the life of a planet, either by a degree of accidental cold or of heat. Perhaps, also, those beings might subsist longer than a planet or a comet—but what is certain is that neither planets nor comets are eternal. Only Nature is eternal, and her divine animator, which is no more distinct from her than life is from our bodies.

"How do those planets and comets die? That is what no man can ever know, but can presume by analogy. The planets dry out as they cool down, like old men; movement and life ceasing, they fall into their Sun, which had launched them from his bosom by virtue of its generative power, and which must absorb them at their death, as the Earth receives us, with certain small differences."

"Are Suns also living beings then?" asked Hermantin.

"They are the second sources of life—which is to say, the means by which the Great Animator communicates it to tertiary beings, which are planets and comets. It is unnecessary to believe that it is by contact with the latter that the planets were detached from the Sun, for what would have detached the comets therefrom? As I said to you just now, both are launched from the center of their Sun by a generative power, a kind of seminal emission appropriate to Suns, which are probably themselves a direct emission of the Great Animator, the unique and omnipotent principle.

"I sensed when you asked me your question as to whether Suns are also living beings that you are surprised that bodies as hot as they are believed in Europe to be can be alive. But that heat is the very life of the Sun. That degree of heat is necessary to animate a body as vast, and to make its influence extend to the planets and the comets. Conclude, therefore, that it is beyond the scope of our organs, we being such limited beings that the extremes in our regard are only a few degrees; that the sun, with all his heat, only has the degree that he needs to subsist and communicate it to us; that he is organized, like the Earth, as the Earth is, like us; but that the Sun is so in a manner much more powerful than the latter.

"Comets are more powerful than planets—for we regard them as newly launched and we believe that their ellipses are gradually shrinking, ultimately to be reduced one day to that of the planets that they will replace as the latter die of old age and bury themselves in their Sun. Oh, how powerfully organized the Great and Sovereign Animator must be, compared to which the Suns are cold! What power of heat and light it must have, compared to which that of Suns is no more than our life and our heat is compared to that of the Star that burns for us!

"Remember this verity: heat is life; the more natural heat a living being has, the more life and generative power it has. It is necessary not to judge, as your European philosopher does, the degree of heat necessary to life by what is favorable to us. Even on the Earth, there are plants and animals for which a climate is too cold or too hot. Your philosopher, in truth is careful to warn that is calculations are made in accordance with the present state of beings existing on the globe, and that beings might exist susceptible of an ever greater degree of heat, for I have read the book of his philosophy attentively.

"Let us return, then, to your errors. Envisage Nature as a living, intelligent Whole; sense the gradation of beings; see, by what is on the Earth, that the warmer a being is, the more intelligent and alive it is. Obtain of the Great Animator an idea as vast as your imagination can comport, and then say: it is far beyond that! By that means, you will see things on a large scale, and you will not remain within the narrow limits within which other animals vegetate."

"Thank you, Father," said Hermantin to the aged Metapatagon. "What you have just said persuades me. But I shall have other questions to put to you. As the force of your genius far surpasses that of other humans, I hope for enlightenment from you that they cannot give me. The questions that I shall ask you are relative to the formation of the first beings that covered the surface of the globe. How do you think your noble nation was born from the plants and animals?"

"I have read in the books of your sages that you Europeans, veritable infants in physics, have a puerile idea of the formation of things, and that you represent the Earth, the Sun and the Stars as formed in the manner of human works. Everything is produced by the Great Animator, in whom everything exists; everything dies, but nothing is annihilated; all the beings that we have before our eyes reemerge from their own ruins; nothing is newly made, but everything that is was not always as it is.

"When the animals and plants perish in the death of a planet, they are only apparently destroyed; they are only decomposed and reduced to their principles: their germs, susceptible of life, their souls, are indestructible, and only await a suitable temperature in order to animate and revivify matter. Thus, when the generator Sun rejects a planet from its center, it makes it a comet by virtue of the force of its impulsion; after thousands of years, it gradually approaches the quasi-circular movement of the planets, and resumes the temperature necessary to charge it anew with vegetables, insets and animals.[54]

---

[54] Author's note: "A proof that the circle of the planets diminishes and that they draw nearer to the Sun is that in a hundred years the year shortens by three seconds; thus calculation can determine exactly how much life remains to out globe, prior to its absorption by the sun." Restif does not carry out the calculation, but if his reasoning were correct (it isn't) it would give a figure on the order of a billion years, much vaster than Buffon's similarly erroneous calculation.

"The germs of plants are revivified first, and proceed by one nuance after another from mosses to trees, and from the sponge to animality; the latter appears to emerge from vegetation, always by one nuance after another, from animal-vegetables like sea-nettles, sea-anemones,[55] etc, which are the first degree, to humans, which are the last of all, passing through all the nuances of animality, of which human being is he known perfection.

"Nature made a thousand trials, a thousand efforts—to make use of our imperfect expressions—before producing humans. Several of those trials subsist as races, such as the various species of monkeys; others are found mixed, such as the beast-people that you have seen in the islands of this hemisphere. There are even some of them in other parts of the globe, but I conjecture that the little people of the north pole, restless and tentative, not wanting to suffer anything in the physical, as in the moral, that does not resemble them, will have destroyed everything that did not fit in with their ideas of perfection, even if it was more perfect than them.

"I am sure that, if there have been tall men of our species among the Europeans, they are small in number, or even absolutely wiped out. They want everything to be on the same level physically, but on the other hand, in the moral and the political they most monstrous disparities have nothing that offends them![56] As for us, respectful children of Nature, we have hon-

---

[55] *Ortie-de-mer*, which I have translated literally as "sea-nettle," is nowadays virtually synonymous with "sea-anemone," but was used more widely in the 18th century to embrace other stinging sea-creatures, including jellyfish.

[56] Author's note: "This conjecture of the Megapatagon is well-founded; one can see in the ancient temple of Belus, the Indian Jupiter, an effigy of every species of beast-people that had inhabited Asia: dog-people, ox-people, monkey-people, etc. It is also the doctrine that the Egyptian priests taught." The so-called Belus Temple in Mysore only appears to date back to the 12th century A.D.; the etymology of the name is unclear,

ored all her works; we have abandoned to monkey-people, elephant-people, lion-people, bull-people, etc., the islands where they were born, and we have let them live in their own fashion; convinced that we are no wiser than Nature, we have extended our justice all the way to the serpent-people.

"Nothing, in fact, is so appropriate to guide humans in the knowledge of Nature than those various beings, which are as many steps that guide us to the sublime elevation of reasonable humankind, kind of animality, brought closer by intelligence to the greatest beings and to divinity itself. Examine all the animals and you will find that gradation, from fish, cetaceans, amphibians, the simplest aquatics, and you will see that all of them come from others by insensible nuances. With almost all the terrestrial germs employed, the species have become fixed where individuals are at this moment, and have remained perfect or imperfect.

"You Europeans, by the very ancient destruction that you have carried out of everything that you called 'monsters,' have robbed yourselves of the means of knowing beautiful truths; so, you have only groped in physics, with respect to everything relating to the formation of animals and humans. Some of you have thought that animals and human emerged fully formed from a clod of earth, like mushrooms, when the Earth was still new; and you have treated as fables and ancient superstition all the traces that the ancients have left you of the doctrine of the first humans, who had seen bipartite beings like centaurs, satyrs, fauns, sylvans or great apes, Anubis, the Minotaur, cerastes, winged men, etc. Your painters and your poets have, in any case, disfigured all of that, as the ignorant always do who set Nature aside and follow their imagination, in composing bizarre beings without analogy.

---

although many sources equate it with Bel or Baal, but Cicero calls Belus the Indian Hercules, and in other mythologies, including Armenian, the name is associated with a legendary king rather than a god.

"As for you, whom your sojourn in these climes has instructed, renounce your errors; admire the march of Nature, and above all, do not annihilate, under the pretext of correcting her, the steps that have led to reasonable humankind, in order to descend into his abysms or to rise up to his perfections."

"I find all that very clear, and more intelligible than all our conjectures," Hermanin interjected, with admiration, "but permit me to return to a question: you have told us how planets die; are Suns eternal, then?"

"Their life must be much longer than that of planets, since they absorb them, but it seems very apparent that each sun only produces each of its comets and planets once, albeit at different times and not all at once, much as animals only produce their young successively."

"There is a lack of accuracy here in the comparison; animals produce their peers, Suns only produce their inferiors."

"Your observation is just, in one sense, but the Great Animator does not produce anything that is his own equal; it is a degree of resemblance that the Suns have with him, because, being immediately formed by his productive power, they have no need to reproduce their peers, but only their inferiors. It is the same with planets and comets; they do not reproduce their peers because the Suns necessarily produce them. Nature follows in that her rule, always one and majestic, although always varied, of only doing what is necessary...

"I shall return to your question. When a Sun has produced all its comets and planets, they grow old, and it grows old with them. They gradually fall into its center, embarrassing it, and end up extinguishing its vital heart; then it falls back itself into its principle, God, or the inextinguishable heat, subsistence and life *par excellence*, who recomposes it, imprints it with new life, and reproduces it again, as beautiful and as vigorous as it was when it commenced the last career that it has followed. The Sovereign Productive Principle, which is everything, which incessantly produces and incessantly receives, can never, in consequence, grow old or die, precisely because it is everything, and its life and heat can never suffer the slightest diminution At least that is all that our reason can conceive of that Great Being, in whom we all are, and who, by that very token, we cannot either comprehend or perceive; whereas we perceive finite beings, however large they are, for, by means of drawing away, we grasp them by means of the organ of sight, like the smallest bodies; as witness the Sun itself, the planets and the stars. But God, who is everything, absolutely cannot be seen from anywhere."

"So everything is alive?"

"Everything. Your Europeans materialists stated the craziest of all absurdities when they put forward that the Whole was blind and dead; it is reasoning like children, or the blind, to submit everything to I don't know what laws of gravity; those laws exist, in truth, but they are the effect of the essence of things and the means of the Sovereign Intelligence, necessary results of his omnipotence and omniscience. That necessity is what you call optimism: everything is made in the simplest fashion, in accordance with the causes that produce it. Matter is one: ever united with some living being it is either in its body, as gross matter, or its emanation, as more subtle matter.

"Air is the emanation of the Earth, of which the land and water are the body; the ether, the mater of light, is the emanation of the Sun, of which a living and active matter is the body, but what is the nature of that matter? Your French philosopher claims that it is the same as that of the planets, because the planets emerged from it. That is to conclude a supposition, plausible in truth, but of which we do not have an absolute certainty. If the Sun is a living being, as our Megapatagon philosophers have no doubt, would it not be more plausible to assert that the planets are excremental emanations of the Sun, as plants and animals are of the planets?

"The extreme vital heat of the Sun launches those planets a long way, whereas those of planets remain fixed to their surface, but if they only had the degree of heat and force that your philosopher supposes at their emergence from the Sun, all those emanations could not remain there; they would be far away, although still in their atmosphere, for it is admitted by your philosopher that emanations are distant from the surface of a star in proportion to its greatest degree of heat. I believe that reasoning to be palpable, and one can thus explain the distancing of comets and planets without having recourse to an accidental impact, a resource unworthy of Nature, which makes everything by slow and sure means.

"Thus, the comets, the first beings launched by the generative and ardent force of the Sun, would have been in an ellipse approaching a straight line. They draw away for as long as force and heat of the impulsion subsists, and they return as soon as those causes cease to act, until they are close to the Sun, which communicates the same reimpulsion to them, but, as I have told you, always diminishing slightly the elliptical direction, in order to revert to the circular, more natural, because the rotation of the sun on its axis. As for the planets, there is every appearance that they were the first comets launched and that they have gradually resumed circular and natural movement around their center. Thus, the motion of the comets is a forced motion; that of the planets, by contrast, is a natural motion."

"I understand marvelously: the matter that we touch is not the body of God, as a certain Spinoza said in Europe."

"You're right, my son. However, not all our knowledge is a certain as what I have just explained to you; we have some that is absolutely conjectural, and which is only founded on the principle, albeit certain, that there is no empty and desert space in nature, and that everything is full of living beings, absolutely varied in their form, their substance and their manner of acting. Thus, we conjecture that the air is filled with living beings ungraspable by our senses, but that it is at a certain height, beyond the range of birds.

"It appears, according to what I have read in your books, and the explanation you have given me of the European doctrine, that people have had a few similar ideas in that part of the world: that your fairies, genii, demons, follets, etc., are a residue of that ancient opinion, which has been long obliterated and lost. But we think here that those substances, ungraspable by our senses are, by that very token, incapable of doing us good or harm, that they can neither see us nor touch us, and that they would suffocate in our air. We suppose that they are more ingenious than us, by reason of the delicacy of their organs.

"We distinguish two principal sorts of them: some are an emanation of the Earth, and inhabit all the regions of the air; they are more perfect than humans, but nevertheless participate in our weakness and our materiality. The others are an emanation of the Sun and only inhabit the ether—which is to say, the space above the atmosphere of our planet, and they are much more perfect than the sehplys, or invisible terrestrial beings; we call those of the sun snizniz.[57] We believe that the entire ether—which is to say, the intermediary space of planets and comets—is populated by these snizniz, which have a degree of intelligence far superior to the sehplys and humans. It pears that your Ancients had some idea of these invisible beings, and that they called the snizniz Angels of Light or

---

[57] Author's note: "Always read these words backwards; this one is zinzins; the one above is sylphes; lower down there are gnomes and ondins." I have left the terms borrowed from the pseudo-Paracelsian classification of elemental spirits in reversed-French rather than substituting reversed-English variants Zinzin does not come from that source, but is nowadays a slang term meaning crazy. It was much scarcer in Restif's time, but it does occur in Étienne de La Barbinais le Gentil's oft-reprinted *Nouveau voyage autour du monde* (1726)—a book that Restif might well have read—whose author credits it to the language of China and says that it signifies anything one wants to mean by it. The "genii" featured in earlier 18th century interplanetary romances, such as those by Tiphaigne de la Roche and Madame Robert, often have equally silly names beginning with Z.

Children of the Sun, and the sehplys Angels of Darkness or Children of the Earth, a tenebrous planet.

We do not stop there, and, always guided by analogies and by the known objective of Nature to animate everything, we think that, in the same way that other animalcule parasites are fund in the bodies of animals, there similarly exist in the entrails of the Earth gross animals that live buried in a profound obscurity, like worms in the human body; here we call them semong and believe them to be very limited. It appears that the Earth has sometimes tried to rid herself of them, and that is the source of your fable of Titans buried under mountains.

"Finally, we think that there might be invisible beings in the waters, and we call them snidno. It is undoubtedly all those different beings that have caused your ancients to say that the Earth was populated by spirits, and that the invisible world was infinitely more numerous than the invisible world.

"But that is sufficient about all those matters, which are nevertheless very familiar to us here, since it is with them that we commence our education and complete it. The moral fills the median interval, and it is supported on the sane notions that we have been given of the Nature of things."

II

"The basis of all our morality is order. It is necessary, we say, that the moral order resembles the physical order. No one among us strays from it, or can stray from it. We are all equal. There is one simple, brief, clear law, which speaks for itself and which humans can never replace. The law is stated in a few words.

"1. Be just toward your brother—which is to say, ask nothing from him, and do nothing to him, that you would not want to give yourself, or have done to you.

"2. Be just to the animals, and as you would like to be done to you by an animal superior to humankind.

"3. Everything should be common between equals.

"4. Everyone should work for the general wellbeing.

"5. Everyone should participate in it equally.

"It is with that single law that everything is regulated; we do not believe that there is any people that needs to have more of them, unless they are a people of oppressors and slaves, for then, I sense, although I have never seen such a people, that there would be a multitude of laws and prohibitions, such as are necessary to legitimate injustice, inequality, and the tyranny of a few members over the entire body.

"Those unfortunate people believe that by doing that they are at least promoting the wellbeing of those who are dominant. They are mistaken; there is no wellbeing except in fraternity, in the sweet sentiment that no one envies me, and my wellbeing costs no one anything, all my brothers enjoying it equally.

"Oh, how can the pretended fortunate of an unequal nation, if they are human, gorge themselves while other humans lack the necessary, amuse themselves while others suffer, and delight themselves while others are crushed by hard labor? If they can withstand all that, their hearts are too hard to savor pleasure; they do not know it; they cannot have humanity; the sentiment of compassion is extinct in them.

"We have some of those unequal peoples in our vicinity; they are the little people who inhabit the island of O-Taïti and other small neighboring islands. Since that unfortunate inequality, those people no longer have mores; they prostitute their women; they have unfortunate societies in which nature is outraged...but I suffer in telling you about those enormities, which you must know as well as we do."

"No," said Hermantin," but we intend to visit those islands, to instruct ourselves and know all our neighbors. I have another question to ask you: here, all are equal; are there, then, no magistrates?"

"Yes, our Elders; all the dignities follow age, and they increase until the final moment of life. They commence as soon as one is an adult, but that is very little at first, since the younger a man is, the fewer inferiors he has who owe him deference. But that deference does not trouble anyone. On the contrary, our young people render with joy to those more advanced in age the services of which they might have need, because they are imbued with this principle: 'You are served as children because of your impotence; it is glorious to return it, as soon as you are adolescent, or you would cease to be the equals of those who have rendered it to you; they would have a right over you, contrary to our holy and precious equality.'

"Thus, one only sees among us children aspiring to emancipation by useful services. When they have worked thus for a time equal to that of their first years of weakness—which is to say, ten years—they are shown the lot of old people, honored, served, revered by everyone, as being acquitted of all the duties of citizens, and one says to them: 'Young citizens, it is now necessary to merit being thus honored and served in your old age. You have been rendered the primary services in advance during our childhood; it is now up to you to in maturity to make in advance the honors awarded to old age. For if you wait to enjoy them without meriting them, when will you acquit yourselves?'

"Our youth is just in spirit; it senses how reasonable those precepts are, and it conforms scrupulously to them in its conduct. From that is born the harmony that you see reigning among us. Everyone who is young works, is occupied, leads an active, useful life without being commanded. It is necessary; it is done; repose awaits at the end of a career. Everything is everyone's; no one can appropriate anything exclusively—what would he do with it? No one can be idle or useless—far from it; it would be a cruel torture to condemn a person to uselessness. Besides which, if you knew how those among us who, in the vigor of age, carry out major tasks, are considered and caressed, and above all, how they are favored and served by women![58] For among us, it is they who encourage good, by the hope of pleasure and the charm of beauty."

"Are women common among you, sage Megapatagon?"

"If, by the word 'common,' you mean that paternity is uncertain and that women behave in a manner that would be contrary to propagation, you're mistaken; the human creature, which does not have seasons of rut and heat, as animals do, must regulate its appetite by reason. But if you mean that women do not belong exclusively to one man forever, yes, women are common among us, and the impetus that they give to virtue is more powerful and less dangerous than all the vile passions about which I have heard from you and read in your books, which are unleashed among Europeans to bring them to labor and excite them to cultivate the arts.

---

[58] Author's note: "The people of cities cannot have the sentiment of this virtue, familiar to villagers. In my childhood, raised among equal men, who all worked, I experienced what the good Megapatagon says here; I only aspired to have the strength to work, because work was honorable, because those who carried out the most demanding work were pampered and caressed. The young women, in particular, welcomed them. It is not necessary to go to the austral pole in search of this verity; it is in France."

234

"Every year, a choice of women in made among us—which does not mean that women marry every year; it is only every two years, because they are nursing. One prepares for the choice by entire abstinence for a month, which serves to repair strength as much as to reanimate the taste for pleasures; in addition, that abstinence contributes to making children vigorous.

"When the day of the choice arrives, all the men and all the women in a habitation, including those pregnant or nursing, arrange themselves in two files facing one another. If those confronted do not suit one another, they change places, and run from one end of the file to the other, until they find a more amenable position and everyone is paired up. Then a general celebration follows, for which preparations have been made, and which lasts about a month, or a lunar cycle.

"It is rare that all the women who are to become pregnant do not do so during that months of pleasure; thus we have very few women pregnant when the choice takes place—about one in five hundred. All of them are ordinarily relieved of bedding at that time. It is permitted to spouses to retake one another. Every year, boys and girls uniting for the first time are admitted to the end of the file, but they do not have liberty of choice like people already married; it is merit that determines espousal to the prettiest girl.

"There is little concern to consult inclinations, because the marriages are too brief to make the husbands unhappy. If, however, before the consultation and on the same day, the young man and the young woman ask to be disunited, liberty is accorded to them, with the restriction that they are obliged to wait for the following year to marry. That divorce hardly ever happens, because everyone is curious about enjoyment, and the liberty that is subsequently acquired to choose according to their taste appears a very sufficient compensation.

"Adultery during the annual marriage is absolutely unknown here, and there is no example of it. Our ancestors had agitated to make women absolutely common and for children to have no other father than the State, and no mother but the homeland, but it was found that the sentiment of paternity is too sweet for men to be deprived of it. In any case, the conduct of fathers toward children, and of the latter toward fathers, is almost the same as if they did not know one another. All the children are the nation's; the father and mother only acquire a little more particular affection. Young people serve indistinctly everyone older than themselves, until the age of fifty; at that age, one is an adult and is served as much as one serves. At a hundred one is considered to be old; we have old people here aged a hundred and fifty, still youthful and fit, and we presently have three of two hundred.

"One can marry at all the ages of life. As we have more young women than young men, the young women who remain are given to men whose wives are nursing. That is why I told you that men marry every year and the women only every two years; that would be impossible without our supernumerary young women.

"All the unmarried, pregnant or nursing women live in a comfortable habitation, separate from the rest of the citizens, throughout the time they have to nurse, until weaning; then the children are placed in the hands of the official teachers, chosen from among the mildest, most active and most meritorious persons of both sexes—in brief, the most appropriate to that precious destination, the most honorable of all functions in our republic. They must also have done their duty in the most exact manner in order to be promoted to it.

"Those educators of youth are as considered and venerated as our priests—which is to say that their person is absolutely sacred. It is true that every individual of the human species is sacred among us, but educators are in a special and particular manner; they are rendered the same homages as people two hundred years of age; they have the best places at fêtes, alongside the bicentenarians; everyone is obliged to obey and serve them. But that law is not onerous; the sacred function with which they are charged renders them dear, and everyone hastens to do everything that might oblige them,

236

since, in serving them, it is the children, the precious hope of the nation, that are being served through them.

"Although young men are not adult until fifty, as soon as puberty is manifest by the beard or the change in the voice they are inscribed in the register of those to be married at the next choice. Girls are nubile at the age of twenty-five, and as there are twice as many of them as boys, that is another reason we have to give them to men whose wives are in circumstances that prevent them being loved.

"Our manner of considering women is to regard them as the second sex; they are, in consequence, subordinate, not as among the people of the neighboring isles of O-Taîti , the Marquises, the Hebrides, and those of Friendship, Society, Amsterdam, etc., where they are treated as vile slaves, and mothers are battered by children, but only as holding the second rank. Thus, every woman must respect every man, no matter who he is. Every man, whoever he is, owes protection and aid to women. Thus, to see our men act, our nation would be taken for the most gallant on earth, but it is not gallant, it is merely reasonable; everyone here serves women, children and the old."

"You have not yet told me anything about your religion, Seigneur."

"Pardon me, but by the idea I have given you of the first principle, I have enabled you to understand everything that our religion ought to be."

"But in what does your worship consist?"

"In one point only: making use of our organs in a manner that conforms to the views of Nature, in not overdoing anything and not neglecting anything."

"You have no temples, then?"

"Yes." He pointed at the ground. "There it is, Four times a year, at the solstices and the equinoxes, four general celebrations assemble the nation, and the most ancient of the elder presents our homage, first to the Mother Earth and then to the Father Sun. After that, the same formula unites both, begging them to bear that pious homage to the Sovereign Being. Here are the three formulae:

"1. O Earth, common mother, powerful daughter of the august Sun, we, your children, have assembled to render you our filial homage: O holy and sacred Earth, our common mother, nourish us!

"2. August Sun, father of intelligence, light and heat, of movement and life, son of God, father and husband of the Earth our mother, we, the children of your august and venerable daughter and spouse, the Earth, have assembled to render you our filial and respectful homage: O holy and sacred Sun, vivify us!

3. Fecund Earth, productive Sun, children of the great God, who has given you being, intelligence and generative power in order to communicate the superabundance of your life to humans, animals and plants, august and powerful deities, bear, with yours, our homage to your divine Father, in order that he might bless us in you and through you. Honor to the mother Earth! Honor to the father Sun! Profound adoration to the Great Being, Father of all, enabling everything, containing everything!

"The nation repeats the final words: honor to the mother Earth, etc. What tenderness those holy words excited at the last fête, pronounced by an old man of two hundred and twenty, sustained by one of two hundred and nineteen and another of two hundred and ten! There was feasting afterwards, games, dancing and pleasures of every sort, for we have for a maxim that pleasure is the most efficacious manner of honoring the divinity, the Sun our father, and the Earth our common mother.

"That ought to lead me to talk about our manner of everyday life, into which diversions enter as an essential part, but certain duties summon me, from which I cannot dispense myself. In any case, it is time for my son to replace me, to explain our usages to you."

Then the sage Teugnil began to speak in his father's stead.

238

"When everyone labors," he said, "there is no difficulty. On the contrary, labor then becomes a pleasure, because that with which each individual is charged never goes as far as fatigue; it only serves to exercise and maintain the flexibility of the limbs; it contributes to rather than harming the development of the mind. Among you Europeans, on the contrary, where inequality reigns, everyone must be unhappy, some for being overburdened with labor and others for want of occupation. Everyone must be very stupid; the laborers are brutalized, the idle numbed or excited by bizarre passions. They must only think about foolish things and extravagances. If anyone among them has common sense, it is perhaps only in the middle class, but they must still be rare, either because of bad example, given either by excessively hard toil or idleness. Have I divined accurately?"

"Very accurately, illustrious Megapatagon."

"Here, on the contrary, the faculties of each person develop in a just proportion; you will not find among us beings who cannot understand what others easily conceive, and although we have among us powerful geniuses who see much further than others, they only surpass them in the faculty of invention; they are easily understood, even in the most abstract matters.

"You have seen the employment of our day. All resemble the one of your arrival here. The day is divided into two equal parts: twelve hours of sleep or absolute rest; twelve hours of action. Included in the twelve hours of repost is the time that men devote to amour, to women, and to living as individuals in the bosom of their family. The other twelve hours are public; they commence at six o'clock in the morning, with the day, and end with it at six in the evening. Occupations are shared out between all the citizens, in proportion to strength and capacity, by the old man who serves as syndic to each quarter of habitation. Each of our habitations has a hundred families, organized in quarters of twenty-five, at the head of which is the most ancient of its elders, called the quartinier; in his absence, the next in line represents him. Old man who have reached the age of a hundred and fifty no longer work, they command. Children under twenty do not work yet, but an old man trains them to do different things in the manner of play, during the hours of recreation. As well as their occupation, they learn to read and write neighboring languages, the true principles of the maternal tongue, and then morality, history and physics.

"When each person has received his occupation from the syndic, he acquits it with care and without precipitation, putting into it all possible intelligence. That labor lasts four hours. People then assemble in a room common to the whole habitation in order to take a meal there, with is prepared by the fellow citizens whose occupation that has been during the four hours. After the meal, there is the rest necessary in this hot climate; the sleep lasts an hour and a half, and then people devote themselves to various sorts of amusements until supper, at the exit from which everyone retires to his private apartment with his wife and children.

"One is not restricted to the same occupation all the time. On the contrary, those who want to change it do not experience the slightest obstacle on the part of the syndics; the citizens are even exhorted to do so, and only those who demand it absolutely always do the same thing.

"The men do all the hard and exterior labor, the women all that interior to the houses, except for métiers requiring strength, where it is a matter of handling metals such as copper or platinum, stone and wood. All needlework is only done by women, with the exception of shoemaking, for we pay the greatest attention to ensuring that they do not do anything that might harm their propriety and communicate something disagreeable to them. Women are submissive and respectful toward men, respected and considered by them as the depositaries of the next generation. Why, in any case, should anyone seek to debase or seduce a woman who might be his someday?

"Our pleasures consist in games, which exercise he body without fatiguing it, and which require more skill than strength. Glory alone, in a land like ours, can be the prize of victory. The women amuse themselves in dances that contribute to rendering their gait agreeable, and games whose skill has the same objective of rendering all their movements easy and graceful. They also occupy themselves in inventing and trying out different sorts of adornments, and combining their soft and flexible voices either with masculine voices or the instruments that the latter play. They also have a kind of game that pleases them greatly, which is to compete between them to produce the most agreeable attitude and the most seductive smile, to find the most effective way of pleasing men in all possible circumstances—for it is inculcated in them from childhood that they are made for men, as men are for the fatherland.

"Thus, among us, work is almost play and play is a kind of instruction. Every day is a celebration, not as in Europe, if it were to adopt our customs, for there would doubtless be a part of the human species that would amuse itself without doing anything, while the other worked without amusement."[59]

"Do you have spectacles—dramatic representations—illustrious Megapatagon?" asked Hermantin.

"Those sorts of pleasures are petty, only worthy of a nation of children," the sage Teugnil replied. "We only want the real, and we do not have the time that we need to savor true pleasures, without manufacturing artificial ones."

"So you don't have fine arts like painting, sculpture, music and poetry?"

"We scorn painting; our pictures are our handsome men and beautiful women, whom we see every day; if the human race were annihilated, and one sole individual conserved were condemned to live eternally alone on the earth, we would find it excusable for him to apply himself to the arts of painting and sculpture, in order to while away his solitude by a deceptive image. Perhaps too, if we had your manner of living, of quitting our fatherland for years in order to travel, we might

---

[59] Author's note: "As in Sparta, so inappropriately praised by Plutarch and J. J. Rousseau."

desire to paint cherished objects; but here, with our mores, painting and sculpture could only be puerility. We hold necessary métiers in much higher esteem than those useless arts.

"We do, however, have a few painters; their small number is employed in rendering the fine actions of our most virtuous citizens, and those pictures are destined to adorn the lodgings of the old men who performed them.

"As for music, I have told you that we have it. It is one of the charms of life to hear the perfected sounds of the human voice, to sing about great men, their pleasures and amours. Poetry is the sister of music; it is an animated and more harmonious way of saying things, but we only adapt it to cheerful subjects; it is ridiculous in terrible subjects, harmful in instructive ones. In brief, we only have three kinds of poetic works: those that celebrate the actions of heroes, benefactors of humankind, of whom one can only speak with enthusiasm; and those we call the Ode and the Ballad; it is forbidden to put any other work of the mind into verse."

"You have dancing?"

"As I have told you, we cultivate it as much as music, of which it is also a sister. Our dances even have something dramatic about them, but less with a view to imitating actions as to bestow grace, grace being among us the principal part of education, especially for women. It is into grace that we put our luxury, as befits a happy and free nation."

"You penetrate me with admiration, illustrious mortal, and each of your utterances is a flash of enlightenment for me. The patagons, to whom we have the honor of being related through our mothers, were right to praise your wisdom. I can assure you that when we return to our homeland, we shall establish all your usages there. So, you do not have, and cannot have, any but agreeable arts made for human wellbeing. Here, there are no trials, no judges, no penal laws, no crimes?"

"We owe all those advantages to equality. Take away that celestial gift, which Nature has made for us but which humans reject among the northern peoples, and all the vices would appear among us in a very short time, as in the other hemisphere."

"Do you have physicians?"

"No, the dangerous and conjectural science of medicine is banned here, as magic and superstition. Physicians are only necessary in vice-ridden nations that need to be soothed of their excesses, but surgeons are honored and we have given them a name that marks the esteem that we attribute to their divine science: that of ruesefer-taâna, remaker of humans, or moé-essahc,[60] expeller of death. Nothing is more honorable among us, by reason of its certainty and its utility."

"Instruct[61] me, I beg you, son of the wisest and most respectable of old men, on your ideas on the foundation of morality.

They are simple: avoid all disagreeable sensations; assemble all those that please legitimately, without excessively softening the organs or rendering them blasé.[62] We have for a maxim that the sole goal of society is to enable men to live together more agreeable.

"Do not believe that with these principles we are effeminate; the work, first of all, to which we are all subject, does not brutalize us but it fortifies us; our games have the goal of making our limbs supple and preventing the indolence of savages; we even practice war, because we might be attacked, and above all we elevate the souls of our young people above the fear of death.

"For that, we have convinced them that all beings, in emerging from the Sun and the Earth to form individuals dis-

---

[60] Author's note: "These two words are composites of the two languages in use among the Megapatagons."

[61] The passage that follows is omitted from the Laffont edition, which resumes with the question: "Do you have authors by profession?"

[62] Author's note: "That is the morality of J.-J. R, but, as my friend has said in a note in his *Contemporaines*, perhaps only in equal peoples. [Joly]"

tinct in appearance, are nevertheless not separate from them, that they are still connected to them and that death only causes them to change location, to exist elsewhere thereafter. In truth, we do not conserve the memory of our previous changes; that is impossible, since the organs of memory have been decomposed, but what does that matter?

"It is sufficient to sense one's present existence, and to make a whole of it by memory and foresight; that is enough to occupy us agreeably; the memory of an almost infinite multitude of previous existences would only clutter up our brain, overload it and destroy our attention to present things; that memory would kill children by rendering them too reasonable; it would eternalize hatreds and divisions in vicious peoples, etc. Sage nature does not want that.

"But analogy shows us that we are only subject to decompositions, and that must be the case; plants decompose and reproduce; every animal draws its life from the same sources; it is the same intelligence and the same matter that constitute it; it is therefore as eternal as its principle, and is so in spite of the death of planets and suns, because the death of those great beings is no more an annihilation than ours and that of the plants.

"Those are the principles that we inculcate in our young people; they are devoted to public wellbeing, to the extent of giving their life with joy, because they are assured of re-existing immediately after the dissolution of the body and thus of being eternally an inhabitant of this beautiful land. We give an extreme attention to the prompt dissolution of defunct bodies, and we regard the most hasty as the most pious. We burn them; burying them in the earth fecundates it, but it slows down the decomposition; to embalm them in order to conserve them is a sacrilege; if we have culpable individuals here, embalming with be the horrible stigma of which we would notify them."

"That way of thinking is very opposed to that of Europeans," said Hermantin, "but it appears to me to be wiser."

"Our youth, in consequence, has no fear of death, and would make excellent soldiers if we were ever attacked by ambitious Europeans. Finally, we render great honors to our dead and their names are conserved for a long time; they are repeated from age to age in every family, with one or two of their finest and most remarkable deeds...

"But to get back to your question about our morality, it only consists of taking the shortest route to the means of being happy, and the one with fewest obstacles; and as unbridled sensuality would have great inconveniences, you can imagine that it is not that route that we take. We know that privations season pleasure by giving it an appetite, so to speak, so we have privations. Similarly, there is a moderation and a measure in our enjoyments; we never take them as far as absolute satiety. But what affirms good morality among us, is that it is not abandoned, as you have said that it is in Europe, to individual fantasy; by means of our equality and out community, moral progress is uniform and public; we practice virtue in the body, and we reject vice in the body: sloth, futility, excess of aliments or lust have all become impossible for us.

A man cannot gorge himself in a public assembly of his fellow citizens; he only takes what is necessary. That fortunate habit has almost extinguished within us gluttonous temperaments, which are recognizable by a dry mouth and poor complexion in the isles of this hemisphere. A man will not commit excesses of debauchery with his wife; a brother in the midst of his brothers, who are fulfilling their tasks, will not neglect his own; he will not become a vagabond in a country where everyone is simultaneously occupied, etc.

Thus, our mores are always assured. In consequence, necessity renders them mild. You can see by our occupations and our pleasures that they could not be more so. I repeat to you that equality cuts off all vices at the root: no more thieves, or murderers, or idlers, or corrupters. As mockery might produce a few abuses among an equal people, it is forbidden;[63] every Megapatagon must abandon that wretched means of showing wit. It is, on the contrary, a tone of generosity and honesty that reigns among us. The truth, above all, is sacred here, and we do not permit the slightest badinage that injures it, even with the intention of subsequently causing an agreeable surprise, and what emerges from our mouths is always what is; that which is not, the ridiculous mask of fable and allegory, is unworthy of the eldest son of Nature, and we leave it to those monkeys that are capable of reasoning, like the ones that you have discovered. That is one of the reasons that all comedy and drama are banished from our regime; that is only good for the people of Monkey Island and the inconsequents of Europe.

"Do you have authors by profession?"

"We have wise men, philosophers who devote their hours of diversion to writing amusing and instructive histories, taking place among us or in neighboring nations. The reading of those works plays a part in public pleasures. Those who compose them are honored as ruesefer-taânas of the mind; which is to say that they are highly considered, but they acquit themselves, like everyone else, with four hours of daily labor, and none of them has yet sought to dispense with that. On the contrary, they are the most zealous and best of citizens.

"As one ought to cite the names of useful men, in order by that means to render them a merited homage, I shall give you a succinct idea of our principal authors. The foremost, one of the most laborious, is the great Seliof-Taâna,[64] author of an

---

[63] Author's note: "The *ridiculum acri* of Horace is stupid. Our present persiflage, the tone of our society, that of our critics, and the expressions that our portrait painters give to faces, are worse than stupid. [Dulis]"

[64] In the first edition this name is rendered as Teraguon, thus making the sarcastic reference to Pierre Nougaret explicit. The version in the Laffont reprint must be taken from a later edition. In *Les Posthumes* Nougaret is disguised as

epic poem in which the majesty of great poetry is combined with the beauty of thought and the importance of maxims. The knowledge extended in that masterpiece is immense; Seliof-Taâna is simultaneously an excellent moralist, a profound physicist and a sublime metaphysician; he is an astronomer, a chemist, a geographer and a musician. It is evident that he possesses fully the foundations of all the arts and métiers, that he is versed in the knowledge of an incredible multitude of ancient and modern languages; and that he knows the customs and usages of all the peoples in the world, as if he had spend his days in the midst of each of them—which comes from the trouble he has taken to interrogating a few castaways whose vessels have been wrecked on our shores.

"In sum, his poem is an ocean of science and enlightenment, which ensures that one cannot out it down once one had taken it up. The subject of that marvelous poem is the Patagoniad, or the first institution of our present regime. The work is full of imagination, because its divine author has been able to divine motives and means as well as all the obstacles and the manner in which they were overcome, and he explains all that in a seductive manner. He provokes, above all, the adoration of the great Yrneh, our first legislator, and the respectable citizens that aided him, such as Nollitâhc, the immortal Yllus, the sage Yanrom, the courageous Norib, the Scassirb, the Sycneromnom and Sednoc, and a multitude of other illustrious citizens who then devoted themselves to public wellbeing, etc.

"Another celebrated author is the modest and naïve Effluosruob-Taâna,[65] who has made sublime odes and ballads

---

"Miléunuefolies," having published a collection of short stories entitled *Les Mille et une folies* (1771).

[65] Rendered Yosorud in the first edition; the journalist Barnabé Durosoy (1745-1792) was another regular object of Restif's bile, similarly castigated in a satirical section of *Les Posthumes* set in the world of discorporate souls (although the

whose naivety and touching simplicity goes straight to the heart, throwing it into a delirious abandon.

The elegant and delicate Epprig-taâna[66] has brought into our language a sweetness and harmony of which our light poets had not yet furnished the example, in which he has been admirable seconded in verse, and above all in prose, by the most polished and cried of our authors, the inimitable Ettesion-Taâdna.[67]

The lucid Zoh'cub is our Pliny, etc.

I shall not talk to you about the likes of To-Taâna, Mar-Taâna, Al-Taâna, Did-Taâna, Er-Tiaâna, Ter-Taâna—who has given us sage views on the education of women, which we have followed—Ux-Taâna and Eiss-Taâna, to whom I should add two less famous because they have less impartiality, enlightenment and taste, named Ua-Taâna and Nai-Taâna.[68]

---

individuals castigated there were still alive when it was penned). Boursouffle means bombastic.

[66] Uaedraf in the first edition; the rather obscure L. G. Fardeau, the anonymous author of *Mariage à la mode* (1774) also features in the same scene in *Les Posthumes*.

[67] Yarducod in the first edition; ditto Alexandre-Jacques Du Coudray (1744-1790).

[68] This entire paragraph replaces two paragraphs in the first edition slightly more comprehensible in their sarcasm-drenched reference to contemporary authors, which read: "I shall not talk to you about the Samohs, the Letnoram[s], the Eprahaled[s], the Trebmelad[s], the Toredid[s] and the Nolliberc[s], nor two obscure writers that we have just lost, Eriatlov and Uaessuor; all those authors, although not without merit, are too far above the first that I named.

"We also have excellent critics whose works, full of taste and impartiality, are the delights of an intelligent nation that loves to see just appreciation of the foremost of talents, that which brings humans closer to their divine author the Sun, and even the father of the Sun, such as Norerf, Reisorg, **T—who has given us sages views on the education of women, which we

"I shall, however, pause momentarily on a man of merit who has written an appreciation of our authors with a sagacity, a justice and an impartiality that grips the admiration of all righteous hearts. He is a respectable elder, a Nestor of literature, an excellent model, whose numerous works in all the genres are as many masterpieces; a man celebrated, even among us, for his veracity, the purity of his mores and his views—in sum, a man who has never masked his sentiments, and whom full of respect for the Sun and the father of the Sun, has always spoken in conformity with the doctrine of sage elders. That divine man, whose name I cannot pronounce without affection and veneration, is named Hier-Taâna.[69]

"His book has become elementary among us; he praises there the sublime knowledge of our sages; great men are treated there with the respect due to them, and a kind of adoration; he also mentions a few petty authors, but in a few words, and one to conserve them a means of future immortality, thus recompensing their zeal rather than their merit. He has not forgotten any of those who merit a place in his book; he has not arbitrarily placed non-authors there solely because they were his acquaintances. As there are no nobles among us, his book is not dishonored by base adulations; as here are no sects, he has never tried to debase the talents of his enemies. He has not affected to turn to odious significance words consecrated by usage to designate amour and lovers of wisdom. In sum, he

_____

have followed—Xueyor and Xueiffud, to whom I will add two less famous because they have less impartiality, enlightenment and taste; their names are Uaeretuas and Yanetnof."

"Samohs" was obviously a misprint; the intended reference was probably to the writer Antoine-Léonard Thomas (1732-1785), briefly famous for the eloquence of his many eulogies.

[69] Reihtabbas in the first edition. The reference is to François Sabbathier (1735-1807), whose mammoth *Dictionnaire pour l'intelligence des auteurs classiques*, which began publication in 1766, was still incomplete when he published its thirty-sixth volume in 1790 and gave up.

249

has been able to made a book whose inventions seem paltry at first glance, a sacred temple in which the nation, in future centuries, will be able to adore true merit."

"Fortunate Patagons!" exclaimed Hermantin. "Oh, if only my respectable grandfather could have the pleasure of seeing and conversing with you! He would admire, above all, how you are the moral antipodes of his homeland, even more perfectly than you by virtue of your situation on the globe. But we shall soon brighten up his old age with an account of everything that you have told us.

"It is not, very wise Megapatagons, that our respectable grandfather does not know maxims as beautiful as yours. He brought into your hemisphere, which is now ours, a religion that teaches equality and fraternity, which he has made a law, and which declares that without charity—which is to say, the virtue by which we love our brethren, by which they are dear to us—we are only vile and unhappy beings. All the precepts of that religion tend to disinterest, to the purity of mores, to beneficence and modesty: all great possessors are cursed therein; if forbids calling anyone Seigneur, on the principle that all are equally the sons of God; it orders one to share ones bread with one's fellows, without exception of individuals, by nation, religion or sentiment..."

"All the people of Europe do not profess that, then?"

"Alas no, illustrious son of the wisest of elders."

"But who, then, are those whose deeds we have read in the books of history that you have given me, in inverse language?"

"They are the same peoples."

"In that case, illustrious Christinians, either you are making fun of me or these peoples are making mock of their legislator and the great God that you say they adore."

"They are not mocking, sage Teugnil, but, drawn by their passions, they follow almost nothing of their religion. Even some of those who, by their estate, ought to practice it, are no more exact; they are the first to violate its fundamental points, although they are most attentive to conserve the prerogatives that it gives them in the eyes of others.

"I don't understand you, noble Christinians; either they profess their religion or they do not."

"They profess it."

"Without following it?"

"True."

"You give me an inconceivable scorn for Europeans! Such a beautiful religion, dictated by the Great God himself—as I recognize by the precepts he has given—is professed without being practiced! Your Europeans are monsters! And among you, on Île Christine?"

"We have put into vigor all the precepts of equality, fraternal charity, community and benevolence, and we are happy in following them to the letter."

"Your conduct in further proof of the folly of your Europeans: they are an abominable people! There are good laws that are not followed! It is corrupt at its very heart."

(That is what an upright man, who has never stifled the voice of nature and reason, thinks of you.)

In the following days, the Christinian princes saw with their own eyes the truth of everything that the aged Noffub and his son Teugnil had said. They visited the whole extent of Megapatagonia with the good and loyal Teugnil, and when they were sufficiently known—which as a matter of a few days—they were permitted to mingle indifferently with the people of that fortunate country.

The sage discourse of the Megapatagons cured the Christinian princes of the blood of their mania for discoveries; they resolved not to search for islands and new lands any longer, and to return home by the shortest route as soon as they were sufficiently instructed.

III

During their sojourn, they had the interesting spectacle of a marriage ceremony, a description of which you will doubtless be charmed to have.

The great day was announced before the preceding thirty, during which all the husbands quit their wives and all the wives their husbands. This, the two sexes were divided into two nations, which no longer had any commerce together except to see one another, without speaking. During that thirty days, all the women became teasingly and coquettishly youthful; once could not see anything more charming, at first glance, than what they were offering in their gallant troops. For their part, the men were no less eager to please; they divided themselves up into regiments and performed maneuvers in front of the women, from whom they were separated by a barrier, and when they rested, the women danced in their turn.

What is the dancing of your Opéra by comparison with those motivated by the desire to please the man that the heart has chosen, seen by lovers already burning with a new fire? As I said, the women danced voluptuously.

All work ceased during the time of amour, but society did not suffer at all, because the cessation had been foresee, and all necessary things had been prepared in abundance It is impossible to describe the delirium of joy and intoxication in which all Megapatagonia participated then. The carnivals of Europe, including that of Venice, are only a sorry image of it. Hermantin shivered with pleasure.

The entire nation seemed renewed; old age had disappeared in both sexes; everyone was ornamented, amiable, cheerful and healthy; they aspired equally to the pleasures that a new choice promised them. Some were more tranquil than others, but a certain contentment spread throughout their physiognomy announced their dispositions; they were the ones who intended to reselect one another. Those women did not wear flowers on their bosom, but they wore them in their hair, like the others. They did not join in the communal dances, but gathered at the barrier to talk to their husbands—a privilege exclusive to them—while all their fellow citizens amused themselves.

Hermantin was shown several couples already advanced in age, surrounded by amiable children, who had never quit one another; although people approved of that, no distinction was made between those who behind thus, because, the elders told the young people from Île Christine: "It is to the liberty to change that those constant couples owe their happiness."

The most delightful spectacle was, however, that of the young people of both sexes destined for marriage for the first time. They formed different quadrilles in one another's presence, striving to surpass one another in their dances, the young men in skill and the young women in grace.

One thing that seemed very extraordinary to Hermantin and his companion was that on the twenty-ninth day, the eve of the choice, the young people of both sexes appeared naked before one another, and carried out thus the same exercises and dances as the day before. Never had such well-proportioned bodies been seen; in that great number, scarcely two of either sex could be found who had the slightest defect.

That was how the preparations were concluded.

The next day, the day of the choice, the entire nation, elegantly adorned, was arranged in several rows along the barriers. The first row was composed of old people, before whom all the women filed. They chose their spouses first, but they had the useful restriction that a young woman could not be chosen two years running by a old man; the following years, she only filed before the younger men, and all those quitting old men formed a final row, which remained motionless, until the older men had made their choice. You will recall that one is not an old man in Megapatagonia until a hundred and fifty years of age.

After the old men came the mature men aged between a hundred and a hundred and forty-nine, then the men in their prime between fifty and ninety-nine. After them were the un-married young men, who were choosing for the first time, and to whom the most beautiful nubile women were given; those who were less so were put among the women already married who could be chosen between men of fifty to ninety-nine.

As soon as the choice was completed and the spouses keeping one another were brought back, a concert was heard of delightful instruments and silvery voices, performed by young people of both sexes who were to be married in the two following years. The young men played the instruments and the young women sang; from time to time the two sexes com-bined their voices. During the concert, whose soft and volup-tuous music was only played on that day, the newly-united couples sat down, their arms interlaced, giving evidence of the first fruits of their passionate sentiments in the most tender speeches, worthy of that delicate nation.

A magnificent feast concluded the celebrations. The next day, only succulent dishes were served; finally, on the thirty-second day of the marriages, work recommenced as usual, after a prayer to the communal mother Earth, the animating Sun and the Great First Principle.

Hermantin and his companions were witnesses to that renewal; the delight and contentment of the husbands of all ages were extreme; everyone appeared to adore one another; or, if a few were ill-matched, they did not worry much about it and at least lived in peace. In any case, there were too many distractions in the Megapatagon way of life for the presence of spouses who did not love one another to become a torment.

After having examined everything, the Christinian princ-es of the blood requested to return home. The aged Noffub and his son Teugnil informed the nation, which assembled to bid their extraordinary guests farewell. They were given magnifi-cent presents, which they took to the ship; they were heaped with blessings and god wishes or her prosperity; and when they were ready to leave old Noffub said to them, in the in-verse tongue:

"My dear children, I know what your conduct has been with the different species of humans that you have discovered; it is worthy of praise, but believe me, do not meddle too much in the affairs of those peoples. Gradually, you would come to regard yourselves as masters and proprietors, which would be a great evil. Maintain equality among yourselves. I shall not tell you to adopt our usages, but conserve your own, which appear to me to be good. We are happy, as you see; it is up to you to make use of your reason, and to draw the consequences. Write in letters of gold, in all known languages, on the principal gate of your city: *Without perfect equality, there is no virtue and no wellbeing.* Adieu."

After having taken their leave of the Megapatagons, the six princes returned to Île Christine with the ship, by the shortest route. On the way, they saw Captain Cook's vessel between the twenty-ninth and thirtieth degrees of south latitude. The English voyager was coming back from the New Hebrides and New Caledonia.[70] They left him and drew away from his route, quite sure that they had not been seen, since he could not have seen their ship, but only the flying princes. However, the latter, after having prescribed the route to their mariners, kept watch on the English captain and saw him advancing toward the coast of New Zealand. They followed him when he left that land, in order to make sure that he would not find any of their islands; they would have given orders in consequence. Afterwards they returned home, where they recounted all the admirable things they had seen and learned.

They told the venerable old Victorin and Queen Christine about the wisdom and the way of life of the Megapatagons, careful not to forget anything essential. The good king and queen were admiring, but Victorin observed that similar usages could not be established among the Europeans, whose ideas were too opposed to them; he therefore enjoined his grandchildren to improve the ancient laws gradually, and not to do anything precipitately, to be perennially

---

[70] Author's note: "This was in 1774."

hopeful, and to conserve friendly relations with the wise and powerful people. The princes conformed with the orders of their grandfather, with a respect so profound that there was a commencement of the introduction of the megapatagon law.

They also talked about the European ship that had been seen in the sea of the region. The old man was troubled, and as soon as his grandsons had rested he ordered them to go and find the vessel in order to discover its destination and to defend the establishments protected by the Christinian Empire if the European navigator attempted to land there.

In order to comply with his grandfather's orders, Hermantin proposed that he frighten the captain during the night and force him to quit the austral hemisphere, making him understand by obvious signs that he would be killed if he ever returned.

The princes departed, equipped with fuses, grenades and fireworks to overtake the ship exploring the region of the pole. They caught up with it beyond the polar circle, on the seventy-first degree of latitude. They deliberated as to what to do. It was unanimously decided that they would leave it to search among the ice-floes, where it would not find anything, that they would keep watch on it constantly, resting on ice-floes enveloped in the skins of sea-martens that covered them entirely, but that they would neither help nor harm to the captain so long as he did not try to land on one of the protected islands. They also promised, in case the vessel perished by accident, to save the crew and transport them to Île Christine.

Nothing like that happened; the captain returned via Easter Island and the Marquise Islands, etc., without having sighted any of the islands they did not want him to find.

I have no more to tell you about now but the new laws established by Hermantin for the entire Christian Republic, after which I shall tell you how and for what reason I have come to Europe, via the Cape of Good Hope, to which the princes carried me themselves and where I embarked for preference on Captain Cook's ship as a passenger in order to penetrate his future designs more surely.

Prince Hermantin, who had the full confidence of his grandfather Victorin, his uncle the hereditary prince and the predilection of his father Alexandre, reflected incessantly, after his voyage, about the beautiful and sage customs of the Megapatagons; he burned with the desire to establish them in our fatherland. He went to see the Patagons of la-Victorique and ask them for their sentiment. They were of precisely the same opinion as Victorin; they advised the young man not to do anything with too much precipitation. In consequence, Hermantin contented himself with setting before the eyes of the Council of State the following law, in order to propose it to the people and try to persuade everyone to agree to it, until one that was more perfect could be promulgated. He took care to tell them that the law was only preparatory. These are the terms in which it was conceived:

Rescript of the King and Queen
to the Community of France-Christinians

Victorin and Christine, by the grace of God, Regent and Queen of Île Christine, Monkey Island, Bear Island, etc., to all our brethren and the inhabitants of thirty[71] austral islands, living under the same law, salutations, joy, repose and liberty. Our very dear and beloved son the hereditary Prince of our Empire, our very dear son Alexandre, worthy support of our power, as well as our very dear grandsons, their sons, and particularly Prince Hermantin, the light of our reign and the splendor of our Estates, desiring to augment national wellbeing, have made various voyages, as everyone knows and has seen.

In the first, they discovered various species of humans, with whom they have acted in a manner worthy of reasonable God-fearing beings full of humanity, only seeking to be useful

---

[71] Author's note: "In addition to those named there were those of Camel Island, Rhinocerina, Hippopotamica, Crocodileante and Insectina, discovered by the governors of other islands."

to those different nations, to which Nature, the common mother, has not given the same perfection of intelligence as to us. But just as they found in the abovementioned islands species inferior to ours, they also encountered beings that are superior in benevolence, sage laws and good usages, in the long sequence of isles that we call il-Victorique, and which might more justly called Patagonia.

There our grandchildren had the good fortune to converse with a people named Megapatagons, separated from us by half a circuit of the globe and almost at the antipodes of France, our ancient homeland, in whom they found treasures of wisdom, enlightenment and public felicity of which we intent to give you a perfect knowledge: to wit, that that equality between humans is the sole source of wellbeing, and, in consequence, of all virtue.

In consequence, we have resolved to publish a new Code of laws, not entirely in conformity with the usages and customs of the illustrious and sage Megapatagons, but which only improve ours and render them more efficaciously good. To these causes, moved by the desire for the happiness and wellbeing of our fellow citizens, with our full royal power and authority, which we enjoy without contradiction, having merited them by the services that we have rendered to present society, which we have founded and hope to make proper increasingly in future, by the maintenance of sacred liberty, statuted and understood, we desire and want the following:

Article 1. Counting from the publication of the present Rescript, all the property of our brethren and fellow citizens will be put in common; work will similarly be shared, but each person nevertheless, during the present generation, will continue his ordinary occupations. Understand only that they will be equally honest and honorable, of whatever nature they might be. We wish them to be fraternally exercised by all our fellow citizens, as by the sons of the same father.

Article 2. We intend that the wives of various citizens should be reputed absolutely equal between themselves, without the distinction of estates that will still be found among men.

Article 3. Children to be born or those who, being too young, have not yet received education and instruction, will be trained for the arts and professions that best suit their capacity, without any regard to birth or to the state of their parents.

Article 4. In order to effectuate with more facility the community of property and the equality of fortune, we want everything to be bought by individuals to be at the expense of the community that we establish by the present rescript, and paid for in proportion to the real needs of the worker and the artist, and not the value of their work. Which is to say that when a worker is charged with children to the number of six, he will be paid for his work double what is paid to the man who has three, and three times what is paid to a man who only has two, and so on, in proportion to the number of children and charges; with the result that the citizen charged with children shall not be more ill at ease than one who has no charge, and that everything shall be proportionate, until we are able to embrace Megapatagon law completely, in all its parts, by establishing common meals.

Article 5. Idleness and uselessness shall be stigmatized vices, capable of leading to be expulsion of incorrigibles from the capital island.

Article 6. Labor shall neither be continuous nor too hard; the hours shall be fixed at six per day, which ought to be well employed. Afterwards, everyone shall take honest recreation, mingling indistinctly, as brothers, all equal and republican.

Article 7. From this moment, all debts, pecuniary obligations and private property cease absolutely, but everyone shall keep his dwelling to live there in privacy with his wife and children, on the product of his labor, as expressed in article 4.

Article 8. No one can delect himself in eating or put more sumptuousness into his clothing than others. Once the most agreeable and comfortable fashion has been adopted, everyone will be obliged to conform to it. But working garb will continue go vary, according to occupation, until differences are absolutely annihilated, as among the Megapatagons. During the house of recreation, however, all men will dress in the same way, and those who exercise dirty professions will take care to clean themselves perfectly before mingling with their brethren.

Article 9. As for women, their costume will be exactly the same for everyone at all times, except when their taste indicates something more agreeable, of which they will always easily obtain permission to make use.

Article 10. It will be the same for youth, boys and girls alike, having no state as yet. They will all dress similarly, with regard to the fabric and tailoring of garments.

Article 11. A magistrate will only be the voice of the law, in civil as well as criminal matters, but civil cases will be almost annihilated by the present law and criminal cases reduced to very few, cupidity being the source of all human crimes.

Article 12. Murderers shall be taken to a sterile rock, where they will be abandoned without provision, even for one day. A person who kills out of anger by striking, or who strikes excessively, shall be punished by flagellation and banishment to one of the most uncomfortable islands; a recidivist shall be punished as for murder.

Arson shall be punished by flagellation and punishment to a small desert island, such as exist in these seas, where he shall be left alone, but with means of subsistence.

Rape shall be punished by flagellation alone, and by subjection to anything that the victim demands, or, if she does not demand anything, punished like the arsonist Brutal insult offered to the sex, if anyone is capable of it, accompanied by the profanation of the propagatory act, shall be punished in the same way as rape.

Atrocious insults shall be punished by humiliation in full assembly before the insulted, provided that the person in question has not responded, in which case both must make honorable amends to the nation, and shall be deprived for a year of a deliberative voice as well as all other privileges of citizenship.

Conspiracy against the State, if it is if the highest level—which is to say, if there has been treason by introducing or attempting to introduce an enemy—shall be punished by death, by the hand of a tiger-man. If it is not with enemies that the treason is conspired, the guilty party shall be relegated to one of our small desert islands, as unworthy of living in society, with fishing equipment.

Article 13. In all cases of banishment, a wife will be given to the banished, chosen from among the most despicable and deformed of the inferior species, while notifying them that the death penalty will follow any ill-treatment to she might suffer; being thus subjected to the aforesaid penalty, the aforesaid wives shall be absolute mistresses of their punishment. The brutal insulter shall have the least ugly, the arsonist one more deformed, the murder worse still, the traitor the most monstrous; his punishment will be less relieved if he ill-uses her. The children of those perverse individuals shall be taken away after weaning to be confided to the public teachers of brute-people, who will conceal the secret of their birth from everyone.

Article 14. Every good citizen shall be honored in proportion to his deeds of note, both for the public good and for individuals. The man who has saved a life shall wear a civic crown of oak and will be advanced ten years toward the privileges of old age, with the consequence that at forty, he will have the privileges of a man of fifty.

The man who has appeased a quarrel with mildness, and who has prevented its effects, shall be publicly thanked and granted two years advance on the privileges of age.

Whoever puts out a fire and brings effective help shall have five years advance of the privileges of old age, and a crown of pellitory-of-the-wall, which will be renewed every year.

Whoever saves the decency of a girl or woman being taken by violence shall have the same five years of privilege and a crown of laurier-rose, which will be renewed every year and placed on his head in the assembly by a twelve-year-old girl.

The man who discovers a conspiracy and saves the State from a plot shall have a laurier crown that will be renewed every year and placed on his head by the oldest of the elders; then all the youth of both sexes will file before him saying "Honor to the god citizen" and he will have twenty years of privilege—which is to say that throughout his life, if he is thirty, he will have the same authority as a man of fifty, etc. The author of some useful invention, either for the needs of life and commodity or for morality and better usages to establish, demonstrated by success, shall have, in the former case, in proportion to importance, five or ten years of privilege, with a crown of pine, which will be put on by the oldest of the elders, and in the second case, a crown of laurier and pine, with ten or twenty years of privilege, according to the importance of the discovery and the service rendered to the fatherland.

Article 15. We establish by the present rescript a new order of rank and dignity among our fellow citizens to replace the one we are abrogating. In consequence we intend that dignities and precedences be given to age, to virtue of every sort, and to great or fine actions, in the fashion nevertheless—as is evident by virtue of the previous article—that the recompense of good and fine deeds by appreciated in years of age, in order to assure that law, founded on Nature, as much as possible by its very exceptions.

Thus, the unreasonable child and the old person will be served by everyone; the more advanced child, by contrast, will serve everyone. Having reached sixteen he will thus have all children down to the age of seven below him, who will owe him honor and deference. At twenty, he will have two classes beneath him, at twenty-five three, at thirty for and at thirty-five five; finally, at forty, he will be a complete man and will commence to be susceptible to dignities.

There will be this difference, between the man of forty and all those below him: that he participates in the administration, in sovereignty, whereas the others remain under the tutelage of the State, of which they will only have the hope and not the reality. From forty to seventy, he will only increase in the capacity to possess dignities. At seventy, old men will become fathers of the nation, and will be charged with presenting its homages to the Sovereign Being, the source of everything.

The most ancient of the elders will be sovereign pontiff, whoever he is; that is why extreme old age will be envied and will bear luster in families. Other elders will rise successively in grade, but the lowest of the grades of sacerdocy will give them precedence over all magistrates and civil officers, who will owe them honor and respect, and will receive their advice with heads uncovered and eyes lowered.

It is thus that we intend and want the old to participate in the honors and homages rendered to the divinity himself, whose ministers they will be. Every priest will be served by the family. Every morning, the first magistrate of the Republic, before commencing his functions, will send the sovereign pontiff a message via two of his sons, who will say: "Wise and respectable Elder, the Chief of the Republic, and the entire

Republic by way of his voice, send you through us the homage of their respect, sage and venerable elder, who has seen us born. Carry our homage to the Sovereign Principle, as a father carries that of his children to his own father."

The sovereign pontiff will reply that he will judge it appropriate, hearing nothing prescribed by the One that puts us, by this present law, above any other living man. But the ministers will no longer meddle in any temporal affair, except in the form of advice; and then they will be heard with respect, in silence, without giving any mark of approval or disapproval under any pretext whatsoever. And in the case that their advice is followed, the magistrate and his assessors will not make any reference to it in their rescript.

Article 16. There will no longer be an individual sovereign. We abandon sovereign power by the present rescript and return it to society, which we want to be ruled in future by elected magistrates. We intend nevertheless that, by a fundamental law agreed by the entire nation, that the princes of our blood will maintain the exclusive and patrimonial right to wear wings, without being hindered in the exercise of that right; but we order them to employ that patrimonial faculty in the service of the State. We intend that any of them who abuses it in order to betray the said State should be punished by death, without nevertheless his crime bearing any prejudice to our other descendants, including his own, who, of all present advantages, shall only reserve that one, for which they shall request the national and universal concession on the part of all their fellow citizens.

Article 17. No mark of honor shall be hereditary. Everyone shall make his own reputation and shall be the artisan of his own glory. Similarly, no one shall suffer the dishonor of his forefathers; both are equally unjust.

Article 18. Women, as well as men, shall be honored in proportion to age, but they will follow the dignity of their husband rather than their own advancement; when they are forty, they will have the title of Matrons; at seventy they will be Priestesses—which is to say that they will exercise conjointly with the priests, and under their orders, various sacerdotal functions, of which the principal one will be to appropriate the temple, to cause arrangement and order to reign there. The priestesses will live with their husbands. Widows will be lodged in common in the vicinity of the temple; all will be honored like the priests themselves, and the oldest will receive on the part of the magistrate's wife the daily message or homage.

The present rescript made and given in our house, formerly the palace, with the advice and consent of our royal family, with no exception, to be published and agreed throughout the extent of our Empire, on 15 April 1776 of the Christinian Era.

Signed:

Victorin, founder and legislator. Christine, Queen.

The Hereditary Prince. Prince Alexandre. Princes Dagobert, Thierry, Hermantin. Clovis, etc.

That law having been published in Île Christine and each of the other islands, delegates were seen arriving from all directions, as many French as night-people, Monkey-, Bear-, Dog-, Bull- and Elephant-people, etc. etc, all of whom begged Victorin and Queen Christine to conserve their royalty.

"Always be our Father and our Mother," they said, "and may our benefactors, your worthy children, reign over us forever. As for the other sage articles of your rescript, we will swear to their observation."

But Victorin was firm in the plan that his grandson Hermantin had suggested to him, and such was the confidence that his grandfather, his uncle the hereditary prince and his father Alexandre had in that young man, prematurely wise, that they left him the absolute master of all the changes to be made in the government.

265

He brought them to a fortunate conclusion.

Victorin and Christine remained the foremost in the State, both became the High Priest and Priestess by right, being the oldest of their fellow citizens, and one cannot express the emotion that was experienced in seeing the founding hero of the State in that office. The Priest, who had sufficed alone for a long time, having just died, at a very advanced age, in order to conserve the unity of religion and sacerdocy, Princes Hermantin, Dagobert, etc. immediately departed with the ship for Europe, where they abducted the Archbishop of ***,[72] who was thought to have died a few years ago, because he was indeed ill, and substituted a cadaver for that Prelate; he it is who organizes are present Ecclesiastics, all elders, in accordance with the law.

It was while returning from that voyage that the princes, passing over the peninsula of India, were witnesses to an *auto da fé* that the Portuguese devotees were about to celebrate in Goa. There was an entire family of wretched Moors, a father, mother, two sons and three daughters, who had abjured Mohammedanism out of fear and had reverted to it out of conviction; two Jewish families what had converted out of interest and had thought to satisfy their conscience by practicing Judaism in secret; and a few Protestants even less culpable, but even more hated by zealous Catholics.

The sacrilegious ceremony was reaching its end; the pyres were built; the unfortunates were being attached to them, mitered and covered by sanbenitos decorated with flames, devils and all the frightful scarecrows of superstition. Hermantin might not have perceived them but for the screams of the Moorish and Jewish girls; he descended somewhat from the extreme elevation that he was maintaining in order not to be recognized by humans, and he then saw that all those poor people were about to be burned. He assumed them to be culpable but resolved nevertheless to save them, intending to

---

[72] "Bethléem" in the first edition. The Archbishop of Bethléem who died in 1777 was Charles-Marie de Quelen.

transport them to one of the deserted islands of the Christinian Republic, but the abominable sacrifice was imminent.

Hermantin shivered. He paused momentarily over the inquisitor's palace, surrounded by his companions, and then approached the pyre alone. It is necessary to observe that during long voyages among civilized peoples, the Christinian princes wore platinum coats of mail impervious to bullets. All the Portuguese, seeing him arrive, took him for an angel; they signed themselves and sank to their knees.

The Prince knew the principal languages of Europe; he untied the unfortunates without any opposition, told them to follow the guide that he gave them, and sent them to walk to the harbor, from which the other princes transported them to the ship. All of that was executed very promptly. When they were safe Hermantin stood on one of the pyres and pronounced a speech of vehement protestation in Portuguese.

"Wretches, who profess a gentle and voluntary religion, what frenzy had led you to make abominable sacrifices to the Divinity? What monster has urged you to honor the common Father of all with human victims? They are impious men plunged into a stupid ignorance who, by a horrible blasphemy, have judged the Sovereign Being by their own bloodthirsty hearts!

"Oh, my brothers, since you are human, return to sentiments in conformity with reason! Throw far from you these infamous inquisitors, who are annihilating the spirit of the religion while they pretend to be conserving the shell! Let everyone in your land be free to think in accordance with his enlightenment and conscience. It is to degrade human beings, to drag them down below the brutes to prevent them to speak and act in accordance with what they think; what is worse still is to blaspheme the eternal reason of which the Divinity has given each of us a spark to guide him, by accusing it of injustice or taxing it with folly! Let any man who persecutes others in order to make them think like him be sequestered on a desert island as a venomous beast!

"No, Portuguese, it is only universal tolerance and indifference to all opinions that can maintain peace. No one has any right over any opinion but his own. The man who is passionate for religion, under the pretext of zeal for God, shows that he knows neither the power of God, since he claims to be protecting it, nor his bounty, since he pretends to be serving it by evil. False and wicked man, God is more powerful than you, and has only to raise his arm! It is an imperceptible mite pretending to aid an elephant!

"Portuguese, the men of all religions are brothers: the author of Christianity declared specifically to the Jews that the good Samaritan was more their brother than one of their brothers who was harsh and pitiless. Regard, therefore, as your neighbor the Jew, the Turk, the Moor and the Protestant, for they are; Jesus has said so, and let the first among you who dares to become a zealot be treated like the fomenters of public sedition.

"Zeal is the most odious of crimes, the most insupportable to reason and common sense; zeal is a venom that renders the man who possesses it more dangerous than the asp and the viper. Portuguese of Goa, heed these words carefully; I, the Flying Man, who has just saved your victims from death, will avenge humanity if you outrage it again! Adieu."

And he flew away, leaving all the people of Goa in such profound astonishment that the next day, the majority of the inhabitants sustained that it was an illusion, that they had not seen any flying man, but that there had been a plot to deliver the patients of the *auto-da-fé*. In consequence the Viceroy, who was of that opinion, has never given notification of that event to his Court, and contented himself with ordering scrupulous searches.

He discovered nothing, as you can imagine, but he is nevertheless convinced that there cannot be any such thing as flying men.

Meanwhile, Hermantin having rejoined his companions aboard the ship where the unfortunates saved from the flames had just been deposited, they drew away from the shore and headed for Île Christine. They put the Moorish family on a small island two leagues around, quite fertile; the Jews, more numerous, were put on one six leagues around; and they were left absolute liberty. As for the Protestants, they were kept on Île Christine. Eventually, the Bishop subscribed to the sage laws of the land and, after having given Victorin the plenitude of Christian sacerdocy, he chose Sheep Island for his diocese, were he is passing his peaceful days in the bosom of innocence.

That is all of the story that I promised to tell you, for I have only one more thing to add.

The wise Prince Hermantin has the satisfaction of seeing that the brute-people are gradually making progress, but in continuing to give them his paternal care, he employs the most efficacious precautions in order that they should not be enslaved. In sum, the new Republic is prospering under our sage laws.

As for me, it is at the invitation of Prince Hermantin, when he departed to monitor the progress of Captain Cook, that I embarked on the island's ship, and when I was some distance from the Cape of Good Hope, the prince himself carried me ashore with rich merchandise, which I have gradually sold. He traced the path of my conduct for me, which consists of being on the lookout here for anything that might be said on the subject of our land, of which I have confided the secret to you in the firm persuasion that you will consent to go and live there when I return there, or, at least, that Prince Hermantin will be able to make you our Resident here and our man of confidence, from whom he will seek information every year of the new discoveries that the English might be attempting.

Conclusion by Salocin Emde Fiter

I shall say no more, honorable reader; one word more would discover what ought to remain forever hidden, and that word would cost me my life. I have only wanted to set before your eyes a new picture.

I have already seen Prince Hermantin twice.

Adieu.[73]

---

[73] The first edition adds one more line: "The man who told me the story has departed; I am the colony's chargé d'affaires." There is also one more note by T. Joly, stating: "My friend alone was obliged to secrecy, so I have not betrayed anyone's."

Afterword
by the Translator

The realization that the pattern of life on Earth's surface must have changed drastically over a vast expanse of time surely occurred to other natural philosophers prior to Benoît de Maillet, but they would have hesitated to voice it—as he did, leaving *Telliamed* to be published posthumously—because it was an exceedingly dangerous opinion to hold. The Comte de Buffon and his contemporary Linnaeus both knew, as a result of their exhaustive taxonomic studies, that evidently-related species must have evolved gradually by differentiation from common ancestors, but Linnaeus was careful only to say so explicitly in personal correspondence, and Buffon only declared it in tentative fashion, specifically excluding humans from the assertion.

The "transformism" of species was difficult to explain because there was little or no evidence of it going on in the present, or having occurred significantly within the timespan recorded by history, during which species seemed to have been constant—and the record of extinct species contained in fossils was still exceedingly patchy and controversial. It was therefore impossible to study the process in action, and possible mechanisms could only be conjectured as corollaries of cosmogonic theories relating to the general transformation of the Earth, which tended to have markedly different accounts of the lifespan of the planet and the precise nature of the forces that had shaped it.

Maillet is rather vague about the beginning of life in the sea, concentrating his arguments on the thesis that land animals originated by the transformation of marine creatures, but it is tacitly inherent in his general thesis that the marine ancestors of terrestrial species must have evolved by a natural process of what would now be stigmatized as "spontaneous generation" from non-living matter, probably on the sea-bed.

Although it did not take long after the publication of comprehensive taxonomic analyses of the Earth's plant and animal species for someone (Erasmus Darwin, Linnaeus' English translator) to voice the possibility that all life of Earth might be traceable back to a single common ancestor and that spontaneous generation might only have happened once—a thesis for which biologists borrowed the term "monogeny" from theologians—the more likely hypothesis seemed to many early transformists that it was probably something that had happened lots of times in lots of places (polygeny), and might still be going on, even though it was frustratingly difficult to find evidence of that.

Restif was a relatively extreme polygenist, but that was not unusual or unreasonable for his time, especially given his similarly-extreme commitment to the idea that creation followed stereotyped patterns (which he later summarized by the dictum that "everything in Nature is type and image") and that it was also cyclical, so that the evolution of worlds, solar systems and the entire universe was a repetitive process, analogous to the life-cycles of living organisms. Indeed, he committed himself to the view, radical even in his own day, that everything in the universe, including worlds and stars, is alive— thus making the spontaneous generation of plants and animals merely a kind of transformism. That idea might seem excessively implausible now, but in an era where the concept of life was dominated by the notion of an inherent "vital spark" of some kind, it could not be reckoned absurd, and the context of changes to the planet's surface offered a useful framework for conjectures as to which the generation and transformation of new life forms had happened much more rapidly in the past than the future.

Maillet, unlike his contemporaries, had not hesitated to include humans in his general evolutionary schema, and when he went in search of "links" between humans and other animals, having no hominid fossils to which to refer, his immediate recourse was to legendary and mythical reports of quasi-human species of various degrees of exoticism, of which there is no shortage in the work of historians such as Herodotus and natural historians such as Pliny, as well as popular folklore and ancient literature. Restif followed that strategy far more elaborately than *Telliamed*, as evidenced by the long essay on "hommes-brutes" appended to the *Découverte australe*, and inevitably came up with a hypothetical account of human evolution far more exotic and varied than the one that would later be based on fossil "missing links" between humans and ape-like ancestors.

Like Maillet before him and Lamarck after him, Restif made the notion of adaptation the key element of his notion of transformism, and like them, he assumed that adaptation was an inherently progressive process: that organisms were in some sense impelled to work for their own improvement—or, as the jargon of the day had it, their "perfectibility." In his view, as in Lamarck's, the mysterious vital spark that provides the definitive feature of life is inherently restless, always and everywhere stimulating change, albeit very slowly. Like Lamarck, Restif imagines that every living being is constantly transforming, and that the very evident individual transformations of growth and aging mask a much more gradual process in which every member of a species is working toward its general transfiguration.

If, however, one imagines transformism, implicitly, as a process of improvement, especially of one chooses to call it "perfectibility," then one cannot help seeing it as something goal orientated—teleological, in philosophical jargon—in which there must be an end-point, or a series of end-points that qualifies as "perfection." Teleology is nowadays a heresy in evolutionary theory; the great triumph of the Darwinian theory of evolution, once the snags had been cleared out of it and it had been firmly welded to the supporting structure of genetic theory, is that it does away with the unnecessary hypothesis of a goal or purpose in evolutionary change. But that was not the case in Restif's day, and he can hardly be blamed, in the context of his time, for thinking that the image of perfection to which all animals ought naturally be trying to aim was that of human being.

Restif's account of animals in the process of evolution is exceedingly generous in that regard; it does not stop, or even pause, at monkeys, or even mammals in general, and although he imagines that the animal species on the various islands of his austral archipelago have all got stuck part-way because the natural motor of their evolution has run out of steam—much as the oysters of his oyster island have been interrupted at a much more primitive stage in the transformist process—he also takes the view that there is still some capacity for further improvement in them, with the aid of the kind of guided education that "superior" species can provide: that proto-humans can become more human in exactly the same way that children can be "civilized" by good education. That fits in very well, of course, with the second purpose of his literary enterprise, which is to argue, satirically, that the European humans who think themselves so nearly perfect, are in fact in dire need of a great deal of re-education in the interests of their material and moral improvement.

There is another improving process mentioned in Restif's account of Victorin's strategy of improvement, which is "mixing," or what would later be called cross-breeding. His assumptions regarding the possibility of different species providing viable hybrid offspring is, of course, wildly exaggerated, but it is only an exaggeration—he knew perfectly well what a mule is. The more interesting part of his hypothesis regarding the much greater possibilities of hybridization is the conviction that it can lead to improvements that the parental species might not have been capable of making on their own. Again, he would have been familiar with the selective breeding of domestic animals for the specific purpose of improving races, and would probably have been familiar with the phenomenon nowadays known a "hybrid vigor," so that assumption too is by no means bizarre, even though it flew in the face of contemporary horrified reactions to the notion of human miscegenation with members of other human classes or races, let alone the sin of bestiality.

Restif's cosmogony is, we can now see, completely wrong, not so much because we now think it absurd to conceive suns and planets as living beings, nor even because modern geological thinking has exposed the oversimplification of Maillet's notion of desiccation being the primary driving force of changes to the Earth's surface, but because of one tiny datum that he thought of as a determined fact, although it was, alas, an error. Restif believed that the Earth's orbit was shrinking: that the year was gradually getting shorter, and that the Earth, in consequence, must be moving gradually closer to the sun. He generalized from that supposed observation to conclude that all the planetary orbits must be shrinking gradually as the planets marched in sequence toward the sun, which would swallow them one by one. That conviction formed the basis of his notion of the transformism of solar systems, and his thesis—utterly mistaken—that planets began life as comets, thus licensing him to talk in terms of "cometoplanets" and eventually to supply them, in *Les Posthumes*, with an extraordinary life-cycle, in which the comets die when they turn into planets, and which are supplied, while alive, with a remarkable population of animal parasites.

Restif based that crucial linchpin of his notion of the evolution of solar systems on a calculation made by the mathematician Leonhard Euler (1707-1783), based on historical astronomical observations that turned out to be mistaken—not entirely surprisingly, given the inaccuracy of the measuring devices that astronomers had at their disposal, although they had worked genuine wonders with what they had over the centuries. It was not Restif's fault that the datum in question was erroneous; his extrapolation of it was doubtless overly bold, taking him into imaginative realms far beyond any previously glimpsed, and since banished to the pandemonium of the impossible, but it was not irresponsible at the time, and can, indeed, be regarded as a triumph of creative rational inference.

We can now see that everything that Restif talked himself into believing about the nature of the universe and the evolution of life was wrong, but that should not lead us to dismiss his endeavors as worthless. Since we have banished teleology from biological evolutionary theory we ought to banish it from literary evolutionary theory too. The evolution of the imaginative literature of the past was not goal-directed; it was not aiming toward the relative "perfection" that is the current state of the scientific or the literary imagination, and it is ludicrous to measure its success or its worth by the extent to which it resembles that "perfection." It is irrelevant that Restif's theories, seen from today's viewpoint, were mistaken; the point is that they were a tremendous advance on anything that had gone before, a veritable *tour de force*. They ran into dire trouble even while they were in development, as the narrative of the companion volume to this one will explain and illustrate, but even that should not disqualify them from respect and admiration, or from the recognition that they were, in their fashion, works of genius.

Restif, of course, did not stop at the conclusions he eventually reached in the *Découverte australe*, in which he does perforce take it for granted that in the present context of Earthly evolution, perfection ought to be reckoned human in form, even though current examples of the form require a great deal of cleaning up, internally far more than externally. Even there, however, the Earth is only at a particular stage of its own evolution, and at a particular level of the cosmic hierarchy. God, of course, is the ultimate perfection by definition, but Restif realized quite clearly that between humans—even cleaned-up humans—and God there might be many stages of further improvement yet to be stained, models of which must already exist elsewhere in the solar system and elsewhere in the universe.

As a conscientious writer of imaginative fiction, even though he knew full well that not only was there no profitable market for such work, but that doing it would earn him far more abuse than praise, he wanted to explore those possibilities, and did, in spite of everything that circumstance threw at him by way of obstacles—which were certainly not spared. Much of that endeavor was crippled, and some of it was lost, but some of it did creep fugitively into print, and eventually became available again for contemplation and wonder in the era of electronic publication, as the companion volume to this one demonstrates.

SF & FANTASY

Adolphe Alhaiza. *Cybele*

Alphonse Allais. *The Adventures of Captain Cap*

Henri Allorge. *The Great Cataclysm*

Guy d'Armen. *Doc Ardan: The City of Gold and Lepers; The Troglodytes of Mount Everest/The Giants of Black Lake*

G.-J. Arnaud. *The Ice Company*

André Arnyvelde. *The Ark; The Mutilated Bacchus*

Charles Asselineau. *The Double Life*

Henri Austruy. *The Eupantophone; The Olotelepan; The Petitpaon Era*

Barillet-Lagargousse. *The Final War*

Cyprien Bérard. *The Vampire Lord Ruthwen*

S. Henry Berthoud. *Martyrs of Science*

Aloysius Bertrand. *Gaspard de la Nuit*

Richard Bessière. *The Gardens of the Apocalypse; The Masters of Silence*

Chevalier de Béthune. *The World of Mercury*

Albert Bleunard. *Ever Smaller*

Félix Bodin. *The Novel of the Future*

Louis Boussenard. *Monsieur Synthesis*

Alphonse Brown. *City of Glass; The Conquest of the Air*

Émile Calvet. *In a Thousand Years*

André Caroff. *The Terror of Madame Atomos; Miss Atomos; The Return of Madame Atomos; The Mistake of Madame Atomos; The Monsters of Madame Atomos; The Revenge of Madame Atomos; The Resurrection of Madame Atomos; The Mark of Madame Atomos; The Spheres of Madame Atomos; The Wrath of Madame Atomos* (w/M. & Sylvie Stéphan)

Félicien Champsaur. *Homo-Deus; The Human Arrow; Nora, The Ape-Woman; Ouha, King of the Apes; Pharaoh's Wife*

Didier de Chousy. *Ignis*

Jules Clarétie. *Obsession*

Jacques Collin de Plancy. *Voyage to the Center of the Earth*

Michel Corday. *The Eternal Flame*

André Couvreur. *Caresco, Superman; The Exploits of Professor Tornada* (3 vols.); *The Necessary Evil*

Camille Debans. *The Misfortunes of John Bull*

Captain Danrit. *Undersea Odyssey*

C. I. Defontenay. *Star (Psi Cassiopeia)*
Charles Derennes. *The People of the Pole*
Georges Dodds (anthologist). *The Missing Link*
Charles Dodeman. *The Silent Bomb*
Harry Dickson. *The Heir of Dracula; Harry Dickson vs. The Spider*
Jules Dornay. *Lord Ruthven Begins*
Alfred Driou. *The Adventures of a Parisian Aeronaut*
Sâr Dubnotal *vs. Jack the Ripper; The Astral Trail*
Odette Dulac. *The War of the Sexes*
Alexandre Dumas. *The Return of Lord Ruthven*
Renée Dunan. *Baal; The Ultimate Pleasure*
J.-C. Dunyach. *The Night Orchid; The Thieves of Silence*
Henri Duvernois. *The Man Who Found Himself*
Achille Eyraud. *Voyage to Venus*
Henri Falk. *The Age of Lead*
Paul Féval. *Anne of the Isles; Knightshade; Revenants; Vampire City; The Vampire Countess; The Wandering Jew's Daughter*
Paul Féval, *fils. Felifax, the Tiger-Man*
Charles de Fieux. *Lamékis*
Fernand Fleuret. *Jim Click*
Louis Forest. *Someone is Stealing Children in Paris*
Arnould Galopin. *Doctor Omega; Doctor Omega and the Shadowmen* (anthology)
Judith Gautier. *Isoline and the Serpent-Flower*
H. Gayar. *The Marvelous Adventures of Serge Myrandhal on Mars*
G.L. Gick. *Harry Dickson and the Werewolf of Rutherford Grange*
Raoul Gineste. *The Second Life of Doctor Albin*
Delphine de Girardin. *Balzac's Cane*
Léon Gozlan. *The Vampire of the Val-de-Grâce*
Jules Gros. *The Fossil Man*
Edmond Haraucourt. *Daah, the First Human; Illusions of Immortality*
Nathalie Henneberg. *The Green Gods*
Eugène Hennebert. *The Enchanted City*
Jules Hoche. *The Maker of Men and His Formula*
V. Hugo, P. Foucher & P. Meurice. *The Hunchback of Notre-Dame*
Romain d'Huissier. *Hexagon: Dark Matter*
Jules Janin. *The Magnetized Corpse*
Michel Jeury. *Chronolysis*
Gustave Kahn. *The Tale of Gold and Silence*
Gérard Klein. *The Mote in Time's Eye*
Fernand Kolney. *Love in 5000 Years*

Paul Lacroix. *Danse Macabre*

Louis-Guillaume de La Follie. *The Unpretentious Philosopher*

Jean de La Hire. *The Fiery Wheel; Enter the Nyctalope; The Nyctalope on Mars; The Nyctalope vs. Lucifer; The Nyctalope Steps In; Night of the Nyctalope; Return of the Nyctalope*

Etienne-Léon de Lamothe-Langon. *The Virgin Vampire*

André Laurie. *Spiridon*

Gabriel de Lautrec. *The Vengeance of the Oval Portrait*

Alain le Drimeur. *The Future City*

Georges Le Faure & Henri de Graffigny. *The Extraordinary Adventures of a Russian Scientist Across the Solar System* (2 vols.)

Gustave Le Rouge. *The Dominion of the World* (w/Gustave Guitton) (4 vols.); *The Mysterious Doctor Cornelius* (3 vols.); *The Vampires of Mars*

Jules Lermina. *The Battle of Strasbourg; Mysteryville; Panic in Paris; The Secret of Zippelius; To-Ho and the Gold Destroyers*

André Lichtenberger. *The Centaurs; The Children of the Crab*

Maurice Limat. *Mephista*

Listonai. *The Philosophical Voyager*

Jean-Marc & Randy Lofficier. *Edgar Allan Poe on Mars; The Katrina Protocol; Pacifica 1, 2; Robonocchio; Return of the Nyctalope;* (anthologists) *Tales of the Shadowmen 1-12; The Vampire Almanac* (2 vols.)

Ch. Lomon & P.-B. Gheuzi. *The Last Days of Atlantis*

Camille Mauclair. *The Virgin Orient*

Xavier Mauméjean. *The League of Heroes*

Joseph Méry. *The Tower of Destiny*

Hippolyte Mettais. *Paris Before the Deluge; The Year 5865*

Louise Michel. *The Human Microbes; The New World*

Tony Moilin. *Paris in the Year 2000*

José Moselli. *Illa's End*

John-Antoine Nau. *Enemy Force*

Marie Nizet. *Captain Vampire*

Charles Nodier. *Trilby and The Crumb Fairy*

C. Nodier, A. Beraud & Toussaint-Merle. *Frankenstein*

Henri de Parville. *An Inhabitant of the Planet Mars*

Gaston de Pawlowski. *Journey to the Land of the 4th Dimension*

Georges Pellerin. *The World in 2000 Years*

Ernest Pérochon. *The Frenetic People*

Pierre Pelot. *The Child Who Walked on the Sky*

Jean Petithuguenin. *An International Mission to the Moon*

J. Polidori, C. Nodier, E. Scribe. *Lord Ruthven the Vampire*

P.-A. Ponson du Terrail. *The Immortal Woman; The Vampire and the Devil's Son*

Georges Price. *The Missing Men of the* Sirius

René Pujol. *The Chimerical Quest*

Edgar Quinet. *Ahasuerus; The Enchanter Merlin*

Henri de Régnier. *A Surfeit of Mirrors*

Maurice Renard. *The Blue Peril; Doctor Lerne; The Doctored Man; A Man Among the Microbes; The Master of Light*

Jean Richepin. *The Crazy Corner; The Wing*

Albert Robida. *The Adventures of Saturnin Farandoul; Chalet in the Sky; The Clock of the Centuries; The Electric Life; The Engineer Von Satanas*

J.-H. Rosny Aîné. *Helgvor of the Blue River; The Givreuse Enigma; The Mysterious Force; The Navigators of Space; Vamireh; The World of the Variants; The Young Vampire*

Marcel Rouff. *Journey to the Inverted World*

Marie-Anne de Roumier-Robert. *The Voyage of Lord Seaton to the Seven Planets*

Léonie Rouzade. *The World Turned Upside Down*

Han Ryner. *The Human Ant; The Superhumans*

Frank Schildiner. *The Quest of Frankenstein*

Pierre de Selenes: *An Unknown World*

Angelo de Sorr. *The Vampires of London*

Brian Stableford. *The Empire of the Necromancers (1. The Shadow of Frankenstein; 2. Frankenstein and the Vampire Countess; 3. Frankenstein in London); Eurydice's Lament; The New Faust at the Tragicomique; Sherlock Holmes and The Vampires of Eternity; The Stones of Camelot; The Wayward Muse.* (anthologist) *News from the Moon; The Germans on Venus; The Supreme Progress; The World Above the World; Nemoville; Investigations of the Future; The Conqueror of Death; The Revolt of the Machines; The Man With the Blue Face; The Aerial Valley; The New Moon; The Nickel Man; On the Brink of the World's End; The Mirror of Present Events*

Jacques Spitz. *The Eye of Purgatory*

Kurt Steiner. *Ortog*

Eugène Thébault. *Radio-Terror*

C.-F. Tiphaigne de La Roche. *Amilec*

Simon Tyssot de Patot. *The Strange Voyages of Jacques Massé and Pierre de Mésange*

Louis Ulbach. *Prince Bonifacio*

Théo Varlet. *The Castaways of Eros; The Golden Rock.; The Martian Epic* (w/Octave Joncquel); *Timeslip Troopers* (w/André Blandin); *The Xenobiotic Invasion*
Pierre Véron. *The Merchants of Health*
Paul Vibert. *The Mysterious Fluid*
Villiers de l'Isle-Adam. *The Scaffold; The Vampire Soul*
Gaston de Wailly. *The Murderer of the World*
Philippe Ward. *Artahe ; Manhattan Ghost* (w/Mickael Laguerre); *The Song of Montségur* (w/Sylvie Miller)

Victor Margueritte. *The Bacheloress; The Companion; The Couple*

CPSIA information can be obtained
at www.ICGtesting.com
Printed in the USA
FSHW022035310120
66710FS